# GOING, GOING, GONE!

A Novel

STEVE HERMANOS

This is a work of fiction. Names, characters, organizations, places, events, and incidents are either products of the author's imagination or are used fictitiously.

Published by Inkshares, Inc., Oakland, California
www.inkshares.com

Edited by Adam Gomolin and Barnaby Conrad
Cover design by Tim Barber
Cover art courtesy of the Helmar Baseball Art Card Company

ISBN 9781950301232
e-ISBN 9781950301249
LCCN 2021935612

First edition

Printed in the United States of America

For Karin—
Laughing together as we travel through time

For Ansel—
My favorite baseball player of all time

# AUTHOR'S NOTE

- What we call the "World Series" was originally referred to as the "World's Series."

- In 1891, the United States Geographic Board changed the name "Pittsburgh" to "Pittsburg."

- We baseball fans spend hundreds of hours every year watching and listening as our sport is described in the present tense. And so it is here.

Life is a comic tragedy.
—Vojtěch Jasný

Baseball is not unlike war.
—Tyrus Raymond Cobb

# CONTENTS

# 1

## Johnny Blent's Thinking

KNEELING IN THE on-deck circle, Johnny Blent's thinking about his brother—and that's exactly the wrong thing to focus on in the middle of the World Series, top of the 9th inning, tie game, runner taking a lead off second base.

Johnny Blent watches the Yankees' pitcher, Guzman, fire a fastball to Rick Brothers. *Ziiiiiiiip*—on the outside corner—perfect strike. Blent is 0 for 3 versus Guzman in the Series. Blent's got to tell himself that he can hit a 102-mph fastball trimming the outside edge of the plate, or the inside edge of the plate, and the slider that looks the same as the fastball until the last seventeen feet and dives into the dirt, making great hitters flail. And Blent knows he's not the best hitter in the world.

His brother Mark's round, stubbly, intense face won't leave his mind. Mark the war hero—shot in the back by friendly fire a year ago. Blent stares at the glossy Yankee Stadium grass, and his batting-glove-clad hand presses his eyelids closed. Fifty-six thousand screaming Yankee fans, flashing lights, rock-concert staccato sound effects—and he concentrates on seeing a long, gray tunnel stretching to infinity, its end a black void smaller than a baseball, smaller than a marble, smaller than a pinpoint. Now, one breath.

Rick Brothers is fooled, hacking a slider, the ball smacking home plate, catcher Shotstein snagging it. Shotstein checks the runner at second base, and tosses to first base to easily get Brothers. Two outs.

## SAN FRANCISCO  4 — 4  NEW YORK

It's Johnny Blent's turn to face Guzman. He approaches the batter's box. After seven weeks in the Major Leagues it still freaks out Blent to see his face on the scoreboard a hundred feet tall by a hundred feet wide. Crappy picture, the color tinted orange, eyes staring up and to the right.

The Giants' runner, Manny Rodriguez, remains marooned on second base. Blent settles into his batting stance, weight on his back, right leg. Blent tells himself, *Guzman, you bastard.*

Guzman brings glove and ball together at his belt. He looks back at Rodriguez, who's taking a big lead off second base. Rodriguez flinches toward third, trying to distract Guzman.

Guzman's angry stare passes across Blent's eyes and settles on Shotstein's mitt. Guzman brings his right leg up, twisting his body, hiding the baseball behind his hip and whipsawing forward, flinging himself toward Blent. The airborne ball's a blur and Blent tells himself, *Trust God*, cranking forward, bat smacking ball—crappy contact—slicing the ball toward the right-field line.

Blent's eyes are focused on first base and getting there. Beyond first, his peripheral vision gives him a view of the Yankees second baseman diving toward the foul line, the ball coming down, *blam*, in a burst of white chalk. Fair ball! It dribbles into right field, where Jefferson picks it up and fires to second base to keep Johnny Blent at first.

Manny Rodriguez scores the go-ahead run.

The Giants' dugout exults in screams, hugs, towel waving, high fives, and sunflower seeds sprayed like rice at a wedding, and the five thousand Giants fans in enemy Yankee Stadium erupt in delight.

## SAN FRANCISCO 5 — 4 NEW YORK

If this score holds up, the Giants will win the World Series four games to one—Blent will have driven in the winning run. He slaps the hand of the first-base coach. He bites his lip to suppress grinning. Left foot on first base, he touches his heart, points to the sky, and looks heavenward.

The Giants' catcher, Pax Molina, strikes out to end the inning.

Manny Rodriguez trots Blent's glove out to the field. "Nice hit, Johnny."

"It wasn't squared up, that's for sure."

"It counts, man! Tight defense, okay? Knock down the ball."

Blent is surprised to see first baseman André Velez emerging from the dugout, flapping his huge glove. Velez is the best Giants hitter, by far, a two-time MVP. But since Velez's knee injury two years ago, his range on ground balls at first has been substandard; statistics prove it. Manager Bucky Martin has, twice, replaced Velez with a lead late in a game, and this lead is as precious as a lead can be. Doesn't every baseball fan know about Bill Buckner's fate in the 1986 World Series when a grounder dribbled between his legs?

Velez hulks to first and gives a thumbs-up to Blent, the rookie replacing the team's über-talented second baseman, who broke his wrist in July.

The Giants' closer, Shiro Hashitawa is in to pitch the ninth. He's a tall, young Japanese guy who doesn't speak English, but throws 98 mph, with a screwball, curve, and killer changeup.

Grounder to Velez, who scoops it up, steps on first. One out.

Lazy pop to right, Rick Brothers camping under it. Two outs.

All the Giants know it's just one more out to a World Series victory, a parade up Market Street in San Francisco, a gaudy championship ring, and a lifetime of glory.

Hashitawa's nibbling at the strike zone, two pitches off the plate, trying to induce Getties to swing. Getties watches a curveball bounce at his feet for ball four, and he jogs to first base.

Pax Molina does a slow jog to the pitching mound.

In the dugout, manager Bucky Martin blurts to the pitching coach, "Stay here! Let them handle it!"

Molina and the infielders converge on Hashitawa. Molina keeps his mask on so the TV cameras can't read his lips. He glares into Hashitawa's eyes. "Throw the fucking ball hard!"

Hashitawa recoils. His English is good enough to understand those five well-used words. "Okay."

Shortstop Rodriguez slaps his glove on Hashitawa's butt, and the fielders retreat. Striding back to home plate, Molina wiggles a thumbs-up at his chest protector, a sign to Bucky Martin and the pitching coach that Molina is satisfied that Hashitawa's mindset has been properly adjusted.

Yankee Stadium thunders, reverberating with 50,000 extended shouts trying to rattle Hashitawa. The first pitch to Jackson plunks the batter in the ribs. Fans roar even louder.

Bucky Martin vaults onto the field, barks "Time!" at the home-plate ump, and strides to the mound. Hashitawa's just proven that he's not up to the pressure, that he's cracked, that he's spit the bit. Martin's got two guys warming in the bullpen: Ricky Magadan, a lefty slidermonster; and Buster Johnstone, a righty youngster who throws heat. Up goes Bucky Martin's right arm to call for Johnstone.

Bucky Martin takes the ball from Hashitawa who looks to be on the verge of tears. Martin grabs Hashitawa's belt, slaps his back, says, "Go ice down the champagne." Hashitawa mopes to the dugout.

As they wait for Buster Johnstone to sprint in from the bullpen, Bucky Martin addresses his infielders, "You guys and your Cristal champagne. It's a waste of fucking money. You can't taste the difference."

"You're cheap, Buck," André Velez comments.

The infielders laugh. Molina smiles. Chuckling, Martin points to the center fielder and to Rick Brothers in right. With the game teetering, he's trying to dissipate this moment of excruciating tension. The outfielders grin and flick their mitts toward Martin.

Johnstone decelerates to the mound, and as is his routine, he barks, *"Ball!"*

Bucky Martin places the baseball in Johnstone's mitt, turns to the dugout. Johnstone's warmups *pound* Molina's glove, the sound penetrating into the raucous crowd. Johnstone is utterly focused on Molina, home plate, and Molina's mitt.

Now it's Rodney Clarke, a big lefty who digs in at the plate. Johnstone's examined video of every Rodney Clarke at-bat of the season. Molina and the fifty-seven people in the Giants analytics department have parsed every Clarke at-bat of his career.

Johnstone tucks his chin to his chest, kicks his left knee high, his right arm reaches back, tendons, muscle, bone flinging forward, the ball zips toward home plate, a slight drift over the middle of the plate, Clarke turning, torquing, *craaaaaaaaaack*, the ball flying high.

The ball zooms high in the black night.

Rick Brothers sprints to the right-field wall and opens his glove, his bare hand pressing the wall padding as he tracks the descending ball. Above Rick Brothers, the arms of fans extend out over the field like tree branches. Glove open, Brothers leaps. The ball smacks a fan's forearm and deflects into the stands.

Fifty thousand Yankee fans erupt at what seems to be a game-winning home run.

Brothers—enraged at what, to him, is obviously fan interference—rushes at the right-field ump.

The ump raises his fist and emphatically nods his head in silent agreement with Brothers that a fan interfered with a ball that Rick Brothers would have caught. *OUT! Giants win!*

Game over, World Series over.

A dozen Yankees sprint into right field and confront the right-field ump.

The cheering transforms to the loudest booing in history.

The Giants dugout empties to join the players on the field in a joyous pile near the pitcher's mound.

The stadium bellows, *"Booooooooooooooooo!"*

The coaches and Bucky Martin trot out to celebrate, are received with long hugs. White World Series Championship caps and T-shirts are distributed. Interviewers thrust microphones at players and coaches. A shaken bottle of champagne sprays.

Standing to the side of the Giants dugout, the flabby umpire crew chief wears a headset over his black cap. He is listening carefully to deliberations at replay headquarters on 6th Avenue in the Chelsea neighborhood of Manhattan, where video analysts and a Major League ump scrutinize and dissect all the shots, data, and AI animation, of Clarke's descending ball, the fans reaching out, and the ball deflecting off a fan's forearm. The big question: Was the ball on a trajectory to land in Rick Brothers' mitt or in the stands?

The crew chief removes his headset as the other umps cluster around him and he delivers the verdict to them. In unison their six right arms rise and hands move in counterclockwise circles: home run. *Yankees win.*

An explosion of Yankees bursts from their dugout, dancing along the first-base line.

The Giants' celebration crumbles, and they sprint to the cluster of black-clad umpires. Bucky Martin races to the crew chief, gesticulating toward right field, underlining, *"The right-field ump made the call! He was there! He saw it!"*

The crew chief shakes the headset in his hand. "They said it was clear, Bucky."

"Bullshit!" Martin sprints past celebrating Yankees, intercepting the right-field ump on his way to the dugout. Bucky Martin's pleas and arguments prove futile.

Giants are pulling off their champagne-damp championship T-shirts, vehemently complaining into TV reporters' microphones, and barking at the umpires as the umpires leave the field. The Giants filter into the dugout under mocking sarcasm pouring down from Yankee fans.

*

Three hours later, on the bitter flight back to San Francisco, Giants are clustered into groups of drinkers, while others bear down on their videos, starting to focus on tomorrow, Game 6.

Johnny Blent is texting with his wife, Darla.

You did your part, honey.
*Not really, no. There's always more to do. I got one lousy hit.*
It was the game winner! Until the Yankees stole the

game! Ur playing great

*I don't know. God. I've got five hits in five games. That's not so great.*

Ur playing great D. No one's better than you.

*I hit .722 senior year of HS. I hit .483 in college! I hit .237 in my 46 games with the Giants. I'm gonna get cut next spring Back to the minors!*

No Ur not! Don't' talk that way.

*How's the baby coming?*

Moving like crazy. Any hour now.

*I'm so excited! I hope I can be there!*

Play ball and have fun and come back when you can.

*My mom's on her way to you.*

We R texting.

*She had to see that crrap at the end of the game. I gave her a hug. She's catching a flight late. Maybe already got it.*

Great. I'm so proud of you.

*For what?*

Just you being you. It's amazing what you're doing. You've been dreaming of it forever. I'll find you a Bible verse.

*I dont know. I need Ted Williams, not Jesus so much. Ha! Hard to have fun right now, sorry.*

Over in the galley, Bucky Martin stands with his coaches, some of whom are getting sloshed. Bucky Martin isn't much of a drinker anymore, but his second plastic cup of cabernet is at least generating a thin salve. It's the worst loss of any of their careers, a World Series triumph wrenched away by unseen replay officials.

The front half of the plane is stuffed with team executives, wives, kids, and reporters. The families know not to mix with players after a bad loss, and this bad loss is unmatched. The reporters observe from afar but don't disturb the players.

The pitching coach rattles his ice, asks Bucky Martin, "You want to say something to the guys?"

Martin licks his lips. The engines whine. Making the situation worse, three days before, NYC rain canceled their off-day. The next game is in sixteen hours.

"Nothing I say's gonna force a guy to get over this." Martin surveys the heads and shoulders sticking up above the seats. "Where's André?"

\*

André Velez is in loose shorts, reclining in a wide leather chair on his leased private jet, a beautiful masseuse digging her hands into his right thigh, which is purple in two areas. She's already worked on his knee, which sports an array of scars from three operations.

Two old friends, Mako and Ernie, sip from cans of Frank-E energy drink—they have an endless supply thanks to André's endorsement contract. His agent sits up front with his business manager. But everyone knows André just wants Mako and Ernie's company right now, and some deep massage on his thigh, hip, shoulder, and neck.

Ernie says, "If you guys weren't thoroughly fucked by New York, the Series would be over, and you'd officially be a free agent for the first time in your life."

"Yeah," Velez agrees. "No more Giants."

Mako loudly mumbles, "They disrespect you too much, man!"

The Giants have been his team throughout his career. His father, Gregg, played for the Giants for parts of five seasons, before repeated knee injuries and a hip injury destroyed him: a two-time All-Star, finishing fifth in MVP voting one year. André witnessed it all, some of it from the clubhouse.

Greg and Andre's mom, Ellin, split when Andre was seven. She was a fashion model, originally from Sweden, a smart woman generally obsessed with herself. He wonders what she saw in his father other than the rich, flashy pro athlete with the perfect body. But they were mixed-race pioneers. André remembers plenty of raised eyebrows when the three of them went out.

Ellin didn't know crap about baseball when she met Gregg. Now, every once in a while, she'll tell André after a game that he's striding too soon or he jerked his head on a certain pitch.

Mako, monitoring social on three screens, says, "It's out, now, that you're not with the team. People are accusing you of going on a booty call between games."

"Ha," André scoffs.

"Want to reply—clear it up? You'll get some mileage out of this."

Ernie, who's been gazing out the window, says, "You guys should see the fires down there," and to André, "Think Ellin will even know you're in the room with her?"

André shrugs. His left shoulder is deeply sore. "It's a nasty way to go out, right? She did it to herself, smoking all those years. Shriveled her. Brutal treatments, a-hole doctors, freaky hospitals, long recoveries, relapses, more chemo, hair loss, radiation, weight loss, weakness. Better if this plane went down right now—poof! I don't want to be taken apart in tiny pieces. Gimme a gun." He mimes putting the barrel to his temple, pulling the trigger. He sings, "Goodbye!"

Mako recoils. "André, man! Don't even *think* about that!"

André gently pushes away his masseuse's hands. "Thanks," he says softly and snatches the backpack at Mako's feet. He pulls out an array of vitamin bottles, and a special bottle containing capsules of "Cherry Seed Oil." He won't get tested for the rest of the World Series, even though his trainer claims the juice is undetectable. Three-and-a-half seasons he's been on it, and two seasons he's been MVP.

An hour later, after landing, he's staring out the open window of the Excalibur SUV at Phoenix. It's 3:35 a.m., the desert-night stars pressing close and awesome, so different than Yankee Stadium where you look up and see a murky New York grayish-red night. But maybe, as a free agent, he'll be a Yankee next year. They pay big. Or he could come to Phoenix.

Riding in the back seat, Mako checks a screen and tells André, "We flipped the narrative. A ton of interview requests. They want to talk about your mother and the challenge of playing in the middle of a World Series while she's fighting for her life. Fifteen-minute answer session at the ballpark?"

André's dad went through stretches where he didn't talk to reporters. But André understands he's got to feed the publicity beast in dribs and drabs and in off-season in-depth interviews. It pays off in endorsement deals.

André emits a single chuckle. The thought of two hundred cheaply dressed dudes and women aiming their recording devices at his mouth makes him sigh in annoyance.

"Yeah, man. Okay. You're good at your job."

"Thanks, dude."

\*

There's a tube in his mother's trachea and an IV drip in her forearm. André watches as the nurse wraps a blood pressure cuff around his mother's upper arm, which is thinner than the three middle fingers, bunched together, on André's hand.

André's sister Eva stands on the other side of the bed, staring at André. Eva's stuffed into jeans and she's wearing a shirt out to cover the weight she's gained, which disappoints André. She was once a high school track star.

Mako places his hand on the sheet, gently pressing the dying woman's ankle. "Hello, Ellin. It's Mako. André played great tonight."

"She should be someplace *nice*," André tells Eva. "Why is she even in here? When's the last time she had a cigarette? That's what she probably needs."

"You're not helping the situation," Eva replies.

"How much longer?"

"A week, two, maybe three. She's dying from not eating."

André leans down and kisses the top of the bony cheek. Her rankness startles him. "Mom needs a bath!"

"I'll tell the nurses," Eva promises and turns to Mako. "Let me speak to my brother a moment."

When they're alone with their mom, Eva tells André, "I've got an opportunity."

André stiffens. "We have to do this in front of her? Can't you call me later? After the Series at least?"

"It's a chain of nail salons in LA. They want an answer."

He set her up in a high-end furniture store that she drove into the ground in fifteen months and cost him a million and a half dollars. Then he invested a million in her first husband's seafood restaurant and never saw much in return before the husband divorced Eva and sold cheaply to a shell company he still controls, stiffing the original investors.

"Who's gonna run the LA nail salons? You live in Phoenix."

"Well I'm thinking, you know, after." Eva nods at their mother.

He assesses his sister, who wasn't endowed with much of their mother's attractiveness, or her smarts. He and she have some resemblance around the eyes. But Eva is pure white. Not him. Eva has broad shoulders and strong legs—ran a good 400 in high school. Ran hurdles. Third in the state one year. Her dad had been a college water polo player. Ellin liked her dudes tall, sculpted and raking in cash.

"Why don't you go be a track coach? Do something you're good at."

Eva sneers, head shaking in disgust or frustration, and departs. André moves away from the smell, to the foot of the bed, looming over their mother. Her blanket looks like a loose beach towel covering plastic toys.

In spring training in Scottsdale, Ellin would sometimes sit in the first row near first base in one of his game-worn jerseys. She was happy to tell everyone that she was his mother. One time, André's first or second season with the team, between innings of a spring game, the field umps were gazing her way and she was offering her mysterious, practiced smile straight at them. André was about sixty feet away from her, noticing her coquettishness and the umps checking her out. He stopped throwing grounders and stalked to the umps.

"Dudes, that's my mom! Go ogle someone else!"

The umps sheepishly replied, "Sorry," and, "She looks like a very nice person." The third ump, Deckinger, silently patted André's shoulder in retreat.

Velez then jogged into foul ground. The fans reached out baseballs, pens and scorecards. He told Ellin, "Stop flirting with the umps!"

"I'm not doing that."

"I saw you!"

"Well, it's the *other* national pastime." She flashed a smile.

Now he reaches down, wraps his hands around her ankles. "You should be some place nice."

She does not move. The IV drips. The fluorescent light makes her look greenish yellow. He hopes she never again sees herself in a mirror; she'd studied elegance, learned it, absorbed it, and that was the world she created, no matter how out of control his father became. The young Swedish model and the street-smart LA ballplayer descended, in part, from Curaçaoan farmers and fishermen. Out popped André. Ellin's second husband, the commercial real estate developer, had been very good to her, but a dick to André, before he keeled over on the 16th green at Scotty Pines. He was the reason they shipped André to Gregg for two years—ninth and tenth grade, which was a disaster with alcoholic Gregg falling apart. André did eleventh and twelfth back in Phoenix.

"MVP."

André Velez starts. *"What?"*

Her head rotates. Chin up. Her eyes remain closed. Mouth parts. "MVP. We're MVP."

Two steps and he gently caresses her head. She returns to her sleep, or coma, or whatever she's in. She does not stir for the remainder of the night, as André periodically dabs a wet cloth into cold water and onto her lips. He doesn't know how long it's been since she's smoked, but she still smells of tobacco.

\*

It's barely dawn in San Francisco. Bucky Martin doubts that many of his players are sleeping. He's twenty-eight stories up in his condo on the side of Russian Hill, with a view over Chinatown, to the downtown skyscrapers, part of the Bay Bridge, and the Bay. He knows he's a lucky bastard to live with this zillion-dollar view, but yesterday's loss was the most devastating he's ever experienced. How do you get a team's mind right after all that?

He pours a cup of ink-black coffee, abandons his phone on the kitchen counter, carries his cup to his white leather recliner, clicks his lamp on. He gazes out at a line of posters of abstract expressionist painters left over from his third wife, Melanie. Eighteen months since *that* divorce. Only two years of marriage. She teaches art history at SF State. It was beautiful for a year or so. Thirteen years younger . . . didn't seem to make much difference. But she turned out to be an argumentative perfectionist, who became meaner and meaner.

He cracks the middle of a stack of new American history books, this one: *Attack and Defend: The Battles of Gettysburg & Vicksburg*. Through two cups of coffee, as the cherry sun rises through South Bay smog, he reads about Grant and Meade, the accidental beginnings of Gettysburg, and Grant's intricate strategy for Vicksburg. He chuckles at himself; he loves touring Civil War and Revolutionary War battlefields and skirmish sites. None of his wives found that particular passion interesting. He yawns.

Professional baseball and regular sleep don't mix. If you can't function on fragmentary sleep, you can't be a pro. And if your team is lucky and good enough to make a run to the World Series, forget about sleep entirely. But since Bucky Martin went from playing—nine years in the minors, and thirty-one games in the Majors as a relief pitcher scattered through San Diego, Houston, and San Francisco—to coaching and managing, deep reading eases his mind.

His apartment looks like a bomb went off in a library—piles of books everywhere. His cleaners do a great job extracting the food and dirt, but since his wife left him at the beginning of the previous season—right when his chemo started—he's instructed the cleaners to leave the books where they lie. And, shit, his son . . . right now Bucky Martin, Jr., is in rehab for the second time.

Rarely is there a third cup of coffee before he departs for his three-mile walk to the ballpark, but today he places a third cup on his dining room table. He sits before his computer. He's never tried to do something like this before, but today is the day. He considers dictating it, but he's enjoying the silence of the morning, so he types:

> To all our fans, players, coaches, and team personnel:
>
>      I can speak for our players and coaches and state that yesterday's loss was the worst of our careers. You just don't lose a game in that manner and be all right with it. I just want you to know that we are going to play the rest of the Series the way we've played the whole season: with intensity and with dignity. The winner of the World Series hasn't had to win 5 games to take the Series since 1921, when it was 5 out of 9 games. So, if we have to win 5 to win the World Series this year, that is, simply, our task.
>
> Sincerely,
>
> Bucky Martin
> Manager, San Francisco Giants

He reads, rereads, doesn't like the word "task"—sounding too much like a burden. He stares out at the city and changes "task" to "what we aim to do."

Not as good as the Gettysburg Address, but good enough.

He types the first strokes of the Director of Communications' email, blurts the last words his biological mother ever said— "Fuck it"—and clicks "send."

# 2

## The Robbery

ANDRÉ VELEZ UNFOLDS himself from the passenger side of his Mercedes and stands in the players' parking lot in San Francisco. Mako and Ernie remain in the Mercedes, talking to Cheech, who is driving André's newest car, his Lamborghini, to meet them.

"What do you mean by 'scratched'?" Mako asks Cheech over the phone.

"How bad?" asks Ernie.

The reply through the phone: "It's sort of bad."

André asks, "Why didn't he send a picture?"

"Where's the picture?" Mako demands.

"I'm coming in."

André picks the edge of his pinkie nail into a shred of crab wedged in his teeth from an omelette his chef, Olé, whipped up at his home in Belmont, thirty-five minutes after his jet kissed the runway at SFO. He can't help but smile as the Lamborghini appears, a yellow spaceship of a car, and carefully pulls in, fat Cheech at the wheel, not making eye contact with André.

Stepping around to the passenger side, André's eyes pop, jaw drops, brow rises, arms go to the sky at the sight of yard-high scratches written across the door panel:

# *DICKWArD*

"*How'd this fucking happen?*" André screeches. "*Who gave you permission to take this car out?*"

Ernie explains, "Cheech thought driving the Lambo would magnetize him some booty."

Cheech sheepishly hangs his head. "I'm sorry, man. I drove it to the Kitty Annex. When I came out at two-thirty, it was like this. The idiots parking the cars said they didn't see anything."

Ernie joins André, for a view of the scratches. "That's a desecration! We can sue those motherfuckers. They should have insurance for vandalism on their property."

"That's stupid!" André growls. "We don't want to be suing a club over this. Makes me look like a whiny rich bitch! This car will never be the same! *Goddamn it!*"

Mako comes around and inspects the scratches. "Dick Ward?"

"*Not Dick Ward!*" André barks. "Dick-*wad!*"

Mako touches the letter in question, "Looks like a piece of an 'r' after the 'a.'"

André presses his thumb onto the scratch, which has scored through the paint and primer into the metal. The whole side of the car, every panel, is ruined in deep squiggles, centered on "Dickwad." He snaps photos of the damage. "Whoever did this is gonna die."

The posse chimes in:

"*Some idiot!*"

"*We'll find out who did this!*"

"*Gonna die!*"

Ernie tries to calm him. "You've got the World Series to win."

"Must've been a Yankee fan who did it," suggests Mako.

André spouts, "Gonna cost the price of the Mercedes just to *repaint* the Lambo!"

Cheech sniffingly asks, "Want me to call the body shop?"

Velez nods. Mako hoists André's bag as they wait for him to begin moving toward the stadium. The huge lattice of light stands, the back of the humongous scoreboard, and the 140-foot-tall left-field hunk of the stadium loom. Velez checks the license plate, black with yellow letters, unscratched. "HR KING9."

They follow Velez into the guts of the stadium.

*

Across the street and twelve flights up, Johnny Blent is doing pushups in his living room while FaceTiming with Darla.

"Quality of sleep?" Darla asks.

"Seven or eight out of ten. I calmed down pretty well."

"Veggie drink for breakfast?"

"Everything in the fridge is wilted and soft."

"You can still use it! Or go down to the Golden Gate Café. They'll make you something. It's good luck."

He's been there with Darla a lot.

"Ooooooh!" she groans. "Contraction. Baby's moving."

"Get your mom!"

"She's here. We'll go. I'll text you when we get there!"

"I'll let *my* mom know."

"I'll text her. I love you so much, Johnny Blent! Go get some hits! Make your plays!"

\*

André Velez and his posse clomp through the curving concourse under the stands, approaching the Giants' locker room. Cheech, checking his phone, informs, "Gloria wants tickets."

Velez blasts a laugh. Gloria *was* his Scottsdale girlfriend, a lawyer who, effectively, stole his Scottsdale home. He hasn't seen her in two months and owes her nothing. Except she regularly offers to let Cookie, André's wife, know about the long, intimately-chronicled-by-her-but-so-far-undisclosed affair.

"You attract the crazy ones," notes Mako. "Arlene's coming too."

"Her place done getting painted? Get her out of the Fairmont, man. I'm sick of bleeding money for her unnecessary crap."

"Okay." Mako continues, "And Cookie will sit with the other players' wives."

"Three of them, three of you. Take care of it."

In greeting, André pats the shoulder of Shannon, the big, smiling clubhouse guard, who reaches up to stroke her three-inch-long, rainbow fingernails across André's biceps, which always makes him laugh. Then he pushes through the double doors.

Teammates are in various states of undress amidst swarms of reporters. In his six seasons with the Giants, André Velez has never seen it so jammed. As usual, everyone notices André's entrance. But not one of his teammates moves an inch or raises their voice to greet him. Brothers brushes past, in white underwear, holding a can of grape Frank-E, shooting a thumbs-up at André.

Like starving dogs, reporters rush at him.

"What about the game last night?"

"How's your mom?"

"How're you feeling?"

"How's the knee?"

The Director of Communications, an old Chicano guy in an orange tie, confers with André, then announces, "In half an hour, André will take questions in the dugout!"

André slides into the manager's office, where he finds Bucky Martin in his stained "lucky" baseball undershirt, gazing toward his framed autographed poster on the wall of legendary basketball coach John Wooden's Pyramid of Success.

André shuts the door. "It smells bad in here, man."

Bucky Martin raises an arm, sniffs the pit. "You weren't on the plane, which is okay. But after a killer of a loss like that, at least tell me before you go off."

"My mom. You know." Velez shrugs.

Bucky glances at a framed photo, him in his first year of A ball, with his two moms.

"And someone just wrecked my favorite car."

Martin bolts up, knocking over his chair. *"You all right?"*

Velez laughs at his manager's reaction at the prospect of losing his bat in the lineup.

"Wasn't a crash, man, don't worry. Someone *scratched the crap out of it.*" Velez raises his phone in its Tiffany diamond–encrusted case and shows a photo.

"Nice car!" Martin comments.

He hands Martin the phone—*"Zoom in!"*—turns and flicks the head of a Willie Mays bobblehead doll on the shelf of bobbleheads that extends all the way around the little office. He flicks a bobblehead of himself, the doll wielding a golden bat in a home-run-swing follow-through.

"Yeah. I see. 'Dickward.' But scratches like that would *improve* my shitty car." Martin hands back the phone and rights his chair.

"I like your post to the team and the fans."

"Thanks. Gotta be a leader, right? I'm not the important one out there."

"We'll be good." Velez reaches across the desk, and they share a firm handshake—both fully aware that after four years together Velez will be testing the waters of free agency this off-season.

"I'm sorry about your mom. She have a chance?"

"No. She did it to herself. Smoked like a chimney."

"Invite me to the funeral, please. I love you, man. We wouldn't be here without you, obviously."

André nods and steps out. Martin sits at his computer, his gaze drifting up to the Willie Mays bobblehead, which continues to nod. He checks his wristwatch, then clicks on a file and today's flowchart blossoms. Even though the Yankees and Giants have played each other for a week, pitching strategy has shifted, and the stats report cautions against Oliveraz facing the Yankees' Johnson. Martin reads the most recent comments from the Head Data Analyst, the Head Quantitative Analyst, the Director of Player Health and Performance. Last night's nightmare of a baseball robbery flashes in his mind again. His eyes latch onto a little grouping of the same Bucky Martin bobblehead—a failed resemblance of little brown pupils in big eyes, ears like orange oysters, black-painted chest hair poking out above his uniform. He scrunches to see, and yes, there's chest hair, some of it not black anymore.

He's ahead of schedule, and it's a window to talk with Buck, Jr. He presses the phone number, which has been sent to him by his first ex-wife, who, as it turns out, was probably the best of the three. When he was with her—Susaline—he was playing AA ball in Rapid City, then AAA in Memphis, then AAA in Fresno. Buck, Jr. was dragged around to new schools, always had to try to fit in as the new kid. Junior never complained much; he seemed to worship his dad. He was a great baseball player, too, drafted by the Giants as something of a favor. Played two seasons at Single-A Pensacola, and that was it. Then, somehow, he found out that drugs was his best friend. The first rehab stint was three years ago. This is number two.

The call is answered. "Solstice Recovery Center."

"Calling for Buck Martin, Junior. This is his father, Buck Martin," adding, "Senior." He wonders if the receptionist is a baseball fan.

"I can take a message."

"Is he available right now?"

"I'm sorry. We don't interrupt the residents' schedule. I will pass along the message and tell him that you called."

"When can I visit?"

"A week from Saturday. Noon to three. You must make arrangements before."

"I'll be there. Tell him that I love him, okay?"

"I'm sorry, but I can't give any content to your message. Just that you called. We have a lot of rules here."

"Can you just draw a heart on a piece of paper and write 'Dad'?"

"I am sorry. He'll call you from our landline. Most residents do not have access to their phones or email."

"Thank you." He gives his number. "Have a good day."

"You too. And you guys got robbed last night."

He laughs. "Thank you," and hangs up. He stares up at the bobbleheads, while an image of his team taking the field forms in his mind.

*

Johnny Blent and Rick Brothers cross the concrete hallway to the passage that leads up a flight of stairs to a rectangle of sunshine and the opening to the dugout. A wasps' swarm of reporters is pressing in around someone in the dugout whom they cannot see. Going up and around the backs of the reporters, Brothers and Blent find a spot at the far end of the bench, where Brothers ties his shoe. Through a bit of movement in the throng, Blent and Brothers see that it's André Velez, seated on the bench, alone, his first-baseman's mitt at his side, one leg crossed at the knee, answering questions.

Blent gazes at the stadium built along San Francisco Bay. Even after a couple of months up in the Majors, he's still awed by its beauty. Blent notices that the red-white-and-blue World Series bunting, which has been up for a week, is slightly faded, slightly sagging, slightly dusty.

"I hope he's out of here when he hits free agency. What a dick," Brothers comments. "Everyone else is a team of Giants, and André's on his own team."

"If he hits three homers tonight and we win, you'll probably want him back."

Brothers chuckles, "Nah." He leans to Blent, Brothers' flowery cologne close. "I keyed his car last night."

Blent recoils. "That Lambo he just bought? I saw it on social."

"After he valeted his car. I pulled past it. Parked down the street. I got a Swiss Army knife. Don't tell anyone or I'll have to kill you."

"He was visiting his sick mom in Phoenix."

"Well fuck him—whatever. He's just visiting his sick mom so other team owners won't only see him as a dick with a big batting stick. He's pumping up his value by plastering over the jerk factor."

"Sure you got the right car?"

"'HR KING9' plate?"

Bucky Martin emerges holding a paper cup of espresso, steps up to the field and around reporters facing Velez. Martin pauses next to Blent and Brothers. "You guys doing okay?"

"Yeah," says Brothers. "Ready. That fucking ball was coming down straight into my fucking glove."

"Yes, sir," replies Blent.

"Let's just pretend it's Opening Day, all right? New season: one game." Martin winks at Brothers and pats Blent's shoulder. "For your new baby girl on the way. Now I gotta deal with the mob." Martin nods his head at the tsunami of reporters turning his way.

Blent wonders how Martin knew that Darla was in labor as he and Brothers start their daily jog along the crushed-brick warning track ringing the field. They circle the field three times, warily eyeing Yankees. They plop down in right field. Blent tells Brothers, "I like Cincinnati and the points on Sunday."

"Versus the Cowboys?"

"Yeah. Ten and a half points. That's a lot."

"Because Cincinnati sucks," chuckles Brothers. "I'll take that bet."

"A hundred?"

"Yeah. A hundred. Isn't that a lot for you, rookie? You should be saving that for diapers."

"With your hundred, that'll make two hundred for diapers."

"Dickwad," Brothers says.

"What?"

Brothers leans close and whispers, "That's what I scratched on his car."

*

An hour later, post-workout, André Velez is in his massage chair. Two winters ago, the walls of four lockers were knocked down to make Velez's expansive sideways locker. No other player has more than one locker. No other player has a massage chair.

Velez wears his white uniform pants with black piping and a long-sleeve undershirt with black sleeves, his body rippling in a slow wave as his chair's rollers press into his back. He wears black eyeshade and groans in relief.

Johnny Blent approaches to within a yard. "Hey, André, how're the legs today?" Blent needs to know because it will determine how close on the field Blent will position himself in relation to first baseman Velez.

Velez replies by flicking his fingers at Blent, as if shooing away a fly.

Blent's never been so deeply insulted by a teammate. His chest pounds. As he steps back from Velez, he's trembling with rage. Then he remembers that Brothers defaced Velez's yellow Lambo: "Dickwad." *That's what you deserve!*

"*Yo, Blent!*" Brothers shouts from across the clubhouse, shaking his phone. "The baby's crowning! Darla put it on social!"

Hashitawa turns to Blent: "Congratulation!"

Johnstone: "Good job, Blent!"

Molina: "I got six!"

Blent gets slaps on the back. Brothers tells the gathering crowd, "Don't jinx it!"

Martin steps out of his office with a collection of coaches. The third-base coach is wiping tears with his uniform sleeve, which, as they notice, quiets a lot of players.

Bucky Martin tells the team, "We're gonna do something a little bit different today."

Brothers shouts, "Thanks for the email, Buck!"

Some of the guys laugh, while others ask their neighbors, "What email?" "Que esto?"

"Thanks." Martin turns to the young, neatly dressed, nervous man from the TV network who, every World Series game, helps corral and orchestrate the team's introduction on the field. Martin tells him, "Please leave."

Shocked as the room silences and thirty-two pairs of eyes focus on him, the TV network man checks the time and states, "We still have five and a half minutes."

Martin chuckles, knowing the guy is pretending to not have heard. "Team only."

The young man pages through his clipboard. "That's not in the script."

"No script today. Out."

Bucky Martin tells the players closest to the clubhouse door, "Bring in Shannon."

When she enters, Martin asks her, "Shannon, how much money is a fiftieth of a share for winning the World Series?"

Shannon shifts her weight and smooths her orange vest. "That would be a shit-ton!"

Everyone laughs.

Martin tells her, "It's up to the players how to divide it, but I'll make up the difference and that's what you're gonna get when we win. But I'd like you to do us a favor."

*"Anything!"*

"In the next five minutes there's gonna be a storm of TV people wondering what the heck we're holding up for. Don't let them in. If you need any beef to keep people back, we got, uh, Mike Shorn here to stand with you." The team laughs. Shorn is 6'5" and 275 pounds of muscle. Shorn laughs.

"Okay, Buck!" Shannon bolts out, leaving the team staring at their manager.

"I want to go out on the field together, all right?" Buck tells them. "If anyone wants to do their usual routine, that's okay. Go ahead. So we wait a few minutes. Hey, Johnny Blent!"

Blent is stunned at being singled out.

"How's that baby coming along?"

The team laughs. Rick Brothers replies, "It's popping!"

Martin asks Blent, "Can you get a livestream going? Mind if we give her some encouragement?"

Blent is pretty sure Darla would love the gesture. He grabs his phone, livestreams to his mom, who states in her thick northern Alabama accent, "It's paused. Five centimeters."

Darla screams, followed by, "I'm all right!"

Blent tells her, "The team wants to say hi."

Brothers snatches Blent's phone, stands on a chair, and holds the phone up. The thirty-seven players and coaches squeeze together. Brothers yells out, "Congratulations!" The team echoes, "Congratulations!"

Darla shouts, *"I ain't done here by a long shot!"* Another breath, she bellows, *"Go win the danged game!"*

The team roars. Martin leads them out of the clubhouse, but instead of crossing the hall to the stairs that lead up to the dugout, Martin goes left, making sure the squad follows along the tunnel, past shocked fans who reach for their phones, past security guards, a cotton candy vendor, the pesky TV coordinator pleading, "You're going the *wrong way!*" They hear the Yankees' names being read, one every eight seconds, as fans snap photos of the Giants, cleats clacking concrete. They take a right to cross under the bleachers.

As they appear in the open courtyard under the gargantuan scoreboard, cheering fans surround them, and those up in the bleachers looking down yell, hoot, snap photos and videos. Far across the field, the Yankees wait in a line stretching from home plate to first base. Martin charges through the bullpen to the door in the center-field fence.

The Giants pour out into the late-afternoon October sunshine, thirty-seven men in spotless orange jerseys, crossing the crushed-brick warning track onto the manicured outfield to the loudest roar any of them have ever heard, a booming catharsis. The team strolls across the field, waving to the cheering fans.

The Yankees stand stoically. Their starting pitcher, Verlinger, pauses in a warmup windup, glances at the Giants, licks his lips. Then he returns his focus to his catcher and throws a fastball high.

# 3

## Edge

AS THE SUN dips west, and the fog blows east to cover the stadium, the Giants take the lead:

| GAME 6 | 1 | 2 | 3 | 4 | 5 | 6 | 7 | 8 | 9 | R | H | E |
|---|---|---|---|---|---|---|---|---|---|---|---|---|
| NEW YORK | 0 | 0 | 0 | 1 | 0 | 1 | 0 | | | 2 | 5 | 1 |
| SAN FRANCISCO | 0 | 2 | 1 | 0 | 0 | 2 | 0 | | | 5 | 6 | 0 |

Top of the 8th. One out. Bases empty.

Deep at second base, just at the edge of the outfield grass, Johnny Blent pounds his glove and sets himself. At first base, André Velez snorts.

The batted ball rises above the top rim of the stadium, arcing into foul territory. Blent races after the ball, tracking it. Blent's peripheral vision sees André Velez lumbering toward the stands, and the photographers' pen, next to the dugout, where the ball looks like it'll be coming down.

Blent yells, *"I got it!"* He has a more direct route to the ball than Velez, who's craning backwards and looking up over his right shoulder. The ball's dropping toward the sunken pen packed with photographers, and Blent, for a split second, has to decide if he's going airborne, headfirst, over the railing and risking breaking his face on the back wall or concrete floor. Blent's flying, glove extended, the ball coming down and he thinks he's lined it up.

*BLAM!* Velez's mitt smacks Blent's mitt, the ball bouncing off Blent's wrist as they collide. Blent falls first, Velez tumbling on top of him, crushing him into the floor of the pen. Smushed face-down, out of one eye Blent watches the ball roll to a stop at the feet of the photographers, who've recoiled into the corner, madly snapping photos of him and Velez.

The first-base ump and the right-field ump stare into the pen like they're looking down a well. Blent finally grasps the ball. The first-base umps arms go out wide: not caught, just a foul ball.

Forty-eight thousand fans moan.

Without a word, Velez lifts himself off Blent. Rick Brothers appears. *"You guys all right?"*

As Velez scissors over the wall onto the field, he gives a wave to the nearby fans, some of whom cringe as they get a look at Blent; a little girl breaks into tears. Blent feels something sticky on his face and touches it, his fingers red. He licks: *ketchup*. On the concrete where he crashed, there's a mass of garlic fries spattered with ketchup. A hefty photographer with his cap on backwards apologizes, "Sorry, Johnny."

Blent lifts his uniform sleeve and wipes the ketchup from his cheek.

As Velez jogs toward first, Blent sprints up next to him.

Rick Brothers asks again, "You guys all right?"

Velez replies, "We're cool."

Blent is not cool. He presses his mitt into Velez's ribs, barking, "That was my ball!"

Velez casually pushes Blent's glove off his ribs. "My ball, rookie."

*"You're wrong!"* Blent shoves Velez.

Velez glances up into the stands, trying to control himself, rage volcano-ing, then heaves into Blent's chest hard, forcing him two steps back.

Without thinking, Blent thrusts his elbow into Velez's chest, screaming, *"I'll punch your lights out right now!"*

While it takes a moment for the shortstop, pitcher, third baseman and catcher to realize that Velez and Blent are on the cusp of a fistfight in the middle of the 6th Game of the World Series, Bucky Martin bursts out of the dugout. The infielders pull Blent and Velez apart as Velez lifts his huge mitt to his mouth to screen his words from one billion baseball lip-readers. He shrieks, *"Don't disrespect me, Junior!"*

While the players and Martin keep Blent and Velez apart, tens of thousands of Giants fans stand appalled and silent, and a considerable number of Yankee fans cheer. A voice from the bleachers bellows, "Hit him Blent!"

Blent screams, *"That was my pop-up!"*

Bucky Martin barks, *"Hey!"* and crooks his finger at Blent. Martin steps up on the mound to join pitcher Hashitawa, Pax Molina, and André Velez.

Blent steps forward, and Martin screeches at him, *"Calm the hell down!"* Velez and Molina share a smile at Blent's expense. Hashitawa is in his own little world, kicking at the dirt, stone-faced.

Blent nods okay and retreats, squirting a jet of carcinogen-removed tobacco juice as he takes his position at second base, having been humiliated by Martin. Over at first base, Velez sniffs and pounds his big mitt.

Staring into the eyes of Hashitawa, Martin says, "You're throwing great." Hashitawa gazes away at the center-field scoreboard, which is showing Martin talking to him, their heads ninety feet tall. Nodding toward Blent and Velez, Martin tells Hashitawa, "Forget that horsecrap." To Molina, "You believe those two?"

Molina smiles from behind his mask and diplomatically says nothing.

Jerking his elbow toward the batter, Martin tells Hashitawa, "Just get this guy."

\*

Walk. Double. Single. Homer. Hashitawa does not throw another strike. The Giants do not get another base runner. Neither Blent nor Velez get another at-bat.

NEW YORK  6 — 5  SAN FRANCISCO   FINAL

The World Series is tied, three games each.

In the clubhouse Velez sits on a padded stool facing into his locker, his uniform pants unbuckled, his undershirt untucked, as he responds to messages. Satisfied that his various women are headed in different directions, he senses the lumpy, poorly groomed presence of seventy reporters standing inches from his back. They'll want to ask him about the bullcrap on the field with Blent.

Across the clubhouse, Blent stands deep in his locker, checking his phone. Dozens of messages. Darla's *still* in labor; the crowning was a false alarm. It was actually the baby's butt!

A reporter asks, "Have a name for the baby?"

"Yeah," Blent spits. "E3!"

The reporters laugh. In a scorebook, E3 means error, first base. That would mean Velez.

"Are you saying it was André's fault you didn't catch that ball?"

Rather than stir up a hornet's nest of controversy, Blent calls Darla. No answer. His message: "Love you, honey! What's happening?"

He pulls off his uniform and storms to the shower. Half the team is in there, no one talking, all wondering how many crappy losses they can endure. At least tomorrow's game will be the last. Do or die. Whoever wins it wins the World Series. There is no Game 8.

Blent soaps up and realizes he should've called his mother, or Darla's mother. The baby might've turned around and be out right now! He feels something poking his shoulder blade.

It's Velez's index finger. "Don't show me up, rookie!"

Swatting Velez's hand, Blent bellows, *"You cost us the game! That was my pop-up! I had it tracked!"*

Velez's big eyes go wide and with both hands he shoves Blent. Brothers and Molina and one of the pitchers start yelling at Blent to shut up. Velez throws a jab at Blent's eye. Before Blent can punch back the others jump between them. Blent goes after Velez. The other guys are screaming at Blent, and Velez is throwing unconnecting haymakers from behind the naked wall of players pushing him and Blent apart.

Blent jumps and grabs for Velez's wiry hair, but his soapy fingers can't hold him. Ballplayers and coaches rush into the shower, pulling at the tangle. They karate chop Blent's hand off Velez, pushing Blent back. Blood trickles from behind Velez's ear into the film of soap on his neck.

Martin bursts into the shower. He's wearing a wrapped, white towel and flip-flops. Everyone's looking at him. He clamps a hand onto Velez's upper arm, the other on Blent's elbow. He marches them out of the shower, through the clubhouse, where reporters and cameramen stare openmouthed, notebooks and phones and cameras pointing like compass needles at the trio. Martin herds Velez and Blent into his office.

Martin slams the door and points at the two chairs before his desk. "Sit!"

"He hit me in the shower!" Blent protests.

"I'm not gonna take any more crap from him!" Velez yells.

Martin pounds his fist into his desk. *"This ends!"* He's squinting and frowning. His naked body looks scrawny. *"Quiet!"* He digs through a drawer while Velez and Blent glare at each other.

Blent asks, "Can I get my phone? The baby—"

*"No!"*

Blent regards Velez. "Do you know what a prima donna is?"

Martin barks, *"Shut up!"* He lifts one of the fat binders on his desk and flings it at the cinder-block wall; the shelves of bobblehead dolls remain motionless. From his desk drawer Martin extracts a fat cellophane-wrapped cigar. He holds it up to them. "This is an extremely rare Dos Fuegos Maduro Cuban. I've been saving it to celebrate winning this World fucking Series. I'd like you guys to lead the way to victory tomorrow. Tomorrow! It's always fucking tomorrow!" Martin points at Blent. "You're a fucking rookie! Show André some respect!"

Velez's chin rises as his lips curl down in a sneer at Blent.

Martin opens a penknife and cuts into the cigar. "You guys gotta play next to each other tomorrow! Calm the fuck down!"

Velez says, "Buck, you shouldn't even be *touching* tobacco!"

Martin looks up. He has sliced the cigar into thirds. Turning to Blent, he says, "André is referring to a bout with cancer, which I won." To Velez, "You're right. I *shouldn't* be smoking a cigar. But this is a fucking crisis!" He closes the penknife and hands one-third of the cigar to Blent and one-third to Velez. The aroma of the tobacco cuts the shower-products scent of Blent and Velez. Martin informs them, "Dos Fuegos Maduro Cuban. They only make it in one field in the whole fucking world. This is a peace cigar, and also a victory cigar. Here's to tomorrow."

"Isn't that bad luck?" Velez asks. "If it's for victory, then we should save it."

"We're doing it now." Martin asks Blent, "Smoke cigars?"

"Sure. When I used to play poker in college. But I prefer my Red Man chew."

Martin strikes a match and holds it out for Velez, who leans across the desk, expertly lighting the one-third cigar. Martin strikes another match for Blent and himself. The three Giants puff their one-third cigars.

Blent rubs his right forearm, a tattoo of a spiderweb with rectangles colored green and red. Above that is "Darla" in thick script, and a fat yellow lightning bolt coming down from his shoulder.

Velez straightens his left knee, *crack, pop, pop.*

Each of the trio spits out pieces of tobacco that have spilled into their mouths, and stare at the swirls of smoke. Martin pinches a piece of tobacco off his tongue. "That's better, right?"

Velez rises, naked, "Got a towel for me?"

Blent mutters, "Maybe the baby by now."

Martin comments, "It's exciting."

The bobbleheads shimmy hard and some are *clacking* into their neighbors' heads.

Velez chuckles and points. His smile fades as a far-off rumbling surges to a roaring rocket blastoff. Bobbleheads tumble from the shelves.

*"What's that sound?"* Fear erupts in Blent.

The room sways, throwing Martin's desk lamp to the floor. Clusters of bobbleheads tumble. The room is rattling, dropping photos and awards from the walls. The bookcase topples. Shelves shake. The desk is vibrating. The noise is louder than any stadium crowd. A falling Bruce Bochy bobblehead knocks Blent's forehead as he rushes at the door. The ceiling collapses inches from his face, halting him. The room throbs, cracking, undulating.

Martin shouts, *"In here!"* and shoves Blent into the space under the desk. Then he pushes in as much of Velez as will fit. Martin crouches next to them, shielding himself with a chair as more of the ceiling falls. The roaring, shaking, cracking, crashing, and rumbling go on and on.

Then it stops. The air is thick with dust. Martin lifts his balled-up shirt to cover his nose and mouth. His cigar is gone.

They crawl out from under the desk. Most of the ceiling has come down.

"Guys all right?" Martin asks.

"My first earthquake," Blent notes.

Martin takes a step toward the door, but a pile of cinder blocks and a steel ceiling beam barricade it. The wall across from the desk is mostly crumbled. Dust hangs in the air.

"Got a flashlight?" Velez asks.

"I don't think so."

Their feet are wet. The carpet is squishy. The office, the clubhouse, the whole stadium, is built on pylons not very much above the waterline.

Martin tugs at the wide steel beam diagonally covering the door, but the beam doesn't move. Velez and Blent climb onto the rubble, trying to jerk the beam, yanking on it, but it's immobile. Martin bangs on the metal door, trying to communicate with the rest of the team, *"You guys okay?"*

There is only silence. They bang on the door. Call out for teammates, coaches and staff. Listen for responses. Nothing.

Icy water numbs their feet.

"Pipe broke," Velez says.

"We might've dropped into the Bay." Martin pounds on the door, *"Hey! Hey! Hey!"*

Velez presses his ear to it. All Velez hears is the sound of his own breathing and his thumping heart, the sounds overwhelmed by a deep rumbling followed by a deafening *CRACK!* and *ROAR!*

Martin shouts, "Desk!"

Velez dives under, his thighs sticking out. Blent and Martin press in against the sides of the desk, just as the rest of the ceiling falls. The building shakes up, down, sideways. The bobbleheads splash onto the soaked carpet, which seems to drop away—with their stomachs—downward. Water is rising. Velez wails, *"I don't want to die!"*

Blent prays aloud, "Dear God, make it stop. Dear God! I'll be good!"

Martin counts, shouting, reaching fifty-two when the shaking stops. Everything is silent again. The trio steps away from the desk. The water is now up to their knees. More material has collapsed to bar the door: A second and third beam, cinder blocks, and broken concrete now only leave a little area of door exposed. A chilly breeze blows in from a wide crack in the wall across from the desk.

Velez and Blent pull away chunks of cinder block and pound the door. Martin yells, *"Guys!"*

*"Hey!"* Blent shouts.

*"We're stuck!"* Velez slaps the door. *"Somebody, grab my phone!"*

The water rises, now waist-high, so cold it's numbing. Martin sloshes to the hole in the cinder-block wall. He can see in perhaps fifteen feet before it's all dark. "Ready to try and get out of here?"

Velez and Blent slosh toward him. Behind them, to Martin's perception, the far wall of cracked cinder block, the tumbled shelves, his autographed John Wooden's Pyramid of Success poster, are all transforming into dirt. The sight frightens him as much as the earthquake did. He takes a last glance at the fallen photo of him with his two moms. The glass is cracked. He rushes into the hole, crawling through the pitch-black, wet opening of collapsed concrete, tangled rebar, broken pipes, wires, and mud. Velez and Blent follow.

Velez splatters Blent, knocking Blent onto a big, sharp rock with a right angle cut like a chair.

"I see the Bay!" Martin shouts.

Ahead of them a forest of boat masts rises in the night sky. Martin breaststrokes forward into the Bay. "I'm out!" He twists in the water to see Velez and Blent emanating from the channel of rocks. But from Bucky Martin's view, there is no stadium.

"All right!" Blent exclaims, stroking to Martin. "We're gonna win the frickin' game tomorrow!"

Velez tentatively pushes off, swimming into the McCovey Cove part of San Francisco Bay. "Damn! Freezing!"

They swim away. Martin does not mention that he does not see any part of the stadium or its ruins.

The black shadows of a wall of masted boats makes them halt. Over on shore there are no lit streetlights. Blent twists, treading water, to look back at the stadium: just dark piles of rocks. He scans for survivors, but the water is devoid of other swimmers. "Is the whole stadium destroyed?" he asks.

The trio treads water, looking back at where the stadium should be.

"I don't see anyone," says Velez.

Martin can't speak, so thoroughly shocked by the apparent devastation.

"Out for a swim?" asks a gravelly voice above and nearby.

In the bow of an anchored schooner behind them is the silhouette of a man sitting on a box.

Martin replies, "We crawled out from the stadium."

"From where? I apologize for my lack of hearing."

Martin asks the man, "You okay?"

"Best place for an earthquake is a boat!" he mirthfully roars, and motions toward shore. "Go around and follow the boats to the embankment. Mind the filth." Something on the boat distracts him, and he barks, *"Put that bottle down, you son of Sodom! The sun's not even up!"*

Martin swims backwards, aching to spot the gleaming office and condo towers across McCovey Cove. He doesn't see any new buildings. He's dazed by the magnitude of the destruction. He asks himself, *Where's the damned stadium?* "You guys see any buildings?"

Blent shakes his head. Velez does not respond.

As they swim toward shore, they're surrounded by bobbing eyeless pig heads encrusted with crabs. Velez yelps, splashing Blent and Martin as he swims as fast as he can without putting his head under. At the edge of the cove, Velez's feet come down in muck. He crawls on hands and his slipping feet make him fall to a knee in the mud.

The three Giants scramble up the mucky embankment. They stand naked and dripping, gawking at men and women carrying buckets, rakes, and shovels, hurrying toward downtown where an orange glow of fire fringes the night.

Blent and Martin swivel north, west, and south, while Velez blankly stares at the empty stadium site—a rocky, weedy, muddy, garbage-strewn point of land.

"What happened to the stadium?" asks Blent.

"Where's the parking lot, man?" Velez grimaces. "Some fucker scratched my Lambo! I'm gonna kill him!"

"Maybe it was a *her*." Blent, despite being at least partly in shock, can't resist taunting Velez.

"It always empties quickly," says Martin. "And after lousy losses, people leave faster. But our team? The whole front office? They all usually stay late, right?"

"Maybe they found a way out," says Blent. "The stadium was built to withstand earthquakes, right?"

"Maybe part of it's still standing on the King Street side," says Martin.

Blent surveys the black cove, looking for other swimmers. None.

*Ar! Ar! Ar! Ar! Ar!* a distant seal barks.

Martin leads Blent north along the Bay. Velez lags back, walking slowly, feet hurt by pebbles. "Man," Velez exclaims, "there's broken glass everywhere!"

Blent realizes he's on King Street, which is now dirt, with no sidewalks. There is a warehouse, a stable of loudly whinnying horses, and an empty lot where Blent is sure his apartment building stood. "My apartment's gone!" His eyes dart from a gas streetlamp to wooden warehouses up King Street. "How could those buildings be here and not my apartment building?"

Where the main stadium entrance should be—Willie Mays Plaza—is an inlet full of wooden boats. Some of the boats are stacked with crates, some crawling with men. The three Giants follow a rough path along the shoreline, amidst garbage and the briny scent of the Bay.

It's all devoid of light stands, bleachers, rows of connected seats, walls of reinforced concrete, turf, yellow foul poles, the 140-foot-tall screen, and *fans*.

Blent lifts his eyes to the stars. "Dear God, where's the stadium?"

"Maybe the parking lot is okay," suggests Velez. "You want to see a fast car, rookie? It can go one-sixty—easy."

Blent does not reply. He steps into the slimy muck and reenters the frigid water. He swims out to where, he figures, they escaped from the stadium, perhaps just fifteen minutes ago. It's water soaking into a wasteland. There's no fragment of stadium remaining. The steel bridge that spanned McCovey Cove is gone. The esplanade behind the stadium is gone.

*"Anything?"* asks Martin from shore.

Blent's aware that he's in shock, as he replies, half watching himself from an angle, "No one! No stadium!"

Velez pats his naked hips, instinctively checking for his phone. He turns to Martin. "You should've taken your phone with you."

"I should've taken a lot of things."

# 4

## They Love Me at the Fairmont!

BLENT CLIMBS OUT, shaking water off as he gingerly picks his way over weeds and broken bottles. "It's like the earth opened up and swallowed the entire stadium." He points at the place in the sky where his apartment stood. "And my house. And everyone in the building."

"Where'd *you* guys come from?" asks a voice behind them.

It's a man in a cart, holding the reins to a gray, swaybacked horse, the cart loaded with potatoes and carrots.

"Right here," Martin replies. "You know where we could get some clothes?"

"Lots of stores on Market Street and Mission, if they're still standing or not on fire."

"Any place giving them out for free?" Martin asks. "We lost everything."

"The churches. They're all over the place—swindlers and hypocrites." In a changed tone, the man asks, "Hungry?" He reaches under his slat seat, pulls out a tin bucket, steam rising.

He tosses a potato to Martin, then one to Blent, and one to Velez, who drops his on the ground.

Blent chuckles, "E3!" at Velez's fielding error. Then Blent's slammed sober by the potential loss of thousands of lives—their teammates, the coaches, the trainers and clubhouse attendants, the batboys, the ushers, the ticket scanners, the peanut and hot dog vendors. And what about Darla and the new baby? Are they all right? Darla might think that he's dead in the earthquake, and she'll have to somehow tell the little girl that her father's dead—dead forever? They'd have a funeral for him—with no body to bury.

Velez asks the potato man, "Want an autograph?"

His bemused smile lacks a number of teeth. "Autograph for what?"

"We're the Giants. We play right here." Velez indicates the inlet.

"Play what?" The man cocks his head.

"Baseball, dude! The *Giants*?" Velez laughs with incredulity.

"We've got other things to concern us than children's games, don't we?" He raises a hand at the fires engulfing downtown. "Here!" An empty potato sack flops to the ground. "That should cover one or two of you." Martin reaches for the sack. Staring at the naked trio, the man adds, "At the least you could say, 'Thank you.' That sack costs three cents."

"Thanks!" pipes Martin. "Pardon our manners!"

The man *humphs*, flutters the reins. The horse yanks the cart forward.

Blent rubs the warm potato over his torso, dissipating his chill. He recalls eating whole roasted potatoes like this, outside, pulled from an open fire, with his grandparents—Memaw and Pepaw—on their farm near Fayetteville, Tennessee. He had a dented metal bat that he took everywhere. Did they see the stadium shake apart? Thank God his mom traveled from Game 5 in New York to be with Darla and not to Game 6 in a stadium that was destroyed.

"Probably everyone moved the cars in the lot," Velez says. "They forgot and left us behind. I'm sure that everyone's okay."

"You're delusional!" Blent's body gesticulates with each word. "Nothing is left!"

Velez doesn't respond to Blent, then bolts along the Embarcadero, losing balance, catching himself, going away from Martin and Blent.

"André!" Martin calls. "Stop!"

Over his shoulder, Velez shouts, "Gonna ask Potato Man to borrow his phone!" He chases the distant cart clip-clopping toward the Ferry Terminal.

Martin leads Blent along the Embarcadero, tracking Velez. A mile ahead rises the Ferry Terminal clock tower. It's the only building Martin recognizes. "Something extremely weird is going on."

Blent scans their surroundings. Normally, an eight-mile-long bridge would be looming and they'd be walking toward it. But it's not there. "Certainly. Yes. Weird."

"What do you think?"

"If the stadium's gone, the whole city could've fallen down," replies Blent. "But if that happened, there would be rubble where the stadium was. But maybe we got hit on the head and we're in some sort of coma all together with Velez. But that doesn't make sense either."

"I read something about collective hallucinations," says Martin. "In Peru. Maybe that's what's happening."

"Or this is the afterlife . . ." Blent's voice dissipates.

Approaching them is a cluster of people of all ages, carrying framed paintings, bulbous bundles, a birdcage with four parrots, and a child's wagon loaded with hardback books. The cluster splits, going around Blent and Martin, giving the naked men a wide berth, a boy gawking at them. Everyone seems to be wearing three, four, five layers—a method of transporting their clothes. Three men are each hauling a steamer trunk, each carrying one end by a strap while the back end scrapes along the ground.

Blent wonders aloud, "Who would drag a trunk when you can buy a suitcase with wheels?"

"Maybe they're historical reenactors," suggests Martin.

"Like the Civil War?"

"More like the turn of the last century."

An ancient car, all fenders and wooden-spoked wheels, chugs loudly past, driven by a man in goggles.

Velez jogs back, huffing. "Potato Man's got no phone."

As the trio approaches the Ferry Building, the growing downtown conflagration alleviates their shivering. A fire engine pulled by a team of horses scurries past. Throngs of worried people—long skirts, heavy coats, bowl-shaped bowler hats, handlebar mustaches, luggage, pets—rush toward the Ferry Building. Others hurry past them, barely glancing at the naked men. But a cluster of kids near a stall selling potatoes and onions giggles at them. Velez waves, "Hey!"

Under a Ferry Building arch, Martin steps up to a fruit stand. The wooden fruit boxes are mostly empty, with only a few apples remaining. The proprietor is a large man next to a hanging scale. Martin asks to borrow a knife. In the bottom section of the potato sack, he cuts holes big enough for legs and creates what looks like burlap underwear. The other two sections of sack are long strips. He winds one of the strips around his midsection. Velez takes the underwear. Blent wraps a section around his pelvis and tucks it in like a towel.

Velez approaches a short man with greased hair standing behind boxes of gleaming salmon on ice. "I'm André Velez. Can I borrow your phone?"

The man sneers, "Get outta here, boy." The short man grabs the shoulder of his partner, aims his thumb at Velez, and makes a comment in Sicilian. Both men laugh. The second one waves the back of his hand at Velez. "Shoo away. No phone-y. Ha-ha!"

The first one asks Velez, "You carry fish?"

"Carry fish? I don't know what you're talking about."

The second man slaps the side of a box of salmon on ice. "Take fish to Oakland. This"—indicating the increasing fire and smoke up Market Street—"no good. You carry to boat. Half cent itch box."

"Half a cent?" Velez giggles. "Know who I am?"

The shorter man replies, "Yeah. You big Black jagass."

Velez's mirth is obliterated. *What did you say?*

The larger fisherman adds, "He say, 'You Black jagass!'"

Triggered, Velez lunges over the fish boxes, grabs both men by their collars, twists his enormous hands, and chokes them. The Sicilians croak, *"fung-oo!" "moul-en-yan!"* as their limbs flail. Other stallkeepers surround Velez, screaming, punching Velez's back and arms. Velez twists harder, and both sets of fishermen's eyes bulge. Martin jumps into the tussle.

Blent is stunned that people would talk to Velez that way. Blent's never heard anyone call Velez "Black."

With Martin and a dozen stallkeepers pulling on him, Velez releases the fishmongers.

Velez asks Martin, *"You hear what those assholes are calling me?"*

Martin and Blent steer Velez across the Embarcadero. They start up Market Street—many of the buildings ablaze—past clusters of dazed San Franciscans either fleeing the destruction or gawking at collapsed buildings.

Blent gazes at the rubble on Market, at a fire blasting out the top half of a green, copper-clad building, at a woman in a black dress wearing a hat with a long white feather and carrying a yapping poodle.

On the ground is a trampled newspaper, which Blent picks up and brushes off. It unfolds into the widest newspaper he's ever held. His eyes drift to the date at the top: "April 16, 1906." He shows it to Martin, who exhales, "Oh shit."

Martin scans their world, then closes his eyes, shrinking into himself. "The 1906 earthquake. We seem to be in it. If that paper is two days old, then today is April 18th, 1906. The day of the earthquake."

Blent shows the newspaper to Velez, who whacks it to the ground. "Fuck the news! It's always bad!"

A rumbling roar. Three blocks up the burning corridor of Market Street, the façade of a building collapses in a cascade of steel and bouncing stone blocks. The reverberation shakes the ground under their feet.

"Did we come out of some weird time-shift hole?" asks Martin.

"That's why I went back into the Bay after we circled the whole stadium," says Blent. "To search for the way we came out. That sort-of rock tunnel. It's got to be there. We've got to find it!"

"Yeah," Martin agrees.

"How come no one has a phone?" asks Velez.

Blent picks up the newspaper and shakes it at him. "Because we're in 1906!"

Velez blankly gazes at Blent, as he rubs the bump behind his ear where Blent hit him in the shower. "Too many fights today. What's '1906'?"

"The year!" Blent shrieks.

"Nah," Velez dismisses the notion with a wave of his massive hand. He steps in the way of a family rushing toward the Embarcadero, the wife wiping soot from her face, girls carrying dolls. Velez blazes a smile—recently laser-whitened—"Can I borrow your phone?" He's waiting to be recognized, his face on myriad billboards and TV commercials selling hamburgers, Mercedes, and Frank-E energy drink. "You guys like baseball?" Velez asks.

"I do!" brightens a boy about five years old.

"I'm André Velez, and I need a phone!"

The parents frown and herd their kids past the strange men in burlap diapers.

In the momentary quiet of a burning city, Martin looks to the sky and snaps his fingers. "Okay, back to the present!" He waits a moment; nothing's changed.

Blent reads the dirt-streaked newspaper:

## HETCH HETCHY RESERVOIR DAM COMPLETE
## THE GIBSON GIRLS OF RENO!
## 50 NEW GLORY NEGROES HANGED

Velez watches firemen loosen bolts on a fireplug and wait for water to fill their hose. The long hose remains limp as only a trickle emerges from the nozzle.

The trio slowly moves up the middle of Market Street past buildings ablaze and onto California Street.

*"Make way!"* barks a policeman in a bullet-shaped helmet. They jump aside for a team of firefighters. Velez giggles, "Look at those outfits, man!"

"We gotta reverse this!" says Blent, gritting his teeth. He lifts a brick off the street and hurls it at a burning building. He picks up another brick and flings it, screaming, *"Damn!"* He hurls another. Another. Another.

*"Don't worry, man!"* shouts Velez. "Onward! Up California! They love me at the Fairmont! They'll give us rooms. Even you, rookie."

"We don't have any money," says Martin.

"I put my out-of-town peeps there all the time. I've dropped a million dollars in that crib. I don't need money!"

As they walk up steep California Street, Blent wipes tears, everything gone.

Martin acknowledges, "We're all feeling it." As they climb the street alongside a row of tall houses, he scans an intriguing sidewalk pile of framed family paintings, silver jugs, silverware boxes, a stained-glass vase, a child's rocking chair, and leather-bound books. The nearest door opens and a woman in a black dress struggles to pull out a rolled rug. Her hair comes loose and spills over a shoulder. The sight of burlap-diaper-clad Velez approaching seems to shock her more than the encroaching fire. She recoils. Velez smiles and yanks the rug to the sidewalk, his back and arm muscles rippling.

The next door up bangs open and a small girl and boy emerge in tears. The little girl exclaims to her neighbor, "Mrs. Johnson! Papa fell! He can't move and the fire is hot!"

Mrs. Johnson's long face turns to the trio of nearly naked men. "Lord help us!"

"Show us!" offers Johnny Blent, aware of the conflicting notions that this is not his time and that these people need help.

"Dude, we're almost there!" Velez points up the hill at the still-standing Fairmont Hotel. "Let's go."

Martin glances down California Street at the encroaching fire. "Right, Johnny? We gotta figure out what we're doing first. This isn't real."

Blent impulsively reaches out and feels the fine wool fabric of the woman's drooping black dress, before she jumps away.

"These people are as real as anyone," Blent answers.

"This is bullshit," Velez comments. "Let's get a room, or two! You guys can share."

Martin suggests to Velez, "Let's just check out the situation here first."

Velez growls, "Fine."

The boy and girl rush in and upstairs, leading the ball-players and Mrs. Johnson around a landing and up two more flights. A man is lying on the floor, robe open, fallen books scattered. He waves an arm and hails, "Good morning!"

Martin is impressed by the floor-to-ceiling wall of books.

Mrs. Johnson inquires, "Where's Justine?"

"Retrieving the auto with Walter. I don't know why they prefer that machine to me."

Mrs. Johnson and Martin laugh. Thick billows of smoke waft past the windows, and the house seems to be heating up.

Blent asks, "Hip? Leg?"

"Pelvis," the man replies. Scanning the naked trio, he grunts, "Perhaps we can find you gentlemen some clothing!"

"We could use it," says Martin.

"They got a clothes shop at the Fairmont," Velez scoffs.

"Ever have back trouble before?" Blent asks the man.

"Nothing too terrible."

The little girl pipes up, "Daddy complains all the time!"

"Every time he sits down," agrees the boy.

Blent reaches under the man to assess the alignment of the vertebrae, the tension of the muscles going down the spine. "Took two chiropractic courses at college," Blent explains as he probes at a spot between sacrum and pelvis.

The man's body jumps, "That's tender! Oooooh!"

"We don't have time for this!" Velez barks. Beyond the windows, thick smoke swirls.

"Broken hip," Blent concludes. "I'm sorry but we're gonna to have to lift you up by your armpits. It'll hurt a lot. We've got to get out of here." To the woman, "Ma'am, take the kids downstairs."

Blent and Velez raise the short, pudgy man to his feet. They lower him, grimacing, onto a chair. Martin and Blent lift the front while Velez grips the chair's back. They carry him down the stairs.

A gigantic automobile, all fenders, big wheels, and wide seats, pulls up to the curb, driven by a reedy, pimply boy wearing goggles. In the passenger seat is a woman with a fine net holding her wide-brimmed hat. Both shriek at the sight of the nearly naked men emerging from their home carrying the man in a chair.

The ballplayers gently set the man down. Velez's eyes pop at the sight of the automobile—wood trim, nickel finishings, red paint.

Bursting out of the auto, the woman admonishes her husband, *"What did you do?"*

"I was reaching for a very important book and lost my balance."

"You love books more than people!" the woman scoffs as she rushes inside.

*"Is this a Finch Touring Car?"* Velez's jaw slackens. "I saw one of these at the Monterrey auction! Shoulda bought it! My oldest is a '38 Dodge. I love that one. My grease monkey wants to make a hot rod out of it, but I like the classic look, you know? Not gonna chop it. Seventeen cars—that's what I'm up to. My Lambo just got keyed!"

The boy driver stares openmouthed at the naked giant talking bizarre nonsense to him.

The woman in the wide hat emerges from the doorway with a bundle of bond and insurance certificates. Embers waft. The fire is eating into the face of the house two doors down. The groaning man grits his teeth as Martin and Blent deposit him in the passenger seat of the Finch Touring Car. The woman herds the two little children. She tells the driver, "Jacques, give each of these men ten dollars."

*"Ten dollars!"* he protests.

"Without them your father would be left to burn to death! Ten dollars each!"

As the son digs coins from his pockets, the woman buries her head in the shoulder of her groaning husband. She straightens and says to Martin, "My husband's armoires are in the top-floor bedroom, please take whatever you want. We are eternally grateful to you all. Be full of care and full of God."

"Amen!" echoes Blent. "Full of God!"

The boy driver transfers a fistful of coins—some gold—to Blent's cupped palms. The boy checks the car's gauges, then sets the goggles over his eyes.

Blent stares at the coins. "Thank you." He has no pockets.

"Where're you going?" Martin asks.

The woman replies, "To my sister's. Hopefully her house is still standing. In Belmont."

"Belmont!" Velez detaches his gaze from the car. Smoke intrudes between him and the family, flattening them into two dimensions. "My compound's in Belmont! Buena Vista Circle! Know it? Can I hitch a ride?"

The driver and the woman recoil in matching horrified looks. The car inches away.

"How about I'll stand up here?" Velez gets up on the running board, the car listing and groaning under his weight.

"Please!" exclaims the man, his painful moan harmonizing with the car's. Velez jumps off.

As the Finch Touring Car eases away, the two little kids wave goodbye to the strange naked men. The car rolls down California, takes a right onto Powell, and disappears in a haze of smoke.

The ballplayers gawk at the sheet of flame consuming the building two doors down, then dash into the house, up past the drawing room and the library, to the master suite. A king-sized bed lies crushed under the fallen brick chimney. Pieces of brick ejecta encircle the bed. A monstrous hole in the roof shows where the chimney fell in.

An armoire door hangs open. Velez pulls out a stack of shirts, forces his arm through a tuxedo shirt, laughing as his forearm jams in the narrow shoulder.

Blent steps into a pair of pants many sizes too small, squeezes into them, but the clasp won't close. He cinches a belt, but it squeezes him hard. A white dress shirt is tight, wearable. A jacket comes up mid-forearm.

Martin crams into a black dinner jacket with satin lapels, and pants with a button-up fly.

Blent loads the fistful of coins into his jacket pocket. He stuffs his foot into an oxford, but even with the back mashed down, it's too small. There are twenty pairs of too-small shoes.

"Let's take two pairs and maybe a shoemaker can widen them," suggests Martin.

Velez chuckles. His shoes are custom-made by an Italian shoemaker in Vegas. "You guys are cheap."

"We don't have any money, André. Except what that kid gave us," says Blent.

The floorboards are getting hot. Smoke is billowing up the stairway, crawling along the ceiling and funneling out the gaping hole through which the chimney fell. Now the front stairway is afire, blocking their way down.

Martin blurts, "Back stairs!"

Down half a flight, they are slammed by an endlessly deep tunnel of fire. Velez shouts, *"Shiiiiiiiiiiiiiiiiiiiiiiiiiiiiiit!"* and they retreat to the bedroom, coughing from the smoke.

Martin yanks on a window curtain, crashing it to the floor. *"Grab a drape!"* Out the window, swirling smoke blocks the view of the street. Martin places a hand on the glass, as hot as a just-bought paper cup of coffee.

"Not goin' out like this!" Velez protests as they each wrap paisley drapes around themselves as best they can. As he hesitates at the front staircase, Velez can see the two stairs below, but the remainder of the staircase is blocked by smoke and fire.

"Deep breath," Martin advises from under his drape, "and go fast!" Martin's down into the fire, disappearing from Blent and Velez.

Blent hesitates, freezes with a thought of his great-uncle Bo, who liked to watch TV in bed while smoking Camels and sipping Busch. Bo and his trailer went up in flames, nothing left of the trailer except its steel ribs.

Head and body covered in drape, Velez rushes past Blent, disappearing down the stairs, into the fire. Blent sucks in smoky air, trips on his drape, and falls, bouncing to the bottom of the flight. He rises and resets his drape, rushing down through fire. He can feel the hairs on his shins singeing as he bursts along the second floor to the stairway, down to the first floor, and finally out to the sidewalk. He throws off the drape as his momentum carries him to the street.

"Watch out!" Martin yells as a steamer trunk tumbling down the steep street—shirts and shoes flying—clips Blent's elbow—worse than getting hit by a 98-mph fastball.

*"I'm so sorry!"* apologizes a man atop the street. *"Are you all right?"*

Martin slaps the fire in Blent's hair, while Velez smothers Blent's burning pants cuffs.

# 5

## This Deep, Stinking Hole

"FUCK THIS FIRE!" Velez screams to the smoke-streaked sky. With his drape clutched across his shoulders, he charges up toward the Fairmont Hotel.

Martin and Blent follow, their newly donned clothes pinching everywhere.

Over his shoulder, Velez orders, "Hang back! Leave this to me!"

Past the Fairmont driveway, Velez bursts into the massive hotel. Blent and Martin wait just inside the front doors, the lobby redolent of perfume, cigar smoke, and humanity. Martin scratches stubble on his chin as Blent extracts, and carefully counts, the unfamiliar coins: two $10 gold pieces, a half-dollar, quarters, dimes, nickels, and five pennies. $23.55. He counts again, reports the amount to Martin, who chuckles, "The kid shortchanged us by six-fifty."

Observing a pair of women in ornate hats, one with a long red plume, the other with a stuffed raven perched atop hers, Blent rasps, "We could be in Hell, right? There's fire. There's smoke."

"Why 1906?" Martin asks. "Why not 1806, or 1006, or just 6?"

"It's God's plan!" Blent declares. "We are chosen for something great!"

Martin considers the God angle as a perfumed woman in a fox-trimmed coat passes, training her assessing gray eyes on Blent before she disappears into the throng in the lobby. Martin notices, but Blent does not. In this lull, Martin's body sags. "Think they have coffee?"

Across the lobby, well-dressed men and women part for André Velez, who winks his eyebrows and offers, "Crazy day, right?" He's waiting for someone to recognize him. He approaches the concierge, a spoon-faced man, who is besieged on all sides by guests:

*"We must get transportation!"*

"We will do what we can regarding carriages and hired automobiles," the concierge replies.

*"Is it safe to drive?"* asks another guest.

"It seems that the streets are passable, but you will have to make that judgment; acquiring fuel will likely be a problem."

*"Is there a hotel with rooms by the ocean?"*

"To our knowledge, all other San Francisco hotels are full."

Velez's arms spread, the drape expanding like butterfly wings to display his naked chest. He asks, "Is Manny here?"

The concierge squints up at the giant. "There is no one employed at the hotel by that name."

"What about Joseph, the general manager?"

"Joseph?"

"Yeah, from Australia."

"There is no Joseph from Australia."

"You sure?"

"Certainly."

"How about Charles, the head chef? He knows me!"

The concierge turns away from Velez to address other guests.

Velez scoffs, bursts away, weaves through frightened couples and wide-eyed businessmen to the reservations desk. "Hey, man!" Velez corrals the attention of a bald, birdlike attendant. "I'm looking for Arlene Tempo. She's here—getting her condo painted. I don't know what room." At least, Velez figures, he can stay with Arlene; she's got a big suite, and there's enough room, including Martin and Blent.

The birdlike man regards Velez with brimming skepticism, then lowers his eyes to flip through a box of reservation cards. "*Mrs.* Arlene Tempo? No one by that name."

"She checked in a few days ago. Maybe she checked out."

"No sir. Perhaps another hotel."

"One of my entourage was here with her when she checked in. Hefty guy—Cheech. Lots of tattoos."

"She's not here. As you can see, we are swamped with distressed guests."

"Can I use a phone?"

The man indicates the hallway across the lobby.

"Thanks." Velez pauses. "Sorry for the clothes. They were lost in the earthquake. Couldn't get back to the clubhouse."

The man blankly regards Velez, not picking up the hint that he should recognize Velez, that *everybody* should recognize Velez, and that to Velez, this *non-recognition* is getting old.

Licking dry lips, Velez charges across the lobby and stops in front of an elaborate display of magazines, newspapers, candy, and cigars. He tells the bellhop, "I've never seen so many newspapers! Everything is ruined outside. You have a phone?"

"Down the hall, around the corner."

"Cell phone? Can I borrow it?"

"You will need a nickel."

"For what?"

"The phones."

"You joking?" Velez decides to change his approach. "Okay, my good fellow. Give me a nickel and I'll give you an auto-graph. My autograph's worth hundreds of dollars."

"Who are you? The president?"

"André Velez. I play baseball for the Giants."

The baby-faced bellhop pauses. "The New York Giants? John McGraw's team?"

"No, man. Give me a piece of paper and a pen!"

The bellhop removes a pencil from behind his ear and offers a sheet of lined paper. Velez signs his autograph, adding below the name his uniform number, "9," and "MVP 2x." The kid gives him one nickel. Velez examines it—"V" on its back. The bellhop specifies, "Charity."

Velez finds the row of booths, each occupied by a man or woman holding a candlestick telephone, each caller either lis-tening intently to the bulky earpiece or enunciating into the conical mouthpiece. To a man wearing a monocle, he asks, "This some sort of 'throwback day'? Don't cell phones work?"

The man's brow squeezes, eyes narrow. He slides into a vacated booth.

Velez tries to remember the numbers for Mako, Ernie, or Cheech; he likes to *snap* his fingers and say the name into his phone; he feels naked without it.

A booth opens. Velez slips in and shuts the door. He's rarely been in an enclosure so small. He lifts the heavy earpiece and articulates into the mouthpiece a 650 number he remembers.

A female voice replies, "Sir, what is that?"

"It's for Mako. Should I say it again?"

"Sir, what city are you trying to phone?"

"I don't know. Lost my phone in the earthquake." He growls, "Goddamned computer!"

"Sir, everyone is cross today. Please calm yourself. Which city please?"

"*Which city?* Just the phone."

"Which city are you calling?"

"I don't know where he is."

"Are you telephoning a residence or a business?"

"A residence, I guess. He lives in San Mateo."

"Should I try to connect you to San Mateo with the last digits you said, 3435?"

"Sure. Yes. Thanks."

"Connecting."

Velez listens to the clicking, pops, and static on the line as he adjusts the drape to cover his chilly shoulder. The voice returns: "That number is not active. I am sorry."

"Wait a second." He remembers Arlene's cell number and gives that. But it does not connect. He tries Cookie's number. And even Gloria's—even though she stole his house, she might help. No luck. The voice tells him, "I'm sorry, sir. There's nothing I can do. I trust you understand. I have many other people waiting. Goodbye."

On the other side of the glass door three people wait. Groaning as he exits, he strides past the newsstand. At the edge of the lobby he cups his hands around his mouth and yells, *"Does anybody have a phone?"*

A hundred people turn to regard the giant in the red-and-orange paisley shawl and burlap underwear, then return to their worried conversations.

Velez trudges over to Martin and Blent and slumps against a pink marble column. He's stunned. He defeatedly asks, "What's going on, Buck?"

Martin takes a deep breath. "It's 1906, André. Somehow, we went from earthquake to earthquake. I don't know how. It's impossible, but we're here."

"Or maybe it's the afterlife!" Blent offers.

Velez turns his hand and raises his middle finger. "The afterlife."

Martin tugs Velez's drape and leads him to the concierge's desk and to the wall calendar. "See that? April 18, 1906."

André Velez focuses on it. His body stiffens.

"It's true, André. I don't know how—"

Velez bolts away.

*"André!"* Martin calls after him.

Velez is easy to follow, head and shoulders above everyone else. Martin and Blent catch up with Velez, who's ripping through periodicals at the newsstand.

"Nineteen-oh-six!" Velez drops the newspaper in his hand and takes up another. "Nineteen-oh-six!" He takes up another. "Nineteen-oh-six!"

"Pay for those, sir!" the bellman yelps. "Hands off!"

Velez pivots to the rack of magazines, grabs a *Collier's*, announces, "Nineteen oh six!" and tosses the magazine in the air. *The Saturday Evening Post*: "Nineteen oh six!" *The Theatre* magazine: "Nineteen oh six!" *Country Life*: "Nineteen oh six!!!" He tears at the stacks of magazines, sending them to the floor. The bellman attempts to tackle him but bounces off and falls. Velez smashes a rack of candy. He spills stacks of newspapers and lays across the papers, rolling over them, facedown, burying his head in the crook of his elbow. *"Noooooo!!!!!!!!"* Tears drip along his arm, and he kicks his bare feet. *"Noooooooooooooooo!!!!!!!!"* He pounds a fist. His body quivers as he sobs. Martin pats his back. Velez swats at Martin's hand, grunting, *"Leave me alone!"* After a few seconds, Velez rolls over. Gazing up at the ceiling, he asks, "Nineteen-oh-six?"

Martin nods grimly.

"I don't know what this is," says Blent. "Maybe we're hallucinating, or the stadium ceiling cracked our heads and we're in a coma—and talking to each other in the same coma. Or this is God's own Hell—I mean the Devil's. Or maybe it's Heaven."

A pair of men in bowler hats stops. One inquires, "Is he in pain?"

"No," Blent tells them.

"Terrible day." They move on.

Martin gazes out the windows at the smoke, at a worried, pasty woman wearing a hat with a stuffed robin on it. "Seems to be 1906."

"You're telling me it's all gone?" Velez asks Martin. "The new Miami condo gone? Kauai gone? Belmont gone?" Velez wipes his tears. He pleadingly looks up at Martin.

"Yeah, André."

"The scratched Lamborghini? My Maybach? *All* my cars? *All* the money? The endorsements? *The posse?* My dudes . . . how are they gonna survive? They can't get *jobs*. And Cookie . . . well, she's probably happy I'm out. She's got big insurance on me . . . very big insurance."

"I don't know how this happened," says Martin.

"I gotta pick up my own *dry cleaning*? I gotta go out and buy my clothes *myself*? And get my own food and *cook* my own food? And the girls? *All* my girls? My God! Every city . . . a whole career's worth?"

*"That's what you're crying about!?"* Blent screams. "My wife is in *labor*—or was—I don't even know if my daughter is born! I'm stuck here with you, you arrogant bastard!" Blent looks at his callused hands. "How does every muscle, my whole *brain*, these danged tattoos, get taken from the twenty-first damn century to 1906?"

The bellhop rushes up with two large men who appear displeased at the sight of Velez sprawled across and crushing an array of periodicals for sale. They latch onto him. "Up, sir. Time to go."

*"Don't touch me!"* Velez rises and storms away.

\*

A few minutes later, Blent stands in California Street, increasingly frightened by the panorama of smoke and relentless flames.

Velez wipes his tears. "You think everyone who was at the stadium is dead?"

"I don't know," replies Martin. "When we were escaping, I saw the walls changing to dirt and mud, parts of the ceiling falling to the floor and disappearing—like they were evaporating. So I don't know if everything was destroyed or not. What I do believe is that we are here." He stamps his foot on the cobblestones. "In 1906."

"Did you have anyone at the stadium?" Velez asks.

"Just our players and coaches and the front-office people. I didn't give out any tickets last night, if that's what you're asking." He wonders, if Buck, Jr. had been around town and offered a ticket, would he have gone to the game?

"We gotta go back to McCovey Cove," says Velez, "and find that hole where we came out of. Right now!"

Martin licks his teeth, missing the effects of his vibrating toothbrush. He gazes at the gargantuan fires, blocking their most direct route to the ballpark site. "I read a few books about today," Martin tells them. "The quake wasn't the main problem. The shifting ground cut the water pipes, so the firemen right now can't get any water pressure. That's why the fires are so out of control. Let's make a big circle around this main fire and get back to the stadium."

"What if that wormhole we went through gets covered up?" asks Velez. "What if it disappears, like a scar healing or something? Like things transforming—what you were talking about with the wall in your office turning to dirt. We've got to get back before it all goes away!"

Blent's stomach rumbles, and he instantly feels guilty that, amidst the human tragedy affecting a whole big city, he's thinking about food.

They join the flow of men and women fleeing west along California Street. Velez rips a hole in the middle of his paisley drape, sticks his head through—*voilà*, a poncho that extends to his knees.

An old man in a too-small blue army jacket is dragging a steamer trunk, one end scraping the cobblestones. "Let me help," says Blent, lifting the back end of the trunk.

Velez turns to a woman grunting under the weight of an ornate clock decorated with gilded bird's nests and vines. "I got this for you, lady," says Velez to the frightened woman, as he hoists the clock to his shoulder.

"That's not necessary!" wheezes her companion, a pudgy man with a purple birthmark on his cheek, a sword on his belt.

"It's fine!" contradicts the woman, then to Velez, "Thank you."

Martin lifts a ten-pound typewriter from the man with the sword. "Where to?"

"The Presidio. The police are directing people there."

"We're just going to Van Ness," explains Martin. "Then left. Nowhere near the Presidio. Sorry."

"What if I offered you twenty dollars to help carry our possessions?"

"Twenty dollars?" As the words spill from Martin's mouth, it is another out-of-body feeling. Martin has drawn baseball paychecks for twenty-five years. Before the world farted them out, he was probably making twenty dollars a minute. "No. Sorry. We'll take you down to Van Ness."

Hundreds of refugees trudge along California Street amidst gently swirling ash, black smoke wafting overhead.

"Where's the sword from?" Martin asks.

"The war between the states."

"You saw *action*?"

The man chuckles. His wife rolls her wide-spaced eyes.

"Sharpsburg. Shenandoah Valley campaign. And, unfortunately, Gettysburg. That idiot McClellan!"

Martin halts, thrilled. "*Gettysburg?* Why 'idiot McClellan'? McClellan wasn't there. Lincoln forced him out in 1862."

The man scratches the border of his birthmark, "I saw McClellan acting, almost sabotaging, our side. I was fifty feet away when a bullet to his right eye took him down. We rallied. But we were slaughtered by cannon off the hills to the south. McClellan failed to secure those hills early in the fight. Casualties were, roughly, even. The South drove us off."

Martin, astonished, asks, "Cemetery Ridge?"

"That's what they called it. Yes."

"And the North *lost* Gettysburg?"

"Driven from the field and all aspects."

"What is 'New Glory'?" Blent asks.

The man stops, his sword rattling against his belt. He asks Blent, "Never read the newspapers, sonny? They don't teach it in school?"

His wife admonishes, "Don't ask him about New Glory. He's an obsessive."

Blent replies, "We're just dumb baseball players."

"Of course I am an obsessive!" the man revs up. "Slave-owning buggers! The cowards fled Mobile, New Orleans, and Pensacola, regrouped east of Havana, and overrode that island. So the former island of Cuba is now called New Glory. They constantly revel in cruelty regarding the small islands of the Caribbean to extend their little empire, all under the protection of the British Navy."

"Shoes!" Velez veers left, carrying the clock toward a shoe repair shop on Larkin Street.

"No time for shopping!" the wife of the man with the sword protests.

"Sorry," Martin tells the couple. "My feet are killing me in these shoes!"

The three men set the couple's possessions down outside the shoe shop. Inside, Blent shuts the door. "You're open?"

The mustachioed shoemaker replies in his German accent, "Am I going to transport three hundred pairs of shoes and machines? No! I vork until the fire tells me, *'Halt!'*"

They examine shoes with leather uppers, chunky heels. There's a pair of boots that Velez can barely squeeze into. "I can pound those open," offers the cobbler.

Outside, the Civil War veteran and his wife negotiate with a man who's holding the bridle to a horse and cart. Martin steps out and helps them load the wagon. The woman drops a silver dollar onto Martin's palm.

Blent pulls on a pair of socks. He tries a pair of unclaimed yellow-brown oxfords, which fit nicely. The cobbler hunches over, softening the leather on the old boots while Velez waits. Blent and Martin cross the street to a mostly empty restaurant, the aromas of bacon and toast and a weak note of coffee. "Apologies. We are closed! Out of food! All I have is bread! And the last of the coffee!"

Martin downs two watery cups of coffee as he and Blent chomp slices of sour bread. They return to find the cobbler pounding a boot. Martin offers slices of bread to Velez, who recoils. "Not gluten-free, right?"

"Sure you don't want it?"

"I'd be shitting all over San Francisco."

$2.25 for Martin's used shoes
$2.25 for Blent's used shoes
30¢ for three pairs of socks
$ 3.00 for Velez's shoes

———

$7.80 total

Martin pays. The shoemaker sighs, "Gott villing ve vill survive!"

"Amen!" Blent raises both hands in praise of God.

Outside, Velez scrapes his slippery soles on a jagged stone. "Which way?"

Martin leads them, jogging along Polk Street, dodging distraught refugees, and tumbled-down houses. The fires are mostly to their left. There's a Victorian mansion engulfed in fire, its neighbors untouched by destruction, so far.

As they cross Market Street, far down the fiery corridor, the Ferry Building and its clock tower are screened, revealed, and screened again by the smoke.

*"Stiff as fuck,"* Velez comments about his shoes. "That guy didn't know what he was doing!"

Their progress at times blocked by fire and smoke, rubble, and police barricades, they snake through SoMa. After fifteen minutes quickly jogging, they find themselves standing at the muddy spot upon which, or near which, they first emerged from the stadium into the McCovey Cove part of San Francisco Bay.

"That's the rock you knocked me into," Blent tells Velez. He steps from firm ground onto squishy mud, grasping a rock with a right-angle chunk out of it, like a chair.

"Sure you remember it?" asks Martin.

"Yeah." Blent nods. "Do you, André?"

"No."

They walk the scrappy ground, toeing broken boxes, broken bottles, a few bricks, rocks, a pile of rotting chicken bones, a broken-off shovel handle, a rusted-apart pail. Blent pulls a shirt up through the dirt. Nothing from the twenty-first century.

From the rock-chair, Velez takes measured steps inland. He points down. "This is probably your office, right?"

"Maybe. I guess so," replies Martin.

Velez chooses a rock, scrapes the ground.

Blent grabs the old, broken shovel handle and twists it into the ground. Martin scrapes with a side of a broken pail.

Each scrape produces a bit of dirt. Martin's pail disintegrates, and he tries scraping with a broken brick. "We need shovels." He stands, hands on hips.

"We gotta find that wormhole before it closes up!" Velez urges.

"Looks like everything's pretty closed up already," says Blent. "There's no passage. No wormhole I can see."

"No, it's not!" Velez insists. "Right, Buck? I'm not staying here!"

"Maybe the hole is still here, buried," Martin suggests. "But the ground doesn't really look disturbed. It's just a scrappy piece of land."

Velez throws down his rock scraper. "I'll look for a way in through the water. We came *out* of the water; we'll *go back* through the water." He pulls off his drape and sloshes into the Bay.

"Your shoes!" Martin warns. "You're wrecking them!"

"I got two hundred pairs of Italian leather beauties waitin' for me!" Velez swims out. He scrambles along the shoreline, dipping underwater, searching crevices.

Martin and Blent watch Velez probing the shoreline. Martin scans the boats anchored in McCovey Cove, wondering where he can borrow, rent, or buy some digging implements. At the end of the Cove, across the street from where they originally emerged from the Bay, is an unpainted barnlike structure with smoke rising from a chimney, a group of people outside of it. "Maybe they have food over there."

"Fuck food!" Velez comments from the water, then, "Goddamn, I'm hungry!" He emerges, dripping, and shivering, "Where're the trainers with the fucking towels?"

They trudge a scrappy path in the wasteland to Third Street. The Royal Palm Saloon emits a stench they can detect well before they step inside. The large room is packed with its ripped-shirt, scarred, unshaven, torn-trousered, filthy, gap-toothed clientele.

"Whoa!" Blent's never seen anything like it.

Dirty and gritty, the ballplayers fit right in. They thread between crowded tables of drunks and lowlifes, some stunned, most hushed amidst the continuing disaster of earthquake and fire and humans trapped in rubble, except for a boisterous group at the far wall—roustabouts playing poker as if the cataclysm were thoroughly immaterial.

Velez sits shivering at a table. His boots clomp wetly on the floor as he pulls them off. Soon they're slurping thin soup and glasses of sarsaparilla.

Returning from the bar with a bunch of ragged newspapers, Martin informs them, "The bartender says there aren't any shovels. They're digging out bodies."

"That's what we should be doing," says Blent.

"Fucking Home Depot," Velez mutters.

Martin opens a newspaper. His chair scrapes the floor as he scoots in. "Listen to this: 'New York 3, Brooklyn 2; Philadelphia 13, Pittsburg 4; Chicago 2, St. Louis 0.' They're spelling Pittsburg without an 'h.'"

Velez and Blent ask, "How much do players make?"— chuckling at their conjoined question.

Martin shrugs.

Velez stands up on his chair, which creaks loudly. Martin gets up and sets his chair next to Velez, so Velez can place one mammoth water-wrinkled bare foot on each chair. Velez shouts, "Excuse me!" Some in the throng notice. His neck veins bulge. *"Excuse me!"* The crowd's attention orients toward him. *"Does anyone know how much money a Major League baseball player makes in a year?!"*

For a second and a half the scrubby crowd stares at him, then blasts into full-throated laughter.

*"I'm serious, man!"*

The crowd erupts anew, laughing at Velez.

He sits, tips up his bowl of soup and downs it.

A burly man with a beard brushing his sweater approaches. "Baseball fanatics?"

"Players," Velez blurts.

"I played a bit in my day! We love baseball—my friends and me! Where do you play? Mind if I take a seat?"

"We play in San Francisco. Here," Blent starts. "I mean, will in the future. Oh, forget it."

Martin clarifies, "Our ballpark was destroyed."

"Sorry to hear it!" He raises his voice so it carries to the bartender, "Four whiskeys two times!" Then to the table, "Thirsty?"

"Still hungry," Velez replies.

"Name's Haley," he winks. To Velez he says, "You were asking how much ballplayers earn. Christy Mathewson pulls in twelve thousand a year, I believe. Frank Chance of Chicago gets fourteen thousand. Honus Wagner of Pittsburg, nine thousand."

"Fourteen *thous*and!" Velez spits. "How about fifty *million*—for starters!"

Haley laughs, revealing his short brown teeth. "Andrew Carnegie, are you?" A bevy of shot glasses are set down. Haley drains one.

Blent asks, "How much does a bricklayer make?"

Haley's fish mouth droops. "Oh, about ten dollars a week."

"How much does a house cost?" Blent asks as they are joined by Haley's friends, a rank-smelling bunch in torn black jackets, one with a peacoat. Three bulky, bearded dudes, one skinny and clean-shaven.

Haley says, "May I present Misters Price, Cummings, Davies and Shaw." Hands are shaken all around. Beers and whiskey shots are set down. "Bottoms up, everyone. Don't be a fancy dancer."

"Not for me," says Martin. "We've got work to do."

"I ain't no fancy dancer!" Velez shoots back his whiskey, face twisting in disgust. "Whoo! Battery acid!"

"We have us some ballplayers here!" Haley informs his friends as he rises, standing behind Velez. "One!"

Walking in briskly from the front door is a skinny man in a denim shirt torn off at the shoulders who goes around the table and stops behind Martin.

"Two!" states Haley, reaching into his back pocket, then, *"Three!"*

The skinny man behind Martin whips out a wooden hammer, as Martin bolts up at Haley, just as simultaneous blackjacks thump the heads of Velez and Blent. Blent crashes to the floor. Velez slumps over the table, unconscious.

Martin dodges the wooden hammer wielder, while the big man's blackjack smacks Martin on the shoulder. As Martin dives after Haley, Haley's blackjack whips Martin's hip. Martin stumbles to the floor, grabbing a fallen beer glass, then rises and smashes the glass into Haley's jaw. The two other men rush at Martin, smothering him, pounding him, and ripping his pants, sending coins clattering to the floor.

Blent gets up, dizzy. He grabs a bottle, leaps at one of the men, and smashes the bottle on the man's bare head. Martin punches his beer mug into the ribs of the skinny one, then starts firing shot glasses at the faces of the others. Blent whips his elbow, catching Haley in the jaw.

As their assailants retreat, Martin and Blent throw shot glasses after them. Blent nails the skinny one in the ear. Martin bounces a shot glass off Haley's throat. Blent fires one into Haley's chest; another pings his nose. Haley and his men try to throw the shot glasses back at Martin and Blent, without accuracy. They pick up a few of the ballplayers' coins.

*"Not in my place!"* screams the bartender, coming at Haley's group with a sawed-off baseball bat. Patrons belatedly—in the hopes of earning a free drink—get between the ballplayers and Haley and his men. Others scramble after the loose coins.

Haley, holding his jaw, backs away. He spits a gob of blood.

*"Get the hell out, Haley!"* screams the bartender. *"No shanghaiing in here!"*

*"Give us our money back!"* Blent screeches.

Martin shouts, *"You bastard!"* Clenching the empty beer mug in his fist, Martin lunges at Haley, but a sawed-off baseball bat smashes against Martin's throat. The bartender, who is the wielder of the bat, screams, "Enough!" as Martin crashes to the floor. Blent helps Martin up to the table. A glass of water with a fish tank's worth of white floaters in it is brought to him.

The attackers flee. Martin and Blent tend to Velez, who opens his eyes. "What the fuck happened?"

"Wow," says Martin. "Almost shanghaied."

"Shanghaied?" asks Velez, touching the growing bump on the back of his head.

"If they'd won," says Martin, "they'd drag us to a boat, lock us under the deck. Then, when we're in the middle of the ocean, they'd let us come up on deck. Our choice would be to work for those assholes or get thrown overboard."

"Shanghaied," Velez mumbles, then louder, "I think I saw a porno where they were shanghaied. Everyone got along just fine."

"That's disgusting," Blent comments. "Is everything sex with you?"

"Yeah, well, pretty much."

Martin counts the coins he's reclaimed. "They stole about eight bucks."

The bartender appears. "I'm Ridley. Terrible day. I apologize that you were attacked in my saloon." He offers his callused hand, and all shake it.

"We need shovels," Velez says.

"People trapped?"

"Sort of," Velez replies. "And a steak, well done."

"Come back later. I might have steak."

"We only have a few dollars," notes Martin.

"A few dollars it is, then. What a day. Did you feel the Earth move like it was alive and angry as Hell? My God!"

Ridley disappears and returns with two rusty shovels and a pickaxe. Martin refrains from mentioning that when he asked Ridley half an hour ago, Ridley said he didn't have any shovels.

Back at the stadium site, through the afternoon, the ballplayers dig a hole into what they figure is the location of Martin's office, occasionally asking each other, "See anything?"

"No."

They joke about being attacked.

An hour or two into it, Velez complains, "I'm digging more than you two combined!"

"No fucking way!" Blent digs in hard.

Martin slams his pickaxe into the dirt, loosing a big hunk. He chuckles at the thought that most ballplayers will compete over anything. Even digging a hole.

As the sun descends behind Twin Peaks, the hole is about eight feet deep and twelve in diameter. They've dug a trench parallel to McCovey Cove that extends in each direction from the hole. They have found no remnant of the stadium. Zero.

"What time do you think it is?" asks Martin, his skull pinging, the result of an insufficient day's worth of caffeine.

"Game time," Blent replies, slamming his shovel into the hole and loosing a hunk of dirt. "My body's telling me."

Velez wipes his brow. "Yeah. We'd be playing the seventh game right now."

Blent asks Martin, "We're not gonna have to stay here, are we? In 1906?"

"I don't know," replies Martin.

"Fuck no!" insists Velez. "But I want that steak."

They carry their tools back to the Royal Palm. Velez plops down at the same table from which they were nearly shanghaied. He guards the tools as Blent and Martin approach the crowded bar.

"What's your theory on how this happened to us?" Martin asks. He knows Blent the least well of anyone on the Giants. Blent's been to three or four spring trainings, starting this past season at Triple-A. When second-base wizard Scuttario's wrist got crushed landing on it after a double play, the team considered trading for an experienced 2B just as a placeholder for the rest of the season, but the nerds touted Blent's defensive metrics. He's gotten some key playoff and World Series hits. He's a good kid, but most good kids don't stick in the Major Leagues. They wind up as high school coaches, or insurance salesmen.

"I think we're cut off," replies Blent. "In all the digging we've done, there's nothing."

"There's nothing," Martin agrees. "It's shocking. Maybe something will change when the tide comes in. But it seems like we're cut off from the twenty-first century. This is just completely fucked. With the seventh game of the World Series to play! That's what's killing me."

"*That's* what's killing you?"

Martin chuckles and changes the subject. "We don't know if Darla gave birth, right?"

"Do. Not. Know!" Blent shakes his head and grits his teeth, his heart ripped to shreds.

"No other kids?"

"No."

"I hope you didn't have a string of girlfriends in every Triple-A city. I sure did when I was your age. I thought I was a rock star for a few years. Then I stopped rising and saw the same small towns again and again, and I realized those girls were moving on to the guys coming up with bigger potential. The girls are sharper at choosing talent than the stats guys."

"It was easy to let all the other guys have 'em. I'm not that way."

"High school sweethearts, you and Darla?"

"Eighth grade."

Martin swivels to try and get Ridley's attention, but he's pouring drinks down the bar. On the wall behind the long, scarred bar, is a list, in large block letters going from ceiling on down, a painted scroll decorated on each side with painted American flags:

| | |
|---|---|
| George Washington | 1789–1797 |
| John Adams | 1797–1801 |
| Thomas Jefferson | 1801–1809 |
| James Madison | 1809–1817 |
| James Monroe | 1817-1825 |
| John Q. Adams | 1825–1829 |
| Andrew Jackson | 1829–1837 |
| Martin Van Buren | 1837–1841 |
| William H. Harrison | 1841 |
| John Tyler | 1841–1845 |
| James K. Polk | 1845–1849 |
| Zachary Taylor | 1849–1850 |
| Millard Fillmore | 1850–1853 |
| Franklin Pierce | 1853–1857 |
| James Buchanan | 1857–1861 |
| Abraham Lincoln | 1861–1873 |
| Thaddeus Stevens | 1873–1877 |
| Ulysses S. Grant | 1877–1885 |
| William A. Wheeler | 1885–1889 |
| Chester A. Arthur | 1889–1893 |
| Amos P. Amboy | 1893–1897 |
| William McKinley | 1897–1901 |
| Mark Hanna | 1901– |

Martin gawks at the list. He grips Blent's shoulder. He glances back at Velez, who's glum, touching the bump on his head.

"What's wrong?" Blent asks.

There's *so much wrong*, Martin doesn't know where to begin. Ridley appears. With desperation, Martin asks Ridley, "That list right? Mark Hanna? What happened to Theodore Roosevelt?"

The bartender waves his middle finger toward the bottom of the list. "I'm no Hanna fan, but the facts are the facts. T. R. is the VP."

"Never heard of Amos P. Amboy," notes Blent.

Martin turns to Blent and sputters, "Thaddeus Stevens was a *congressman*! Never president! And Cuba is 'New Glory' now? It means that everything is different, or *can* be different. All that history I read over the years . . . You just have to wonder *what else is different*."

"Want the steak?" Ridley asks. "Fifty cents each. How's the bumps and knocks?"

"Yes, three steaks please. Got a place for us to sleep later?" asks Martin. "We've got nowhere. Gonna be cold tonight. *Is baseball the same?*"

"The same as what?"

"Sorry."

"Might have a room upstairs."

"Thanks," says Martin. "We've got more digging to do."

"Find anybody?"

"No, it's not that."

"Good."

"Please save a room. We're hungry, so steak would be great."

A filthy, dusty bearded man pushes past and sotto vocco, tells Ridley, "Box of dyno outside."

Ridley's eyebrows rise. "Full?"

"Minus two sticks. Railway dyno."

After the steaks, Ridley shows them to a dusty upstairs room. There's a sagging single bed and mattress, no pillow, a small rug on the floor. The muffled roar of the bar comes up through the floorboards. "I've got to charge you seventy-five cents each," Ridley half-apologizes. "The missus, she keeps accounts."

"We've only got a dollar and fifty-three cents," Martin tells him.

"I'll take the dollar-fifty. There's a toilet down the hall. Please keep it clean." Ridley departs.

*

On a baseball field, you never ask, "Are you tired?" You assume a guy wants more practice, more reps, wants to get better, wants to be on the field. They dig holes hour after hour, deep into the night. Two miles away, the city continues to burn.

Velez regales them with the story of how his lawyer in Scottsdale, who became a girlfriend, tricked him into signing the deed of his house over to her; now he can't get the house back. Martin asks Blent to tell them about his brother, the war hero. Blent tells them about his grandparents' cabin on Lake Panchoo, lighting fires and going wild with Mark, who could usually keep up fine with Johnny's antics. When Johnny was eight and Mark six, Mark followed Johnny up a tall tree, fell out, and broke his leg. Another time, Mark crashed his bike chasing Johnny on a ride; he wrecked the bike but walked away with a scraped elbow. "Mark loved his country and would do anything for it. Made the ultimate sacrifice."

"What about you, Buck?" Velez asks. "Tell us something we don't know about you."

"Right now, I'm just freaked out as hell that Mark Hanna is the president, when he's *not supposed to be*. And the South *won* the Civil War, or at least didn't surrender and fled to Cuba. Shall we call it a day?"

In the dingy room above the bar, Blent tells Martin, "You take the bed, Coach."

Velez purses his lips, nods. He and Blent stretch out on the rug. Velez wraps himself in the drape-poncho. "This is as fucked up as it can get!"

"You think?" asks Blent.

Martin says, "St. Louis. That's the nearest major league city. They have two teams. The Cardinals and the Browns. The Browns became the Baltimore Orioles in 1954. But right now, they're the St. Louis Browns."

"What about San Francisco?" asks Velez.

"Minor League. Pacific Coast. The New York Giants moved to San Francisco in 1958. The same year the Dodgers moved from Brooklyn to LA."

"Sixteen teams in the Major Leagues." Martin rattles them off. "No divisions. No playoffs. The winner of each league goes to the World Series. I mean . . . unless baseball's fucked up like the list of presidents. But from what I read in that newspaper, it's the same. God."

# 6

## Dick Ward

"HOLY SHIT!" Velez jolts.

It's the first light of dawn upstairs in the Royal Palm. Blent sits up, his neck sore from sleeping with his arm as a pillow.

"My boots!" Velez wiggles his toes on his bare feet. "They're gone!?"

"Did you sleep with them on?" Martin asks.

"Yeah."

"Then someone snuck in and cut the laces," Martin says. "I was out like a log."

"Can we go back to that shoe store?" Velez asks Martin.

"We only have three cents, André."

Velez shrieks, jumps up, hops onto the bed. Blent jumps, too, not knowing what's wrong. Velez is pointing at the floor; there's a cockroach the size of a quarter crawling through the wall. Martin and Blent crack up laughing, not regarding a cockroach as much of a problem compared with being ripped through time.

At the stadium site, the tide has risen. The chair-rock's seat is submerged, its back sticking up like a shark fin. Velez steps down into the largest pit, examining their work in the light of day. His bare right foot plops into water, a result of the risen tide.

"This was your office," Velez concludes, voice deadened by the pit. "I'm sure of it."

He extracts a square of cloth from the dirt wall—*from our time? A baseball uniform?* Turning it over in his hands, though, it looks to be from the era in which they've been thrust. A rough weave, detectable even in its half-disintegrated state. He climbs out and hands the cloth to Martin. "What do you think?"

"It's nothing." Martin removes his shoes and descends. He places his hand on the side of the hole. It's possible that he glimpsed this very dirt transforming from his office's white-painted cinder block. He says, doubtfully, "Maybe this dirt can *change back* into my office."

Velez and Blent stare into the pit, to gauge if it's transforming, while seagulls squawk, a faraway argument in Italian rolls on, and a boat creaks, *bang*, up on their little piece of scrap land.

A man, a woman, and a boy about eleven years old climb out of the rowboat. They pause by the holes. They, too, hold shovels, pails. The woman wears thick gloves. Gloves protrude out of the man's back pocket.

"Where'd you get the gloves?" Velez asks. He shows a bleeding hand.

The woman sneers, "What are you doing, digging *here*?"

"Mind your own freakin' business," Velez retorts.

"There are people trapped in falling buildings, and you guys are digging a stinking hole to China. Come with us to dig real people out of houses. There are bodies in the streets. Our church is organizing search parties."

"What church?" Blent perks up.

The kid replies, "Bohemian Church of the Archangel."

"You know the Restored Church of Christ?" Blent asks.

"No," the family responds in unison.

Blent turns to his two comrades. "Maybe I can get some food and make a few bucks."

"I'm frickin' starving," says Martin. "I'm going with Johnny."

"If I find the hole, I'm not waitin'!" Velez warns

"Just leave a note to mark the spot," Blent suggests. "Or leave your potato sack underwear."

"Good luck, rookie," Velez says. "Don't let any houses fall on you. See ya, Buck."

Blent and Martin help the Bohemian Church of the Archangel track down and make an account of its membership of 287. Foodstuffs are brought to the church, which is dusty, smoky, and undamaged. The basement kitchen is firing up as chunky-armed cooks produce pot after enormous pot of goulash, chicken stew, boiled vegetables, and bricks of bread.

At the end of the day, Blent and Martin wrap six plates of stew, chicken, and vegetables in a blanket, tie it to the end of a charred two-by-four, and walk with the laden blanket dangling between them. Picnicking at the edge of the biggest hole, Velez voraciously eats while Blent and Martin chomp roast chicken. They convince Ridley to let them sleep in the filthy room atop the Royal Palm for another night.

\*

They get to work early every day. Velez digs at the stadium site, while Blent and Martin shuffle between working with Velez and helping the church people.

By the foggy dawn of day six, they've pounded a hundred pieces of scrap wood into the earth, staking out the four bases. They outline the field, the Giants' dugout, the tunnel from dugout to the concourse, the clubhouse, all of the lockers, Martin's office, and the escape route to Willie McCovey Cove. The wiggling, rising, and receding waterline cuts off almost all of the outfield.

Velez hammers a stake where the third-base coach's box should be. Blent and Martin have scrounged buckets, another shovel, and a hammer. Digging out rubble, Martin has found a few books, including a battered Bible for Blent. They've made a few dollars in tips, some of which goes to Ridley.

"That's it!" Blent drops his shovel. "I'm done! Let's go to St. Louis and try out. I'll never see my wife again!" He raises his hands to Heaven, then covers his face and sobs.

Martin shakes his head at their fruitless digging. "The wormhole's gone. This is a cosmic accident. We're fucked, André. Face it."

"Just let me dig, goddamn it!" Velez steps down into a hole, disappearing.

Martin rips a piece of hardtack he bought from Ridley and hands the rest to Blent, who's drying his eyes on his dirty sleeve and continuing to sob. Both sit on the cold ground, chewing the leathery dried meat, while shovelfuls of dirt fly out of the hole.

Velez's head pops up. "You know what?" he barks. "Get me a box of dynamite, and we'll turn over the rest of this earth."

"We've turned over every goddamned inch," Blent sobs.

"Not deep enough in most places!"

"Then you'll be ready to get out of here?" Martin asks.

Velez swallows and gravely nods. "Fuck yeah. Yeah. Yeah. Nineteen fucking oh six."

Fifteen minutes later, Martin and Blent are walking up Market Street, where steam shovels belch smoke as the city is digging out and rebuilding. The stalls at the Ferry Building have reopened, where the price of a bushel of apples has jumped from twenty cents to a dollar. Business has never been better at the funeral parlors and cemeteries.

Soldiers with rifles guard a bank building. A corpse is covered by an Army blanket.

"Pulled from the rubble?" Blent asks a young soldier.

"A looter!" a short man behind them declares. He's less than five feet tall, dressed in a spotless black suit, tie, gold-rimmed spectacles spanning his shiny pink face.

"Clear away!" someone yells from across the street. A pair of steam shovels raises a fallen brick wall as sections of brick break off, sending up dust clouds.

Blent feels something jabbing his stomach: the little pink man's pen. "Thirty-five cents an hour!"

"For what?"

"Recovering goods. We want honest workers. It took us five days to dig down to this level." The little man waves his pen like a conductor's wand over the site, where scattered men and women are climbing on the rubble field. One extracts a bolt of cloth. Another is walking across the rubble holding two canvas mannequins, which he sets down alongside an array of furniture, intact glassware, china plates, oriental rugs, pillows, stacks of folded sheets, dresses, suit jackets, and pants.

A minute later, Blent and Martin are out on the rubble field. They spend hours excavating goods. At the end of the day, exhausted, they lean together as they push over a chunk of bricks the size of a twenty-first-century refrigerator. They rock the chunk back and forth until it rolls backwards, and they jump out of its way. Martin shrieks as a shard of glass protruding from the bricks slices his thigh. Blood oozes. He squeezes the two sides of the wound. "Well, there goes my swimsuit modeling career."

The cut is jagged.

"You need some medical help," Blent tells him.

"You a doctor?" Martin asks sarcastically. "And also a chiropractor?"

"I always dreamed of med school."

"Holy shit!" says Martin, gazing down at a spot revealed by the thigh-slicing hunk of bricks, a smashed nest of pocket watches amidst broken glass shards of a crushed oak display case. They carefully remove bricks, uncovering dozens of gold and silver watches.

"This might be a few hundred dollars," Martin says quietly.

Blent licks his lips, fighting the urge to steal.

Martin wipes the sheet of blood dripping down his thigh. "This might get us to St. Louis."

"Those men have rifles."

Martin glances at a group of soldiers sitting in the street a hundred feet away. "I sort of don't really care anymore."

"What did you men find there?" the diminutive boss yells from the edge of the rubble.

"Nothing!" Martin replies.

"He caught us," Blent whispers.

The boss makes his way toward them. He snaps his fingers at a guard with a rifle, who follows.

"It's a body!" Blent yells.

The boss and guard halt.

*"Dead?"* asks the boss.

"Big mess, sir!"

"Man or woman?"

Martin removes his grimy shirt, spreads it next to the watches. "It's a child."

Other workers climb toward them, half-curious, but fully eager to take a break. Blent bellows at them, *"Back to work!"*

*"Back to work!"* the boss echoes, resuming his wobbly trek.

Martin and Blent pile the watches—about sixty of them—onto the spread-out shirt. Martin rolls it up tight and wipes blood from his leg onto the bundle. "My leg is okay," Martin tells Blent. "Don't care if I'm bleeding."

Blent says, "I'll make it seem heavy—like there's a head in there."

The boss and the guard are closing. Martin hands the shirt full of pocket watches to Blent. "You're so fast, take the watches. I'll veer off and draw their attention."

"Rifles up and down Market Street."

"Those kids don't know how to shoot."

"How do you know?"

"Coach's instinct."

Martin and Blent scamper over bricks, chunks of concrete, and shattered glass, heading to the uptown side of the lot. The boss yells, *"Come here!"*

Martin replies, "He's got the head!"

Blent carries it like a baby, shielding it from view. "It's stinking and bloody!"

Workers stop and soldiers stare. The little pink boss retreats to the edge of the rubble where he waits for Blent with a cluster of three soldiers holding rifles.

"I've got the one on the left," says Martin.

"We're assaulting men in uniform."

"Yeah." Martin picks up a charred brick.

"What ya got there?" a soldier motions with his rifle.

"The baby's head," replies Blent.

The boss squeaks, "Give it here!"

The moment they're out of the rubble, Martin bursts forward, knocking the biggest soldier to the ground.

Blent smashes the brick against the chin of a soldier, who crumples. "Sorry!" Blent apologizes.

Martin twirls a fallen rifle far onto the rubble.

*"Soldiers!"* the boss screams behind them.

Blent and Martin sprint past a horse with frightened eyes, past a teetering truck, past a cart carrying a recumbent stone sculpture of Saint Mary. Just ahead, a soldier turns and raises a shotgun as Blent bashes his forearm into the soldier, flattening him. A woman in a heavy black dress shrieks.

A rifle shot whistles waist-level between Blent and Martin, pinging off the street in front of them. Police whistles blow.

"Two more blocks!" Blent grunts, "then left!" Blent bursts ahead, leading Martin, who chugs behind, losing ground like in a nightmare, as another rifle crackles.

They flee through SoMa, police whistles trailing them. They snake through alleys, slow to a jog. Six blocks later, they walk, panting, with the realization that they seem to have gotten away. They giggle with elation, full of adrenaline.

Back at the stadium site, checking for pursuers, Blent unties the bundle and spreads out the watches. Velez wipes blood off his just-smashed thumbnail and licks his mossy teeth. "Good job." He throws the shovel down so hard its blade end bounces higher than their heads. He screams, "Dynamite!"

*

*Boom!* The first explosion sends a parabola of dirt chunks rocketing sixty feet high. They jump in the hole and dig through the loose dirt. It's where they figure Velez's locker, phone, massage chair, and clothes should be, but all they find is rocks, mud, and clumps of plant roots.

*Boom! Boom! Boom! Boom! Boom! Boom! Boom! Boom! Boom! Boom! Boom! Boom! Boom! Boom! Boom! Boom! Boom! Boom! Boom! Boom! Boom! Boom! Boom! Boom! Boom! Boom! Boom! Boom! Boom! Boom! Boom! Boom! Boom! Boom!*

Nothing. Bereft of any shard of the twenty-first century other than themselves, they stare out across the churned field in the settling cloud of burnt paper casings and nitroglycerin. Velez shifts his gaze to where he last saw his precious Lambo, before Game 6. Almost feeling the indentations in the side panel, he mumbles, "Dick Ward."

# 7

## Stupid Little Gloves

EVEN ONE-QUARTER tumbled down and half-charred, San Francisco looks beautiful from a ferryboat pulling away. The ballplayers stand on deck, in new suits of thick wool, their faces clean-shaven.

Wiggling his toes in a new pair of boots, Velez checks out two worried-looking windblown women, one in a tight-waisted jacket and billowing skirt. Martin cradles a fat roll of newspapers and books, the wound in his leg nicely sewn up by an enterprising veterinary student for five dollars. Blent spits a jet of tobacco juice into the Bay, the tobacco harsher and less consistently moist than his normal de-nicotined chew; this stuff has kick.

As Martin ponders the Ferry Building clock, the hands stuck at 5:12—the moment of the earthquake—he fingers the chain on an Estrella del Norte pocket watch with a cracked crystal clicking away in his vest. For a seven-dollar finder's fee, Ridley, the Royal Palm proprietor, directed them to a no-questions-asked jeweler. Watch by watch, he denigrated each one's quality, deeming thirty-three only good for the metal, twenty-three *maybe* reparable, and ten functional. After an exhaustive negotiation, during which Velez commented, "This is worse than salary arbitration," and Martin decided to keep the working Estrella del Norte watch, the settled price for the remainder of the watches was $172.80. It was enough for the dynamite, enough then to bathe, shave, and clothe the three men, to take a room at the Fairmont for $9, to pay for a sumptuous steak dinner, and to purchase train tickets to St. Louis, where two Major League teams play: the Browns in the American League, and the Cardinals in the National.

As the ferry crosses, and San Francisco shrinks, Martin spots what he's quite sure is Green Street, and the block where his condo tower stood—or rather, should rise—in fifty-six years. His elbow reassuringly squeezes the bundle of paper and history books. But this history is not so reassuring. This world of 1906 is not the one recorded in his books at home.

Trailing his hand along the boat's railing, Velez approaches the pair of women, "Hey! Where're you headed?" Two men holding soda bottles suddenly emerge on deck, eyeing Velez, their steps quickening. Velez doffs his hat, which the wind zips away into the Bay. The cluster around him laughs. He knows *never* to intrude on another dude's girl; the world has always been abundant with women. So don't get into a fight over a girl—ever! He just laughs, "Easy come, easy go!"

Reveling in the surge of chewing-tobacco nicotine, Blent claps his hands and announces, "Time to play ball!"

Martin spins, blasting, *"What the hell are you so happy about?"*

Blent has never seen Bucky Martin erupt in this manner. Blent apologizes, "Sorry!"

"No. *I'm sorry*. I'm outta line. It's weird, leaving San Francisco. Even though it's not our time, obviously, it's still the same hunk of the world." He changes tone. "You guys *are* gonna play ball. With your skills and dedication, and conditioning, this *will* work out."

Velez, who caught the last part of Martin's statement, says, "I can smack the ball and impress anyone. And Blent can probably slap his cheap hits. What are *you* gonna do, Buck?"

"Me?" Martin replies. "Hell, I'll be the towel boy."

\*

Packed with earthquake refugees shivering in the cold night, the train winds its way through the snow-blanketed Sierra Nevada Mountains as Velez vents to Blent about the lack of video games, and dearly missing the TV show *Murder by Dawn.*

The next morning, changing trains in Truckee, near Lake Tahoe, Martin exclaims, "Hey look, a ballplayer!" as a young man boards with a baseball bat resting across the top of his canvas bag.

After the train gets underway, Martin brings over the absurdly long bat, and the kid, who says he plays at St. Mary's College.

Velez grips the bat and rises to the aisle.

"You hit with this log?" asks Velez.

"I hit three-twenty-two last season."

"Fifty ounces and thirty-nine inches?" Velez estimates the dimensions. Most of his bats are thirty-two ounces and thirty-one inches, though he'll switch up to thirty-three, thirty-four, thirty-five ounces, depending on how he feels, and who's the pitcher.

"Good guess. You're exactly right."

"Not a guess. I'm a frickin' MVP! Twice!" Velez chokes up the handle, trying to get a good feel.

"I'm thinking of going up an ounce or two," the blond kid says. "More oomph."

The twenty-first-century ballplayers share a glance, knowing that bigger bats can be a hindrance. Power is generated from the speed of the bat combined with the force of the contact crushing the ball.

Velez takes his batting stance, looks up with gleaming eyes. "Feels good!"

Martin asks the kid if they can see his glove, if he has a baseball. "Mr. Blent and Mr. Velez are professional baseball players."

"Where's your equipment?"

"Wiped out in the frickin' earthquake," Velez replies. "You don't know what I lost!"

"How did the earthquake destroy bats and gloves?" the kid asks. "It burn up in a fire?"

"You ask a lot of questions," says Blent. He holds his hand out for the bat, but Velez raises his elbow to keep Blent away. Blent grabs for it.

"Let Johnny try it," Martin attempts to intervene.

Velez hands over the bat.

Blent takes a turn, hunching into his righty stance. "This thing's a tree."

The kid retrieves a ball and his glove, which is about half the size of a Major League baseball glove. Blent, respecting the unwritten commandment that you never blithely shove your hand into anyone else's mitt, asks, "Mind if I try?"

"Fine."

He puts it on, pounds it. Tosses the ball into the pocket. It's like a nine-year-old's glove.

"That looks like something for walking around Boston in October." Velez sneers. "How can you catch with that?"

Blent hands the ball to Martin. It's the same size as balls in the twenty-first century. It's scuffed, dirty, the leather feels somehow thicker, and Martin can slightly compress it.

He hands it to Velez, who examines it.

Martin asks, "Can we buy the bat?"

The kid scratches a golden sideburn. "How much are you offering?"

Martin has no idea what a bat costs in 1906. "What do you think is fair?"

"Let me consult my father. He's up there. He bought it for me. And I did say I was looking to buy a new one."

Soon the father—portly, jowly, pale—trundles down the aisle. He smells of salami. "Where are you headed?"

"St. Louis."

"Where have you played?" He pulls a greasy cloth from his back pocket and wipes his nose.

"San Francisco," Velez replies.

"Didn't see you," he says. "I would remember." He reaches in his jacket, removing, indeed, a small salami wrapped in a white cloth. He unhinges a pocketknife, slices off a finger's width of salami, and offers one in turn to each of them.

"We're gonna play ball in St. Louis," Velez says.

"Oh?" he responds. "Maybe they'll look at this fellow." He nods at Blent. "But they do not let Negroids play in the Major Leagues."

"*Negroid?*" Velez's face contorts. Martin and Blent jump between him and the man.

Recoiling, the man asks, in a friendly tone, "Then what are you?"

"I'm from LA!" says Velez.

"What's that?" the man asks.

"I'm half Swedish!"

"Mulatto?"

"Why do you fucking care about my skin, you asshole?"

The man sniffs. He pulls the bat from Blent. "No bat for you."

\*

That night as the train bumps through the Wyoming plateau, distant hills in the moonlight, the car is dimly lit at each end by a bare bulb. The coal stove spews dust, minimally diminishing the frigid air jetting in under the doors. Velez is taking a long time in the bathroom, and Blent waits his turn. On the other side of the door Blent hears Velez, unmistakably, retching. Velez emerges sweating, shivering, wiping his mouth. He recoils at the sight of Blent.

"You all right?" Blent asks.

"Ate something bad." Velez brushes past.

"Glutinous bread?" Blent asks, half joking.

"Must be."

Later, while families crammed in nearby try to sleep, the trio leans together, heads almost touching. Blent is chewing tobacco and spitting into a spittoon, one stationed at each end of the car, for chewing riders to borrow. To Blent, Velez doesn't seem sick anymore.

"Abraham Lincoln lived to 1881," Martin says. "He had three terms in office. He died from pneumonia. Confederates invaded Cuba and renamed it New Glory. Since then, they've been taking over islands in the Caribbean. They invaded Panama—took it away from Colombia. They raided New Orleans in 1899 and burnt a lot of it down. All protected by the British Navy. New Glory is a slave society."

"Slave society?" Velez asks. "When will people ever fucking learn?"

"*Shush!*" a voice in the darkness admonishes.

Blent toes the slipping pile of newspapers. "I just read an article about Henry Ford making cars in New Glory."

Velez offers, "The butterfly effect."

"The butterfly effect?" Martin asks.

"Don't you watch science fiction?"

"I'm not really a science fiction fan."

Velez scoffs, "You don't know what you're missing. It's the theory that if someone is able to go back in time, then the littlest thing that is altered, like the flapping of a fucking butterfly's wings, would create a chain reaction of differences that would become huge."

Martin shakes his head at the concept.

"Yeah," Blent says. "I get it. If we can find the point in the past when the history of this world began diverging from the one we know, then that might untangle this timeline we're on. And the fact that we are here—that we moved through time—could have possibly changed things in itself, further."

They silently consider the implications.

Martin says to Velez, "Meanwhile, we have to make up something about you. It's 1906. It's unfortunate we have to even think about it. The color of your skin."

"What about the color of *your* skin?" Velez asks sarcastically. Turning to Blent, "Not you, you pink grapefruit."

"It seems that even in this different world, there aren't any Black men playing in the Major Leagues." Martin apologizes, "I'm sorry, but what color do you think you are?"

Various women over the years have commented on "how nice" Velez's skin is, or what a nice color it is, but never *which* color it is. A light *café au lait*, perhaps. "I don't know. What about you? Italian or something?"

"One of my moms was Jewish."

"*One* of your moms?" Blent asks.

Martin chuckles. "Yeah. Didn't you know I had two moms? That's like, the first line of my bio," he jokes. "They were great. My bio mom was Jewish. We never met the sperm donor. He might've been Italian originally. I did a DNA test. It showed Piedmont area. But also Russian. Hungarian. Irish."

Velez stares at his hands but cannot see any color in the dark. "The women I wind up with, their favorite color is *green*."

"All right, Casanova," says Martin. "We've got to have a plan, a story that works in 1906."

"Whitey ain't asking *you* to lie about who *you* are."

The train sways hard, *clacking* Velez's and Blent's heads together.

"*Ow!*"

"*Shit!*"

"Before Jackie Robinson broke the color barrier," Martin says, "they used to let Indians play. They often called them 'Chief.' Chief Bender, Chief Meyers—those two guys are ballplayers in the newspapers. Think about it."

"*Indian?*" Velez asks. "The only Indians I ever meet are across a blackjack table. Dealing. And one of my accountant's assistants."

"'Chief Velay,'" says Martin trying out the name. "That's not bad, right?"

"Velay?"

"Just has a nice ring to it. It obscures your whole background."

Blent offers, "How about 'Chief Coyote'?"

"'*Chief Coyote*'?!" Velez squawks. "How about we call you 'Chief Crackerhead Dipshit!'"

*

Next afternoon, as the hands on Martin's pocket watch show two o'clock, the train chugs across the Missouri River. St. Louis is covered in a brown-yellow haze, the product of a hundred smokestacks lining the Missouri and Mississippi Rivers, and tens of thousands of homes and businesses burning coal.

"There's no Arch!" Velez comments. Other than church steeples and the smokestacks, only a few office buildings poke up above the rooflines. "I can't believe we were just here. It sure doesn't *look* like St. Louis."

They were just in St. Louis when the Giants swept the Cardinals in the playoffs, staying in the most high-tech hotel in town. But now, other than the contours of the rivers, they don't recognize anything.

Blent gazes out the open window at a man pushing a cart of green apples; a horse-drawn cart piled twelve feet high with pots, pans, and washing tubs; a man screaming, *"Up! Up!"* whipping a cane into the ribs of a brown horse, supine, only moving its head. Blent shouts, "Hey! Leave that horse alone!" but engenders no reaction.

Stepping off at Union Station, the three teammates have no possessions other than a few books. Blent is carrying a fifteen-pound typewriter in a case for an older man who claims to be a journalist. At the end of the platform are two porcelain water fountains marked "White" and "Colored." Blent purposefully grabs the handle of the "Colored" fountain, and drinks.

Velez ponders the fountains. "This is fucked."

"You all right?" Martin asks him. "Missouri wasn't as segregated as the Deep South in 1906—I don't think—so this is weird. Maybe the alternative timeline we're on. But maybe Missouri *was* this segregated."

The older man relieves Blent of the typewriter. "You're not in California anymore! Welcome to the rest of America, gentlemen!"

A block from Union Station, the trio studies a restaurant menu painted on a window. They're soon devouring twenty-cent beef tenderloins, twenty-cent pan-roasted catfish, five-cent mashed potatoes, creamed spinach, and cup after cup of watery coffee. Cheek stuffed with gristly meat, Blent jokes, "Think they make Frappuccinos?"

Velez grunts. "My guys used to spend, like, a hundred bucks a day on that diarrhea."

A crowded, horse-drawn streetcar deposits them at Robison Field, which is surrounded by a six-foot wall of unpainted slats containing a murmuring crowd. There's a section of grandstand running from halfway between first and home to halfway between third and home, the back row of fans visible from the street.

"Are you serious?" Velez whines. "This is a big-league ballpark? Are we in the worst part of Mexico or what?"

Blent snorts, "I played in bigger stadiums in Little League."

Referring to the sign facing the street above the grandstand, Martin notes, "It says 'Robison Field,' so this is Robison Field." Under the sign, fans are trickling out of the gate, leaving the game as the distinct sound of a bat *smacking* a baseball is heard, followed by the crowd lustily booing. A fan in the top row yells, *"My mother pitches faster than you, Sallee!"* inducing scattered laughter. Blent, Martin and Velez are thrilled.

At the gate, they find a man slumped on a stool, his suit jacket dusty, his pants repeatedly patched at the knee, shoes with holes on the side. He tells them, "Game's almost over. Price is still the same." Beyond him, through the rectangular tunnel under the grandstand, Velez and Blent can see the pitcher, the shortstop and the center fielder. A pitch *pops* the catcher's mitt.

*"Strike!"* the umpire bellows.

The crowd cheers.

"At least it *sounds* like baseball," says Velez.

The announcer intones, "Now batting, Frank Chance!" to a mixture of applause and booing.

"Frank Chance of the Chicago Cubs!" Martin exclaims. "Frank Chance of Tinker to Evers to Chance!" Martin tells the gatekeeper, "These men are ballplayers. We're here from California. San Francisco. We'd like to meet Manager McCloskey."

"San Francisco?" The weathered face turns serious. "I hope you didn't lose anybody."

"We lost everything, man!" Velez shakes his head. "We don't have a team anymore or teammates!"

The gatekeeper waves them in. "Anyone asks for a ticket, tell them to talk to Old Davey."

They emerge into the middle of the grandstand. The green field is spread out before them—nine fielders, a batter, a home-plate umpire, and an umpire between second and third. The bases are loaded. The coaches at first and third are screaming at the pitcher, who's tall and incredibly thin. The pitcher winds and throws a straight pitch that doesn't seem all that fast to the twenty-first-century ballplayers, and the batter cracks it above the second baseman's head into right field. The crowd boos as the runner from third scores, followed by the runner from second scooting toward home in his baggy uniform.

"Move, please!" a man bellows behind Martin.

They drift up the wooden stairs, staring at the men on the field with no names or numbers on their backs. A man in a suit on the field lifts a four-foot megaphone and announces, *"Now batting, Frank Schulte!"* Boos are mixed with a few cheers. The scoreboard above the right field wall:

|          | 1 | 2 | 3 | 4 | 5 | 6 | 7 | 8 | 9 | R | H | E |
|----------|---|---|---|---|---|---|---|---|---|---|---|---|
| Chicago  | 2 | 0 | 1 | 0 | 0 | 1 | 1 | 0 | 3 | 8 | 9 | 1 |
| St. Louis | 0 | 0 | 1 | 0 | 0 | 0 | 0 | 0 |   | 1 | 2 | 3 |

A man nearby rises, announces to his seatmate, "I can't watch this massacre anymore," and brushes past Blent, Velez and Martin.

In the bleachers, a brassy song blasts—men and women standing with trumpets, clarinets, drums, and tuba.

The pitcher, Sallee, winds up and hurls the pitch. The batter cracks one past Sallee's shins, up the middle, the ball rolling into center field. Two runs score. More boos.

Droves depart.

## CHICAGO   10 — 1   ST. LOUIS

"It's been way too long," Martin says as they settle into a vacated compartment—four spindle-backed chairs to a square of low wall. These boxes line the first row of the grandstand. Martin chuckles. "This is what 'box seats' means!" They are in their own little box.

Blent leans his forearms on the wall separating grandstand from field. "Baseball is a beautiful sight."

Non-ballplayers are allowed on the field—a cluster of photographers just ten feet from the catcher, scattered policemen eyeing the crowd, a boy in a white suit and cap with a wicker basket scanning the grandstand, "Last chance for lemonade!" The field itself is splotched with innumerable dirt patches and shaggy grass. Velez points at the St. Louis first baseman, "How can he catch with that little glove?"

The megaphone announcer bellows, "Now batting! Johnny Evers!"

Evers is 5'4" and looks like he weighs as much as an eleven-year-old girl, his face drawn, pinched.

The catcher's chest protector dangles below his crotch. He's got a wire mask, but no shin guards. He's squatting about eighteen inches farther back than a modern-day catcher. That little extra bit of distance the ball needs to travel—eighteen extra inches from pitcher to catcher, eighteen extra inches from catcher to second baseman—excites Blent. It could translate into scads of stolen bases.

Evers works the count to three balls, one strike. On a sharp-breaking curveball, he lines out to the first baseman, the ball smacking mitt just as shouting and screaming are blossoming out of the left-field stands. Six bullet-helmeted policemen are converging on a cluster of men in bowler hats. Martin scans neighbors in the box seats, and to a man sporting a handlebar mustache directly behind, Martin asks, "What's going on?"

The man glances across at the situation, dips his head to spit tobacco juice, then looks up and explains, "Gamblers. That's their spot. Every year or so the mayor announces he won't tolerate gambling at the ballpark, and so, here's the result."

One of the policemen is punched, knocking his bulbous helmet askew. The policeman replies by wielding a billy club and striking his assailant. Two others attack a different policeman and are beaten into submission. The police shove their quarry down the planks, out of the stands, and onto the field. Some fans boo and others applaud as police march the gamblers to the left-field corner and out a door in the wall, to the street.

Bottom of the 9th. The Cubs take the field. Martin points out the shortstop, second baseman, and first baseman. "Tinker. Evers. Chance."

The pitcher's face is round and determined. There is something wrong with his hand. Martin asks, aloud, to no one in particular, "Three Finger Brown?"

"Yes," answers the man behind them.

"Oh my God!" Martin shifts excitedly.

Velez leans to Martin. "Who's Three Finger Brown?"

"Ever go to the Hall of Fame?" Martin asks.

"No. My dad didn't want to see jerkwads he knew on the walls forever."

"Three Finger Brown is there. One of the greatest pitchers. Check his pitching hand."

Three Finger Brown throws a curve—arcing and "lazy" by twenty-first-century standards—that bends into the catcher's mitt.

*"Strike!"* the ump hollers.

Three Finger Brown's right hand is missing his index finger, and the middle finger corkscrews the wrong way. Martin explains, "Caught it in a threshing machine when he was a kid."

Martin asks the man behind him, "Which guy is McCloskey?"

He points to the third base coach. "McCloskey."

"Coaching third?" asks Martin.

"Most of them manage from the third-base coacher's box. Where are you from?"

As the last out settles into the glove of Chicago right fielder Frank Schulte, the remaining fans hurl their garbage toward the field, much of which falls short, landing on the first few rows of fans. A few of the right-field victims of the garbage shower charge up the aisles to slug the hurlers, who slug in return. Policemen sprint along the bleachers to the fight.

As Martin opens the low door separating grandstand from field, he steps down and his foot catches in a hole. *"Shit!"* He crashes onto his right side. Velez and Blent help him pop up, swipe dirt off his hip and knee, and they rush after McCloskey, who is disappearing through a passageway next to the bench, followed by his dejected players in clattering cleats. Martin bolts ahead, squeezes past the spindly, sweaty, losing pitcher, and catches up to McCloskey.

Lagging back, Velez asks Blent, "Know anything about McCloskey?"

"Nothing." Blent nods at the departing Cubs team. "But *those* guys, one of the best teams in history. A bunch of Hall of Famers."

"The earthquake?" McCloskey stops, sniffs and rubs the side of his veiny nose.

"Could you use two great ballplayers?" Martin asks.

McCloskey stares hard at Martin, pearls of sweat clinging to oversized pores on McCloskey's cheeks. "I'm going to beat the shit out of you if this is a waste of my time."

Velez mutters to Blent, "What a piece of crap field."

Blent is thoroughly relieved to be standing on a baseball field, even a scrappy one, the soft ground on the bottom of his soles. "Well," he says, "it's the only one we got. What the heck else are we gonna do in 1906? Be garbagemen? We're lucky it's not 1806, or 1506, or 606. There was no baseball then."

McCloskey and Martin emerge from the passageway followed by six grumbling Cardinals. McCloskey offers his hand to Velez, while scrutinizing Velez's face. "Chief Velay, huh?" McCloskey is short and his uniform accentuates his bulging gut.

Velez glances at Blent and Martin. He smirks. "Chief Velay."

While he maintains his hold on Velez's right hand, McCloskey's left jumps up Velez's arm, checking the rippling forearm, steel-hard triceps, and shoulder like an unripe melon. He lightly punches Velez's massive thigh. McCloskey gasps and repeats the handshake and checkout of Blent.

"Can you musclemen hit a baseball?"

The losing pitcher, Slim Sallee, growls as he steps out of his cleats and kicks them in Velez's direction. Sallee is as tall as

Velez, looks like he weighs about half as much, and he is white as a porcelain cup. McCloskey barks, "Bennett. Cleats! These gentlemen are survivors of the earthquake in San Francisco." Bennett, giving hard looks to the "survivors," steps out of his cleats. Four other players drift onto the field in the emptying ballpark.

For Velez and Blent, the gargantuan bats on the ground are a problem. Martin tells McCloskey, "We use a shorter bat in California."

*"Why the hell would you do that?"* McCloskey chides. *"Use the biggest stick you can handle!"* Players nearby chuckle.

Blent takes up a pockmarked bat at the edge of the bench and asks McCloskey, "Can I cut this? You have a saw?" McCloskey's face twists. He nods yes. Martin, Velez, and Blent take turns holding the abused, cleat-stepped-upon bat, testing its weight, examining it for cracks. Meanwhile the gatekeeper brings them a rusty saw. Blent sets in to cutting, trying to cut four and a half inches off the top of the bat.

A baseball rolls to Velez's feet, now shod in the sweaty cleats. He leans down, but stops, unsure if he wants to touch the ball: black, brown, yellow, looking like it's been chewed, pissed and shat upon by packs of dogs.

"You guys actually practice with this?" asks Velez of Grady, the catcher. Velez has never, in his entire life, from his earliest memories tossing a ball with his dad at the age of four, on through to the Majors, ever touched a ball so ratty.

"Why don't you go the fuck back to California?" Grady replies.

The quick result of Blent's sawing is a bat with a flat top. Velez grabs it out of Blent's hands, and strides toward the batter's box.

"All right Bugsy!" McCloskey bellows at the pitcher. "Let's see what these yannigans can do!"

The pitcher, Bugs Raymond—face puffy, bags under his eyes—looks like a pork butcher. After tossing a warmup, he whines at McCloskey, "Why do we gotta do this?"

"You have yet another appointment with a bottle this afternoon?" McCloskey replies.

The other players laugh. Martin glances into the stands where, just like in the twenty-first century, the lowest-paid baseball employees are the ones gathering the trash. Bugs Raymond motions with his mitt for Velez to step into the batter's box.

Velez approaches the left side of home plate and digs his back foot into an already-existing hole. Sallee's long, sweaty shoes squeeze the side of Velez's feet, but the cleats are providing a good hold. The bat feels okay, still two or three ounces too heavy. Velez chokes up one hand's width. He instructs himself, mumbling, "Turn off the head. Hit the ball."

Bugs Raymond winds up and fires a zipping fastball.

"*Strike!*" Grady makes the call and tosses the ball back to Bugs.

It looks odd with Grady squatting a foot and a half farther back than a twenty-first-century catcher, not under Velez's left elbow. Velez lets the next pitch go by, assessing its movement: a meaty 82-mph fastball. Velez taps the plate with the bat, and coils.

"You gonna swing, Chief?" Grady asks. "What tribe are ya?"

"I don't like talking while I'm batting," replies Velez.

"I'm interested, Chief! What tribe?"

"Um..." Velez blurts, "Ewok."

"Ewok? Never heard of them. What's that?"

"Shut up."

Bugs Raymond winds up, throws. Velez waits, then attacks the ball—like a sword smashing a low-charging enemy's skull. The ball sizzles through the air over first base and down the line in right.

Bugs Raymond sneers as he picks up a ball behind the mound. He eyes Velez, who nestles into his crouch, weight back on his left foot, ankle, knee, and thigh. Raymond winds, and the pitch breaks halfway to home, angling toward the outside of the plate. Velez hesitates, gets his weight behind the ball, and pulls it hard over Raymond's head into right-center.

McCloskey, in appraising Velez, does not move a muscle.

"Big Indian motherf—" Grady stops himself. He pounds his mitt.

Bugs winds up and zips a fastball down the middle that Velez waits on, *craaaaaaaaaack!* up into the sky, the sound reverberating throughout the grandstand. The trash sweepers stand to try to locate the ball, gray against the clouds, as it carries, carries, carries, dropping beyond the right-field fence. *"Woo-hoo!"* a high-pitched child's voice exclaims behind the wall.

A fielder yells through a broken slat, "Toss it back!" He opens a door in the fence and races through, yelling, "Give it!" A second later, the sound of a child's protesting squeal wafts over the field.

McCloskey reaches into his back pocket and tosses a ball to Raymond, who inspects it as he paces around the mound, then expectorates a gob of tobacco juice onto it.

Velez is astonished. *"Can he do that? Spit on the ball?"*

Grady and Bugs Raymond laugh.

Martin nods his head. Spitballs are legal.

Bugs Raymond toes the pitching rubber, rocks back and fires a fastball. To Velez's point of view the ball increases in size as it rushes at his forehead. Velez yanks out of the way, crashing onto the dirt.

*"What the hell!"* Blent yells, dropping the two on-deck bats he was swinging, starting toward Raymond. The outfielders start jogging in to back up Raymond, but Blent stops and

retreats. *"Watch it!"* Blent roars, doubly upset because there are no batting helmets.

Martin doesn't react, matching McCloskey's impassiveness.

"Got away from him." McCloskey leans forward and spits tobacco juice onto the yellow grass.

Velez brushes off his pants, elbow, picks a pebble out of the heel of his hand, wipes the shiny brown-red scrape, grips the bat. He stares at Bugs Raymond, expecting something low and away and that's what's coming, straight on the corner, knee level. Velez hesitates, reaches and pulls it into the air, high, down the right-field line.

*"The other guy!"* McCloskey orders.

"Only four pitches?" Velez wheels toward McCloskey. "I'm just feeling good!"

The ball lands beyond the fence.

McCloskey shouts, *"You'll do what I say, Chief!"*

The players in the outfield laugh.

Taking the bat from Velez, the handle warm, Blent asks, "He got anything?"

"A curve. Obvious. Nothing breaks late. Wait on it."

Blent digs in from the right side of home plate, relishing the feeling of cleat breaking dirt, twisting the ball of his back foot into a secure hold.

"You his brother?" Grady asks, stepping forward to kick a pebble off home plate.

"Oh, I wouldn't say that," Blent replies. "Where you from?"

"Near Wilmington in Delaware."

"That's nice. Now I gotta work. Talk later."

Bugs Raymond winds up and fires a fastball on the outside edge of the plate. Blent spanks it, sharply, to right field. Raymond is pissed off. He lets a gob of tobacco juice fall onto the ball and rubs it in, then spits into his mitt. The next pitch starts high and outside, then darts across the plate. Grady chuckles as he tosses the ball back to Raymond. Raymond winds up and lets loose, aiming the ball at Blent's ribs, then it breaks toward the plate and Blent fouls it off. Next is a fastball at the knees. Blent cranks it into the left-field gap. Over the next ten pitches, Blent lets three wide ones go past, fouls off one, slaps one down the right-field line, zips four into the gaps, and yanks one over the fence in left.

*"Enough!"* McCloskey waves his hands.

Martin asks him, "What do you think?"

"What do I think?" McCloskey lips the tobacco out of his mouth. Twisting his cleat, he grinds the shreds into the ground. "I think I'm happy there was an earthquake in San Francisco."

# 8

## Your Dog Is Speaking to You

MCCLOSKEY WALKS THE trio out of the ballpark and gives them directions to Neal's Sporting Goods on Tucker. "Let them know I sent you. And go to the Terminal Hotel. Use my name. I'll meet you at nine tonight."

Up on the streetcar, gazing at the passersby, Velez and Blent smile out with a bit of triumph. Life is beginning to feel normal.

"Hey!" Velez points at a window painted with a crystal ball cupped by female White hands. "Madame Mosha! Fortune! Let's check it out!"

Sticking to baseball, Martin says, "I'm surprised he didn't want to see you guys in the field. But you did enough."

They find Neal's Sporting Goods. They test the bats, absurdly heavy. They finger the rudimentary catcher's equipment, walk the aisles of basketballs, hockey sticks, rubber balls of varying sizes, jump ropes, tennis racquets, boxing gloves. Most everything gleaming dully, they are engulfed in aromas of wood, leather, rubber, and varnish.

Velez squeezes a white-as-snow baseball that his hand mushes into lopsidedness. "You gotta hit it pretty perfect to get it over the wall." He offers the ball to Martin.

"This is why they call it the dead-ball era," says Martin.

"The *what* ball era?"

"There aren't a lot of home runs hit now," Martin explains. "They hit the ball differently. It's place hitting. Not home run hitting. Later on, they named it the dead-ball era. They started making the ball harder around 1920."

Blent tries on a baseball glove. It looks like a ten-year-old's glove. There is a miniscule pocket, a tiny bit of webbing between thumb and forefinger. "This is the biggest one they got!"

Velez asks Martin, "You sure they don't have designated hitters in this league?"

They buy two gloves, one bat, two balls. Using McCloskey's name, they buy two pairs of baseball cleats on credit.

Out on the sidewalk, rain clouds have covered the sky, thick drops sprinkling as Blent and Velez jam their hands into their new gloves. Velez tosses a ball to Blent, skimming the tip of his glove and bonking Blent in the eyebrow. Velez laughs wickedly.

\*

Blent's dreaming mind is at eye level with his daddy's dogs, running, chasing the hairy butt of a boar near his cousin Mikey's friend's cabin an hour outside of Huntsville. Foam is dripping from the dogs' wagging tongues, splattering Blent's face. Blent's mother-in-law is standing over him, arms on hips, the handles of red, blue, green, gold, black shopping bags running up her forearm. The shiny bulging bags look like second, third, fourth, fifth, sixth, seventh, eighth stomachs. His daddy's lead dog, Buster, looks back, eyes wide and serious, and barks.

Velez is in the shared hallway bathroom, wiping the back of his hand on his mouth, having puked into the toilet. He rubs his hands over his face, smooths his hair, pops out of the bathroom to the hall, and quietly enters the first room on the right.

Blent stirs awake in his bed nearest the door. Martin is balled up in his clothes, sleeping on the stained sofa.

Blent softly asks Velez, "How you doing?"

"What a shithole," Velez mutters. "I'm going downstairs."

Blent flings back his cover and leaves a note for napping Bucky.

At the enormous dining room, a bulbous, twelve-foot-tall clock loudly strikes its chime eight times. They order, and when the waiter departs, Velez glances at the tablecloth, at the carpet, at his shoes. "I was taking something my trainer called 'cherry seed oil.'"

Blent stares at Velez's saggy, ill, sad face. Silverware clangs plates. The loud murmur of a hundred conversations. Blent is shocked that André Velez seems to be confessing that he took performance-enhancing drugs. "Cherry seed oil?"

"That's what my trainer, um . . . called it."

"How often?"

"A lot." Velez's face twists.

To Blent, he looks nauseous.

Velez continues, "A regular schedule, especially during the season. No one ever detected it."

"What did it do?"

The weary expression partly dissolves in a half smile. "Made me feel strong, man."

"How long were you on it?"

"This last season."

"You hit .312 / .402 / .533."

Velez sniffs and nods. "And the season before that."

"You hit .322 / .411 / .521."

"And the one before that."

"Two seasons ago and three seasons ago were your back-to-back MVPs."

He tells Blent he doesn't know what was in it, but Blent asks him if he thinks it included a substance like testosterone, or growth hormone.

"Maybe."

Blent saw guys in the minor leagues get significantly stronger in just two or three weeks. Some of those guys were caught by drug tests, their careers derailed. Blent closes his eyes at this admission.

"Don't judge me."

"You're a fraud. Your MVP seasons are frauds. This is almost as bad as getting sucked back to 1906! I feel cheated! Every guy who's not on it is cheated! Don't you understand that it's cheating?"

"You ever try anything like it?" Velez asks.

Blent lets out a chuckle at the complexity of the prospect of taking performance-enhancing drugs. Everyone in their baseball world knows it can be the difference between a life stuck in the minor leagues and ascending to the Majors. It can be the difference between an average major leaguer and an All-Star. It can be the difference between a sometimes-All-Star and a Hall of Famer. On the other hand, you have to be a chemist to know what's going into those drugs and the effects on your body. And it's cheating.

"My wife told me, 'I want a healthy Johnny Blent, not an unhealthy superstar Johnny Blent.' You realize what she was turning her back on, potentially? Everything you got—the big house, the vaycay houses, all the toys. Your fucking Lambo."

"I was still an All-Star before I took the stuff."

"That's my point!" Blent shifts his chair away and spits on the floor. "A weight lifter in college who lived in my dorm offered to get me testosterone. I told him, 'No.' And a guy at a gym at home wanted to give it to me."

"You're a better man than me."

Their food is set down. Blent orders a scotch, telling Velez, "You're making me drink." He saws into his steak and eats while absorbing Velez's confession. Around a full mouth of food bathed in scotch, Blent barks, "So it's the withdrawal from this 'cherry seed oil' that's making you sick?"

Velez nods yes and winces so deep it creates a dimple in the middle of his forehead. "My trainer said everybody was doing something and only the stupid ones got caught. I knew it was against the rules, sure, sure." He sucks in a cheek. "One time my girlfriend in Scottsdale . . . I told her the truth. She asked me, 'How can you be certain that you're the best if you take that stuff?' I laughed at her. But that chick was smart. So smart she stole my house from me, had me sign a quitclaim deed and some other shit. Stole it."

"What did the cherry seed oil do?"

Velez sips his soup and wipes his chin. "An extra fifteen, twenty feet on fly balls. Quicker bat. Strong as the season goes on. Can concentrate fine even though it's 115 degrees on the field. You just get caught up in it, you know?"

"*I don't know!* I wasn't sure I'd *ever* make the bigs. I only made it 'cause Scuttario got hurt."

"You're clean, man. Very good. You get a medal."

"You're an asshole! You made all this money and won two MVPs and took us to the World Series."

Velez's angry expression at being called an asshole disappears as he retches. "Maybe there wouldn't be any World Series for Johnny Blent if I wasn't on the cherry seed oil." He bolts up, napkin to mouth, to find a restroom.

After a silent dinner, they bring Velez's plate of food up to the room for Martin, who jokes, "I thought you guys ditched me."

Blent watches Martin eat, burning to know if Martin has been aware that Velez was on the "cherry seed oil."

Knocking on the door. Velez opens it, and there's Manager Honest John McCloskey, puffing a cigar, a bundle under one arm, the other holding a bottle in a bag. "The Californians!"

McCloskey steps sideways through the small space between beds and sofa, sets the bottle of bourbon on the table, finds a glass, and plops into the only chair. McCloskey heaves the bundle of gray flannel onto Velez's bed. "That's two uniforms."

"No smoking in here," Velez warns, receiving a reply of McCloskey's raised eyebrow and staring gray eye. Blent adds, "Please."

"Health fanatics?" McCloskey considers his cigar, sets it in an ashtray without crushing it out. "How about a drink of liquor? Against that too?"

Blent checks out a jersey—thick, heavy wool—"St. Louis" across the front. The back is blank: no name, no number.

"Well, gentlemen, here is my proposition. Next up is New York for three games, then Philadelphia for three. Then we go on the road." McCloskey points a red, callused finger at Blent. "You and Bennett will alternate at second." He points at Velez. "You and Burch will alternate in right. Six-game probation. Then I'll decide. If you're in, then you get a contract for the year."

"Great!" Blent blurts out, elated.

Velez has got a pinched expression as if his mouth is full of peeled lemons. He leans back on his pillow, crossing his arms and squinting.

Martin asks, "What more do you want to see from these guys before you can give them a contract right now?"

"I want to see if they trip all over themselves. I want to see if they are consistent. I want to see if they are better than the guys I already got. I haven't seen them play the field. Maybe they can only hit. None of my guys are going to like this arrangement at all. But it might make the team better."

Velez says, "My agent used to say, 'Can you give us twenty-four hours?'"

McCloskey's nostrils flare as he squints. "'Agent' for *what?*" McCloskey rises. "Practice is at noon tomorrow. Either show up ready to kick, or don't show up and go back to California. Whatever your no-smoking hearts desire."

Martin asks, "What's the pay?"

"Twenty dollars each."

They ponder the three-dollar-a-day room, the one-dollar dinners. They've got about four dollars remaining.

Velez chuckles at the irony of twenty dollars.

Martin counters, "We can't afford to live here. How about forty dollars each?"

"You can get a cheaper hotel," McCloskey says, digging in his pocket. "Twenty-five dollars each. Fifty total. That's it."

The trio shares a glance. Martin shrugs. Velez nods. Blent smiles boyishly and gives a thumbs-up.

McCloskey lays two twenty-dollar gold pieces and a ten-dollar bill next to Martin's glass of bourbon. He stands and demonstrates the team's elaborate coaching signs, makes sure his new players understand. He sticks the cigar in his mouth, grabs the bottle. He blows a nimbus cloud of smoke toward their beds, laughs, and exits.

"We're going to that fortune-teller!" Velez insists. "I wanna get the fuck out of here!"

"A fortune-teller is *utter* heresy!" Blent shakes his head.

"I ain't staying in 1906," Velez snorts.

Martin wolfs down the leftover steak. "I'm willing."

\*

A fifteen-cent horse-drawn cab ride clip-clopping over cobblestone streets leads the three ballplayers to a glass door with a yellow curtain behind it. As Martin and the heavily rouged Madame Mosha negotiate the price, Blent tells her, "I'm Restored Church of Christ. I'm born again. So this, to me, is really against God."

Velez blasts, "What does that have to do with it?"

Madame Mosha reaches out for both of them, "I like everyone's viewpoints."

Martin hands her three dollars.

"Born *again*, darling? Please tell me what that means. You gentlemen are *very* fascinating. California is so *very* exotic." Her perfume smells like ripe peaches.

Blent begins explaining his church's theology.

*"We want to return to our time! Now!"* Velez wails.

Madame Mosha's gray eyes settle on Velez. "Which time is that?"

As Velez tells her, Martin and Blent shift uncomfortably, trying to discern if Madame Mosha thinks they're out of their minds. But Madame Mosha listens as if she's heard all that the human imagination can conjure. She locks the front door and leads them down a hallway to a room where she lights a stub of incense, excuses herself, and slides away between a curtain.

The walls are festooned with carnival and African masks. The trio sits at the round table.

Martin asks Velez, "You try this before?"

"My main Miami girl goes. She took me once. It was freaky, man, the stuff that woman knew about me."

Madame Mosha reenters, lights candles, turns off the overhead light, and sits. "Hold hands, stare at the candle. Close your eyes."

The ballplayers feel very odd holding hands, Blent on one side, Velez on the other of Madame Mosha's little, soft, moist hands.

Madame Mosha says, to no one present, "Darlings, yes. These men are from the future. They came back to us—and we are happy to have them—but they want to go home. Gentlemen, please say 'yes'—let the spirits know you want to communicate with them."

"Please help us!" says Velez.

"Yup," blurts Martin.

"Yeah," Blent agrees.

"Spirits of the future. We are here. Will you listen to us? Please come to us. We look up to you. Please. *Oh my!*"

*"What?"* Velez asks.

*"Oh!"* Madame Mosha flings up as if her butt is being chomped. *"There's a disturbance! A giant disaster!"*

"Exactly!" says Velez.

"Please talk to us!" pleads Madame Mosha, and instantly a distant *whoo-oooo-oooo* is heard from beyond the walls.

"What's that?" Velez asks.

She whispers, "The spirits are turning to us. Oh? Come back? Yes, come back. May I ask, who are you?" A pause. "Mister Blent's pet?"

*"Which dog?"* Blent exclaims.

*"Ask about Cheech and Mako and Ernie!"* Velez pleads. *"Did they get out okay? How about Cookie? Anyone die?"*

"I'm sensing a very large dog."

Blent explains, "My daddy's got a lot of big dogs! They're hunters!"

"Brown. Short hair."

*"Buster!"*

"Are you Buster?" she asks. "Yes, and you miss your friend? Your dog is talking to you, Mr. Blent. Please welcome Buster."

Blent swallows. "Hello, Buster. How are you all getting along?" Tears sting Blent's eyes. "Do you miss me? How is Darla? Have you seen her? Is there a baby girl? Annabelle Jackson Lee? Have you met her?"

*"Ruff! Ruff!"* something barks, not near, not far. *"Ruff!"*

"Buster?" Blent asks. "That sounds more like your sister, Peppi! Is it Peppi?"

*"Ruff! Ruff! Ruff!"*

"Darla is fine," Madame Mosha interprets. "Yes, there is a little girl."

"I'm a father!" Blent exclaims.

Velez squeals, *"Ask Buster how we can get back!"*

Addressing Buster, Blent asks, "What do we do to get back?"

Martin coughs hard and pulls his hands away.

"Don't break the circle!" Blent protests.

"Glass of water." Martin rushes out.

Blent opens his eyes.

Madame Mosha takes Blent's hand, "Buster is still here! He wants to talk to you."

"I'm listening!"

From down the hallway Martin bellows, *"André! Johnny! Party's over!"*

Madame Mosha says, "Come home, Buster. It's lonely."

*"Guys!"* It's Martin's voice, blasting into the room in the same ethereal-sounding tenor as Buster's. "Woof, woof, woof," Martin says. *"Come here! See this joke!"*

Blent storms out and finds Martin down the hall, standing at a doorway and ordering some unseen person, "Don't move!"

Blent turns the corner. Standing against the far wall is a shrewish, bespectacled man holding a black phone receiver to his ear, a wire snaking into the wall. He's wincing guiltily.

Martin tells Blent, "Here's your ruff, ruff, ruff."

# 9

## Bastard's Good

THE BALL FLICKS off Blent's glove, past his head. Velez guffaws. Blent retrieves the ball in the outfield grass in the silvery morning.

Velez and Blent are wearing the tiny fielding gloves on their right hands, each in their heavy, gray, flannel uniforms. Their caps have shorter bills than any caps they've ever worn. Blent's is a half-size too small, squishing his skull no matter how he tries to stretch it.

"Maybe you guys should take off the mitts for a minute," Martin suggests. "You're basically catching barehanded anyway, and these gloves are just padding. Catch it on the ball of your index finger."

"Screw this," Velez whines. "How am I supposed to catch a line drive? I haven't played outfield since high school!"

"Practice," replies Martin. "Little kids can catch with these gloves."

Blent tosses the ball, adding, "Sometimes I practice with a flat glove with no pocket."

"Right. Soft hands," says Martin.

"These little kids you're talking about get bumps on their heads?" asks Velez.

"Probably," replies Martin, as Velez completely misses a ball that smacks his cap off.

A few minutes later, Martin hits the first grounder of the day.

Velez follows the side-to-side bouncing of the ball in the patchy ground, then stabs at the ball, which hits a pebble and scoots under him. *"How do they play on this fucking field?"*

Martin hits some long fly balls. Tracking one, Velez steps in a hole and falls. Sweat blobs spread through Martin's shirt, and it's foreign for him to be working out his players in street clothes. His shoes can't bite into the ground like his good old Puma cleats. He throws batting practice—inefficient with only two baseballs. Velez smacks one to right.

"Very nice!" McCloskey exhorts, walking onto the field, in uniform, stomach bulging.

Martin sets the bat down. His place on the field quite undefined, Martin will leave McCloskey's team to McCloskey.

Two and a half hours later, the ballpark is mostly full, with fans eager to see the New York Giants, who wear black uniforms with "World's Champions" on the front—no name, no number on the back. There's a tall man beginning to toss a ball beyond the third-base dugout. He has a well-proportioned body and an open, handsome face. Observing from the front row of the grandstand, Martin gasps, skin tingles: It's Christy Mathewson. Martin glances out to right field where Velez and Blent are seated on the grass, stretching, oblivious to Mathewson, one of the greatest pitchers of all time.

Martin is politely asked to move out of the box seats. He climbs the aisle, and finds a seat fifteen rows up, about a third of the way up the grandstand. Except for the box seats, the tickets denote a section of the ballpark, not specific seats.

As the teams drift to the benches, Martin focuses on the fans. Most of the men wear black derby hats with a curved brim. A pack of boys in shorts, floppy caps, and dirty jackets bolts past. There are no sneakers, no sweatsuits, no one talking on phones or reading phones, no overflowing trays of greasy food, no plastic cups of beer, no music blaring from a thousand speakers, no nightmarishly large TV above center field, no Air Force flyover, no broadcast booth, no luxury boxes, no third, fourth, or fifth deck, and significantly fewer obese people. There are no bullpens and no dugouts—just benches with wooden roofs.

On the field, the announcer lifts his long conical megaphone. "Batting for Bennett, Johnny Blent! Batting for Burch, Chief Velay!" He repeats the announcement toward left field, then toward right.

| NEW YORK | | ST. LOUIS | |
|---|---|---|---|
| C | ROGER BRESNAHAN | 3B | HARRY ARNDT |
| CF | GEORGE BROWNE | 1B | JAKE BECKLEY |
| LF | MIKE DONLIN | CF | HOMER SMOOT |
| SS | BILL DAHLEN | C | MIKE GRADY |
| RF | SPIKE SHANNON | LF | RED MURRAY |
| 3B | ART DEVLIN | SS | GEORGE McBRIDE |
| 1B | DAN McGANN | 2B | JOHNNY BLENT |
| 2B | BILLY GILBERT | RF | CHIEF VELAY |
| P | CHRIS. MATHEWSON | P | BUGS RAYMOND |

Roger Bresnahan, the New York catcher, steps up to home plate, twirls his bat through the strike zone, and steadies his hands at his back shoulder.

St. Louis pitcher Bugs Raymond looks worse than the day before—baggier bags under his eyes, puffier face. Over at second, Blent bends in his crouch, astounded at the patchy infield grass and the pebbles dotting the basepath. Velez, in right, glances at the center fielder, Homer Smoot, who motions for Velez to step in closer.

Bugs Raymond winds and fires a fastball on the outside corner. *"Strike!"* the home-plate ump declares. Though it's an overcast, chilly day, by the time Bugs has thrown the nine pitches it takes to strike out Bresnahan, Bugs is already sweating hard.

The next batter, George Browne, slaps an outside curve toward the hole between second and first. Blent dives, knocks the ball down, scrambles to it, and fires from his knees to nip Browne. The crowd erupts.

Velez yells, *"Way to go, Blent!"*

Blent flaps his stiff little glove at Velez, a twenty-first-century superstar standing amidst crabgrass and patches of dirt.

Bottom of the 1st. As Christy Mathewson warms up, McCloskey approaches Blent and Velez, trying to explain Mathewson: "He's got the fastball, the curve, the outshoot, the mini-outshoot, the drop, the spitter—and look out for the slow ball; it'll twist you like a corkscrew." Velez and Blent glance at each other in confusion. McCloskey jogs to the third-base coacher's area—no chalked box, just a worn oblong dirt patch in foul territory.

Mathewson gets Arndt to fly to left fielder Donlin.

Jake Beckley hits a deep fly to center, the ball knocking the heel of George Browne's glove and dropping to the turf. Browne picks it up, fires toward shortstop, and screams, *"Fuck!"* at himself, which most in the ballpark hear.

Beckley stands on second, clapping his hands.

Homer Smoot, the center fielder, walks on four wide pitches. The guys on the bench mutter, "On purpose," and indeed, it looked like Mathewson wanted no part of Homer Smoot with a man on second.

Mike Grady waits on a curve, knocking it to shortstop Dahlen, who grabs it and takes it to second base for the last out of the inning; Mathewson's strategy of walking Homer Smoot is vindicated.

## NEW YORK  0 — 0  ST. LOUIS

Bottom of the 3rd. With one out, Blent steps into the batter's box for his first official 1906 at-bat. His back foot chops at the dirt, digging a toehold. He crouches into his stance, opening his eyes wide to maximize the scope of his vision. The heavy, baggy uniform feels odd. The lack of a batting helmet feels odd. Mathewson winds up and whips a fastball on the outside corner. Strike one.

Blent steps out of the batter's box and glances up at the stands at Martin, who's looking on stock-still. Blent shudders with deep relief that he's playing ball, that fellow refugee Velez is on deck.

The umpire barks at Blent, "Get in here!"

Blent resets and takes a curve that looks outside. The ump calls it a strike.

"Ooooh!" the crowd moans.

*"No!"* McCloskey screams near third base. *"You are blind today, Billy!"* The ump's head, wire mask screening his face, rotates toward McCloskey. McCloskey adds, *"I know a fine optometrist across the river!"*

Scattered fans hold up spectacles:

*"Here you are!"*

*"These work well!"*

*"Here's an extra pair!"*

No balls, two strikes.

Bresnahan, the catcher, tells Blent, "You know who is about to strike you out? That's Christy Mathewson. He threw three shutouts in the World's Series last year."

Mathewson winds up. Another curveball—off the plate—a sucker pitch. Blent doesn't bite.

Mathewson winds, hands above his head, kicks and throws. *Fastball*, Blent's unconscious mind determines, his weight shifting forward, bat pulling through the zone, as the ball tails away—a late-breaking curve—swinging bat nipping it, Bresnahan snagging it for the third strike. *"Out!"* the ump bellows. The crowd *groans*. A fan behind third base yells at Blent, *"Yannigan!"*

Blent gawks in astonishment at Bresnahan, at the ump, at Mathewson, who in triumph coolly observes Blent. Bresnahan and the ump chuckle at Blent.

Head down, Blent trudges to the bench. As he hands the bat to Velez, he says, "Good fastball. That last one was a slider, a little tail on it. Fooled me."

"Yup," Velez notes and strides to the plate, digs in, and glances at McCloskey going through hand signals that add up to nothing. Velez addresses Mathewson. He stares at the spot above Mathewson's right shoulder where he expects the ball will be released. No reason to look at the body. Look at the ball.

"You boys from California?" asks Bresnahan.

"Don't know," mumbles Velez, trying to ignore Bresnahan, staring at the pitcher and mumbling to himself, "Stay behind the ball."

The pitch tears the air, straight and eighteen inches off the plate. *"Strike!"*

Fans boo. McCloskey unfurls a string of curses at the ump. But Velez nods, understanding that the ump is making his point about who is in charge. Mathewson holds the ball at his belt, winds up, hands over head, then forward in an easy motion—curve, outside—Velez lets it go, and it slices the same few cubic inches of space as the previous pitch, eighteen inches off the plate. *"Strike!"* More boos. Near Martin, a fan yells, *"Swing the bat!"*

The next pitch starts out at Velez's shoulder, Velez unflinching, expecting it to curve back, and it does, looking like it's going to nip the edge of the plate, Velez pulling his hands in, lashing at it, grounding it in the hole between first and second. The second baseman knocks it down, but the first baseman dove for it and is sprawled on the ground. Velez chugs hard toward first, unoccupied. But Mathewson cuts over. The second baseman throws a perfect lead to Mathewson, Mathewson catching the ball and stepping on the bag a half step ahead of Velez, whose bulging left shoulder knocks Mathewson's right on the way past. Mathewson shoots Velez a killer look. Three outs.

As New York jogs off the field, Blent hustles out to Velez, who, hands on hips, stares at the tops of the carriages parked beyond the outfield wall, some with spectators standing in the carriages taking in a view of the game along with their horses. Blent brings him his glove.

Of Christy Mathewson, Velez blurts, "Bastard's good."

Top of the 5th. New York's sixth-place batter, Art Devlin, smacks a curveball to right, inches in from the foul line, Velez picking it up on the backhand, firing to second, Devlin hook-sliding away from the tag: *"Safe!"*

Devlin on second. No outs.

The next pitch is a fastball away that Dan McGann crushes to left-center, the ball splitting Murray and Smoot and bouncing toward the wall. McGann is not fast, but he easily makes it to second base, knocking in Devlin.

## NEW YORK 1 — 0 ST. LOUIS

After two quick outs, and Dan McGann on second, Roger Bresnahan smacks a ball sky-high to right field. Velez settles under it. Martin in the stands, and Blent near second, each hold their breath, hoping Velez's new, little mitt and his athletic ability are up to the task of catching the big pop fly, because if he *does* drop it, the run easily scores, if he *does* drop it, the Californians' stock will crash. Velez's feet shift left, back, forward, the ball coming down—down—down—down—*plop* into his glove. Velez jogs forward, exhaling through his poker face as if the catch was easier than tying his shoes. Three outs.

Bottom of the 5th. Blent leads off. Mathewson rocks back, hands overhead, fastball whooshing toward the inside corner, and Blent uncoils, bat cracking ball, the ball tearing the air above the shortstop. It splits the outfielders, the center fielder running after it. Blent's cap falls off as he rounds first, motoring for second, the ground choppy, legs churning as the ball comes in late. He pulls up at second. The shortstop, Bill Dahlen, snaps his mitt onto the ball. Dahlen, grizzled black stubble, a round face older than Velez's, shoots a sneer at Blent.

Blent smiles, not in retort to Dahlen, but at life itself, at the satisfaction of smacking a double, no matter the year or the century. The announcer on the field points his megaphone at the stands and booms, "Batting eighth, Chief Velay!" Shouts of *"Chief!"* greet Velez as he steps into the left-handed batter's box and takes his stance.

Mathewson settles with his glove and the ball at the "World's Champions" on his chest. He checks Blent at second, then looks in at the catcher. Mathewson winds and fires, a fastball away, Velez letting it go by. The ump calls it a ball though it was closer than the ones he called strikes on Velez's first at-bat. Bresnahan flicks a handful of dirt away from the plate, before tossing the ball back to Mathewson.

Mathewson takes the ball, sets at his chest, looks in to Bresnahan.

McCloskey screams, *"Look out!"* as Mathewson whirls and fires the ball to second base—Blent is frozen, noting the shortstop toward third and the second baseman toward first—but it's center fielder Browne who is rushing in, taking the throw from Mathewson, tagging Blent. *"Out!"*

Blent experiences the Jog of Shame back to the bench, and it feels terrible no matter what the century—a pickoff by the center fielder.

*"Wake up!"* McCloskey screams across the diamond at Blent.

In the stands, Martin whispers, "Damn!" He knows he should've seen the center fielder creeping in and yelled out to Blent. He hasn't seen that play since he was managing his first season in Single-A.

Velez taps the plate with the sawed-off, top end of the bat. Velez squints at Mathewson, who fires the ball straight down the middle, breaking wide of the plate. *"Strike!"*

The crowd moans. A fan yells, *"Swing the bat!"*

Velez reaches down, rubs dirt in his palms, re-grips the bat, stares out at the spot—ten o'clock from the pitcher's head—where Velez expects the ball to separate from Mathewson's hand. Mathewson fires the ball—straight and slowish. Velez holds his trigger, then flashes his body into the ball. *Thhhhhwaaaaacck!*

The ball rises and Velez watches the gray speck against the gray sky as he sprints toward first base. The right fielder rushes back, back, back, bumping into the fence as the ball smashes onto a carriage, bounces high, and disappears. Velez howls, "Ha!" as he slows to his home run trot.

Martin has risen with the rest of the cheering, roaring crowd. Velez trots around second, checking out the applauding throng in the grandstand—just five or six thousand, but they're all into it; rounding third, he shakes McCloskey's hand—"Good one, Chief!"—and jogs along the scraggly base path to home plate.

## NEW YORK   1 — 1   ST. LOUIS

Over the next few innings, Bugs Raymond tires, and New York racks up four more runs. Martin notes that Bugs looks like he is in dire need of a month of rehab, a fifth of gin, or a relief pitcher. But McCloskey leaves him in.

## NEW YORK   5 — 1   ST. LOUIS

Bottom of the 9th. Two outs. Runners on second and third. From the batter's box, Blent stares out at Mathewson. Blent's seen Mathewson's fastball, curve, and slider—aka outshoot—which breaks inward to a right-handed hitter like Blent, who cocks his body like a rifle trigger with his hands back. He's guessing fastball. It's a curve that begins moving toward Blent's ribs then slices the inside edge of the plate. Strike one.

Blent tongues the chaw of tobacco in his right cheek, tells himself, *Gonna be a fastball.*

That's what it is, a fastball with a little movement toward the outside. He's diving for it, contacting, body rotating—down and through—almost like slicing a golf shot—into right field. Single. Two runs score. Sweet.

## NEW YORK   5 — 3   ST. LOUIS

Velez retrieves their shared bat and strides to the plate. He digs in, checks McCloskey, who touches elbow, cap, knee, belt, belt: meaningless. Velez turns his attention to Mathewson, who sets at his chest, glances over his left shoulder at Blent taking his lead at first. Everyone who's been paying attention is mightily aware of Blent's earlier pickoff off second base—and adding to the shame, by the center fielder. Mathewson flinches, throws to first, and Blent dives back safe.

Blent dusts himself off and waits for Mathewson to set his foot against the pitching slab before starting his lead again. He glances down at his cleat firmly pressing into the corner of first base, a little pillow compared to the solid rubber squares of the twenty-first century.

Loudly clapping his hands, partly to try and distract Mathewson, and partly in pure joy, Blent takes his lead. Mathewson kicks and fires a fastball zipping for the outside edge. Velez rotates hard, the ball smacking the ground, bouncing twenty feet in the air. Mathewson fields it, firing to Dan McGann at first. Out. Three outs.

## NEW YORK  5 — 3  ST. LOUIS  FINAL

\*

That evening, Velez and Blent enter the enormous barroom at the Terminal Hotel. The row of ten gargantuan chandeliers are unlit; one is down on the floor being operated upon by a trio of technicians. Behind the shiny bar, which is about ninety feet long, a bartender's hand is a blur as he's chipping a block of ice into a mound of rocks ready for drinks.

Blent and Velez are slowed as men slide off barstools and offer congratulations on the pair's productive debut. Happy male faces shine.

"Thanks a lot," Velez replies, shaking a hand, slapping a shoulder. It's a feeling that makes his every particle boisterously alive.

Blent is cornered by a trio of round-faced men in suits and bow ties offering to buy him a drink. "Maybe later." The two ballplayers weave their way through the huge, smoky room crowded with men—watch chains curving 'round waists, hair slicked back with parts in the middle, thick mustaches waxed at the tips, brown teeth, fat cigars. A piano is being played, but it is barely heard. The music of the room is three hundred men loudly burbling.

They find Bucky Martin seated in a leather club chair, sipping scotch, unfolding *The St. Louis Star.*

The waiter explains the chandelier situation, "The power for the hotel blew up this morning," then emits a frustrated sigh. "That Mr. Edison is merely a great salesman, and he's going to burn us all up."

Velez orders a scotch, Blent a sarsaparilla. Martin shows them the sports page. "You guys are in the box score. How'd you feel out there?"

Blent examines the paper—his name, and "Chief Velay."

They share laughs about the uneven ground, the dirt patches, the holes, the rocks, the swale in right field. They marvel at the terrible fundamentals of most of the players, and how weird it feels not to wear a helmet in the batter's box. They reconstruct McCloskey's elaborate razzing of Christy Mathewson and New York manager John McGraw's raw cursing at Bugs Raymond.

"Did you see that wine bottle flying out of the stands at the New York right fielder?" Velez asks. "I found it out there in the sixth inning. A fan yelled, 'I'll take some.'"

Martin's amused expression toward Velez changes to an ingratiating smile. "That was a nice home run."

"Thanks."

"But this is a dead-ball league," Martin states.

Velez looks on coldly.

"After the homer, you got nothing on the inside half of the plate, right? Nothing at all."

Velez sucks in his cheeks and squints.

"They already have you pegged as a pull hitter. You can't be a pull hitter in this league."

"It's how I was about to get a gazillion-dollar contract, man." He leans back, crosses his legs, inspects a chip in his thumbnail.

Martin taps Velez's knee. "The only thing inside is gonna be straight at your head. Every hitter I saw today is trying to hit outside pitches the other way. They go with the pitch. It's because of the ball, the nature of the ball, how it's made. It's not gonna fly as far. You already know that."

"You sure?" Velez challenges. "Everything isn't exactly the same, right? There's this whole New Glory thing that's got everybody freaked out. The presidents are different, right?"

"You definitely cannot hit it as far."

"A homer is a homer is a homer."

"Yeah. But that fence in right is about 260 feet. The ball went 275."

Blent sits back. It's the first time he's ever witnessed Martin suggesting a change to André Velez.

Martin drains his scotch. "If they pitch you outside, hit it to left field."

"That's not my game, man. What are you worried about? That moron manager is gonna cut me? Ha! I'm better than anyone out there!"

"On the inside pitch—yes. But not on the outside pitch. And you can't pull this squishy ball over the wall when it's outside, right? You just roll it to an infielder, or the pitcher, or at best bloop it. This is *serious*." Martin turns to Blent, "Your approach is good."

"Thanks, Coach."

"Can't we talk about something else?" Velez whines.

"Yeah. Let's go over scoring in a scorecard," Martin says. "So we're using the same notation. You guys ever follow a game with a scorebook?"

Blent nods, "Yeah."

Velez sneers, "I'm a hitter, not a pencil pusher."

"Now you're gonna be both. You might be scoring games as we could compile data that no one else gathers in 1906." He fishes in his coat pocket, fat with train schedules and ripped-out articles. He pulls out his scorecard from the day and lays it on the table. There are rows and columns of numbers and notations in his barely decipherable handwriting, written on a card that was preprinted with the names of the St. Louis lineup along one side. "Pug Bennett" is scratched out and "Blent" written in, "Al Burch" scratched out and "Velay" written in. There are rectangular advertisements for a car repair shop, Coca-Cola, and a tire shop.

"The basic idea is that each position is assigned a number 1 through 9; pitcher is 1, catcher 2, first baseman 3, second baseman 4, third baseman 5, shortstop 6—don't ask me why shortstop is 6 and not 5, it's just the way it's always been—left fielder 7, center fielder 8, right fielder 9. Okay?" Blent nods; Velez looks on. "So, when I write '1-3' it means that the ball was hit to the pitcher and the pitcher threw it to the first baseman for the out. '6-3' means the ball was hit to the shortstop and over to first for the out. '8' means that it was a fly ball to the center fielder."

Martin points to a square on the top line with "F7" in it, in the row for New York catcher Roger Bresnahan. The fifth inning. Martin asks, "What does that mean, 'F7'?"

Velez replies, "Fly out."

"Right. '7' is left fielder." He points to another box, "5-3."

Velez replies, "Shortstop to first?"

"Almost!" Martin says.

"*Third* to first," says Velez.

"Correct!"

"You actually learned something in 1906," Blent comments.

*

The next evening, after their second 1906 ball game, Martin is sitting in the same club chair, with a glass of the same scotch, perusing that evening's *Post-Dispatch*:

|          | 1 | 2 | 3 | 4 | 5 | 6 | 7 | 8 | 9 | R | H | E |
|----------|---|---|---|---|---|---|---|---|---|---|---|---|
| New York | 0 | 0 | 1 | 0 | 0 | 1 | 1 | 0 | 0 | 3 | 7 | 2 |
| St. Louis | 0 | 2 | 1 | 1 | 0 | 0 | 3 | 0 | x | 7 | 9 | 1 |

By Alexander Cline

Behind the pitching of Gus Thompson, the St. Louis ballers managed nine hits and seven runs, the first four runs coming off New York's Hooks Wiltse, the last four surrendered by his re-placement, Red Ames, who fared no better.

Newcomer Johnny Blent, batting third, rewarded his team by making four hits in five at-bats, including a triple in the third inning. Mr. Blent added three swipes of second base, his only blemish coming in the eighth inning, a fly out to left field, when the game's fate was long decided. Beckley, Arndt, Smoot, and Grady made two hits each.

Velez sits heavily in the chair opposite Martin. Blent settles in with a touch of triumph, having outplayed André Velez.

"The pitchers are *pussies*," Velez whines. "They're scared of me. They pitch everyone else inside, but I get nothing."

Martin nods in sympathy.

Velez's mouth turns down, and he stares at the wood-paneled wall, laces his fingers behind his head, looking as disappointed as anybody about his two days' tally of one hit in eight at-bats. In the third inning, after Velez struck out, McCloskey admonished him, "You can't try to hit a home run each time, Chief! Place your fucking hits!"

*

The next morning, a rapid knocking on the door wakes Blent, who opens it and there's McCloskey in a suit and overcoat, the shoulders speckled with rain. He holds a china cup of coffee.

"I'm sorry about the early hour, gents," says McCloskey. "But I have business to discuss." He high-steps around the edge of the sofa, damply sits in the lone chair, sips his coffee.

Velez snorts as he pulls his underwear on—scratchy as hell compared to his normal silks. McCloskey reaches in his coat and drops a contract on the bed in front of Blent. "Eight hundred bucks for the year. Sign at the bottom above your name. You're smart—I figure you can read. Go to college?"

McCloskey swivels to Velez, "You've got work to do." To Martin, "I don't know if the pitchers are stupid in California, but no one taught your big fellow to hit to left field."

Velez protests, "What the hell you talking about? I hit a homer my second at-bat! I can destroy these pitchers!"

"One for eight," McCloskey replies. "That's what I'm talking about. You're not a big-league hitter. Maybe you will be one day, but not now. And this is not a debate. All I care about is winning, and your approach won't win games. It'll win fly-ball exhibitions."

"Fuck you."

*"What?"* McCloskey's face twists as he rises to challenge Velez, who is over a foot taller, broader, younger, quicker, stronger.

Martin shoots up between them, explaining to McCloskey, "He's upset. So am I, to tell you the truth."

Blent asks McCloskey, "How much does a decent house rent for in this town?"

"Thirty-five, forty dollars a month."

"With eight hundred bucks for the season I probably can't buy a car."

McCloskey chuckles. "You don't need a car."

Blent concludes, "I gotta think about it."

McCloskey exhales hard as his hands slap the skirts of his coat. "You fucking Californians. Think all you want. Practice is at noon. This rain will let up." McCloskey aims a finger at the uniforms hanging on the coatrack. "Which one's yours, Chief?"

Two hours before game time, from their rag-dried seats in the third row of the empty grandstand, Martin and Velez watch as Blent hands the signed contract to McCloskey. McCloskey checks the signature, orders "follow me," and walks with Blent past home plate, where they are met by the Giants' manager, John McGraw. McGraw shakes McCloskey's hand, then shakes Blent's hand. McGraw says something to Blent.

*"What!?"* Blent replies, jaw slack, body bowed forward.

McCloskey and McGraw laugh.

Blent steps away, hands on hips, staring at the ground, walking to the grandstand.

Martin rushes down the aisle, to the chicken-wire screen. "What's going on?"

The sun behind Martin's head makes Blent squint as he tells Martin, "I've just been sold to New York."

# 10

## World-Famous Polo Grounds

THE TRAIN SWAYS, almost knocking Blent into a table of well-dressed diners. He spots Martin and Velez halfway down the dining car, each of whom sits in front of the cheapest dinner possible—a side dish of carrots and green beans, and glasses of water.

Blent slaps a fifty-dollar bill onto the table. "An advance to me from Mr. McGraw. He said he won't pay for berths for you guys. But if I want, *I* can pay. I talked to a porter and there's one berth open. Fixing it up right now. You guys can take turns lying down."

"Thanks," says Martin.

Velez's lips press into a half smirk / half frown. He waves for the waiter, orders, "Big steak."

"Me too!" declares Martin.

"And a scotch," Velez adds. "A *good* scotch."

"Wait a second," Martin tells Velez. "We gotta pinch pennies." To the waiter, "Regular scotch for both of us."

Blent's debut with the New York Giants: a single and a double—two for four. Two clean double plays, each time feeding the ball to shortstop Bill Dahlen, who offered Blent subtle nods of approval.

Blent tells them, "McGraw says there might be an apartment for rent across the street from him on the West Side of Manhattan. An easy ride to the ballpark. He thinks it's thirty-five dollars a month."

"Going back to New York!" Velez snorts. "We were World Series champs—*stolen by video replay bullshit*—and now I'm not even gonna get the good scotch."

*

Their first morning in New York, Blent steps up into an open carriage that he is sharing with third baseman Art Devlin, left fielder "Turkey Mike" Donlin, and the catcher, Roger Bresnahan. Each of them wears a snow-white uniform with "World's Champions" emblazoned across the chest. Donlin grips the collar of his uniform and shakes it like a flag, making "World's Champions" ripple, igniting the others in laughter.

"If another team was wearing these," Devlin says, "I'd spike them till they bled."

Blent feels multiply fraudulent: He is not a World's Champion, and this isn't even his century. There are ten carriages, four players or dignitaries per, each drawn by a pair of horses, and the parade starts from the 5th Avenue side of Madison Square Park, in full view of the Flatiron Building, where the Giants keep their offices. There are two bands. A banner states: "WORLD'S CHAMPION GIANTS." All along Broadway, New Yorkers pack the sidewalks, office workers lean out open windows, cheering, shouting, "Mathewson!" "Turkey Mike!" "McGraw! McGraw! McGraw!"

An hour later, the parade passes Martin and Velez, who are standing outside of Dirk's Restaurant, on 85th Street and

Broadway, the smell of bacon, pancakes, greasy steak settling around the thick crowd. Martin cups his hands to his mouth and bellows in the direction of Blent's carriage, *"Hey Johnny! Johnny! Johnny! Hey!"*—snagging Blent's attention.

Standing up, Blent shouts at Velez, *"Don't worry, Chief, you're next!"*

Velez raises his middle finger at Blent. He tells Martin, "He can go *'Chief!'* himself! Where's the fucking ticker tape?"

A Hasidic man under a furry hat—his hands gently touching the shoulders of two small boys jumping on their tiptoes to see the ballplayers—assays Velez with a sharp look.

Velez smirks, "Sorry for cursing, dude."

Martin replies to Velez, "I think they've invented ticker tape. But maybe not the ticker tape *parade*."

Another band passes—tubas, drums, trumpets, flutes, multiple sets of reindeer bells. A dozen men in white caps and uniforms follow, each with a garbage can on wheels, shoveling and canning manure. There are horse-drawn omnibuses, the rumble of the subway underground, a big car grinds past. The crowd dissolves.

A stooped man in rags, bare feet, wearing a length of dirty, navy-blue cloth as a shawl—reminding Velez of his San Francisco drape-poncho—rattles his dented tin cup at them.

Velez explodes, "Man, I don't have one single fucking penny!"

The man recoils.

"Let's go," Martin says, and starts up 85th Street.

Velez doesn't move. "I need to go for a walk."

"What about the game?"

"Not going. I don't give a rat's ass about it—1906 or no 1906, world-famous Polo Grounds, or no world famous Polo Grounds. I don't want to watch it or talk about it or even *think* about baseball."

"Okay." Into Velez's huge palm Martin pours a dollar bill, three quarters, and a dime. Velez chuckles at the pitiful amount.

Martin writes out the address of the apartment he's about to view and the address of McGraw and Mathewson's apartment. Handing the scrap to Velez, Martin says that if he fails to rent the apartment, he will make sure that Mathewson or McGraw knows where he and Blent will spend the night. "Don't worry," Martin says, "We'll get our lives together."

Velez doesn't look at Martin as he twists away.

Martin is headed to 66 West 85th Street. He pulls the note from his pocket, written by McGraw in thick, blue ink:

> These gentlemen are with my new ballplayer, Mr. Blent. Please consider them for any available apartment.
>
> Thank you.
> John J. McGraw, manager
> New York Giants

As the aroma of freshly washed sheets wafts out of a below-street-level laundry, Martin wonders how much a hand-written note from John J. McGraw would be worth, at auction, in the twenty-first century. Five thousand dollars? Ten thousand? He passes a cobbler hammering, a cabinetmaker sawing a board, and a junk shop crammed with dull old beds and picture frames. These men and women behind the store windows did not, a few minutes before, emerge to see the World's Champion Giants parade up Broadway.

\*

Velez crosses 79th Street. There are no traffic lights, no signs with the flashing green or red hand, just a guy atop a stand in the middle of the intersection with a whistle in his mouth pointing at cars, horse-drawn carriages, horse-drawn buses. The traffic cop's not doing much good as far as Velez can tell; people and traffic are going in every direction. As he dodges cars, horses, and pedestrians, Velez debates himself about going to the game.

He stops near the entrance to the subway and steps out of the flood of humanity. He's staring over the traffic on Broadway at a mostly finished building covered in scaffolding. The building takes up the whole block between 78th and 79th streets. It's about fifteen stories tall. It looks sort of familiar, especially the crenelated façade. Maybe he sped by it in a tricked-out SUV in the past few years, zipping off to clubs after games. Maybe he remembers it from way back when his father played ball, the two trips his dad took him along on the road. The building's stone is fresh and white.

"Pardon me," a man apologizes after his briefcase whacks the side of Velez's knee.

Velez gazes at the masons up on the building troweling cement. A rope hoists a block of stone, dangling six flights up. On the ground below it, a team of grunting men pulls it higher.

Most of him doesn't want to go to the Polo Grounds. He asks himself what the point would be, other than to see, really see, if everybody is hitting the ball the other way, and no one can make it as a pull hitter. At least his body's got the day off, another day free from violently twisting his torso, snapping like a bear trap at the pitch again and again and again. At the end of his father's career, his dad's hip was so jacked his right leg was two inches shorter than the left, and his girlfriend had to get under his armpit to help him out of bed. But what else is Velez going to do in this world? Mooch off Blent? Be Blent's posse? *"Ha!"* Velez blasts, earning a frightened stare from a passing white woman in a wide red hat decorated with plaster parakeets.

He's never paid for a ticket to a baseball game. Down the concrete steps, he descends to the subway.

*

An hour later, Blent is digging his right cleat into the hard-packed dirt at home plate. Teammate George Browne takes a short lead off first. Blent looks at McGraw in the third-base coacher's box, who bellows at Blent, "Come on now!" Then McGraw turns to the Boston pitcher, Pfeffer. *"Your mother's a fucking whore!"*

Unflinching, Pfeffer checks the runner at first, kicks, and fires a fastball. The pitch rising at Blent's head, he twists away, crashing to the dirt. The crowd boos Pfeffer. New York players and McGraw scream threats at him. Blent gently chuckles as he brushes himself off, glancing around at the little grandstand, the bleachers, at the fans—men in neckties and derby hats, scattered women in dresses, at the arc of crowd sitting on the grass, forty deep, behind a temporary rope barrier marking a parabola along the deep outfield. It's extremely weird to have that arc of fans watching the game *on the field.*

The next pitch is straight, ripping the air at the outside corner. *"Strike!"*

The crowd spews curses at the ump. McGraw adds, *"That's horseshit!"*

Blent tells himself, *Damn. Good location. Maybe 93. Man up. He's gonna do the same thing. I can make it in this league.*

Blent chokes down the bat, his bottom hand still two inches from the knob. The same pitch zips, heading a touch farther outside, letting Blent unleash, cracking the ball down the right-field line—fair! The right fielder races after it, but the ball scoots past. Browne, the base runner, is on his way to third. Blent's foot crushes the inner corner of first base, as he's flying, digging for second. Seeing the right fielder slinging the ball toward home, Blent decelerates into second base, the roar of the crowd enveloping him.

Hands on hips, panting, he asks the field ump, "Time, please!" The field ump bellows, "Time!" Blent jogs a few steps back to pick up his cap.

*

"That a boy!" Martin exclaims under his breath. He is seated in the fourth row behind home plate. He's already covered his scorecard with notes about the Boston pitcher's tendency to lick his lips before he throws a curve, about the third baseman playing too shallow, about the positioning of the outfielders—Boston's and New York's.

"His first name John?" a sportswriter asks another in the pit of sportswriters clanging on little typewriters and a bevy of telegraph operators tapping out the description of the game on wires whose tendrils connect to a web crisscrossing North America.

Martin steps down the aisle and leans over the edge of the pit. He recognizes some of the writers from the train ride from St. Louis. As he realizes he's just about the only man in the stands who is not wearing a derby hat, he announces, "I was John Blent's manager in San Francisco, if any of you have any questions." A few writers glance away from the field at him, but none acknowledge him. Trying to fight the feeling of humiliation, he turns up the aisle.

\*

Velez is seated on the ground in left-center. He paid a quarter for the privilege of sitting on his ass, surrounded by a boisterous mass of humanity behind a line of ropes in the deep outfield. Velez thinks he sees Martin standing up and waving at him from the stands. It's hard to tell from so far away.

Velez is surrounded by cheerful boys, men, and some women. The men and boys are dressed in dark pants, white shirts—some with collars, some without—and dark sports jackets of varying ripeness. He is not one to throw stones about clothes as the knees and elbows of his suit are smeared in gray dirt.

And now there's Blent—Goddamned Blent!—leading off second base. He considers shouting, *"Don't get picked off by the center fielder!"* but doesn't open his mouth. He can't tell who is who from the back because none of the players have numbers or names on their uniforms.

"Now batting, Joe McGinnity!" a guy with a megaphone announces from near the New York dugout. Fans roar. Velez sighs hard and picks a blade of yellow grass.

A *knock*, the crowd roars. The third baseman stabs the ball shoulder high and fires it across to first—sort of a weak throw, it seems to Velez. Blent slides into third. McGraw pats him on the back. "Bastard," Velez mumbles regarding McGraw and all 1906 managers. "Gotta be kidding me." A man nearby is loudly munching a pork chop, holding it in a grease-stained handkerchief. On the other side, a father and son are crunching apples. Everyone smells bad—or maybe it's just him—no, packed in tight on the subway, it smelled like a minor-league locker room. *That lousy pitcher is nothing. A nibbler. Just stay off the outside crap and hammer something. Slam it. I could destroy this guy. Kill him.* He shouts, *"Fuck!"*

The next pitch is a fastball that Bresnahan whacks to center, and the crowd rises around Velez, but Velez knows it will land in the center fielder's glove. Inning over, the fielders jog toward the dugout. Velez groans as he stands, turns his back on the players, grinds his teeth, squeezes his fists till the nails dig in his palms, picking his way through the seated crowd, walking away from the game. He walks alongside a standalone section of bleachers to a gate in the eight-foot-tall wooden fence.

\*

Martin is hunched over his scorecard, going over the inning's pitching chart. It's a way to analyze the pitcher's tendencies. He's running out of space on his card, and he figures he should go buy another rather than ask the writers for a sheet or two of paper. He doesn't want to be unprofessional, and this includes mooching *anything*, even a sheet of paper.

"That's quite an elaborate scorecard. What's your system?" asks a young man in the seat next to Martin.

Martin hesitates. He does not want to reveal much. Twenty-first-century statistics will be a gigantic advantage for Blent, and eventually, hopefully, for Velez. But statistics disseminated erode any advantage. To the young man with deep-set brown eyes, Martin replies, "I am charting pitches for Mr. Blent. I am a good friend of his."

"The new player?"

"Yes."

"I am the son of the man who pays Mr. Blent's salary." The young man extends his hand, "John Brush, Junior."

Martin shakes hands. Referring to his position in the aisle, Martin asks, "Is it okay that I'm sitting here?"

"Certainly," Brush, Jr. replies. "Packed ballpark. Beautiful sight."

Martin looks up in time to see McGinnity wind up and fire a fastball on the outside edge of the plate.

\*

Velez clomps a foot up on the rail of a bar. The sun pours in, highlighting ten thousand dust motes, and the collection of chicken bones stacked up above the light fixture. He is somewhat lost downtown, having ridden the Elevated Train, then walked and walked. "What kind of whiskey you got?"

The bartender—short nose, piggy face—replies, "What kind of money you got?"

"Something old and good. I usually don't drink during the day."

"Five-cent, ten-cent, or twenty-five cent?"

"The twenty-five. On the rocks."

Across the street, there's a large woman sitting in a chair on the sidewalk. A sign over her door: "FORTUNE." Velez clenches his teeth. He sips the whiskey and ice. "This is all right," he tells the bartender.

The bartender removes his toothpick, spits. "I'm glad as all hell."

A little kid races in, his jacket and shorts fluttering, skids in the sawdust, announces, "Bresnahan grounds out! Blent singles! Devlin double play!"—some drinkers cheer, others groan—"Three to two Giants! End of the seventh!"

Drinkers toss pennies at the kid's feet. He picks them up and rushes out. Velez is always surprised that people who do not play baseball have so much attachment to who wins and who loses.

"Anyone want to bet they lose?" asks a fat man on a bench.

"What's your odds?" replies a man across the room.

"Three to one."

"Gimme six to one."

"Sheesh! Stop wasting my time."

"It's a long season yet," says the second.

"A long season for you to not place any bets."

The barroom erupts laughing.

Velez tells himself, *Should be "Velez" that little kid says.* *"Velez hits a homer!" They don't know what home-run hitting is!* *Stupid soft baseball.*

He drains his glass, sets it on the bar, aims his finger at the glass, bends his thumb like a trigger and shoots, which makes the bartender smile.

*

## BOSTON  4 — 3  NEW YORK

Bottom of the 9th. Browne on first. No outs.

Blent relishes the feeling of his spikes biting the ground as he approaches home plate. The game's been swift, with zero pitching changes. Battling the same pitcher four or five times in a game tilts the advantage to a good hitter. Blent has seen Pfeffer's fastball (degraded over the innings and now about 85 mph), his curve (breaking away from Blent), a half slider (breaking in), and a changeup.

What he deeply doesn't like is that the ball is various shades of brown. At least the few clouds are not dimming the sunlight. With New York down one run and Browne on first base, the third baseman is pinching in a few steps, expecting a bunt. Manager McGraw signals Blent, touching knee, belt buckle, shoulder, shoulder: swing away.

Blent will try to refrain from swinging at anything outside, and if it's good, go with the pitch and hit the darned thing *hard*.

On a 3-and-1 fastball, middle-out, he blasts it to right-center, the right fielder chugging, diving, not touching it. The ball is absorbed by the outfield throng beyond the rope lines, and the umpire declares it a grounds-rule double. Blent stands on second base, the cheers enveloping him for the fourth or fifth time this day. In his mind's eye, he sees his mother and war-hero brother in the kitchen unloading the steaming dishwasher and smiling at him. He squats on second base and rubs his face, pretending there's something in his eye.

"You all right?" the base ump asks.

Blent refocuses. He looks over at Browne, on third, catches his eye. Browne points back at Blent and nods in approval.

*Crack!* Art Devlin strokes a single down the left-field line, scoring Browne. Blent hits third base—the soft bag like taking one nightmarish step in sand—legs pistoning. There are twelve thousand pairs of eyes on Blent as he tells himself, *Pick up your feet! Pick up your feet!* Racing toward home, the ball thuds grass, and Blent drops into a slide. The ball bounces to the catcher; Blent's aiming his feet at the catcher's left foot blocking the plate. As the mitt and ball come down on Blent he feels the catcher's foot give way, the mitt hitting Blent's shoulder.

Blent doesn't know if he's safe or out, and a roaring pain shoots up his leg.

"*Safe!*" the ump shouts.

"*Nooooo!*" the catcher protests.

The fans erupt in thunderous exultation, scream in triumph, swarm the field, jump in ecstasy, boys and drunks trying to snatch players' caps.

BOSTON   4 — 5   NEW YORK   FINAL

Martin rushes down the aisle, edging between celebrating fans. *"Please! Please! Please!"* He pushes them out of his way and scampers onto the field toward home, where a huge pile of fans and players covers Blent. Blent pops up, wincing, face streaked with dirt.

"Fun game!" Blent dryly comments to Martin.

*"You all right?"*

"Ankle."

\*

Eight and a quarter miles away, Velez lets out a belch that echoes in the run-down Bowery bar within which he's already consumed four drinks. It's his third bar of the day, this one redolent of turpentine and vomit. He lays out the remaining contents of his pocket on the plank that serves as a bar: a dime and two pennies. To the reflection in the mottled mirror behind the bar, Velez shouts, *"I don't want to hit the ball the other way! That's for wimps! For little guys!"*

Outside, a pack of boys shouts, *"The Giants win! The Giants win! The Giants win!"*

Inside, no one reacts. The bar is populated by half a dozen people whose overriding purpose is to drink as much as possible for as little money as possible. Velez points to his coins and asks the bartender, "What'll this get me?"

"Two more," replies the turnip-shaped woman missing most of her teeth, adding, "And a two-cent tip."

"Ha! Okay. Two whiskeys. If they really *are* whiskeys." Over the years, his posse has mentioned that he's not a very good drinker when it comes to quantity. *Quality* . . . yes. He appreciates Cristal, Remy Martin, expensive wine, caviar! . . . and his favorite: sushi flown in from the Tsukiji fish market in Tokyo. He picks up a shot, says to the bartender, his voice sounding to himself like it's down a tunnel, "I like eating at home. Don't like four-hour meals. Know what I mean?"

"Sure." She wipes her rag at a puddle on the bar.

"I don't get it—why people sit in one place, eating, eating, eating, four hours. Gets *boring*! The French Laundry can go fuck itself. You feel me?"

"Feel you?" She squints. "No, I don't *feel* you."

"Sorry. Didn't mean no disrespect."

"You babble."

"I like my chef—you know, surprise me! Fix whatever you want—everything's great!"

"You employ a chef, do you?"

"Damn straight!" Velez reaches for his other shot glass of booze, but the bar is undulating and spinning into itself. He raises the glass, but misses his mouth, pouring the shot on his neck and shirt.

*

Christy Mathewson's 1906 Cadillac is rolling down 8th Avenue under the Elevated train tracks. In the Cadillac are Mr. and Mrs. Christy Mathewson, Mr. and Mrs. John McGraw, Henry—the driver/mechanic—and Blent.

McGraw tells Blent, "A good soak in hot water, then a wrap in a hot towel will take the sprain out of it," which, to Blent, is exactly the *wrong* approach. In college, Blent took a course in sports medicine and nutrition, along with two off-campus courses in chiropractic. The hot treatment that McGraw suggests will increase rather than decrease the swelling.

Meanwhile, it is hard for Blent not to stare at Mrs. Mathewson: perfect skin, perfect chin, cheeks, nose, broad unblemished forehead. Her black hair is bunched up loosely, undulating in the breeze as she gazes out at passing New Yorkers. She turns to Blent: "Does it hurt much?"

From the front seat, tall, handsome Christy Mathewson interjects, "*Of course* it hurts! But we don't talk about how much it hurts, right, Johnny?"

Blent tries not to groan. "Right."

Mrs. Mathewson reaches for Blent's lower leg, and to the concerned glares of Mr. and Mrs. John McGraw, she lifts Blent's foot and places it on her thigh atop her blue dress. She explains, "My cousin is a nurse." Blent appreciates her Southern accent. He grunts, "Thank you, ma'am."

As the car bounces in the flickering shadow of the El tracks, Mrs. Mathewson says, "I think I detect a south Tennessee or north Alabama accent."

"Exactly."

"Can you guess where I'm from?" she asks as she begins surreptitiously stroking his shinbone. To Blent, her touch is like an explosion that has forced this 1906 world into an extra dimension.

He tells her, "Ma'am, I need to readjust," and with pain corkscrewing up his leg he sets his foot on the floor. Now he's scared to look at Mrs. Mathewson. "North Carolina. Piedmont."

"That's right! We Southerners must stick together!"

McGraw raises his hand in objection. "As long as you're not New Gloryers!"

Half an hour later, inside their newly leased apartment, Martin removes Blent's sock, revealing a blue, black, red ankle, looking like a hunk of uncooked bacon, about twice its normal size.

"The bathtub work?" Blent asks.

"Shit. Didn't think to test the bath. Should have." With their livelihood in the balance, he asks the next question, "Think anything's broken?"

Attempting to flex the foot, Blent winces, "Don't know yet. I could use ice. A lot of it," adding, "I'm pretty sure they have X-rays in 1906. Did you see where André went?"

The last words are obfuscated by insistent knocking. Opening the door reveals Mrs. Critz, the landlord with whom Martin negotiated the monthly rent down from $27.50 to $23.25. She's a nervous woman a bit older than Martin. She and her two standard poodles peer in at Blent. "Is your friend all right?"

Martin introduces Blent, and asks Mrs. Critz, "Could you tell me how I can get a lot of ice?"

Her eyes go wide at the sight of the damaged ankle. "I'll send a boy around to the Dublin House."

# 11

## A Quarter Deer

"WHAT IS WRONG with you!?" André Velez's father, Gregg, shouts as he towers over him, spoon-sized, tan-yellow cockroaches crawling over his father's neck and shoulders. Gregg shakes his head at André and turns away. "Wait," André says. André's head pounds; his body is freezing, sweating and numb. He groans, "Damn!" and sits up.

He is surrounded by broken chairs, piles of garbage, a quarter deer—or something as big as a quarter deer—rotting, red guts out and covered with flies. He shrinks into himself and realizes he's in an alley, his bare toes flexing up at him.

"The shoes again!" He groans, wretches and vomits. His shoes, yet again, have been stolen.

A few cold blocks later, on Broadway and 4th, Velez side-steps a shattered bottle, the pavement frigid, the sky lightening to a cobalt blue. A little white guy sneers as he passes. Velez has found one penny in his pocket, four cents short of the subway. He's dizzy and sweating. He asks a boy sitting on a stack of newspapers, "Which way is Fifth Avenue?"

The kid points up Broadway.

Velez offers, "If you give me four pennies, I'll give you twenty dollars later."

The kid looks up with an angelic, dirt-streaked face. "Get lost, bum."

His head pounding, mouth agape, Velez considers the four directions of the New York grid, the wind chilling his throat. He shuffles up Broadway, picks his way uptown, and makes it to Union Square with his hands in the pockets of his filthy pants. He finds a bench and cranks his dirty right foot under his left thigh, trying to warm at least one foot.

Across the path, a bench is occupied by an old, white man in a wrinkled white suit and a black scarf. He is sipping from a china cup and eating a bread roll. He brushes off crumbs. Pigeons swoop to the path.

Velez's stomach growls as he remembers a stripper—was it Atlanta or San Diego or Houston?—talking about eating pigeon in Egypt. Not bad at all, she said. He knows he can snatch one of those pigeons poking crumbs in the path and snap its neck, but he doesn't have a place to cook it. And he's never killed anything bigger than a moth.

The man in the black scarf crumbles his roll and tosses a cloud of pieces, attracting the whole flock. Velez rises, kicking at the birds, which flutter up, pooping. He kneels and sweeps crumbs together, getting one palm full. Returning to his bench, he picks out bits of dirt and a twig, then keeps his head down as he munches on the breadcrumbs.

"Do you actually have to do that!?" asks the man sipping coffee. "Here!" The man tosses an oval biscotti through the air.

Velez snatches it. "Thanks! I wish I could pay you for this. I got one stinking penny!"

"Not an issue for me today."

Velez shivers as he crunches into the biscotti. "This is my first day in New York. I mean, I've been here before, but first since the earthquake."

"San Francisco?"

"Ya-huh."

The man watches Velez chew. "Would a cup of coffee suit you?"

Velez hesitates to take charity, telling himself he's a bum, a bum, a bum. "Okay, man. Yeah. Thanks. I used to be worth a lot of money—a lot! Now, this." He slaps a bare foot.

"Enrico!" The man raises a hand, conjuring the sleepy, long-aproned waiter from the park's café.

"*Sì, signore?*"

"Can you make a coffee so strong it will raise the dead?"

The waiter's guffaw tilts his head back.

"Bring that for my friend here. But first please bring us a pyramid of your bread rolls, and an assortment of sweet rolls."

The waiter aims his rueful expression at Velez, then, "How is *your* coffee?"

He raises his cup, as if toasting. "To my liking, thank you."

Giving Velez the stink eye, the waiter stomps away.

"Thank you," says Velez. "You're saving my ass."

"You are certainly welcome." He reaches into his white jacket. "Do you mind if I foul the air with my see-gar smoke?"

Velez chuckles. "You a comedian? You remind me of people in LA."

"El. A?"

"Los Angeles. You remind me of actors."

Coffee and rolls are brought and set on the bench beside Velez, who devours a roll. Gazing into the coffee cup, amidst the silhouette of tree branches and buildings, he is startled at the ragged outline of his reflection. He sips. In thanks, he nods at the man, who in reply flourishes his cigar. "To the great God, Coffee!"

Velez answers questions about the earthquake, recounting swimming into the Bay, crawling through the mud, being buck naked. He leaves out the most important part, though—being ripped through time. On his fourth cup and fifteenth roll, he explains that people want him to pretend that he's an Indian. And beyond that everyone wants him to slap the ball to the opposite field. "If I can hit, then I can hit, no matter my name or how I look, right?"

"Would be nice if the world worked that way."

"And they want me to *change* my name!"

"Oh?" the man's eyebrows rise like frayed sections of rope. "I do not think it's such a tragedy to change a name."

"Why's that?"

"Because many, many years ago, I chose another name. Now some people call me Mister Clemens. Others call me Mark Twain. Others, no doubt, call me nasty names when I am not in their presence." He crosses the path, holding out his right hand.

Velez's massive hands cover the bony hand. "Mark Twain? You shittin' me?"

Twain laughs hard, doubling over. Addressing the pigeons pecking under Velez's bench, he bellows, *"You shittin' me?"*

\*

Uptown at the 20th Precinct, the gray-faced police sergeant leans over his gargantuan desk and asks Martin, "Is this fellow simple in the head, or in some other way dangerous?"

Martin considers dropping the names McGraw and Mathewson, but he's quite sure that McGraw wouldn't want his name bandied about to try and find a player he considers of no use. "No."

"Is he the type who does stupid things when drunk?"

"He's not used to being alone."

"I'll telephone some other precincts," says the sergeant. "That's all I can do. But if you ask me, he sounds like a simpleton."

*

Midmorning, Velez walks past the steel skeleton of the in-construction Plaza Hotel and into Central Park. He's wearing a new pair of shoes courtesy of Mark Twain. The Irving Place shoemaker suggested ankle boots, but Velez said, "No, man, just regular shoes. I've had too many ankle boots stolen."

A problem for Velez is that somewhere he lost the scrap of paper with the addresses for the new apartment and for McGraw and Mathewson's. He's pretty sure it's 86th or 85th or 87th or 84th Street near Broadway. Crossing Sheep Meadow, boys are playing baseball—six fielders, a few hitters. Velez sits, watching a kid take a weak swing at a weak pitch, the plop of the ball in the catcher's mitt. "Stay behind the ball!" Velez suggests. "It's not a raw egg—nail the heck out of it!" The kids take nervous glances at him.

The boy at bat swings at the pitch too early, missing by two feet. *"No!"* Velez rises. *"Let me hit!"* he says, holding his hand out for the bat. The kid at the plate, stunned that this giant is asking to play, hands the bat to Velez. It's a kiddie bat, a bit short for Velez, but the weight feels good. "Okay!" Velez rolls his neck, takes an easy practice swing, cocks his body. As he's focusing on the kid pitcher, the trees beyond the outfield are moving too much. "Pitch it!" he hears himself say. The ball is on its way. Velez isn't tracking it normally—with his eyes—instead using a sixth sense. *Wait on it,* he tells himself, *wait, wait.* Shwoosh! The ball rockets away. He can't see the ball go, but it *feels* like a great hit. He turns and dizzily hurries behind a nearby tree and vomits a few times. "Damned rotgut."

Velez returns.

"You all right, mister?" a kid asks warily.

"Shoot, yeah. I drank something bad. Hey, I was Most Valuable Player two times! Let me get some hits, then we can play a game."

The kids erupt:

*"I'm on his team!"*

*"Me too!"*

Velez wiggles the bat, standing next to the round newsboy hat they're using as home plate. "Pitch the ball outside!" he tells the skinny pitcher, pointing the end of the bat at the spot he wants it. The skinny pitcher lobs it in. Velez shifts his back foot, steps toward the ball with his right, and strokes the ball on a low arc into left field, telling himself, *That's opposite-field hitting right there. It ain't cracking the ball, that's for sure,* and to the pitcher, "Again! Same pitch!"

While the outfielders yell— *"Hit it here!" "Hit it far!" "Hit it out of the park!"*—the pitch arrives slowly. Velez shifts his weight back, waiting, slapping it to left.

\*

Blent is gazing out the bay window, sipping coffee that Martin cooked in a pot borrowed from Mrs. Critz. *"Oh shoot!"* Blent's coffee sloshes out of the cup as he notices his puggish new manager charging across the street. "McGraw!"

"Probably seeing if you can play today," says Martin.

"Don't you find it weird that he and his wife live in the same apartment with Christy and Mrs. Mathewson?"

"We're in 1906. Doesn't that beat everything for weirdness?"

McGraw bounds up the steps and into the first-floor apartment, all business. "How's my second baseman?"

"Not broken," Blent grunts. He lifts his foot and, trying not to react to the pain roaring up his leg, minisculely rotates the ankle.

"Can you stand on it?"

Blent stands, craning to the left. "I'll be good to go."

Martin interjects, "Johnny never missed a game for me."

"Just when I took bereavement leave my first year of A-ball."

*"Bereavement leave?"* Spittle accompanies McGraw's words. *"What the hell?"*

"When my me-me-maw died—great-grandma."

*"You left the team for that?"* McGraw, for the first time in their presence, looks baffled. "Is California on another planet?"

Martin is about to conjure an excuse, when they're distracted by the high-pitched shouting of excited children, *"There he is! There's McGraw! McGraw! McGraw! McGraw!"* McGraw, Blent, and Martin turn to the bay window to see Christy Mathewson smiling brilliantly, walking across the street toward them, the center of an entourage of exultant boys and girls, along with Velez, who is smiling too, disheveled, pointing the kiddie bat at Martin and Blent.

\*

After two dozen pancakes, a pound of bacon, eighteen scrambled eggs, and half a loaf of toast are downed at Dirk's Restaurant, they head to Amsterdam Avenue, Blent limping along, to the St. Agnes branch of the New York Public Library, the new library redolent of drying varnish. They seek to pin down when their world diverged from this.

Blent and Martin plop stacks of history books on a table while Velez examines *Autos Today*.

Blent scans *The Anthology of Famous Scientists*. "A lot of these people live in New Glory. Hey, this could help: Alexander Graham Bell lives in New Jersey."

"New Jersey?" Martin asks. "I specifically remember that he was Canadian."

Velez lights a cheroot Twain gave him.

Martin approaches the librarian's desk. "Is there any way of finding out where Alexander Graham Bell lives?"

Wearily, the librarian replies, "Of course."

As they pore over the history books, as far as they can decipher, they agree that everything seems to be the same going into the Civil War. In this world, the South won the Battle of Gettysburg in July 1863 and also broke the siege of Vicksburg, defeating General Grant.

"What triggered the divergence?" Martin wonders aloud.

"Maybe it's been triggered more than once," says Velez. "Maybe there's not just one timeline. Maybe this happened to someone else."

Nearby a reader hisses, *"Shhhhhhhhhh!"*

Velez blows a cloud of cigar smoke. He turns his head toward Martin, but he doesn't look *at* Martin. "Coach, there's something else."

"Yes, André?"

"Well . . . It's just . . . I don't know how to say this, but . . ."

"But what?"

"I was on the oil."

"What are you talking about?"

Blent crosses his arms and sits back.

"Performance enhancers," Velez says.

Martin closes his eyes, absorbing the news. Opening his eyes, Martin asks, "Really?"

"I'm sorry, man. PEDs. Yes. I was on them."

"Why are you telling me this now?"

The librarian scurries at them. "There is no smoking of cigars—or pipes! You may smoke a cigarette! Final warning!"

Tired, confessing, teamless Velez whines, "Man, gimme me a break!"

Martin snatches the cigar, throws it down and stomps it. *"That's lying, André!"* Martin storms away.

Velez asks, "How's it lying?"

*"It means we didn't win honestly! You cheated! We cheated! Everybody cheated!"* Martin's voice echoes. Library patrons hiss.

Martin and Velez rumble out separately. Blent limps after them, to find Velez on the sunny sidewalk telling Martin, "I'm sorry, boss. I'm so sorry. And I'm not the only one! Everybody was doing it!"

"Not me!" Blent protests.

"Did you know about this, that he was on performance enhancers?" Martin asks Blent.

Blent shrugs, frozen, embarrassed. "He told me a few days ago."

"What if we missed the playoffs every year 'cause I wasn't on it?" Velez asks.

Martin seems shrunken, ill, confused. He wipes his eye and nose. "A team doesn't hide secrets from each other. Or else it's not a *team*." He trudges away, downtown.

Blent and Velez watch him go. Velez walks alongside limping Blent toward the apartment.

"Feel better?" Blent asks. "It's called confessing."

"You confess in your cock-ass religion?"

"No, we're not Catholic."

"You need some treatment on that ankle." Velez's eyebrows are lowered, chin compressed. He squats, covers his face with his hands, and weeps hard.

Clusters of people—1906 people—pass them, some looking at crumpled Velez with concern. A puffy woman in a bonnet makes eye contact with Blent, who fends off a query by telling her, "He's okay."

Blent pats Velez's back, smears off dried pigeon poop, but Velez brushes off Blent's hand. He stands and leans against the redbrick building, crying into his forearm, a prodigious amount of tears and snot dripping, his face contorted.

Just to try to get him to stop, Blent tells him, "It's okay, man. Buck will understand. He *has* to understand. He has no choice. It will all be fine."

Velez convulses with crying.

"You'll start to play ball and get a car nicer than Mathewson's—or *two* cars. You'll get a condo, or a house, a mansion . . ."

Velez's crying does not abate.

Freaked out, Blent tries another tack. "It was Rick Brothers."

Velez's convulsions do not abate.

"The guy who scratched your Lamborghini," Blent repeats, "was Rick Brothers."

Velez's crying regulates to a staccato. "What are you talking about? Brothers? You serious?"

"The Kitty Annex. He told me. He saw your car at the edge of the parking lot."

"Why would he scratch my car?"

"He didn't like you."

Velez wipes his face on both jacket sleeves. "Why didn't he like me?"

They begin walking up Amsterdam. Blent's weak ankle is now just deeply sore. "You weren't such a good teammate. You were obsessed with yourself. You were an asshole."

*"Really?"*

"The guys used to say, 'It's one team plus André Velez.'"

Velez's mouth puckers. "I guess, maybe, I was a dick, maybe, sometimes."

"Affirmative."

\*

An hour later, Martin returns to the apartment. He's gnashing his teeth as he and Velez eye each other. "I'm going to the game," Martin says. "You can come along."

In silence, they walk to the El station on 81st Street. In silence, they ride the train. In silence at the Polo Grounds, Martin buys two tickets. There's a line of people in front of a popcorn vendor, the kernels popping, the air perfumed with the aroma of butter cooking corn.

Velez asks, "Can I have a nickel?"

Munching from his bag of popcorn, Velez follows Martin into a grandstand box behind the pit full of two dozen reporters and eight telegraphers. On the field a white-suited vendor scans the stands, a wicker basket under his arm, a hand-painted sign on the basket, "SAUSAGE 15¢." Martin's arm shoots up. *"Over here!"* He doesn't offer to buy a sausage for Velez. He shifts his chair to the side of the box, as far away from Velez as possible, then, holding his sausage, addresses Velez, "Is there anything else that you were doing that you didn't tell me about?"

Velez glances around. "I had lots of girls."

"Anything about *baseball*, the *team*, *cheating*."

"No."

Martin examines his scorecard, while Velez contemplates the varying states of physical conditioning of the players warming up on the field.

Martin asks, "How are you feeling? You have withdrawals from the shit you were on? Is that why you were sick in St. Louis?"

"Honestly?" Velez replies, and to Martin's increasingly reptilian visage, Velez admits, "I feel weaker. I'm not Superman anymore. I feel all my old injuries—ankles, knees, hip, shoulder, neck. It's the way I felt the past two winters, when I stopped taking the stuff. I gotta find a gym, pump some weights."

Martin gazes out at Christy Mathewson warming up on the pitcher's mound, tells Velez, "Mathewson won 373 games in his career. Over 2,500 strikeouts. An ERA a bit above two. A WHIP near one."

"In St. Louis, I hit a homer off him." Velez tips up the bag of popcorn, a last cluster of popped kernels rolling into his mouth, not deeply respecting any pitcher—alive, dead, past, present, or future.

\*

Blent's on the bench. His foot throbs with each heartbeat, but the cleat is on. The foot is so swollen he had to tie an extra quarter length of shoelace in order to close the shoe. McGraw determined Blent should give the ankle a day off. Blent takes a pouch of Red Man from Hooks Wiltse—a guy who weirdly looks like a deer on hind legs, or, perhaps, an undertaker. Red Ames, another pitcher, is on the bench. And Frank Bowerman, who catches when Bresnahan plays center field. That's it—four guys on the bench with Manager John McGraw.

Christy Mathewson takes the ball, inspects its nicks and abrasions, nods at catcher Bresnahan. He winds and fires a curve that drops three feet—the batter flailing at it. Mathewson's toe wipes the pitching rubber. He rocks back and fires a rising fastball that rips the air—the batter resists. A ball. Mathewson, with a hint of frustration—either at the umpire or himself—slaps his glove onto the returning ball. He rocks back, and the pitch looks like a changeup, but bends in toward the batter—a slider—the batter hitting a dribbler fifteen feet up the line toward third. Catcher Bresnahan explodes after it, pounces, straightens, and zips the ball to first. Out by two steps.

Martin wonders where Mathewson would fit on a twenty-first-century team. Would he be the ace, a reliever, a closer? His stuff is good enough to keep him out of the minors, that's for sure.

*"Strike three!"* the ump bellows.

New York jogs off the field. Mathewson ambles toward the bench, affecting nonchalance. Martin looks down at his score-card, which he has neglected to score, having been so absorbed in watching Christy Mathewson.

Catching Martin's eye, with a serious expression, Velez blurts, "Sumbitch is good!"

\*

After the game, squashed together in the packed Elevated train, Velez tells Martin, "I want some batting practice."

Martin pushes away. Like the chemical-therapy drugs that fought off his cancer three years ago, Martin's disappointment in Velez makes Martin feel thoroughly sick. "Throw it to yourself."

But by the time the train makes the next two stops, Martin considers the other players he's managed who've been suspended for using PEDs, but no one as great as André Velez. It's all different now; there are no PEDs in 1906. Martin pokes Velez in the kidney.

Velez turns a cold expression.

"Batting practice," Martin blurts. "It'll be good for me too."

In Central Park a half an hour later, Martin throws a bean-bag toward home plate, which is a square of brown butcher paper retrieved from a trash can, weighted with rocks.

Cocking the kiddie bat, Velez eyes the incoming beanbag, flicking his bat at it, spanking it toward third. Martin holds up another beanbag, just like batting practice—showing the ball to the batter before the pitch. Martin pitches the beanbag at the outside half of the plate. Velez hesitates, steps his right foot toward the incoming beanbag. Right elbow leading the swing, his wrists snap as the bat smacks the beanbag over where third would be. "There you go," Martin encourages.

"Why you hittin' beanbags?" It's the snot-nosed kid, whom Velez recognizes from the early-morning pickup game.

"Softer than a baseball, right?" Martin explains and pitches another beanbag toward the outside of the plate. Velez strokes it into left field. Martin continues, "So you can't hit it far. You gotta hit it where it's pitched."

"You're turning me into a frickin' singles hitter!" Velez shouts, smiles, his voice carrying across the Great Lawn, where couples stroll, a red Irish setter runs after a twirling stick, kids play ball, three kites with tails loop in the air. The roar of car engines is distant and sporadic; it's quieter in the park now than in the twenty-first century. "It's more like tennis than baseball!" Velez says. "Sometimes soft hits, sometimes hard."

"Yes!" Martin throws a beanbag.

Velez swats it to left.

The kid rumbles after the beanbags and dumps them at Martin's feet. "Can I hit?"

"Not today, kid," says Velez through his dead-serious expression, feeling the sweaty lather on his torso, the familiar, weightless movements of his knees, hips, ankles, wrists, shoulders, and neck.

The snot-nosed kid soon loses interest and stomps away, wiping tears.

Velez eyes an incoming beanbag, wrists it over shortstop.

"I think you've had enough." Martin's sweaty, elbow aching.

"No! A hundred more!" Velez tells himself, *Gonna be the best fucking slap hitter this league's ever seen!*

# 12

## Bell's the Man to Figure It Out

THE NEXT DAY the trio is riding a train rolling through New Jersey.

"I specifically remember learning in second grade that Bell was Canadian," Martin says.

Velez blurts, "Things are messed up. What else is new?"

Martin says, "Thomas Edison and Henry Ford are New Gloryers."

Getting off in Little Silver, they take a carriage away from the salty ocean breeze. Half an hour later, they arrive at a compound of houses and barn-sized structures, various chimneys emitting toxic smoke.

At the largest house, a butler greets them.

Velez says, "We are here to see Mr. Graham Bell."

"Mr. Bell is occupied."

Martin persists, "We have a question to ask him. He might find it of great interest—great scientific interest."

"I can pass the question to him, if you would care to write a note."

Blent asks, "Is Mr. Bell a religious man?"

The butler winces. "No more than the average person."

"Mr. Bell like baseball?" Velez asks.

"Games are not a pursuit of his," the butler replies, and adds, "but his sons do play."

"Mr. Blent here plays for the New York Giants. And we'd like to meet Mr. Bell and his sons."

The butler escorts the trio to a secretary, who, after everything is explained again, brings them to a room that smells of burnt rubber. It's full of vacuum tubes and copper wire, a pile of assorted bicycle parts, and a skeleton leaning face-first into a stack of papers. A bearded rotund man with tired eyes, pasty skin, greasy hair, offers his hand. "Gentlemen. How may I be of assistance?"

Velez chitchats about being ballplayers, the San Francisco earthquake, then says, "You see, Mr. Bell. We did go through an earthquake, but it's well over a hundred years in the future, the twenty-first century."

Bell recoils as if blown by a hurricane. "The future?"

Velez repeats his statement.

Bell's jaw clenches as he steps toward the door. "I have heard a lot of unusual claims in my life. Why are you here?"

Velez says, "We want you to help us figure out a way to get back."

Bell opens the door. His secretary pops to attention.

Bell waves them out. "I'm not your man. Good luck with your search."

Velez stops halfway out the door. "Ever hear of a cell phone?"

"A what?" Bell gently pushes Velez's elbow along.

"You hold it to your ear." Velez mimes holding his beloved old phone. "And there are no wires. You can walk around outside with it. Take it anywhere. In your automobile."

Bell squints at Velez. "No thank you." He shuts the door.

The carriage ride back to the train station is silent until Velez comments, "I can't believe he wouldn't be interested in cell phones."

"I hope that doesn't fuck us up even more," Martin wonders, "if we divulge inventions of the future."

Blent puts his aching foot up on the door of the carriage. "We'll get back to our time."

"Based on what?" Velez sneers.

"Based on faith."

\*

Four mornings later, Martin sits on the living room sofa, the table before him covered in a sea of newspapers and hand-calculated statistics. He's reading about the Giants' 4–3 loss to Boston.

> In addition to being ejected from active participation in the game at the Polo Grounds yesterday, Manager McGraw of the champion New Yorkers, annoyed at what he considered some uncomplimentary remarks hurled at him as he was leaving the playing field, struck a man in the eye with his fist, and then went to the clubhouse. The man assaulted refused to give his name, but he claimed that McGraw's attack was un-justifiable, and when he demanded of a policeman the arrest of the manager, the officer replied that he did not see the occurrence, and furthermore he

> could not make an arrest without
> a warrant.

Sniggering at the article, Martin's eyes return to the Major League standings. Even though he's memorized them, seeing the standings printed in a newspaper makes them seem more real:

| National League | W-L | PCT. | GB | | American League | W-L | PCT. | GB |
|---|---|---|---|---|---|---|---|---|
| N.Y. | 13-4 | .765 | — | | Phila. | 9-5 | .643 | — |
| Chi. | 12-6 | .667 | 1½ | | Clev. | 7-6 | .538 | 1½ |
| Pitts. | 10-6 | .625 | 2½ | | Wash. | 8-7 | .533 | 1½ |
| Phila. | 9-8 | .529 | 6 | | Det. | 7-7 | .500 | 2 |
| Bosn. | 7-10 | .412 | 8 | | Chi. | 7-7 | .500 | 2 |
| St.L. | 6-9 | .400 | 8 | | St.L. | 7-8 | .467 | 2½ |
| Cin. | 7-14 | .333 | 10 | | N.Y. | 6-8 | .429 | 3 |
| Brkl'n | 4-13 | .235 | 11 | | Bosn. | 6-9 | .400 | 3½ |

New York won the first two games against Boston, and all three versus Pittsburg. Blent played the last two games, his ankle slowing him down, but not slowing down his bat. In his five games in a New York uniform, he's hitting .320; on-base percentage .416; slugging .525. Martin knows it's a small sample, only twenty-three plate appearances, but he is extremely relieved that Blent seems to be sticking in the Major Leagues.

Regarding the stats, Forrest from the *Post* introduced Martin to F. C. Lane, from *Baseball Magazine*. F. C. is a statistics nut who, at his office on 5th Avenue and 18th Street, showed Martin batting and pitching records for the past three years, the batting broken up into hits, singles, doubles, triples, homers, walks, and strikeouts; the pitching into wins, losses, strikeouts, and walks. Martin asked to borrow the master sheet, then at home calculated on-base percentage and slugging percentage—he loves OPS. But the pitchers' statistics are quite useless. Stats like BABIP can be compiled. WHIP—walks plus hits per innings pitched—can sort of be calculated because number of games pitched is tracked, but not number of *innings*, because it's assumed that pitchers toss complete games, which is not always the case. So past seasons' WHIP figures aren't completely accurate.

Velez clonks through the front door with his sack of ten baseballs, his bat, and batting tee made out of a pipe and a slab of wood. His collarless shirt is soaked through with sweat. Glancing at the coffee table piled with stats, he comments, "See the ball, hit the ball."

Blent emerges from the bathroom, the limp 99% gone. Velez sits on the sofa, which Martin uses as a bed. Velez isn't particularly aware that his pants-covered rear is centered where Martin's face contacts the sofa.

Martin scratches his neck. "I'm trying to figure out if André and I can go on this road trip—Pittsburg, Cincinnati. Seven games. We have enough money for food if we stretch it out, and we just paid the rent."

Blent is staring out the window as Mrs. Mathewson walks up her stoop. She's wearing a tight cotton jacket and full skirt, riding boots, black hair in a neat ponytail. She turns to dig her key from her handbag. Lovely cheekbones, lovely face.

"But with train and hotel," Martin continues, "maybe we could go to Pittsburg, but then we'd have to come back here, and we'll have zero until Johnny's next paycheck in two weeks. It's tight." He holds up a sheet of paper with pencil-marked columns. "Here's how much base salary you're making. Here are our expenses: rent; weekly food; subway fare; extras, which includes all booze and food out." The players look on without much urgency. "On one hand, I'd like to go along and help with charting and putting a game plan together for you—" He slaps the pile of papers. "There are only four or five pitchers a team, so scouting the whole league—only seven other teams—won't take much time. On the other hand, I need to get a job and help put some numbers into the 'INCOME' column."

Velez stands motionless, pretending to disappear, not wanting Martin or Blent to tell him to get a job. What would he do? Hoist a rope tied to a giant block of stone like the guys building the Apthorp House Apartments on 79th and Broadway? Tend bar and deal with drunks all night? Be a bouncer? On second thought, that last job—bouncer—doesn't seem so bad. Stand at the door, check out the ladies, intimidate jerks. On third thought, it *does* seem bad—freeze your buns off, stand in one place all night, deal with *drunken* jerks. "Hey, let's ask McGraw for a tryout. I'm ready."

Martin licks the stubble below his lip. "McGraw's got his team set. It's gelled. They're playing great. We wait for an injury, or if someone is seriously underperforming. Johnny will let him know you're ready, and you want a tryout. But there are two other teams—the Highlanders, and Brooklyn."

Velez and Blent share a glance, each considering the pros and cons of not playing on the same team.

"And I'll get some stupid job somewhere doing some stupid damned thing. There is eight dollars and fifty-four cents on the table. André and I will make it on four bucks and change each."

*"Four bucks for two weeks?"* Velez squeaks.

Across the street, Mrs. Mathewson emerges in a fresh outfit—blue chiffon dress trimmed in black, and a matching hat with a pouf of black lace. She's holding a Bible. Inwardly Blent asks himself, *Is it Sunday?* Outwardly he says, "You should come on the road, Buck, and chart the pitches."

"Well, you can chart their pitchers when you're between innings on the bench. And André and I can go to the games in Brooklyn, and I can chart two sets of opposing pitchers and hitters in each game. That's a good use of two nickels subway fare, twenty-five cents admission, and a scorecard. Not a bad way to spend the afternoon—eh, André?"

"I ain't a *watcher*!"

\*

John Brush, Sr., the New York Giants owner, is trying something new. It is the 4:17 a.m. train, destination: Pittsburg—all in the name of not having to pay for hotel rooms for the night. Blent, McGraw and Mathewson ride in Mathewson's Cadillac. Henry, Mathewson's driver/mechanic, guides the big car down Broadway. Ghostly, bundled-up pedestrians move through the shadows. Blent looks over at Mathewson, wrapped in an overcoat, wondering what Mathewson would think if Blent told him that he, Velez and Martin are from the twenty-first century: probably not a friendly reaction.

At the station, a pack of newsboys coalesces, voices echoing,

*"Hi Matty!"*

*"Hi Mr. McGraw!"*

*"Hey Champs!"*

*"Go beat Pittsburg!"*

Mathewson signs offered scraps of paper; McGraw pushes past well-wishers to join Bresnahan and Devlin, who is beaming, on his arm a woman with a fox-trimmed coat and a rhinestone tiara. "The fat-ankled Californian!" Devlin teases Blent, introducing him to "Miss Markey, the best actress in New York!" She scrunches her little face in an embarrassed smile. Their four eyes are matching bloodshot.

Hours later, Blent rises from a nap, stares out at a pasture of Pennsylvania cows. It's strange to be chugging away from Martin, from Velez, alone with his new team for the first time. The feeling reminds him of going off to college—but at least he knew plenty of people there. This is more like going off to Single-A—he'd been at spring training, but then he got on a bus with his team and two days later they were in Minot, North Dakota, freezing their asses off. Darla drove their car up to set up a home for the summer.

Bill Dahlen, the shortstop, leans his elbow on the seat in front of Blent. "You're a square guy, right?"

Not exactly knowing what Dahlen means, Blent replies, "Sure."

"When we get to Pittsburg, we're going in big on today's game. I've got a hundred. Devlin's going two hundred. Donlin's got a thousand."

"Wow." Blent is making eight hundred dollars for the entire season. He's noticed the men congregating at the front rows of the left-field bleachers at the Polo Grounds, openly taking bets. In his time, every clubhouse in the big leagues displayed signs warning about gambling in any form—for or against—though some players certainly gambled in casinos or on other sports.

"You're betting on *us*, right?"

Dahlen chuckles. "We got even odds. Deacon Phillippe is pitching for them, and he's excellent. But, yeah, we're not betting against our own team. A lot of us are betting fifty dollars. You want in?"

"Okay."

*

At Tip-Top Shoes on Broadway, the jangling doorbell announces Bucky Martin's presence. There are two customers. The five salesmen assess him as a prospect and one rises—three-piece suit, gold watch chain, gleaming black shoes. "May I help you?"

"I wonder if I may speak with the manager?" Martin asks, his voice weird and distant to himself. Only two other times in his life has he asked for a job—as a teenager looking for work at his favorite burger joint, which he didn't get; and at an ice cream shop, which he did.

"I am Ernest Jones," a mustachioed, mutton-chopped fat man snorts. "How may I help?"

"I am looking for employment."

"Selling shoes?"

"Yes, that's right."

"Do you have any experience?"

Martin blinks. "I sold shoes in San Francisco. All that's gone now." This statement silences all in the store.

\*

At the edge of Columbus Circle, Velez stops at an apple cart, picking out two, handing the man a dollar bill. He examines the silver quarters and dimes he receives in change, then chomps an apple as he walks down Broadway toward Times Square. There is no neon, no two-hundred-foot-long poster of a super-model in panties. But there is an eighty-foot tall billboard of a jaunty man touting Old Mill Cigarettes, a billboard for Pepsin Gum, another for Hershey's. Velez picks at a piece of peel stuck in his teeth as he gazes at a cluster of men in derby hats, one of them relentlessly motor-mouthing, reminding Velez of his first agent.

He peruses the lineup card on a stand near the door of the Saintsbury Theatre:

# ADMISSION STARTS AT 15 C E N T S ! ! !

Order Of This Program Subject To Change

### BURT JORDAN AND ROSA CROUCH.
SENSATIONAL, GROTESQUE AND 'BUCK' DANCERS. A GOOD ACT!

### THE WHITE TSCHERKESS TRIO.
A MAN AND TWO WOMEN WHO DO A SINGING TURN OF THE OPERATIC ORDER. THEY CARRY SPECIAL SCENERY WHICH IS VERY ARTISTIC AND THEIR COSTUMES ARE ORIGINAL AND NEAT!

### SARAH MIDGELY AND GERTIE CARLISLE.
PRESENTING THE SKETCH 'AFTER SCHOOL.' THEY ARE A 'KNOCKOUT'.

### THEODOR F. SMITH AND JENNY ST. GEORGE-FULLER.
REFINED INSTRUMENTALISTS.

### MILLY CAPELL. EUROPEAN EQUESTRIENNE.
THIS IS HER SECOND WEEK. ON ACCOUNT OF THE VERY PRETTY PICTURE THAT SHE MAKES SHE GOES AS STRONG AS SHE DID LAST WEEK.

### R. J. JOSE. TENOR SINGER.
THE VERY BEST OF THEM ALL!

### THE NELSON FAMILY OF ACROBATS.
THIS ACT IS COMPOSED OF THREE MEN, TWO YOUNG WOMEN, THREE BOYS AND TWO SMALL GIRLS. THE GREATEST ACROBATIC ACT EXTANT!

### JAMES THORNTON. MONOLOGIST AND VOCALIST.
HE GOES LIKE A CYCLONE. IT IS A CASE OF CONTINUOUS LAUGHTER FROM HIS ENTRANCE TO HIS EXIT!

### BURK AND ANDRUS AND THEIR TRAINED MULE!

A woman walks out of the theater, her face shielded from Velez's view by her wide hat, the skirts of her blue dress rustling, her boots *clip-clipping* on the sidewalk as she passes, and he glimpses the side of her face. Cute chin. Small, round cheekbones. Young. A sprig of curling black hair. Her frilly shirt goes high up her neck.

Usually, girls would follow *him*. He mumbles, "Life ain't so easy now, dude," and he walks after the girl. He follows, about twenty yards behind, around the corner and she steps up and pushes through the door of a five-story building. He considers whether to make a move or not—he's got $1.95 in his pocket. His verdict: He's a nothing in this world, so he's got nothing to lose.

He pushes open the green door. She is almost to the top of the narrow stairway. She glances over her shoulder, stops, turns toward him. "Are you the strong man?" Her pleasant tone reverberates against the marble-slabbed walls, and it reminds him, oddly, of the distant sound of the dynamiting of buildings in San Francisco.

The strong man? He doesn't know what to say. She starts to turn away. "I *am* strong, if that's what you're asking."

Her hand flutters up. "Pardon the question." She continues on, out of view, opening the door to a noisy office.

He gazes up at the empty stairway. Someone's banging a tune on a piano in one of the offices. Did she have an accent? Or was it the voice echoing? He retreats. There's singing and piano coming from the next building too. He examines the roster of offices, each name next to a little black buzzer.

2nd Floor: Traub Talent Ag'y.

Stepping around to Broadway, he mutters, "Screw me." *Gimme a pile of sushi! Rick Brothers . . . Dang!*

A few steps away, a wiry man in a white suit and cap is shoveling horse manure into a garbage can.

"My future." Velez gazes out at a horse-drawn bus, at a policeman on a platform in the middle of the street, at the pedestrians. Velez sucks in a lungful of New York air and shouts, *"Fuuuuuuuuuuuuuuuuuuuuuuuuuuuuuuuuuuuuuuuuuuuuuuuuuuuck!"*

\*

Below Times Square, Martin zips along in a subway train headed for Brooklyn. He plans to chart the Brooklyn-Cincinnati game with his fresh supplies: an accordion folder, thirty pages of blank paper, and three sharpened pencils. His *New York Times* is folded into a small rectangle, and he's reading the article under a headline: "New Glory Overwhelms Trinidad."

He's scheduled to start at Tip-Top Shoes in the morning and he's wondering if this is the end, if his baseball life is over. In his mind's eye, he can see himself leading spring training in Scottsdale with the San Francisco Giants; 6:45 a.m. meetings in his office with his coaches over paper cups of coffee; the huge blank eye of the television camera at the end of the dugout in San Francisco aimed straight at him; bouquets of microphones inches from his mouth; bantering with reporters; shaking the hands of some of the legends of baseball; the mental chess match against the manager in the opposing dugout; and winning—his Major League record of 412 wins and 309 losses; plowing through the playoffs; on the cusp of winning the World Series. Zap. Gone.

As the train squeakily decelerates into the Fulton Street station, he opens his eyes and a young woman is holding out to him a white carnation, plucked from a bouquet that she's transporting; he takes the flower; she smiles and says, "Take a deep breath," and steps off the train.

Martin regards the green stalk between his fingers. "Thanks!" he yelps as the train door closes. The woman turns the other way.

\*

Velez is bent to a brass viewfinder as he cranks the handle on a wooden Mutoscope in a Broadway amusement arcade. The illuminated flip cards show a man juggling four balls, riding a unicycle, juggling bowling pins, and blowing fire out his mouth. The cards end, the light inside the machine clicks off. The sign above the next machine shows a cartoonish Black face with red lips and white teeth holding a slice of watermelon. He blurts, "Goddamn!" He drops a penny into the Mutoscope and cranks the handle. The machine's light illumes and the flip cards: a cartoon of a big Black woman in a red kerchief shooing Black kids out of a kitchen, with the caption, "Mammy's Realm;" a cartoon of a bunch of little kids with spiky hair falling all over each other, captioned, "Pickaninny Pile;" a cartoon of an old Black woman with a stick about to come down on the back of a man who is probably her husband, titled "Sassy Mammy;" a cartoon of a skinny, barefoot man sitting against a tree, captioned "Massa's in the Cold, Cold Ground;" a cartoon of a beaming Black man in old clothes way too large for him, "Massa's New Hand-Me-Down."

To the white man nearby wiping the brass on a machine, Velez asks, *"What's this racist shit?"*

"People laugh! You don't like 'em—don't watch!"

Velez scowls, inspects the title card above every machine, notes two more with cartoonish figures of Black people acting foolishly. He meets the man with the rag in the sunshine at the front of the arcade. "Don't people complain? That racist stuff's disgusting!"

"What's disgusting is our government banning Mr. Edison's New Glory machines. They get 'em in Europe. Better than Mutoscopes!"

"What if I gave the owner of this place a thousand dollars to get rid of those three nasty sets of cards and an agreement to never let anything like them in here again?"

The man chuckles. "For a thousand dollars, the owner would sell you his new wife."

Velez pats the man's shoulder and walks away.

\*

Martin gawks at the mass of trolleys and fans thickly surrounding Brooklyn's Washington Park, everything wheeling like a gargantuan, stirred stew. He chuckles at the astonishing visual feast of the old ballpark, and at the prospect of analyzing a 1906 baseball game.

\*

In Pittsburg, the starting lineups:

| | NEW YORK | | | PITTSBURG |
|---|---|---|---|---|
| CF | ROGER BRESNAHAN | | CF | GINGER BEAUMONT |
| RF | CY SEYMOUR | | RF | BOB GANLEY |
| 2B | JOHNNY BLENT | | LF | FRED CLARKE |
| LF | MIKE DONLIN | | SS | HONUS WAGNER |
| SS | BILL DAHLEN | | 3B | TOMMY LEACH |
| 3B | ART DEVLIN | | 1B | JOE NEALON |
| C | FRANK BOWERMAN | | 2B | CLAUDE RITCHEY |
| 1B | DAN McGANN | | C | GEORGE GIBSON |
| P | HOOKS WILTSE | | P | DEACON PHILLIPPE |

Bresnahan strides into the batter's box. Blent stands next to Cy Seymour, ondeck, just as a boy in a white suit, announcing, "Get your lemonade!" brushes past him, scanning the grandstand. Blent's eyes sting, the result of the yellow-orange haze, smoke constantly belched from the hundred steel mill smokestacks lining the rivers. From inhaling the smoke, just like on the trains from San Francisco to St. Louis, Blent can sense the dimensions of his lungs.

At home plate, the catcher, George Gibson says to Bresnahan, "Heard you put money on the game."

"A little birdie tell you?" Bresnahan replies.

The umpire blurts, "I got money on the game too," and the three laugh.

Bresnahan flies to left. Cy Seymour flies to center. Blent chops the ball down the line past third for a single. Phillippe fires a pickoff throw to first, and Blent gets a hand under Nealon's tag. Rising, Blent shares a significant look with Mathewson, who is the first-base coacher.

"He's got a good move," says Mathewson.

"Very observant, Mister Mathewson," Blent retorts.

Mathewson cackles at the joke.

Across the diamond, McGraw is screaming, *"Phillippe, you fucking infant! Suck your thumb! Shake your rattle!"*

Two pitches later, McGraw touches nose, bill of cap, belt, belt: the steal sign. As Phillippe lifts his front leg, Blent explodes toward second. Head down, legs churning, he senses the white light of God is emanating from second base as he races for it, the ball crossing his field of vision as he slides, the ball ticking off the second baseman's glove, Blent popping up and zipping for third, McGraw's fist of a face staring at the ball coming in, *"Down! Down! Down!"* McGraw shifting and pointing both hands to the outside edge of the bag. Blent slides in right at McGraw, as Leach blocks the short-hop throw. Safe!

Donlin strokes a single to left center, knocking in Blent.

NEW YORK   1 — 0   PITTSBURG

Bill Dahlen grounds out to shortstop for the third out.

Bottom of the 1st. With two outs, Fred Clarke slashes a single that whistles past Wiltse into center field.

Honus Wagner up. As Clarke breaks for second, Wagner takes a low curve that Bresnahan catches at his ankles, straightens, firing to second, the ball tailing between the mound and Blent's glove. Safe!

Wagner smacks a hard single to right-center where Seymour fields it and launches it over the infielders, bouncing on one hop to Bresnahan as Clarke slides in behind him, while Wagner races to second. Dahlen squints disgustedly at Seymour, who should have thrown in to second to hold Wagner at first. Blent, not wanting to humiliate Seymour, rubs his cleat over a patch of dirt, thinking of his fifty-dollar bet, thirty of which is a loan from Turkey Mike Donlin.

NEW YORK   1 — 1   PITTSBURG

Bottom of the 4th. Fred Clarke leads off with a double. With two outs, Tommy Leach doubles home Clarke. Blent takes the throw from Seymour. Blent glances at Donlin, who shouts, *"We'll get 'em!"*

NEW YORK   1 — 2   PITTSBURG

Pencil-thin second baseman Ritchey smacks a ball that splits Donlin and Seymour. Leach scores. Ritchey cruises into third with a triple.

NEW YORK   1 — 3   PITTSBURG

Hooks Wiltse settles down and Deacon Phillippe keeps the Giants off-balance.

Top of the 9th. Dan McGann cracks a liner up the middle that Wagner, leaping at it like a monstrous mountain lion, snares in his glove, evoking gasps and curses from the New York bench.

McGraw sends up Spike Shannon for Wiltse, and Shannon works a walk. Bresnahan doubles, sending Shannon to third.

As Cy Seymour approaches the plate, Phillippe wipes his brow, taking heavy steps around the mound. From the on-deck circle, Blent appraises Phillippe, knowing that in the twenty-first century, no way Phillippe would be out there; right now, it would be a fresh pitcher throwing 100 mph.

Seymour takes a 3–2 curveball wide for ball four.

One out, and the bases are loaded for Johnny Blent as he strides to the plate, the Pittsburg fans screaming:

*"Country boy!"*

*"Go home!"*

*"Welcome to the big leagues, fuckface!"*

McGraw at third is clapping, "Okay now Johnny, Johnny, here we go!"

Gibson, the catcher, says, "You're from California, right? You have an orange tree? Man, I'd love to wake up, walk outside in the sunshine, pick me an orange and peel it right there!" Blent concentrates on Phillippe, but intruding on Blent's mind is the fact that he'll owe Donlin thirty dollars and his next paycheck is a hundred. Thirty-five is rent, so that leaves three adults not much to live on for two weeks.

"Time!" Blent yells, hand to eye, pretending there's a bug in there.

"Time!" the ump complies.

Blent is bent over, wiping his eye. He finds that tunnel, thinks of Mark, his brother the hero. Then the tunnel again.

McGraw lays his hand on Blent's back. "You okay?" McGraw leans in to Blent's ear, "Look for an outside fastball and drive it." He winks at Blent in a way that makes Blent relax, and McGraw jogs away.

The fifth pitch is an outside fastball. Blent smacks it. It plops fair inside the right-field foul line, halfway to the wall. Spike Shannon scores. Bresnahan scores. The right fielder, Ganley, picks up the ball as Cy Seymour rounds third hard, McGraw windmilling, *"Go! Go! Go!"*

Blent blazes past second, and cruises into third. The New York bench is hooting and tossing their caps in the air. "Johnny!" "That's the way!"

Hands on hips, Blent stares in at the bench; he wants to smile but doesn't want to seem like a rookie.

### NEW YORK  4 — 3  PITTSBURG  FINAL

*

That evening, Martin is leaning against a lamppost on Columbus Avenue next to the newsstand at the base of the iron stairway leading up to the 81st Street Elevated train station. A wagon pulled by gray horses halts, and stacks of the *Evening Mail* and the *New York Post* thump the sidewalk. As the newsstand owner slices the twine and Martin bends for a *Post*, the horse nearest exhales on Martin's neck. Martin recoils and wipes his neck, places an Indian-head penny on the thick, dirty palm of the newsstand operator.

The sports headline reads: "Giants Best Pitts 4–3."

"It was a gritty game in Pittsburg this afternoon . . . " Martin scans, moves to the box score. Blent's line: 3 for 5, one double, one triple, two runs batted in, zero errors. Pressure in

Martin's shoulders releases as he slaps the paper and says to the newsstand vendor, "My friend! Johnny Blent! The Giants win!"

"Baseball very good!" replies the unshaven, chain-smoking, bulbous-nosed man in a Spanish accent. "Mister Mathewson nice, nice man!"

"Yes!" Martin starts home, the view of the trees of Central Park to his right, distant New Jersey at the horizon to his left. But his elation turns blue. He feels more severed from professional baseball than at any time since he signed a contract two days after his nineteenth birthday. Men in derby hats cross in front of him. A woman in a beige dress stands with a leashed white Scottie dog which is pooping on the sidewalk. A pair of men in long beards and fuzzy hats argue in Yiddish.

*"Hey!"* It's Velez, charging at Martin, the men in fuzzy hats parting as they let Velez through, without pausing their argument.

Velez is carrying the bag of baseball equipment. *"Where you been?"*

"At the Brooklyn game. I got a job."

"Doing what?"

"Selling shoes."

Velez considers asking if they need more salesmen, shudders at the notion. "The sun is disappearing. I gotta hit, okay?"

Martin nods in the direction of home. "Can I take a piss first?"

"No, man! Let's go! I've been waiting for you!"

Martin holds up the newspaper. "Blent won. 3 for 5."

"Good. We're keepin' a roof over our head today."

# 13

## God's Earwax

BLENT SITS AT the little desk in his hotel room, writing a report with Bresnahan's fountain pen. While on the bench, he tried to take notes, to help Bucky Martin analyze the opposition, but found it too distracting from his normal mental engagement with the game. Now he writes, "Phillippe pitches hard, and mixes in junk. Main thing is nibbling the corners. Then sneaks in a fastball. Knocks you down." The blue ink is making blotches, smeared on the side of his hand.

"Don't break my fucking pen!" Bresnahan snaps it from Blent.

A jaunty knock on the door, Donlin striding in, black suit spotless, a white carnation in his lapel. As if they were tiny, sleeping puppies, Donlin gently sets two stacks of bills on the desk. He tells Blent, "There are a ton of guys in the bar who want to buy you a ton of drinks. And McGraw has ordered us to go to some moronic dinner in an hour. At least it's paid for."

The Giants are whisked to a private men's club on 18th Street. A professor from the Carnegie Technical School, who grew up in Manhattan a Giants fan, is hosting a dinner for his hometown team. Waiters in long aprons pass hors d'oeuvres and drinks and a case of New Glory cigars, as the host and his friends from the world of industry and academia mix with the ballplayers. Downing glasses of twenty-year-old scotch, Turkey Mike Donlin removes his cigar, mounts a chair and raises his voice, "Listen to this one, boys!"

Blent sips a glass of seltzer with a dash of scotch, watching Donlin sing out:

*"I've got a manager named McGraw,*
*He's a swell sort, just like my Paw,*
*He'll practice you the hit and run,*
*And then you'll hit and then you'll run! A ton!"*

Donlin bellows, "Everybody!" and thirteen voices:

*"A ton! A ton! A ton! A ton! A ton! A ton! A ton! A ton! A ton! A ton! A ton!"*

McGraw, at the side of the room, thumbs hung on his belt, elbows akimbo, shines his broad smile as ballplayers and businessmen slap his back. Donlin picks up the solo:

*"Till your tired body moans,*
*Your belly aches and groans,*
*But Mac is our leader true,*
*I wouldn't play for anyone else, would you?"*

Blent pushes out into the crisp evening, a horse-drawn carriage cutting in front of him. Odors of mildew and cooking onions and garlic seem to emanate from nowhere. Belching smokestacks loom in a line that stretches as far as he can see. He starts walking in the direction of the hotel. Aching, he's never been away from Darla this long since they both showed up in eighth grade—though they weren't dating, she was *around*, she was *there*. Now she most likely, most reasonably, thinks he's dead, nursing their baby girl.

Straight ahead stands St. Vladimir's, a brick-and-stone church. *Don't think*, and his legs, of their own volition, take him up the steps. Inside is cool and reeks of candles. Old women in headscarves are scattered amongst the pews. There's the water bowl, and he's frozen about whether to stick in his finger, whether the real God, his God, will strike him down or remove heaven runs from his score.

"Are you of the faith?" A rotund, many-chinned priest appears.

"Catholic?" Blent asks. "No, I'm not. Restored Church of Christ."

The priest's eyes narrow.

"I guess you don't have it up here," Blent says. "It's small."

"This is a church of Christ, is it not?"

"Of course. But not the one I'm used to."

The priest introduces himself as "Father George," and waddles to the front pew, where they sit side by side. Blent explains, "The problem, is, Father, that I don't think I'm ever going to see my wife and baby girl again. How do I get back?" His words dissolve in the cavernous cathedral. He recounts the earthquake and playing for the Giants and leaving Martin and Velez in New York.

Father George asks, "Isn't that part of your profession? Traveling from city to city, being alone? Pittsburg is chockablock with people from Poland, Ukraine, Germany, Italy—people who will *never* see those loved ones again."

Blent tries not to stare at the hairs sprouting from Father George's nostrils and turns to the marble steps leading to the pulpit. "Still, if they make a lot of money, they *can* travel back. *I* can't. It's all gone. My whole life. We went through a wormhole, or something. It disappeared. I can't explain it. Father, I'm from the future."

Father George's eyes widen, mouth forms a silent O.

"The twenty-first century. We found ourselves in 1906."

Father George does not change his expression as he slides away along the pew.

"Can I pray about it, at least?"

"Well," Father George replies. "You did say you were in the Church of Christ—"

"*Restored* Church of Christ."

"Perhaps you can find better comfort there." Father George smooths his pockets, checking for his wallet. "Please be our guest for now to pray. God listens."

Blent tells his departing black back, "When it comes to me, God's got wax in his ears!"

There is no answer. Blent stares at the varnished Christ up on the cross hovering above the pulpit, and Blent covers his face, muttering, "Jesus, sweet Jesus." Tears are pressed between fingers and face.

Blent walks down 18th Street, staring at his stiff 1906 shoes striking the brick sidewalk. The coal dust in the air stings his eyes. Snippets of harsh-sounding languages. Most of the shops are closed, but the food joints are stuffed with steel workers. He scans the street, looking for a steeple, doing a 360. If he had a phone, he could search for a church like his. Blent steps in front of a huge man in overalls carrying a lunch pail. "Church? Do you know one?"

"Ch-ch-ch?" The man points inland. "You go . . . up."

A few minutes later, Blent's in the middle of a cobblestone intersection deciphering the names of the three churches. He concludes they're all Catholic and steps up into St. Ignatius. In a pew, he finds a Bible. The words look bizarre, a language with accents under the "c" and cross hatches across the "l". The second church's door is locked. In the third church, the Bibles are in yet another indecipherable language.

He dejectedly walks through a Pittsburg that has some-how lost its "h." A blast of laughter from a packed saloon catches his attention. Blent plops onto an abandoned apple box, stares at the saloon, thinking that the reality those men are feeling, backslapping, telling stories, is more real than any book, holy or not. The books help form one's outlook, but the moment-to-moment presence of a conversation—the main plane of reality is life as lived through the senses, not a construct of the mind, not trying to convince oneself of anything. As if God were speaking to him, a phrase, fully formed, pops into Blent's mind: "Atheism is a big step forward."

He chuckles, telling himself that the phrase is silly, while simultaneously, he tries to ignore the chill down his spine.

*

Velez's dreaming mind sees the pitch curve in toward him. He twists, bat following through, ball rocketing away into the night, high, the crowd rising as he watches it clear the San Francisco stadium wall, the line of water cannons blasts, the roar of the crowd like a hundred jet engines. *Yeah, you're going now.*

Opening his eyes, he groans at his white wall full of gray toe prints—*why on the walls?*—from its previous occupant in his tiny room. In the kitchen, converted out of a closet, Velez's attempt to make coffee results in a bitter brew. He pours a bit into a cup and fills the rest with cold water. The woman he saw in Times Square and followed to the office building—could he ask her out? But he doesn't have any money to take her anywhere.

Across the street, the Mathewson/McGraw front door opens, and Mrs. Mathewson emerges, catching Velez's attention. She's wearing a blue jacket and skirt, blue-gray top hat with a blue ribbon dangling. He rushes out and catches up to her on Columbus Avenue just as the El rumbles overhead. With a shocked expression at his appearance, she waits to respond until the clattering of the train dissipates. "Mister Velay?"

He asks, "May I walk a bit with you?"

"Are you going this way?"

"Where are you headed?"

"To Claremont—the stables."

"You own a horse?"

"I do. I am most pleased with him."

"Would you show it to me? What's its name?"

"His name is Nanny."

"I met this girl. Can I ask some advice?"

\*

In Pittsburg, Blent sits up in bed, a band of sunshine blinding him. Roger Bresnahan emerges from the hallway, telling Blent, "We're betting again today. And I'll take you to Horne's to buy a fresh suit. Yours smells like the back of my balls."

Blent doesn't want to bet again, doesn't want to think about money when he's on the field. But he wants to fit in with his new team. Most of the guys are older than he is. It's an older team than any twenty-first-century team. And they look older, their faces crinkled in season after season without sunblock. And though occasionally he'll spot a pedestrian in sunglasses, he hasn't seen a player wearing them on the field.

"Five bucks today, all right?" Blent decides it's a respectable sum that won't let down his teammates.

"Sure."

Unlike many of the New York players that day, the girth of Blent's wallet does not significantly shrink as Mathewson departs the game in the sixth inning with numbness down his right arm. Pittsburg wins 4–1.

\*

The next day, Velez is up before dawn. His legs are sore in odd places and his thighs and ass hurt. The previous morning, after he walked with Mrs. Mathewson to the stables, she borrowed a horse for him. He hadn't been on a horse since he was a kid, but by following Mrs. Mathewson he got the hang of it. While riding side by side at a conversational walk, Mrs. Mathewson suggested that he write a note to the woman at the Traub Talent Agency. Then she leaned across and took his hand for a long moment. This shocked him, then pleased him. It was timeless. She led him and his horse, Echo, to a part of the park called the Ramble, where she tied up the horses and led him on a path secluded by low, leafy trees. With a view of the lake, she spread a blanket, and they made love as swiftly as the unbinding of Mrs. Mathewson's habit would permit, in a very straightforward but, to Velez, and seemingly to Mrs. Mathewson, pleasing manner. He'd never done it so rushed before, and it was elating. Afterwards, he stood naked amidst the trees at the edge of the Boat Pond and shouted across the water, "Hello, 1906!"

Now Velez sits at the coffee table and riffles through Bucky's portfolio for a pencil and a blank sheet of paper. As he writes, he realizes that the only handwriting he does in the 21st century is to write out his name on baseballs and photos and whatever else fans shove in his face. His signature is a bunch of squiggles, so he slows-the-fuck down. There's an artistry to this. In 1906, he can't just text, "Wassup?" With deep concentration, each draft getting clearer and nicer-looking, he's satisfied with the look of the fifth.

> Dear ma'am,
>     I met you two days ago on the street on Broadway. I followed you to your office. You thought I was a strong man. I am a baseball player. Would you care to have a

*cup of coffee with me one day? If so, please reply to this address.*
*Sincerely,*
*André Velez*
*66 West 85th Street #1A*
*New York*

He wonders if it makes any sense. Across the street, Mrs. Mathewson emerges from her doorway in a red riding habit, descends the stoop, and heads toward Columbus. Velez takes the letter and rushes out, his inner thighs barking from yesterday's activity. After a moment of chitchat during which Velez doesn't sense that she's at all embarrassed, he shows Mrs. Mathewson the letter.

"I haven't ever written anything like this in, like, my whole life, so like, tell . . . um, me if it's bad, okay?"

She reads as she walks, her boots clip-clopping. She stops, and her face broadens into radiance. "André, it's perfect!"

*

The Giants lose to Pittsburg. Over the next two days, they lose twice to Cincinnati. Blent's hitting well, *likes* the dead ball. He's got a small, but significant, increase of control over where it's going when he hits it. And it forces him to plan to which section of the field he's trying to hit, rather than just only trying to hit the ball hard.

*

Meanwhile, Martin has been lacing shoes, studying the different brands and styles, learning the layout of the dimly lit basement stockroom, accessed by a ladder that goes straight down a hatch in the store's floor. All day long the salesmen climb up and down that ladder.

He returns to the apartment to find Velez in a suit, tweaking his looks in the clouded wall mirror. Advice has come from Mrs. Mathewson these past few days, on their rides to their trysts in the Ramble. Riding his horse back to the stables, he never brings up the new woman, Nicole.

Nervously redoing the knot of his tie, he asks, "I look all right?"

Martin replies, "What do you have to worry about? You're an expert on women."

"Not really. I *had* girls, yeah. In the past—future—whatever the fuck it is. I'm nobody here. I haven't even *talked* to this chick. I just wrote a note, and she wrote back, so I wrote another. Now I'm all psyched out and nervous. I feel like a fucking rookie."

"Pretty nice suit."

"A little small, huh?" The cuff rises up his forearm. "Mrs. Mathewson gave it to me. Long story. Don't tell Christy." Fingering the trio of five-dollar bills in his pocket, also courtesy of Mrs. Mathewson, he refrains from mentioning it.

As Velez rides the IND subway, he smells steel and horse manure. He checks his shoes. He rubs his fingertips across his sweaty palms. He realizes he has no plan. He wasn't the plan-maker: Mako, Ernie, or Cheech did the planning, or the girl did the planning, or there wasn't a plan beyond "Meet me upstairs in my room." He hasn't gone out on a first date since ninth grade, and that was with an eleventh-grade girl.

He emerges from the Subway at 23rd and 7th Avenue, starts walking, and only when he gets to 8th Avenue, does he realize he's gone the wrong way. He backtracks. Approaching from the opposite direction is a man in a top hat, smoking a cigar, a woman on the man's arm in a shiny black dress, the man glancing warily up. Velez doffs his bowler hat, a castoff from Art Devlin that Blent snagged as Devlin dropped it in the locker room trash bin. Velez brushes at the scrapes on its side. Up ahead looms the Flatiron. He wonders why, in the twenty-first century, they so rarely make buildings as beautiful as these. One of Velez's places, a new condo in Kauai, one face of the building is sheer blank glass.

He finds the Belgravia Hotel. Inside at the front desk, a sign: "A Hotel for Women." He likes that idea—a hotel full of jiggity. After giving his name to the dude behind the desk, he takes a seat in the lobby amidst three other gentlemen who are hiding behind newspapers, all taking glances at the elevator doors.

The elevator opens, emitting Nicole in maroon and a wide black hat, and he recalls that first glimpse of her outside the theater on Broadway. Velez pops up. She smiles nervously and extends her gloved hand. "It is a plez-ure to meet you." He wonders if it would be polite to ask her where she is from.

"Ah! Parlez-vouz Francais?" asks Velez.

"Oui! Et vous?"

"En peu. It's been a while."

She leads him to the sidewalk where his meager French crumbles. As he asks her about life working for the talent agency, he doesn't know where to put his hands—whether to touch her or not. He stuffs his hands in the stiff material of Mathewson's pants pockets.

Nicole tells him, "You will have to see me perform! I do all sorts of plays and parts. I work in the agency, so in the mornings, I take care of the accounts—the money—and in the afternoons and evenings, I am often onstage. I would like to play a long-running part, but right now I fill in when actresses are ill or otherwise indisposed. It is rather thrilling, throwing myself onstage, often improvising, muddling through with the other actors. I try to make it amusing for myself. A lot of it is vaudeville."

"I'd love to see you perform. I used to watch a lot of"—he's about to say "TV" but substitutes—"performances. I like crime shows. And sci-fi."

To Nicole's query, "Crime shows?" Velez haltingly at first, then more fluently, describes his favorite *Murder by Dawn* episode in which the killer strikes by traveling through the city's sewers.

Nicole brightens. "Thrilling!"

"Yes. That's the idea! You should see *me* perform—on the baseball field. But I don't have a team right now. Ever see a game?"

"No." She asks, "Where are we going?"

"It's a surprise." Their destination was Jane Mathewson's idea.

He recounts the earthquake, skipping the part about time travel, about digging, about Martin and Blent stealing watches and almost getting shot, and says, "We earned enough to buy train tickets out."

"Perhaps this is a forward question. But did not you and your two friends have other friends or relatives in San Francisco who could help you?"

Velez is stunned by the question, the obvious fact that after the earthquake there was no one else in the world for him other than Johnny Blent and Bucky Martin. "All my guys were gone. My car. Everything."

"Please pardon me for asking you to recall a terrible time."

"No, no!" Velez waves aside her concern. "Forward, backward, whatever! It's fine."

Under the wrought-iron sign for Süchow's Restaurant, Velez ascends the stoop. Mrs. Mathewson told him that the

German restaurant is the perfect place for a first date. Noticing that Nicole is not in his presence and has halted on the sidewalk, he scoots down to her.

"They won't have me in there," she explains.

"Why?"

Her hand goes up to the side of her neck. "My skin."

"What about it?"

"André, I'm part Negro. And you?"

"Me?" Again, he's got to concern himself with *what he is*. "I'm one hundred percent American!" He gazes at her in the dim streetlight. He can't discern her color; her face is radiant. She removes her hat, and he protests, "No, don't do that." She thrusts her face up, asking, "Can you see me?"

"I do see you, and you're beautiful." Perhaps her complexion is *café au lait*. "Are you telling me that this restaurant *won't let you in?*"

"That's right."

"They can do that?"

"Of course, this is America."

"This is complete bullsh—" He checks himself, takes her elbow. "Trust me." They ascend the stoop. Inside, to the maître d' manning the podium, Velez declares, "I have a reservation. My name is André Velay."

The maître d' glances at them, glances at Nicole again. "I am sorry, sir, I do not see your reservation, and we are full today."

Over the maître d's shoulder, an archway decorated with gold-painted twigs frames the huge dining room. There are dozens of empty tables. Velez slaps a five-dollar bill on the podium. "I think you can find us a table." Nicole seems frightened.

The maître d' states, "No. I'm sorry. You will have to leave." He pushes the money away.

"Why will we have to leave? And you're not sorry."

"That is our policy. Don't blame me. I don't make the policy."

"You're just a moron, is that right?"

Nicole says, "André, let's go."

Velez has seen guys get kicked out of clubs for being too drunk or starting fights. But he's never been asked to leave anywhere in his life. *"No! Give us a table! Right now!"*

The maître d' spins away. Scattered diners glance haughtily at André and Nicole.

She says, "I know of some very good restaurants in Greenwich Village."

Velez reassures, "We're gonna eat here. Don't worry."

The maître d' returns with three large white waiters, a large white cook, and a tall, thin white man in a crisp suit, a pink carnation in his lapel, the latter of whom says, "You will have to go."

Velez asks, "Who are you?"

"Horst Schmidt. An owner. We are asking you pleasantly one last time to depart." The cook points a wooden spoon at Velez and comments in German, "He looks odd too."

"We just want to eat. We hear the food is good."

The maître d' moves forward and the four others surround Velez and push him toward the stairs. Velez shoves them away.

*"André!"* Nicole half-shrieks, half-cries.

Velez tells them, *"You're assholes!"* He yells out into the huge dining room, *"The food here sucks!"* Nicole exits ahead of him. He feels the rage in his chest and neck as his blood pounds.

Outside on the sidewalk, Nicole asks, "Is that really your fight?"

He watches two couples—all four of them white-skinned, but as they pass and ascend the stoop, the men seem pink. An ice wagon is backed up, the iceman and Süchow's kitchen staff trundling eighteen-inch blocks of ice down a chute into the basement. Velez strides to the chute, picks up a block, tests its weight. At first the kitchen workers and the iceman are amused that this well-dressed man is hoisting an ice block, but then he takes a second block, balancing one in each hand at shoulder level.

"What are you doing?" Nicole asks.

"Sorry. I gotta do this."

The iceman and the kitchen workers stare. Velez carefully walks up the stoop. He places one block at his feet. The other he brings in toward his body, then thrusts out, as if he's an Olympian and this ice block is a gargantuan shot put, which accelerates over the balustrade, obliterating the plate glass window to the right side of the entrance. He lifts the second block and takes it to the other side of the stoop. *"No!"* the iceman yells as the amused kitchen workers laugh. The maître d' and the owner appear in the doorway just as the second block is airborne and smashes the second window, shattering "Süchow's," the gold-painted lettering.

"That's on you," Velez points at, and calmly informs, the owner and maître d'. He offers Nicole his elbow, guides her between the basement chute and the ice truck.

Behind them a whistle is blown.

"Oh, God!" Nicole gasps. "They're calling the police!"

"Do we run or do we stroll?"

"I'm scared to be arrested."

"Why?"

"Don't you have any fear?"

"Cockroaches."

She glances back. The stoop at Süchow's is packed with people pointing at them. "We run!"

\*

Martin stares out at 85th Street, watching a newsboy running toward the El. He would love to go out and buy a meal or a drink, but he is down to sixty-two cents and he plans to see tomorrow's Brooklyn-Cincinnati game. Using the kitchen knife, he sharpens his lone pencil. He thinks of his son back in the twenty-first century—wonders if Buck, Jr. is sober now— He ponders his his ex-wives, his last wife, Melanie. He writes:

> May 24, 1906
> Dear Melanie,
>     Yes, look at that date. 1906. This makes no sense—writing to you—since you are beyond a century in the future. You're not born, your parents aren't born, your grandparents aren't born, your great-grandparents aren't born. I've never written you a letter.
>     I just hope that, in your time, if after the earthquake I am dead, then you're OK with that and are mov

He stops. As he reads, his astonishment at the conflicting concepts multiplies exponentially. How insane it would seem to a stranger reading the letter over his shoulder or picking it out of the trash. She's the one he misses talking with the most, about art and history. What a crappy marriage. Perfectionism is a downfall. She got more and more condescending. He's not perfect, of course. A nasty divorce. He writes:

> You're probably happy I'm dead.

He balls it up, and on a clean sheet:

Dear Buck,

I miss you. Are we surviving? Yes, barely. Johnny Blent is with the Giants. Velez spends his early mornings jogging in Central Park. Then he takes batting practice from me, and he works with weights at a boxing gym on 97th Street. The ballplayers today don't work with weights. Some of them are in terrible shape, but they can throw or hit and so have a job. Fundamentals, wow, what a mess most of them are! You could make it here—if you practiced and got your old swing back.

But, I am nothing more than a shoe salesman. But we are alive, very much. I am getting a big kick out of watching baseball in 1906. <u>We know Christy Mathewson and John McGraw.</u>

Maybe I'll go out now, just for a walk, just to see that people are alive.

I hope that you don't miss me too much.

I love you,

Dad

\*

After tough steak and okay roast chicken at a coffee shop on 14th Street, Velez helps Nicole into an Electrobat carriage, a skeletal steel machine powered by a battery. It would be terrible in nasty weather but is lovely in the sixty-five degree evening. The Electrobat takes them up Broadway to the St. James Theatre, where a bawdy version of *King Lear* is playing. Nicole greets the woman in the ticket booth, "Hello, Karen."

"Miss LeVanche! What a pleasure!"

"Do you think Mr. Rose would mind if I have two passes?"

"I don't see why Mr. Rose has to know at all." She jots a note, slips the paper under the glass. "The bald ticket taker, not the short ones."

Velez and Nicole are ushered to the fifth row. Velez scans gargantuan lunettes and frescoes, cupids painted on the ceiling. He can't recall being in a theater so ornate. Not even in Vegas.

The play is about an old man who divides his kingdom into three to give to his sons. The sons insult each other, draw swords. They fight, there's blood. There's murder. Nicole touches his arm, whispers, "Don't worry. It's not real." Her eyes crinkle up at him.

In the second act, Velez moves his hand to feel atop her skirt for her leg, startling Nicole. With both of her hands, she removes his big paw and returns it to the armrest, pats the hand once, and folds her hands in her lap.

Afterwards, walking down Broadway, the wedge of the Flatiron Building a gray silhouette against the night, Velez turns her down a side street, takes her shoulders in his hands, leans down and smooches her. She kicks his shin on an old, deep bruise.

*"Ow!"* He limps away in a circle.

*"Who raised you?"* she shrieks. *"The wolves?"*

He rubs the shin. "You bitch!"

She storms away.

"Hey!" He limps after her. "Please! Hey! I'm sorry."

She wipes tears with the back of her hand. He catches up.

"You can walk with me, but do not touch me!"

"Damn, I'm sorry. I'm so sorry. I'm really sorry."

"Foul language."

"I'm just a stupid ballplayer, okay?"

Outside her hotel, she holds out her gloved hand.

He gently shakes it. "May I call on you again?"

"Perhaps." She adds, "I had a very nice evening—mostly. You really are brave for talking to them the way you did at Süchow's."

A million people have given him a million compliments, but those million people always *wanted* something from him, so how could he be sure that they were sincere? She seems one hundred percent sincere. "Thank you. I had a great time. I am so sorry about that bit before on the street. It won't happen again. You are really cool."

"'Cool?'" she asks. "Cold?"

"No—I'm sorry—wonderful! *Merveilleuese!*"

She minutely nods and turns into the lobby. He watches her exchange words with another woman. The elevator opens. As Nicole faces forward in the elevator, she glances across the lobby and through the front doors . . . at him. Her face relaxes into a smile as the elevator door shuts.

# 14

## The Flatiron

THE NEXT DAY is Martin's half day at work, set free at one o'clock. Safely beyond Tip-Top Shoes, he scurries along Broadway, buying assorted newspapers at the stand outside the 86th Street subway station, zips down, and he's on his way to see the game in Brooklyn. Martin studies the standings in the *New York Times*.

| National League | W-L | PCT. | GB | | American League | W-L | PCT. | GB |
|---|---|---|---|---|---|---|---|---|
| N.Y. | 19-7 | .731 | — | | Phila. | 16-7 | .696 | — |
| Chi. | 21-9 | .700 | — | | Det. | 13-9 | .591 | 2½ |
| Phila. | 16-12 | .571 | 4 | | St.L. | 14-10 | .583 | 2½ |
| Pitts. | 13-12 | .520 | 5½ | | Clev. | 11-9 | .550 | 3½ |
| St.L. | 12-14 | .462 | 7 | | Wash. | 12-11 | .522 | 4 |
| Bosn. | 11-16 | .407 | 8½ | | N.Y. | 10-12 | .455 | 5½ |
| Cin. | 10-19 | .345 | 10½ | | Chi. | 8-13 | .381 | 7 |
| Brkl'n | 7-20 | .259 | 12½ | | Bosn. | 6-19 | .240 | 11 |

In a grandstand seat, Martin arranges his scorecard. Unwinding his portfolio—he inadvertently included the letters to Melanie and Buck. There is someone familiar in the row ahead of him, tries to put the name to the young man's flabby face: It is John T. Brush, Jr., son of the Giants' owner. Martin met him at that first game at the Polo Grounds. Why is he at the Brooklyn game with the Giants in Philadelphia?

After quickly debating himself, Martin leans forward and taps Brush, Jr.'s shoulder, refreshes Junior's memory, asks if he can take the seat next to him.

"Absolutely!"

As Martin reaches into his portfolio, he notices the side of his hand is stained brown from shoe polish. The odors of leather and polish and sweaty men's feet have burrowed into his olfactory nerves, and he hopes, by the end of the game, they'll be replaced by the aromas of roasted peanuts and cut grass.

He wonders if Brush, Jr.—his bottom eyelids red-rimmed and saggy—drinks at lunch or if this is a hangover from the night before. Maybe both.

Brush, Jr. cracks a shell, pops the nut in his mouth.

Martin arranges his spray charts and pitching grids into an order that matches the day's lineup, then contemplates small red blisters from lacing shoe after shoe.

| CINCINNATI | | BROOKLYN | |
|---|---|---|---|
| 3B | HANS LOBERT | LF | JACK McCARTHY |
| 2B | MILLER HUGGINS | SS | DOC CASEY |
| RF | FRED ODWELL | CF | HARRY LUMLEY |
| 1B | SNAKE DEAL | RF | BILL MALONEY |
| C | ADMIRAL SCHLEI | 1B | TIM JORDAN |
| CF | FRANK JUDE | 3B | PHIL LEWIS |
| LF | JOE KELLEY | 2B | WHITEY ALBERMAN |
| SS | TOMMY CORCORAN | C | BILL BERGEN |
| P | CHICK FRASER | P | HARRY McINTIRE |

Brush, Jr. shifts his bulk. "Johnny Blent is doing well."

"Yes!" Martin looks up from his charts. McIntire is warming up on the mound. Hans Lobert stands a few feet from the plate, ready to hit. "I have another ballplayer with me from California, Chief Velay, who would help the Giants, possibly even more than Blent. Velay would be a big upgrade over Dan McGann at first base."

"McGann's not having his best year, that's true. But it's only a month into the season."

"Five and a half weeks. McGann is hitting .213. His on-base percentage, which adds walks, is .312. That is terrible. Mr. Velay will hit .320. His on-base percentage will be over .400. He will drive in a lot of runs."

"Is that a fact?" asks Brush, Jr., amused. "Then why isn't he in the major leagues?"

"I've been pitching batting practice to Velay every day. I wish Mr. McGraw would give him a—" Lobert drops a bunt down third that Phil Lewis charges, barehands, takes an extra step to steady himself, and fires to first. *Safe!* The Brooklyn crowd boos. The reserves on the Brooklyn bench scream at the base ump.

Regarding the papers stacked on the portfolio on Martin's lap, Junior inquires, "What kind of notes, may I ask, are you taking?"

To Martin, Junior's expression is one of sincere curiosity. But Martin is keenly wary of sharing this information. If it were to be disseminated, the competitive edge that the information reveals would be filed down; the more people who know, the smaller the advantage. But there is another angle to explaining some of the information to Brush, Jr. Martin shows the spray charts and says, "These will help plan a defense. Also, I keep track of walks, hit batsmen, runners caught stealing—statistics that are very valuable, in my opinion, but are not compiled by the newspapers, or anyone else." Martin nods his chin at the three dozen sports reporters and telegraphers in the pit fronting the grandstand. "And I am charting pitches. This helps Mr. Blent—a lot—and would help any hitter. It would make them aware of a pitcher's tendencies."

The flab in Junior's face is motionless as his eyes dart between Martin and the charts. "Truly?"

Gauging Brush, Jr.'s interest, Martin keeps up a commentary on his methods as the game progresses. He won't mention OPS—he doesn't want anyone else to know about OPS, on-base percentage, plus slugging percentage. It's too easy to calculate, and it's such a powerful metric.

Junior's attention locks onto a vendor lugging a tray of sudsy beers in glass steins. He asks Martin, "May I buy you a beer?"

Thirty-three minutes after the final out, Junior leads Bucky Martin into an elevator in the Flatiron Building. On the twelfth floor, a glass door is painted with gold letters:

### NEW YORK NATIONAL
### BASEBALL CLUB
### JOHN T. BRUSH, SR., PRES.
### JOHN J. McGRAW, MGR.
### J. T. ABERNATHY, SEC'Y.

Martin is not prepared to meet the president of the Giants. The lion's share of his papers are at the apartment. While Junior goes in to talk with his father, Martin takes a seat in the antechamber, across from a pasty secretary, sparse hair combed over a bony face, who is typing at a clattering typewriter as Martin riffles through his portfolio trying to conjure a presentation. The wall is festooned with framed newspapers with fat headlines:

"New York Champs!" "WE WIN!" "McGrawmen Victorious!" "MATTY THE HERO!" There are also black-and-white photographs of past teams. Junior's smiling, slightly drunk, shiny face emerges from the doorway: "He'll see you."

Brush, Sr, a small man with a triangular face, pushes up from his glass-topped desk. Taking a cane in each hand, his partly crippled body inches toward Martin, the right hand transfers its cane to the left and he offers his hand. "You were Mr. Blent's manager, and *he* is doing well!" Leaning around Martin, Brush projects his voice, "Abernathy!" Back to Martin, "I apologize. My time is limited today. My son has told me about your papers, and being a financial fellow, I do appreciate the dime-and-nickel-and-penny accounts. Are your methods so precise that they attain such a level of predictability?"

"Not really, sir," Martin replies, noticing a blackboard on the far wall, a neat hand having written up-to-the-hour National League standings, showing New York and Chicago tied in first place. "It is a way of examining the history of what a player has been doing. For instance, I chart where a player hits the ball." Martin pulls out two balls-in-play charts, one for Honus Wagner of the Pirates, the other for Frank Chance of the Cubs.

"As you can see here on the Wagner chart—and this is only based on six games—his hits are sprayed to all fields. But there are fewer to right."

"That is no great discovery, Mr. Alexander Graham Bell!" Brush comments sarcastically. "It is akin to telling me that the sky is blue." Abernathy, having appeared in the office, titters through his nose at his boss' quip. Brush waves over Abernathy to join them in considering Honus Wagner's chart.

"Yes. I agree," says Martin. "Frank Chance, here, has a cluster of hits and outs to right-center, and a cluster of hits down the left-field line. So the idea is, if the right fielder plays close to that cluster—where he will be able to catch the balls on the fly—it will either force Chance into an approach that is less comfortable for him, or the right fielder will take hits away from Chance. And if the left fielder plays closer to the line, and perhaps shades the center fielder over so there isn't a big gap between left and center, then that will force Chance out of his comfort zone too. The aim is to try and make a .320 hitter into a .275 hitter, with hopefully less power."

Brush, Sr.'s eyes widen as he scratches an ear. "I am sure that Mr. McGraw, were he here, would say that he is aware of that information."

"Certainly. But you play so many games in baseball that, over time, these little edges give you more outs in the field. I know it from experience. It helps to have this information on paper—precise, scientific, objective—rather than just being aware from experience. It's a bit like being an illiterate, yet intelligent, tribe. Now"—Martin smacks the papers—"here is our dictionary." He sees that Brush, Sr. is intently following, and Martin adds, "Are we better with the invention and skillful *use* of the dictionary, or not? I say certainly we are." Martin tacks. "Here's a statistic that's very useful in evaluating players. It's called BABIP—batting average for balls in play. You strip out walks and strikeouts and home runs. Just balls that are hit in the field. It's very useful to see if a certain hot stretch or cold stretch is a fluke, or not. BABIP normalizes batting over time. No one else has this information."

"Tell them about slugging percentage," says Brush, Jr., scrutinizing the contents of a set of decanters by the window.

Martin asks if he can turn the chalkboard around. Abernathy flips it to its clean side.

"I'll use Turkey Mike Donlin's statistics from last year. His average was .356, so we know he is a fine hitter. Beyond that he hit 162 singles, 31 doubles, 16 triples, and 7 home runs. So, here is the power of slugging percentage, gentlemen. I multiply a double by two, a triple by three, a home run by four, and I add up the sum of those numbers and add them to the singles. This statistic is total bases. For slugging percentage, I calculate it the same way you do batting average. Batting average is the number of hits divided by the number of at-bats. Slugging percentage is the total bases divided by the number of at-bats. So Donlin's average last year was .356. He had 300 total bases. His slugging percentage was .495, which was third best in the league." Brush, Sr., and Abernathy seem to be transfixed. "Now, let's compare him to Tommy Leach, third baseman of the Pirates. He hit .312 last year. Who do you think is better, Donlin or Leach?"

Brush, Sr states, "Donlin, obviously."

Martin explains as he writes, "Here's Leach's year. 92 singles, 33 doubles, 8 triples, 2 home runs. It's a .533 slugging percentage—versus Donlin's .495." Senior studies the numbers. "It's fairly close, but I would also say that Leach's position, third base, is more of a skill position. If you rank the hitting ability of third basemen, Leach is the best in the National League. Donlin is the eighth-best outfielder. Few people would agree with me, but I would argue that Tommy Leach is a more valuable player than Mike Donlin. So by ranking every player in the Major Leagues this way, we can get the best of other teams in trades, we can analyze the strengths and weaknesses in teams. It's a wonderful tool." Wanting to end before he gets kicked out, Martin concludes, "Well, gentlemen, here I stop. Right now, I am a shoe salesman. Before that I was employed in baseball my entire life. I wish to get back in that employ. Since my former second baseman is your second baseman, I wish to be employed with your franchise. I have a plethora of statistics. The proposition is to engage in some concerted, systematic gathering of information, then it would be synthesized by me, and, perhaps, others—" Martin nods at Brush, Jr., who salutes with a glass of rye. "Then the findings would be presented to you. I *know* it will give you an edge. It will give you an edge in games. It will give you an edge in trades. You will have knowledge that no one else will have." Martin considers somehow telling them that the Giants are up against one of the best teams in the history of baseball, the 1906 Chicago Cubs, and he also considers erasing the blackboard—the figures are on display for the taking: the slugging percentage calculation. But he surmises that Brush, Sr. could probably reconstitute the calculation from what has already been explained. Martin taps his papers together.

Senior asks his son, "This appeal to you, John, compiling baseball charts?"

"It might make all the difference. And it won't cost much."

Senior asks Martin, "Please tell us a bit about your background. Where you were raised. What your parents did. Are they alive? Where they are from."

Martin makes up some anodyne history, and regarding what he figures Brush, Sr. is really after, concludes, "So I'm part Russian and part English."

"Good enough," Senior nods. "And these statistics, is this catching on in California?"

"No." Martin is aware that he is about to take the credit for the work of an army of baseball statisticians and historians. On the other hand, hopefully, this is his ticket out of the shoe store, and maybe those statisticians and historians—knowing the predicament of being wrenched through time and out of baseball—would forgive him. "The system is all my own. It can be scaled up or down. You can have one employee—me—going to as many games as I can. Or you can build a team of people scouting every league game, scouting the American League and the Eastern League and the International League and the Western League—looking for talent. How many people you want to hire, and what it's worth—that's a business decision.

Also, the more people who know about these equations and their value, the more likely the knowledge is to spread, and your edge will erode."

"Sounds like crafty intelligence work!" Brush, Sr. sniggers. Abernathy seconds, "Good one!"

\*

Seated on a tiny stool, a meaty, damp-socked foot emanating a wretched bouquet of odors mere handsbreadths from his face, Bucky Martin feeds a yard-long shoelace through a MacKenzie Topper, which has nineteen eyelets on each side. There are six other left-foot MacKenzie Toppers, all freshly laced by Martin, each replaced in its box, each box stacked up, none of the left-foot MacKenzie Toppers being a sufficient fit for this customer: a flatulent man eating from a bag of grease-dripping sausages, his long silver watch chain accentuating the rotundity of his abdomen.

The doorbell jingles, and in walks Brush, Jr., a smile slicing up in the face as he spots Martin, who hesitates for one second, then abandons the nest of shoeboxes. "Hey!" his customer objects.

Brush, Jr. extends his hand, pulls Martin close. "Twenty dollars per week agreeable?"

As Bucky Martin and Brush, Jr. ride the subway to the day's Brooklyn-Cincinnati game, Junior fleshes out the arrangement: Martin will travel with the team, or to other cities to scout teams; his travel expenses will be paid; he will have a two-dollar *per diem* for meals on the road; Brush, Jr. will assist.

\*

The next morning, Sunday, Blent clangs down the iron stair-way of the El. Clutching his leather satchel, he strides up Columbus, turns right onto 85th, jumps up the stoop, and presses the buzzer to the apartment. There is no answer. He peers in through the living room window at a pair of pants on the sofa and an abandoned coffee cup.

Over the clip-clop of a horse-drawn ice wagon and the rumble of the El pulling away, Blent hears familiar footsteps. It is Mrs. Mathewson in a cream-colored dress and matching gloves, clutching her Bible. Henry, the Mathewsons' chauffeur, stands astride their large automobile.

"Hello!" Blent waves at Mrs. Mathewson and bounds down to meet her. "Matty and Mr. McGraw will be back later. They stopped off outside of Newark to scout a college pitcher."

"Christy telephoned."

"May I join you at church?"

In the back of Mathewson's automobile, Blent and Mrs. Mathewson chitchat about the Giants as they speed past the Dakota Apartments. To Blent, the awareness of his attraction makes him feel like he's a cheater. It frightens him, despite the fact that Darla is in another millennium.

"How is your ankle healing?" she asks.

The automobile jerks forward. Henry apologizes, "Sorry, ma'am!"

"It's fine!" Blent inches away.

Down 5th Avenue the car agglomerates onto the stopped traffic outside St. Patrick's Cathedral, where many of New York's muckety-mucks, and their families are ascending the stairs. Blent is mentally listing the many transgressions of Papism as he is awed by the structure pointing to heaven in multiple spires.

As they find spaces in the balcony at the end of a pew, Blent whispers, gesturing at the stained-glass saints, the opulence of the well-dressed crowd, "I don't believe in all this, you know. It's too . . . *rich*."

"Just enjoy the hats with the birds on them," Mrs. Mathewson suggests. "I like to see who's here."

She's so close that Blent feels the warmth from the side of her face.

She adds, "It's almost like bird-watching. Or hunting ducks."

"You hunt?" Blent's body twists in surprise.

Cardinal Jonathan Donohue's bass voice booms, in Latin. Mrs. Mathewson shows Blent the passage in her Bible. "So the Lord shall make bright clouds, and give them showers of rain, to every piece of grass in the field."

Blent gazes at the stained glass, the bigness of the nave, almost like an indoor stadium, or a basketball arena. Mrs. Mathewson points down at the second row. "The French ambassador. The Italian ambassador. And do you see the man on the aisle? That's Vice President Roosevelt. Yes, I do hunt. Pheasant mostly. I enjoy it."

Blent leans on the wood railing, watching Vice President Theodore Roosevelt adjust his pince-nez, cross his legs, run his fingers to the side of his mustache. Something warm and soft on the back of Blent's neck makes him flinch: Mrs. Mathewson's hand.

"Is that okay?" she whispers.

"Ummmmm," Blent replies, looking around, freaked out. Mrs. Mathewson's hand feels very nice. "No." He nods, contradicting himself, then whispering, "I'm married, still."

He's shaking, moving away, the sexual excitement coursing through him.

"Do you ride?" she asks.

"*Shhhhhhhh!*" from the next pew.

He stands up, nods at Mrs. Mathewson's questioning gaze. "We've got practice, I think. Bye."

He trudges up 5th Avenue, irritated.

*

That afternoon, Velez picks up Nicole at her hotel, and she leads him to another New York theater. Under the marquee, she opens her handbag and unfolds a newspaper. "Vandal Attacks Süchow's" is the headline of an article, which calls him "a negroid" and them "the negroid couple."

"You've impressed some people," Nicole tells him.

The play is a melodrama of love and deceit. Velez watches with a big grin. But it's too obvious that the guy with the heavy black eyeliner is the killer. A bit more mystery would be enjoyable. The lead actress is Mabel Hite—cute, white, auburn ringlets. Her fiancé, Giants left fielder Turkey Mike Donlin, sits in a box on the side, feet up, smoking a cigar next to backup catcher Frank Bowerman.

After the play, standing outside, beyond the protection of the marquee, a drizzle makes the black cars and the streets of Times Square glisten. Velez watches Donlin and Bowerman climb into a car and roll away. A short bowling ball of a man grabs Nicole's sleeve, and Velez slaps the guy's hand down.

Nicole exclaims, "Tony!" To Velez, she explains, "He's an admirer of what you did at Süchow's!"

"*You're* the man! Nice to meet you! Would you want to be interviewed?"

Velez squints, clarifies, "I just got mad. That whole situation of not letting people into a place because of their color is disgusting. No interviews, no."

Tony tells him, "Süchow's is very influential. We've been asking everyone all year to not eat at those restaurants. It is a strike. We have a list of two hundred and six."

"Strike?" Velez cackles derisively.

"Süchow's was crowded when we tried to get in."

"Whites are not supporting us enough. Make sure no one goes to Süchow's, Carmelo's on Prince Street, Max's on University Place." Tony hands Velez a printed sheet listing the 206 restaurants and bars.

"Have any of these places changed their policy because of your strike?"

Tony rubs his jaw. "Not yet. But we did get the city council to put it on the ballot; that was a massive victory. Abolishing racial restrictions in any public establishment."

"Rich people voting to give up their high-and-mighty, my" —with an apologetic glance at Nicole—"poop-don't-stink status? Not gonna work. Believe me. I know. I used to be rich."

Tony asks Nicole, "Where'd you find this genius?" To Velez, "What would you suggest?"

"I don't know, man. Breaking random windows probably isn't the answer either. But I wish you luck."

"What are you?" Tony asks. "You don't seem white *or* Black. You probably look different in different light."

"*Tony!*" Nicole admonishes.

"Apologies that I'm not so polite."

Velez cracks a smile at Tony's phrasing. "I don't know, man. Why worry about what exact color you are unless jerks are trying to keep you out of places or keep you drinking at 'Colored' water fountains?"

"I'd like to know where are you from, Mr. Velay?" Nicole asks. "You know, your heritage?"

"Mom's from Sweden. Dad's family originally from Curaçao."

"Curaçao!" Tony exclaims.

Nicole adds, "New Glory invaded in '99. Enslaved the population to work on plantations. When's the last you heard from them?"

"My family?" Velez's eyes flutter while he wonders if he has relatives, right now, in Curaçao. Were they taken to New Glory? He doesn't remember shit about them, just his father saying, "We're from Curaçao, partly. But it doesn't matter."

After dinner at a Times Square restaurant that isn't on the strike list of 206, Velez and Nicole stroll down Broadway. He is thoroughly impressed that, starting with nothing, she's carved out a nice life in New York. "I think you can do better onstage than that play—though I liked it!"

"What do you mean?"

"It wasn't scary enough, wasn't thrilling enough. You knew who did the murder from the second minute. I think we could come up with something really exciting." As they stroll, he recounts some fun crime show plots, scared that if he touches Nicole, she'll kick him in the shin again. He refrains from making a move all the way back to her hotel and the date ends with the same amount of touching as at the end of the first one: a lingering handshake, perhaps lingering two seconds longer this time.

\*

Two weeks later, Martin is riding the train from Philadelphia to New York. He's gazing at the spray chart of Philadelphia catcher Red Dooin. There are three dots representing hits down the left-field line, and four down the right. From his recently purchased, secondhand valise he removes a fresh sheet of paper, sets it atop his portfolio, and writes:

Dear Buck,

I landed a job, I have hooked on with the Giants as a scout, sort of a superscout. Doing statistics. It is quite a thing to get a job with no one helping you—no connection. Just impressing them with my knowledge of the game. I hope that you would be proud.

I hope that you don't miss me too much. I guess that you do. I am fine. Oddly, very oddly, I am pretty happy though missing you is part-way killing me.

Well, I just got to see the Cubs—Frank Chance, Joe Tinker, Three Finger Brown, Frank Schulte, Harry Steinfeldt play ball against the Phillies. I sat in the front row for the three games, charting every play, and as many pitches as I could. I saw a Red Sox-Philadelphia A's game. I saw Cy Young pitch! He's got a paunch, and he's about 40, but the ball zips in. He pitched against Rube Waddell, who throws flames and is extremely odd. The things the Red Sox players were yelling at Rube Waddell! We would've laughed together.

While paying my 50 cents yesterday I noticed a handbill for the Philadelphia Giants vs. the Cuban X-Giants. I asked the man selling programs if he knew anything about it and he said, "Nigger ball." They toss around that word all the time. Then the man said, "I've seen 'em play. They're better than the Phillies. And if that Rube Foster is pitching, you should see him. Fast and smart."

So this afternoon I watched Rube Foster pitch for the X-Giants. Three hitter—one decent slice over second base, the other cheap infield hits. No runs. He's a big, barrel-chested guy. Throws about three-quarters. Right handed. Intense. A real ballplayer. He might be number two or three on the New York Giants. Maybe number one considering Mathewson's arm issues.

And the other team had a catcher—Bruce Petway. He's the only guy I've seen here who actually <u>SQUATS VERY CLOSE</u> behind home plate the way modern catchers do. All the other catchers squat back a foot or two or three behind home plate. They're scared of getting whacked with a bat and you can't blame them because the catchers don't wear helmets. No one does. Bruce Petway. He nailed the first two runners at second. Perfect throws right on a line no higher than the pitcher's head. He picked a runner off first. Shut down the running game. He hit a double but he's got a long swing and that might get him into trouble. After the game I introduced myself to him—told him I'm a big baseball fan, told him I work for the New York Giants--I asked him where he learned to squat behind the plate so close to the batter and does anyone else do it? He told me he figured it out himself. I suggested he get shin guards. He laughed at that, said the other players would laugh him out of the league for being soft.

*Then Rube Foster came over. Petway introduced me and said about Rube Foster, "This man's the reason we all get paid."*

*Foster runs their whole league. He looked at me, and just his eyes and expression--he seemed to be extremely smart--I don't know. He seems to be as smart as Christy Mathewson. "Could I win in the National League?" asked Foster and before I could answer, he asked, "How about this fellow?" --meaning Petway. For a few moments I could not respond, because of course they would do well in the National League. Foster said, "Thank you for coming to the game."*

*Unfortunately, oddly, the Giants have had a bad streak since they hired me. Won five and lost eight. At the Giants' offices I sat with McGraw before they went on their latest road trip, showing him charts of St. Louis, Chicago, Pittsburgh, and Cincinnati. McGraw grunted and looked at me with one cocked eye, and took up all my pages intending to take them with him. I told McGraw I'd make copies for him and bring them to his house. I am quite sure that he took the copies on the trip.*

Martin puts the pencil sideways in his mouth, like a horse bit. He stares out at the thick-leaved trees sliding by, at distant smokestacks exhaling lines of smoke. He gazes at a horse-drawn lumber cart; a man a hundred feet in the air sitting atop a vertical steel girder, swinging his hammer at a bolt; a drainage pipe spewing red fluid into a creek; a floating dead horse. He pulls out his OPS chart.

National League

| | Team | Pos | OPS |
|---|---|---|---|
| Honus Wagner | Pit | SS | .875 |
| Harry Lumley | Bro | RF | .844 |
| Frank Chance | Chi | 1B | .843 |
| Harry Steinfeldt | Chi | 3B | .840 |
| Mike Donlin | NYG | LF | .839 |
| Johnny Blent | NYG | 2B | .811 |
| R. Bresnahan | NYG | C/CF | .811 |
| Sherry Magee | Phi | LF | .766 |
| Frank Schulte | Chi | RF | .745 |
| John Titus | Phi | RF | .724 |
| Miller Huggins | Cin | 2B | .711 |
| Jimmy Sheckard | Chi | LF | .699 |
| Fred Tenney | Bos | 1B | .688 |
| Tommy Leach | Pit | 3B | .686 |

# 15

## Asbury Park

*"SHULZYCKI! WHAT THE HELL is wrong with you? You're the worst fucking umpire in the league!"* McGraw screams and rushes the home-plate ump. Polo Grounds fans are booing; Shulzycki deemed Bowerman's tag missed Cincinnati's Miller Huggins hook sliding into home plate, scoring on a sacrifice fly.

Shulzycki turns his back to McGraw, picks up the bat, and hands it to the batboy.

### CINCINNATI 5 — 3 NEW YORK

*"I'm talking to you!"* McGraw screams, eyes bulging, face and neck reddening, neck veins popping. *"Why don't you go back to fucking Asbury Park and get a job handing out towels on the fucking beach!"*

Shulzycki spins to McGraw. "Shut the hell up!" he says, which cranks McGraw to a higher degree.

*"Don't tell me to shut up you blind-as-a-bat bastard! I'm trying to win a ball game here! You're fucking incapable!"*

Miller Huggins brushes himself off, jogs past McGraw and spreads his arms, tauntingly showing the safe sign to McGraw.

McGraw barks at Huggins, *"Fuck off!"*

The vast majority of the crowd delights in every McGraw curse that carries to the stands. Many women are covering their ears, smiling with embarrassment. Polite fans sit with folded hands, suppressing laughs at the outbursts.

McGraw repeatedly kicks dirt at Shulzycki. *"You should be a sausage vendor but that would be an insult to all the other sausage vendors!"*

Much of the crowd roars in appreciation.

Face purpling, eyes bulging farther, McGraw reaches in his back pocket, pulls out dollar bills and throws them in the air as he goes nose to nose with Shulzycki, *"Take the El! Go to Penn Station! Take the Long Branch line! Transfer to Asbury Park!"*

"Stop right now, John, or I'm running you!"

McGraw's purple, fist-of-a-face shouts, *"I should be fuck—"* then the face stops moving. McGraw chokes, chokes again, gags *"—ing."* Eyes pushing out, mouth agape, stuck-out tongue desperately wagging side to side, face the colors of a spectacular sunset, the crowd roaring and cheering, McGraw focuses pleading eyes on Shulzycki, who inquires, *"John?!"*

Then John McGraw collapses to the Polo Grounds dirt.

\*

Late that afternoon, Velez, Blent, and Martin are staring out the living room window at the pack of reporters gathered in front of the McGraw/Mathewson residence. Velez's brow is corrugated, mouth open in terror: Martin has told them that he's certain, that in their history, John McGraw *did not* die in 1906. McGraw won the 1921 and '22 World Series. He managed the National League in the first All-Star Game, in 1933, and also that McGraw compiled one of the top number of managerial wins in baseball history. But here, in their world, McGraw has died at the age of thirty-three, a sole World Series win under his belt.

The *New York World* headline: "McGraw Out Forever."

Martin mutters, "I feel responsible."

"It wasn't *our* fault we were yanked through time!" Velez whines.

Blent gazes at the reporters across the street and a phrase pops, *Too bad it wasn't Matty.* The fact that he would think that disgusts him.

"If you go outside, they'll ask you for a quote," Martin tells Blent.

"Here's my quote: 'He was a great Goddamned manager.'"

Velez and Martin chuckle at straightlaced Blent's curse. The Mathewson/McGraw front door opens. Mathewson and Jane step out. Mathewson, somber, starts talking.

"I'd like to hear this," Martin says.

"Then go on out," Velez urges.

Martin shakes his head no and sits in his chair, having just completed an intricate mental calculation that includes Brush, Jr., Brush, Sr., and National League President Harry Pulliam, the calculation concluding with Martin as the New York manager. "Not if I want to be manager."

Velez lifts the window, as, across the street, Mathewson begins, "Everyone on the team is extremely saddened. We have lost the best manager any of us has ever had, the best manager ever. Mrs. McGraw, however, has lost her husband, the manager of their life together, their marriage. Though ours is a tragic loss, her loss is much larger." After a respectful silence that lasts two seconds, a reporter barks, "Any chance of a statement from Mrs. McGraw?"

"No," Mathewson says. "Not at this time."

"How do you feel about it, Matty?"

"In shock. Stunned. Leaderless. He taught me everything I know about pitching at a higher level."

"How about you, Mrs. Mathewson? You have anything to say?"

"No," she replies. "Well, perhaps. Mr. McGraw was a gentleman in the truest sense of the word."

Her gaze rises, and it seems she is looking at Blent and Velez.

\*

JOHN J. MCGRAW has died in fourth place.

National League

|  | W L | PCT | GB |
|---|---|---|---|
| Chi. | 24-12 | .667 | — |
| Phila. | 26-15 | .634 | 2½ |
| Pitts. | 21-14 | .600 | 3 |
| N.Y. | 16-14 | .533 | 5 |
| St.L. | 20-20 | .500 | 6 |
| Cin. | 14-23 | .378 | 11½ |
| Bkl'n | 12-24 | .333 | 12 |
| Bosn. | 11-23 | .324 | 12 |

\*

Up Broadway, a single black horse pulls a caisson with the rosewood coffin of John J. McGraw, followed by a marching band playing a dirge, then a flock of walking dignitaries: former Mayor—now Vice President—Theodore Roosevelt and Governor Mitchell in the company of lesser politicians, then Giants' employees Abernathy and Martin, players Mathewson and McGinnity on foot, then the same horse-drawn carriages used in the opening-day parade nine weeks before.

The front carriage is occupied by Brush, Sr., and Mrs. McGraw, who is aided by Mrs. Mathewson, and two of Mrs. McGraw's Baltimore relations. Their ride is fragranced by a blanket of 600 black-stained roses, which spans and droops over both sides of the carriage. Brush, Sr. emits series after series of sneezes.

There is no roar or applause from the watching crowds, just tears, and individual shouts:

*"We love you, Mac!"*

*"Thank you, Mr. McGraw!"*

*"What do we do without you, Johnnie?"*

Six carriages back, Blent rides with Devlin, Donlin, Dahlen, Wiltse, and Bresnahan. They wear black stripes of wool serge, or felt, on their right sleeves. Blent's was sewn on by the landlady, Mrs. Critz.

Devlin says, "I wish that band would play a snappy jig."

Donlin reaches into his sock garter, "Here you go, fellas," and pulls out a pint of whiskey. The bottle is passed and drained in less than two minutes, the empty tossed by Wiltse over the side, shattering on the pavement at a pause between dirges.

Inside the confines of the Polo Grounds, the caisson halts atop home plate. The walls along the playing field have been draped with black bunting. An eight-foot megaphone is set on a stand.

Brush, Sr. wheezes a short speech, followed by Mathewson who annunciates a speech fit for a valedictorian. Vice President

Roosevelt eschews the megaphone, his high, flinty voice dying and unheard across the outfield in the packed bleachers.

When it is over, Martin takes his seat in the grandstand. Brush, Jr. plops down next to him. Accompanied by a strong puff of scotch breath, Junior tells him, "It's Abernathy."

"Abernathy!?"

"Yup."

"J. T. Abernathy!?"

"Yup."

"For *manager*?"

"Yup."

"The J. T. Abernathy who works in the office?"

"Yup."

"Has he ever managed before?"

"Nope."

"Has he ever *played* before?"

"Perhaps in grammar school."

Martin stares out across the field, the scattered players, the bleachers, the El gliding to a stop, the Bronx in the distance, the spot where, he estimates, Yankee Stadium stood, and will hopefully, rise again—and the memory of losing Game 5 on the replay-reversed call twists his guts hard.

He asks Junior, "Why Abernathy?"

"My father trusts him. My father thinks that with your statistics, the importance of the manager diminishes. My father can pay him . . . well . . . Abernathy's already on the payroll."

"Doesn't your father want to win?"

Brush, Jr.'s face turns to the clouds, his scruffy eyebrows conjoining. "His main concern is not losing customers."

Abernathy remains on the field in the company of Brush, Sr., who canes his way to the New York bench, where Senior introduces their new manager to each of the players. Brush, Sr.

takes Abernathy to meet the umpires, O'Day and Shulzycki, the latter of whom is trembling and wiping his eyes.

The Giants lose the continuation of the McGraw-collapsing-and-dying game, 7–5. Then they lose the regularly scheduled game. In Boston, the Cubs win. The Giants fall 6½ games behind.

After a day trip to Baltimore to attend John McGraw's funeral, the team travels to Boston to face the lowly Beaneaters. In the fifth inning, after a Boston single, double, triple, and double, rendering the score 3–2 in favor of Boston against "Iron Man" Joe McGinnity, Abernathy approaches the pitching mound where all the infielders gather with Bresnahan. Abernathy waves in Red Ames, a lefty who's been warming up on the sideline. The players stiffen.

McGinnity erupts at Abernathy, "Are you serious?"

Abernathy recoils. "Yes, of course I am serious. I wish to give the team a fighting chance."

Bresnahan says, "You can't do this to Joe."

Blent sucks in his cheek. In the twenty-first century, it'd be the right move. But here, when a pitcher feels unmanned to be removed early, it's reckless for a new manager trying to earn respect. Abernathy seems to be unaware.

McGinnity flicks the ball in the air and stomps toward the right-field clubhouse. The ball lands at Abernathy's feet. The Giants lose 7–3.

Abernathy's style is to sit on the bench when the Giants are at bat, a sheaf of Martin's charts on his knee, a player coaching at third, usually Hooks Wiltse or Mathewson. At least a dozen times, the third-base coacher has looked over to Abernathy, seated in the dugout, and a player on the bench will nudge Abernathy, "Are you gonna call for a play here?"

"Oh, now?"

"Yes."

"What would you suggest?"

Mathewson and Wiltse soon begin calling their own plays.

When the Giants are in the field, Abernathy spends much of his time along the foul lines in the outfield, making minute adjustments to the outfielders according to Martin's spray charts.

With the Giants 1–9 under his stewardship, before a game at Brooklyn, Abernathy decides, in consultation with nobody, to start Christy Mathewson at first base and bat him sixth in the order. Dahlen and Spike Shannon grumble about being dropped in the batting order *for a pitcher*! And everyone in the world of baseball wonders how a pitcher with a .212 lifetime batting average is going to transform into a heavy-hitting first baseman. Over the course of his next twenty-five at-bats, Mathewson knocks a single and a double. He pitches five good innings before his arm goes dead and Red Ames finishes during the only Giants win over that span, against Cincinnati. Abernathy's record is 2–16.

The next day is June 21, 1906. Having charted the St. Louis–Brooklyn game, Bucky Martin rides the subway to the Flatiron. As he emerges into daylight, he asks the corner news vendor, "Giants?" and the reply is croaked out accompanied by a cirrus cloud of cigarette smoke and the flash of the man's two remaining teeth, each the color of a different species of bark. "4–2 Philly, top of the ninth."

His key unlocks the door to the empty office. The ticker tape machine is silent and Martin reaches into the basket below, where the tape drops and curls upon itself. He pulls the tape through his hands, reading scores from around the league. As the ticker clacks to life it spits out: NY2 PHI5 F WSPKS LMTHSN.

"Is that you, Mr. Martin?" Brush, Sr.'s reedy voice.

Martin tears off the piece of bad news and brings it in to Senior's office, where Martin is surprised to see not only Senior, but Junior too. The chalkboard has been updated in Junior's hand with all the scores, except Giants-Philadelphia.

Senior indicates the strip of ticker tape. "The score?"

"Yes, sir. It's not too happy."

"Post it, please."

Martin erases Brooklyn and New York, and exchanges their positions:

NATIONAL LEAGUE

|  | W-L | PCT | GB |
|---|---|---|---|
| Chi. | 36-17 | .679 | — |
| Pitts. | 33-19 | .635 | 2½ |
| Phila. | 33-26 | .559 | 7 |
| Cin. | 24-32 | .429 | 13½ |
| St.L. | 23-31 | .426 | 13½ |
| Bkl'n | 18-29 | .383 | 15 |
| N.Y. | 18-30 | .375 | 15½ |
| Bosn. | 19-32 | .373 | 16 |

Senior exhales hard, knobby jaw jutting, pondering the standings as Martin wipes his chalk-dusted right hand on a cloth at the base of the blackboard.

Senior states, "Well, Mr. Martin. My experiment with Abernathy has been a thorough, utter, and complete disaster. We were within striking distance of Chicago when Abernathy took over, five games out—if memory serves—and look at us now. In the company of Philadelphia, St. Louis, *Brooklyn!— Brooklyn for goodness sake! Boston!* Terrible teams, indifferent teams, are leapfrogging us! We were World's Champions last year! We have the *same players*!" He emits an exasperated wheeze. "Chicago is coming in for the next three days. Time is critical. My son here claims that you are a baseball savant.

Do you have confidence you can turn our season around? I am willing to give you a try as manager."

Relief and closely guarded happiness flash from Martin's comprehending mind through the nerves of his body, and certain muscles along his spine relax for the first time since the earthquake crushed his previous world.

Face emanating light, Martin replies, "I'm your man. Thank you, sir."

He heartily grips Senior's bony, weak hand, then Junior's fat hand. Martin has a hundred ideas for improving the team, and since he was hired as a scout he considered writing them and organizing them, but he never wanted to jinx the possibility of this very moment. He picks out his top upgrade. "I suggest, first, sir, to attempt to sell Dan McGann and replace him with Mr. Velay. I've been working with Velay and he will give the team a significant boost."

"McGann *is* having a poor year," Senior notes.

"My focus is to catch Philadelphia, Pittsburg, Chicago, and win another World's Series. Buffalo of the International League is weak at first base."

Brush, Sr. gives Martin a sharp look. "McGraw usually makes—previously made—all the inquiries." Brush gestures with some reverence at the candlestick telephone McGraw used to conjure deals. "He knew everybody."

"I'll do it! Happy to! Who is the Buffalo contact person?"

Brush, Sr. bellows at the door, *"Abernathy!"*

For a moment, Junior and Martin share a significant worried look that Senior's mind has blanked, that he has forgotten Abernathy is not in the antechamber, but with the team in Philadelphia. Senior's withered face breaks into a grin and his consumptive lungs wheeze a laugh like a damaged accordion. The joke is, that before Abernathy knows it, Abernathy will be returned to the antechamber. Martin and Junior crack into laughter.

*

Early evening, Velez is dining with Nicole at an inexpensive shoebox of a restaurant on 6th Avenue, where the owners greet her with a smile. In forty-five minutes, she's to appear as Lady Macbeth in the "out, out damned spot" scene, and later on the same bill, to assist a magician. She's already done Lady Macbeth once today, and the magician's assistant two times. Velez asks, "Why don't they do the whole *Macbeth*?"

"The producers think the audience will not sit for so long," she says, her words tinged in her French accent. "They like little sensations, nothing too sustained." She forks a tiny triangle of pork roast.

"You don't seem to be nervous."

"I am the performer. It is not the words that I speak—as long as my English is clear. It is the emotion that I show. As long as I understand what I am doing, there can be no problem. And I understand these roles."

"I admire you."

She seems embarrassed. "In what way?"

"Your career is awesome."

"Little parts here and there. I do not think so."

"To be doing what you love. Love! And making some money. One day I'll be raking in the dough. I'm itching to get on the field. We'll have money. A lot more!"

"As you say, André, the money is not so very important—of course it's important to have enough. There is a saying: 'He who knows he has enough is rich.'"

Velez ponders all of his gone riches. "I like that a lot. You come up with it?"

"No. Confucius."

An hour later, seated in the middle of the half-full theater, Velez is enthralled by Nicole's Lady Macbeth. Her English accent, to his ear, is perfect. Between acts he buys four hunks of fudge, and when he returns to his seat, up onstage is a guy riding a unicycle juggling batons of fire. Nearby, a man greets a friend with a slap of a rolled newspaper on the shoulder, and loudly informs, "The Giants canned Abernathy!"

\*

On the field before the next day's game, while the Giants are playing catch, Martin stands by the bench, cups his hands over the sides of his mouth, and roars, "Everybody in!" He claps his hands. Mathewson, Wiltse, Bresnahan, Turkey Mike Donlin, Art Devlin, Red Ames, catcher Frank Bowerman, George Browne, Bill Dahlen, Spike Shannon, Cy Seymour, Iron Man Joe McGinnity, Blent, and André Velez, who grandly fills out his new uniform, all gravitate toward Bucky Martin.

Martin is wearing a uniform too. The flannel collar, which is shaped like the collar of a golf shirt, irritates his neck. He begins, "Gentlemen, some of you know me, and some of you do not. I am Bucky Martin. I am your new manager."

"Yay," Turkey Mike sarcastically groans, eliciting chuckles— some nervous, some cynical.

"I have been the manager for this man"—Martin points at Blent—"and this man"—He points at Velez. "This is André Velay. Some call him, Chief. He plays first base." Donlin, Devlin, Dahlen, Browne, Bresnahan shift uneasily. Martin continues, "The Christy-Mathewson-at-first-base experiment is officially over."

"Hoo-rah!" Roger Bresnahan sings. Others clap. Some chuckle. The bodies of the players lose stiffness as they begin to realize that Martin, unlike Abernathy, just might be a baseball man.

"Now, Mr. McGraw was a great manager. We are going back to some of his ways. Some, we are not. I want you to listen to me and trust me. We did things a bit differently in California— " Blent smiles; Velez stands still, for the first time in his life nervous about fitting in with a new team. "But we won a lot and we're going to win here. I want your best efforts and I don't want any griping. Let's have fun, and let's kick ass!" All the players are now amused. "Put your hands in here!" Martin holds out a hand and stands sideways; Velez and Blent place a hand on top of Martin's. Never having seen this formation, the other players catch on and most reach in. But Turkey Mike Donlin, Red Ames, McGinnity and a few others stand back. Turkey Mike raises both hands, as if surrendering, "Mr. Martin! Mr. Martin! A question."

"Sure."

"Where is Danny McGann?"

For a shard of a second Martin hesitates to share the news. "Dan McGann was sold to Buffalo this morning."

Turkey Mike spins away up the first-base line. McGinnity, Ames, Dahlen, Bresnahan, Wiltse, and Devlin peel away, and Martin's attempt at a happy cohesive start to his tenure has thoroughly failed, with only eight hands overlapping in the center of the circle. He considers abandoning his rah-rah spirit-building exercise, but decides to forge on, ordering, "Blent, give the word of the day!"

"All right. Kick ass!"

"On three, we say 'kick ass!' One, two, three— "

Eight voices of varying enthusiasm raggedly overlap. *"Kick ass!"*

Velez slowly jogs to the owner's box where Brush, Sr. sits with Nicole. She is radiant in a red velvet hat trimmed with lace and white freesia, the wide brim of which has already thrice smacked Brush's ear. On the other side of Nicole, Mark Twain smokes a cheroot as he signs his name on a wrinkled scrap tendered by a boy.

Velez gives a nod to Brush, Sr., who that morning signed Velez's contract—$650 for the year, prorated—with a $100 advance. Within two hours, Velez spent the $100 on two new suits, six shirts, a dozen collars, four ties, a gold tie pin, three pairs of shoes, and a fifty-pound bag of roasted coffee, which he delivered in a horse-drawn carriage to Mark Twain's house on 5th Avenue near Washington Square Park, inviting Twain to that afternoon's game. Now Velez holds up a scuffed ball and says, "Mr. Twain, would you like to throw out the first ball?"

"The first ball?"

"The ceremonial first ball. I'll tell the announcer."

Twain chuckles. "May I introduce someone to you?" He turns to a pale, thin man. "This is my particular friend, Mr. Tesla. Mr. Tesla, the esteemed baseball man and coffee aficionado, Mr. André Velay!"

Velez leans in toward the small man in a well-tailored suit, his wrist like the thinnest part of a baseball bat. "You the automobile maker?"

Twain's hearty guffaw is heard by most in the ballpark. Tesla's face cracks a smile.

Twain explains, "He makes just about everything else in the world *other* than automobiles! If you've never before met a genius, Mr. Velay, now you have! In two days, out on Long Island, Mr. Tesla is going to demonstrate how to throw electrical currents across the Atlantic Ocean! But this evening Mr. Tesla is performing an electrical demonstration that will thrill the masses, and I hereby invite you!"

Martin steps away from the bench, across the choppy, worn grass to home plate, where he shakes the hands of umpires Rigler and O'Day, and the Chicago first baseman / manager Frank Chance.

| | NEW YORK | | | CHICAGO |
|---|---|---|---|---|
| CF | ROGER BRESNAHAN | | CF | JIMMY SLAGLE |
| RF | GEORGE BROWNE | | LF | JIMMY SHECKARD |
| 2B | JOHNNY BLENT | | RF | FRANK SCHULTE |
| LF | MIKE DONLIN | | 1B | FRANK CHANCE |
| 3B | ART DEVLIN | | 3B | HARRY STEINFELDT |
| SS | BILL DAHLEN | | SS | JOE TINKER |
| C | FRANK BOWERMAN | | 2B | JOHNNY EVERS |
| 1B | ANDRÉ VELAY | | C | JOHNNY KLING |
| P | HOOKS WILTSE | | P | MORDECAI BROWN |

Martin's strategizing puts Bresnahan in center field because he's caught four days in a row. And Martin doesn't want to install Velez in the middle of the batting order right away. That would further ruffle feathers, and it would add pressure on Velez—though, to Martin's thinking, pressure has never been Velez's problem. Martin wants Velez to hit his way up the order.

Downey, the announcer, informs the crowd through his megaphone, "Ladies and gentlemen! Throwing out the first ball of the afternoon, Mister Mark Twain!" The crowd cheers, enjoying the concept of a ceremonial first ball. Twain's white suit matches the color and the rumpled quality of the suits worn by the refreshment vendors. Photographers aim their boxy cameras at Twain as he holds the ball up near his shoulder, then launches it through the air—moments of boyhood flashing through his mind.

Velez snags the ball as the crowd applauds, hoots, and laughs.

Jimmy Slagle steps into the batter's box, and, initiating the Bucky Martin Era, Hooks Wiltse strikes out Slagle.

Bottom of the 2nd. Two outs. Frank Bowerman huffs atop second base after a stand-up double as Velez digs his back foot into the batter's box, his first big league at-bat since his one-for-eight in St. Louis. He crouches into his stance, worrying if the lack of "cherry seed oil" will render him impotent, if he'll get cut forever. He stares out at the pitcher, mumbles, "Come on, you bastard!" He realizes the catcher is talking to him, but he successfully tunes it into a sound merging with the crowd.

One box over from Nicole, a man's jowls shimmy as he shouts, *"Smack it, Chief!"*

Nicole asks Brush, Sr., "Why do they call the pitcher Three Finger?"

Three Finger Brown sets at his chest, checks Dahlen, gazes in toward Velez, fires a slider off the plate.

*"Strike!"* Rigler, the ump, bellows.

Velez frowns.

*"No way!"* Martin shouts from the third-base coacher's box. *"That was low!"*

Rigler stares at Martin. Bowerman leads off second. Brown sets, rocks, fires a fastball that wickedly breaks in, something flying off it. Velez jumps back, the ball continuing, a sharp punch to the ribs. He thinks he hears Nicole shrieking amidst the *ooohs* and the fans' shouting at Brown. Velez closes his eyes and braces his body. He doesn't want the other team, or his new teammates, to see him wince. He turns to the catcher, Johnny Kling. "Spitter?"

"Welcome to the big leagues, Chief."

"I been here before." Velez trots to first.

Hooks Wiltse slaps a single over Frank Chance's head, scoring Bowerman.

Martin claps, "Now that's what I like!"

## CHICAGO   0 — 1   NEW YORK

Top of the 3rd. One out. Bases loaded. At first base, Velez kicks a pebble into foul territory and bellows at his pitcher, "Come on now Hooksie! You the man, man, man!" Frank Schulte, on a first-pitch fastball, rockets the ball into right field, knocking in Three Finger Brown and Slagle.

## CHICAGO   2 — 1   NEW YORK

Schulte steals second well ahead of Bowerman's throw.
Sheckard on third, Schulte on second. One out.
Wiltse hurls an outshoot, which hangs up, and Frank Chance yanks it—a shot down the third-base line. Art Devlin is airborne, the ball smacking in the pocket of his glove, his momentum rolling him onto his shoulder and back. Sheckard is twenty feet off third toward home. If Devlin tags third base, then Sheckard will be out for a double play. It's a race for third base, Devlin diving headfirst, Sheckard sliding cleat-first.
*"Safe!"* yells the field ump.
Devlin stomps to his feet. "No way in Hell!"
Martin bolts up, instinctively looking around for a replay monitor, for coaches to give their opinion, though he saw Sheckard getting back safely. Instead, here, now, he's got five sets of eyes staring up at him, from bodies in baggy uniforms seated on a pine plank in a dugout with puddles and a cracked wall.
Solo crowd voices shout:
*"He was out!"*
*"Out, goddammit!"*
*"Out, you blind bastard!"*

Blent's and Martin's eyes meet, and Martin understands the urgency of Blent's expression. Blent has seen enough 1906 games to know that managers react.

Martin cuts across the field, shouting, *"Out! Out! Out!"* The crowd growls in appreciation.

"No," the umpire, Hank O'Day, shakes his head as Martin gets up in his flat, hard face. "You can go back to the bench, now."

For a split second, Martin is about to retreat, but he knows McGraw would have had his say, and Martin wants the fans to know that he, too, is a battler. "Don't tell me to go back to the bench! I'm the manager of this team!" His head's bobbing like a barking dog, arms flailing, the actions for the ballpark of fans, but the next words are intended for O'Day. "You don't intimidate me, even if you got this call right, which you did!"

A smile slits across O'Day's face.

*"Okay?"*

O'Day asks, "Shall we get on with this afternoon's contest?"

*"Good idea!"*

Ten feet away, Art Devlin gazes at Martin in astonished appreciation. Martin jogs over, slaps Devlin's butt, *"Great play!"* and jogs toward the bench.

Many fans are on their feet applauding: *"You tell 'em, Buck!"* *"You show 'em, Bucky Boy!"*

Steinfeldt knocks a single to center scoring Sheckard.

The Giants battle to establish a lead.

## CHICAGO  3 — 5  NEW YORK

Top of the 9th. Hooks Wiltse's trudge from bench to pitching mound is tired and determined. Martin's fingering the abundance of flannel at his thigh as he weighs not pulling

Wiltse versus making enemies right away. Martin refrains from ordering another pitcher to warm up.

Doc Gessler, pinch-hitting for Three Finger Brown, slices a bouncy grounder to Blent, who flips to Velez for the first out.

Slagle flies to left. Two outs.

The crowd rises. Thousands of widened mouths, opened throats, emptying lungs are aimed at Hooks Wiltse. Martin stands without volition, earning a distracted glance from Wiltse. Martin's enveloped by the sound, a sound he has missed these many months, a sound he feared he might never again experience from the playing field.

Sheckard waits on a curve and chops it past Wiltse, fielded by shortstop Dahlen near second, who flings the ball to Velez, who stretches out to get it, before Sheckard's foot slams the bag. *Out!*

*"Yeah!"* screams Bowerman. *"Wooooo!"* exclaims Velez, jogging in, patting Wiltse's back.

Velez holds his hand above his shoulder. Blent lustily slaps it—the first high five in the history of the Major Leagues.

Walking off the field, Martin raises his vision to the stands, and finding Brush, Sr., tips his cap, then nods at National League president Harry Pulliam. He gives Brush, Jr. a thumbs-up. Junior shakes his sheaf of papers in triumph. The stands are 60 percent full. Martin knows that with winning comes fans.

Velez holds his cap in his hand so no kids or drunks can snatch it as he takes congratulatory pats on the back from swarming fans. He pushes through to Nicole and Mark Twain. Twain's back is turned to the field as he jabbers with admirers. Nicole, alone, looks up at Velez. She dabs a handkerchief at her tears.

*"What's wrong?"* The glow of his first victory with the New York Giants is extinguished. *"But we won!"*

"Yes. I am so happy for your performance." She sniffs. "You were wonderful. I hope your rib is not hurt from the Three Finger."

Velez hugs her. "Is that why you're crying?"

She weepily gestures at the Cubs pushing their way through the fans toward the clubhouse beyond the right-field fence. "The Chicagos. Such sad, sad faces. Why must it be that one team must lose?"

CHICAGO  3 — 5  NEW YORK  FINAL

# 16

## Tesla's Sparking

AS VELEZ AND BLENT enter the Bellamy Theater on 17th Street between Broadway and 5th Avenue, they are each handed a baseball-card-sized sheet of dark green glass. Onstage Mark Twain is finishing his introduction of Nikola Tesla, "His work was so effective in New Glory that he electrified the entire island. There is so much electricity that the bulbs burn all night! Nobody gets any sleep, and it's been said that the lack of sleep explains their general orneriness and irascibility!" The crowd laughs. "Now we're lucky to have him. In two nights, he's giving a demonstration at his facility in Wardenclyffe that will change the world, ladies and gentlemen! The world! Meanwhile, he's been straightening out our electrical generation systems so that we, too, might be the beneficiaries of consistent power and light! But unlike New Glory, we'll know when to turn it off!"

A huge flash makes the audience wince, and lit in three spotlights, skinny, little Nikola Tesla stands onstage, arms raised. Behind Tesla is an array of technological apparatuses, including two ten-foot diameter glass globes, one at each side of the stage. The audience wildly applauds.

"All right dude," Velez mumbles from the middle of the orchestra seats. "Show me something."

Tesla dons inky goggles and announces, "Now I will control lightning!" Striding to the back wall, he flicks a switch, darkening the theater. The glass globe stage left begins to glow. Tesla strides to the other globe, and it, too, soon glows. "Please employ your dark glass!" The crowd glances around at the odd sight of everyone holding rectangles of almost-black glass across their eyes.

There's a high-pitched whine, then lightning leaps from one globe to the other, vibrating in an arc between the globes.

Frightened shouts emerge from the crowd:

*"Wooo!"*

*"Fantastic!"*

Suspended from the ceiling, a globe illumes above Blent and Velez.

Telsa shouts, *"Now!"* and the bolt moves off the second globe and leaps to the one above the audience.

The audience gasps.

More glass globes suspended throughout the theater illuminate, and soon bolts of lightning are leaping and dancing, criss-crossing through the theater in a vibrating web of lightning.

\*

At the office six blocks away, Martin stares at Brush, Sr.'s chalkboard. The Giants are 14½ games behind Chicago. Brush, Jr. is sorting ticker tape scraps, compiling the day's statistics. Martin takes a sip of scotch, which to him tastes thinner than twenty-first-century scotch, then tells Junior, "I want you to add another two statistics: runs scored, and runs against. For us, for Chicago, Pittsburg, and Philly. The statistic will tell us a lot. Sorry to pile this on your workload."

"I can go back through the box scores." There's a yard-high stack of newspapers in the corner, regularly mined for statistics.

"I think you should start following Chicago."

"What about the Pirates? And Philadelphia?"

Martin knows that if the Giants can ascend the standings, the Cubs, one of the greatest teams ever, will be waiting on top. Even though they lost the 1906 World's Series to the White Sox, they set the record with 116 wins in a season. "Let's focus on the Cubs. They're real."

Junior's eyes narrow as he gazes out the windows. In the red sky above Broadway, thick columns of smoke rise. "There's a fire."

*

At first, the audience figures that the flames spreading on the ceiling are part of Mr. Tesla's show. But then lightning starts climbing a curtain to the ceiling. Twain rushes onstage and grips Tesla's shoulder, frantically pointing to the expanding fire. Half of the audience guffaws at Twain's gestures, while the mirth of the other half subsumes in fear. On the other side of the theater, fire jumps from globe to wall and spreads.

Screams. Dark-green glass rectangles are crunched underfoot as the audience rushes through two narrow doorways. Tesla switches off the lightning, but flames are rapidly spreading on all walls, across the face of the balcony, and on the ceiling.

Velez asks, *"How come no one's moving?"*

"It's like getting off an airplane. Just one or two little doors. No emergency exits here." Burning cinders drop onto Blent. *"Shit!"*

Someone yells, *"Stay calm everybody!"*

In the thickening smoke, the crowd is coughing and shouting in panic. Affecting calmness, the light of the fires flickering off his face, Velez asks Blent, "You think this is how we're
dying?"

"The stage! There's got to be an exit back there!"

"You sure?" Velez asks.

"No!"

Velez scissors over the seats, while Blent walks on their arms
toward the stage. Pieces of burning ceiling fall. Panicked shouts
and screaming continues. Velez and Blent make it to the stage,
share a glance, then look back at the crowd. A woman is passed
out in the aisle, her husband screaming at her, *"Gloria! Gloria!"*
People walk over her.

Velez scrambles across the seats to the aisle, reaches
under the woman. He hoists her. Blent scoops up two small,
freaked-out boys in one arm, a girl in the other. Blent sets the
kids on the stage, and they scamper for the stage exit, which
does, thankfully, exist.

Velez hands the passed-out woman to Blent, who grunts
with her weight, deceptively heavy under her big skirt. Swaths
of red-orange fire seem supernatural through the smoke. Velez
helps Blent carry the woman into the cool night.

They set the woman on a stoop across the street. Blent
inspects her wound—a medium-deep cut on her temple. The
man soothes her in German, then he turns to Velez. "Tank you!
Tank you, zur!"

"No problemo, man . . . Gloria, huh?"

Blent rips off the tail of his shirt, wipes away the blood
dripping down her face, wipes the wound on her scalp. Winds
another strip around her head. Blent tells the man, "Clean the
wound and get a clean bandage on it."

Meanwhile a horse-drawn fire engine remains stationary in
the middle of the street, but no water is being sprayed onto the

fire. A voice emerging from the theater announces, "Everyone's out!" A few steps down, firemen brandishing axes are screaming at men sitting on a barrel who also wield axes. One in the street yells, "Get the hell off, you sons of whores!" and the reply is, "This is *our* street!"

Velez screeches at a fireman, "What are you waiting for?"

"These pricks here won't let us fight the fire!"

"Aren't you all firemen?"

"Different companies! This is *our* fire!"

Clanging bells announce the approach of yet another horse-drawn fire engine. The men on the barrel cheerily remove it, revealing a fireplug. A hose from the new engine is carried over.

*Craaaaaaaack!* goes the theater's roof, emitting a geyser of sparks up into the night, as the roof collapses. Blent watches the German couple slowly walk away up the street, hugging.

\*

The next day in the Polo Grounds clubhouse, Brush, Jr. hovers over a bench in front of the lockers, laying out a line of Chicago spray charts. Junior seems stiff and chaste, rarely having rubbed shoulders with players.

Martin gathers the team. "Excellent game yesterday. Let me tell you some tendencies of today's Cubs pitcher, Ed Reulbach, which you might not know. If he throws two curveballs in a row, he almost never throws another curveball—so look for a fastball, or an outshoot." Martin waves at the row of spray charts, one chart for each Chicago batter:

**Jimmy Slagle**

**Jimmy Sheckard**

**Frank Schulte**

**Frank Chance**

**Harry Steinfeldt**

**Joe Tinker**

**Johnny Evers**

**Johnny Kling**

"These charts show where the Chicago hitters hit their balls; they show outs and hits. Let's cheat a step or two here and there toward the clusters of hits and outs. Mr. Brush here and I call them spray charts. You are not allowed to share this information with anyone—not with other teams, not with the newspapers, not with your wives, not with your mistresses." Many of the players chuckle, and all gravitate toward the charts.

On the day, Velez goes 2 for 3; Blent slices two singles to right and rakes a double down the line in left, going 3 for 4. "Iron Man" Joe McGinnity shows grit and determination, pitching a complete game:

|          | 1 | 2 | 3 | 4 | 5 | 6 | 7 | 8 | 9 | R | H | E |
|----------|---|---|---|---|---|---|---|---|---|---|---|---|
| Chicago  | 0 | 0 | 2 | 0 | 0 | 1 | 0 | 0 | 0 | 3 | 6 | 2 |
| New York | 0 | 0 | 1 | 1 | 0 | 3 | 0 | 0 | X | 5 | 9 | 1 |

*

The next morning, Velez loudly snores off a night of ten-dollar-a-game pool with Turkey Mike Donlin, Bresnahan, Dahlen, Devlin, and McGinnity at the pool hall on 14th Street part-owned by Highlanders' first baseman Hal Chase, a night that ended for some of them at a brothel on Gramercy Park, with Velez staring up at the façade of the brothel, while Dahlen and Devlin urged him, "Come on, Chief," "They don't bite," while Velez debated himself whether to join them or not, and what difference would it make?—he was *in the wrong century.* "No, guys. I got a girl."

Martin studies the pitching chart of the Cubs' Jack Pfiester. He sips at his coffee cup, gold rimmed with a pattern of tiny purple flowers. "Johnny?"

"Ready, boss."

Martin, carrying his coffee cup, followed by Blent, walks out into the soft June morning. Martin rings the buzzer for the Mathewson/McGraw apartment. Mrs. Mathewson answers, a pinched smile in the confident, concerned face. "Mr. Martin. Mr. Blent. Please come in." She crinkles her eyes at Martin. "Congratulations on your first two victories."

"Thank you. Are you coming today?"

"It's really not for me. It's too tense watching my husband pitch. I can't sit still for so long. I'd rather be *doing* something." She offers Blent a significant look.

"You sit at church," Mathewson comments from his leather chair in the tall-ceilinged living room; theirs is an apartment with more volume, brighter, larger in every way than the Martin/Blent/Velez apartment. Mrs. McGraw has remained in Baltimore, her plans regarding New York uncertain, so there's even more room.

Mathewson's in suit pants, collared shirt. His hair is oiled. Feet in shined shoes rest on an ottoman. He sets aside his *New York Times* and stands up to shake hands.

"I'd like a word," says Martin, weirded out, once again, that he is actually shaking the hand of Christy Mathewson.

"Sure, Mr. Martin."

"Please, call me Buck."

"Please, sit down. We can talk here."

Martin takes a seat on a spindle-backed chair. Three chessboards rest on the window bench and there's a chess/checkers table. "It's your day to pitch."

"I appreciate it. I'm not much of a first baseman." Mathewson smiles.

"I want you to pitch well. But I need to know exactly what's going on with your body."

Mathewson raises his right arm, twists it palm up, showing with his left hand the burn coursing around his elbow and up into his biceps. He twists the hand so the palm faces out, points to a fiery knot of pain in his shoulder.

Martin turns to Blent, who has been watching Mathewson's every move.

Blent asks, "May I?" Mathewson assents. Blent prods and pokes, repeatedly asking, "Does this hurt?" and "Please describe the feeling," as he explores the hand, wrist, forearm, elbow, biceps, triceps. He glances at Mrs. Mathewson who, from the opening to the room, is staring at them.

He stands behind Mathewson's chair, pulls Mathewson's arm straight, digs in the shoulder, *"Oh!"* winces Mathewson.

"Apologies." Blent lowers the arm. With his fingertips on each side of Mathewson's spine, Blent counts each vertebra, up to the base of Mathewson's skull, noticing the twisted neck vertebrae—the cervicals. Blent digs the tip of his finger in on the right side between cervical four and cervical five. "Pain?"

Mathewson's words are clipped, as he points with the other hand, "Goes along my head, down into my shoulder, arm."

"If you are willing to let me manipulate your spine, I think I can relieve some of the pain."

"Truly?" Mathewson queries Blent about his background and knowledge, concluding with, "Will it keep me from pitching today?"

"I have hopes that it will let you pitch *better* and farther into the game."

To Jane, whose eyes are wide, jaw clenched, Matty asks, "Think it's all right?"

"I've seen a trainer do it with a foal whose hip was out of joint. So, it could work."

The dining table is cleared, three blankets are added to provide cushion as Christy Mathewson lays on his stomach. Blent asks Mathewson to roll onto his side. Blent stands on a chair to provide the correct angle. He drops onto Mathewson's hip, causing the hip bones to spread apart, *craaaaaaaaaackkkkk!*

*"Whoa!"* Mathewson exclaims.

"Relieved?" Blent asks.

Mathewson assesses the level of pain: diminished. *"Yes!"*

Blent checks the spine, noticing a bit more movement now in the lumbar. Blent moves to the head of the table and reaches under Mathewson, Blent's fingers pulling on the base of the skull, tractioning, a bit slippery from Mathewson's pomade. "That feels good," Mathewson comments.

"Now I am going to do a movement that is always a bit scary the first time—manipulate your head to release the pain in your neck. That is the object. It may not work the first time. And we'll only try this one time today. We can try another day if you wish."

"Go ahead," Mathewson says.

Mrs. Mathewson reappears at the doorway, in her dark dress, tight at the waist, which she often wears to church. "I can't watch." She clomps toward the door.

"Stay here—" Mathewson pleads, then *craaaaaaack!* The sound pulls Martin's attention away from appreciating Mrs. Mathewson's waist, to his pitcher, who exclaims, *"Wow!"* Mathewson reaches for the side of his neck. "Oh my goodness! It's gone!"

"What's gone?" Martin asks.

"The pain! The tightness! Almost all of it!"

A knock on the front door. Martin opens it and there's Velez. He points at his wrist, indicating the time.

\*

The trio rides the Elevated downtown to Christopher Street. Stopping at a bakery on Bleecker, they munch pastries and a crispy, warm French bread as they cross Washington Square, its benches crammed with students, the men in suits and ties, the women in skirts and puffy blouses, many reading from little hardbound books and smoking cigarettes. While tossing a chunk of bread at a cluster of pigeons, Velez steps on a sharp pebble that spikes his foot. "These shoes have no *cushioning*! *Man*, I gotta invent sneakers!" Martin's cackle and Blent's laughter echo against the inside parabola of Washington's Arch as they pass through.

At 21 5th Avenue, a redbrick mansion, Velez brushes bread crumbs off his suit, then knocks on the door. A white curtain in a ground-floor window is quickly closed. The odor of manure from the street is rich, as is the spicy, mossy odor of the shrubbery fronting the mansion.

The door opens just enough for the over-stooped, over-questioning, eyebrow-raised expression of Mark Twain to emerge into the daylight, asking, "Who wishes to enter the castle of Count Mofongo?" The trio cracks up.

Twain straightens, "Gentlemen." With some tenderness he reaches for Velez's hand. Velez introduces his friends. Blent and Martin blink in astonishment at meeting Twain, and that André Velez is on casual terms with him.

As they step inside, from the other end of the foyer, a group of serious, hard-looking men examines them. One determines, "Giants players."

Of the security, Twain comments, projecting his voice, "That's how our government is wasting its money—on these able-bodied loungers!" The security guards laugh.

Velez asks Twain, "Tesla here?"

"He *is* here. But not in any mood on account of the fire. His demonstration at Wardenclyffe for tomorrow has been canceled. He is being threatened with various lawsuits."

"I promise he'll find it very interesting to talk with us."

Twain winks. "You shittin' me?"

Velez's body shakes as he guffaws.

On the third floor of the mansion, Twain knocks on a door. "Nik, we have some distinguished visitors! The California baseball players!"

No answer.

Velez knocks hard. "Mister Tesla, we want to talk with you about the future!"

No response.

The others start away, but Velez bangs on the door. *"We want to talk with you about a telephone without wires! You carry it with you anywhere! You can call anyone in the world!"*

The door clicks and opens. The room looks more abused than a ballplayer's hotel room. Twain yanks a curtain open, asks, "Soup?"

Wearing the same suit as the night before, Tesla replies, "I don't care."

Twain strides out and downstairs.

"Cell phones," Velez starts. But Tesla's looking at the floor. As Velez and Blent dive in, trying to explain cell phones and the way they think the technology works, Tesla's body loses its flaccidity. He sits back with a leg crossed, strokes his chin. Blent adds, "We went to see Alexander Graham Bell about this, but he didn't even want to talk with us."

Tesla flicks his wrist, "That dolt," as a servant brings in a tray and sets it on a table before the fireplace. Tesla asks, "Are you scientists?"

"Just ballplayers," Velez replies.

Martin utters his first words in Tesla's presence. "Mr. Tesla, we're from the future." The ballplayers exchange glances.

Tesla's eyelids flutter. His head tilts down, seems to be examining them with his peripheral vision. "The future?"

They explain their predicament in detail. Tesla steeples his fingers. The edge of his tongue darts out the corner of his mouth.

"So we dug and *nothing*," Velez explains. "No tunnel or wormhole. Here we are."

Tesla's questions: "When in the future?" "How did this happen?" "How else have you tried to return?" "Who else knows?" "What were you doing when you came back to the past?" "How do people derive their electrical power in the future?" "Is electrical power sent wirelessly?" "What kinds of advances, would you say, has your society over ours?" One statement: "I have thought this possible."

Twain returns, looking many years older, sunken. "Clara—my daughter—is ill. I'm off to see what I can do."

Blent rises to shake Twain's hand, fights an urge to look at his own hand, just touched by Mark Twain. As Twain is saying to Tesla, "Eat the soup!" Martin adds, "It is an honor, sir."

Twain waves off the sentiment. "It's an honor to have such talented ballplayers and their manager in my home!" Twain grimaces and departs.

Blent asks Tesla, "Do you believe us, that we're from the future?"

Tesla strokes the side of his skinny face. "It is a most fantastical claim! Permit me to consider it. I will leave my contact in Chicago. Mr. Westinghouse has assembled my laboratory. When you play your game in Chicago, you can call on me."

*

At 2:01, Jimmy Sheckard, Cubs left fielder, lines a bullet over Johnny Blent's head into right-center for a single.

At 2:03, Harry Steinfeldt, Cubs third baseman, blasts a shot that kicks up dirt from the mound as it scoots into center for a single. Sheckard to third.

At 2:07, Frank Chance cracks a high fly to left. Mike Donlin shouts, "I got it!" as he settles under it, waiting, the ball smacking his glove and falling to the crabgrass. The crowd groans. Sheckard scores. Steinfeldt scores. Chance cruises in to second.

## CHICAGO  2 — 0  NEW YORK

Mathewson strikes out Frank Schulte and Johnny Evers to end the inning.

Top of the 3rd. Johnny Kling rips a shot into left-center that Turkey Mike Donlin charges, the ball bouncing over his glove. The crowd groans. Browne, playing center, backs up Donlin and gets the ball in to third to hold Kling to a double.

Next to Martin on the bench, Hooks Wiltse mumbles out the side of his mouth, "Maybe Turkey Mike's on the take today." Each of the reserve players glance at Martin, who's never, *ever* suspected one of his players of betting on a game, or throwing a game for a fee.

*Intentionally muffing plays?* Martin feels very alone. He would like to ask Mathewson, on the mound, what he thinks of the Turkey Mike Donlin situation. He wonders what McGraw would have done, and instantly, as if channeling McGraw, Martin pops up from the bench and declares, "We're not having any of that shit on this team!"

He starts out onto the field, claps his hands and to the home-plate ump, "Time, Mr. O'Day!" Martin spins to the bench. "Spike! Left field."

Every player in earshot stiffens as Spike Shannon takes a few moments to find his glove under the bench. Shannon jogs toward left. Martin crosses the first-base line, gives a significant look to Velez and Blent. "You guys might need to back me up."

"What's up?" asks Velez. Blent steps in toward the pitcher's mound.

Spike Shannon slows in the outfield grass. Turkey Mike Donlin points a finger at himself, "For me? Why?" Donlin's face is a twisted gnarl.

Spike Shannon replies, "Ask the new boss."

Donlin takes a quick glance at the nearby stands where the knot of gamblers stares on in horror. Donlin jogs in. Devlin and Dahlen watch him pass as Turkey Mike fixes his stare on Martin. *"Are you taking me out?"*

"Let's go sit on the bench," Martin uses an even tone. He hasn't fought anyone since his second year of minor league ball, and he unclenches his hands. "Come on, Mike. Rough day. Let's take the day off."

*"'Cause I dropped one damned ball? 'Cause that one just popped over my glove?"* His eyes are black marbles of rage. *"I'm not perfect, you damned yannigan!"*

"No one's perfect," Martin says mildly, as he wonders what kind of lightning-fast calculation is going on in Turkey Mike's head. The fans stare, silent. On the roof of the grandstand a seagull *squawk squawk squawks*. If Donlin insults him one more time, Martin decides he will have to respond.

Donlin starts his jog toward the bench, and as he passes Martin, Donlin's shoulder knocks Martin's shoulder. Martin fills his lungs—deciding whether he should accept the insult, whether it will undermine the respect he is trying to construct with his team, or if, on the other hand, by taking Donlin out of the game, Martin has already sufficiently made his point.

On his way back to the bench, Martin passes Dahlen. "How you feeling, Bill?"

Dahlen's huge smile reveals stained teeth and a cheek-ballooning wad of tobacco. "Good, Skip! Real good!"

Martin stops at the pitcher's mound. The intense face of Christy Mathewson gazes down. "My arm feels like new. I'm a little wild, but I'm getting better."

Bresnahan, the catcher, jogs out to join them. Velez, Blent, Devlin, and Dahlen walk in. Martin doesn't want to show any preference to Velez and Blent, so he addresses Mathewson. "I would like to sweep the series from these Chicago bastards. Make a point. What about you?"

"Agreed," replies Mathewson stonily.

Devlin, Blent, and Bresnahan growl in approval. "Yeah," says Velez.

Umpire O'Day walks out, removing his mask. "Time to break up the tea party."

Martin says, "There are some guys in the left-field stands who would like to buy us more than tea." Everyone, including O'Day, gazes out at the cluster of gamblers in boater hats, staring back, pissed off at Martin for tearing up the day's elaborate blueprint for a haul of gambling money.

"How much could they be offering?" asks O'Day, almost to himself.

"They tried that stuff with me," Dahlen replies. "Two hundred bucks."

O'Day whistles. "*Verrrrrrry* tempting!" Bresnahan and Devlin double over laughing.

Martin takes his seat on the bench next to Wiltse. At the other end, Turkey Mike Donlin sulks.

On the next pitch, Johnny Kling pops up sky-high in foul ground. Velez rushes toward the bench, snagging it, his big body's momentum carrying him toward the bench, and there's

Turkey Mike right in front of him gazing up into space. Velez considers, in defense of his boss, letting his whole body continue on and crushing Mike. Deciding to leave the disciplining to Martin, Velez veers away, almost tripping on the team's bats, which are neatly arranged in front of the bench like a fallen picket fence.

Bottom of the 4th. Velez knocks another single.

Mathewson singles, advancing Velez to second.

Bresnahan hits a slow roller into a 3–6 fielder's choice. Velez to third. Bresnahan on first. One out.

After fouling off five two-strike pitches, George Browne walks.

Blent hits a fly ball to medium-deep right. Velez tags up at third, Schulte firing a strong throw that is tailing up the line, Kling snagging it two steps toward the pitcher's mound, spinning and lunging at sliding Velez. *"Safe!"* bellows O'Day, triggering a roaring crowd. Velez pops to his feet, grinning.

## CHICAGO  2 — 1  NEW YORK

Spike Shannon singles, scoring Bresnahan. Devlin singles, scoring Browne. Dahlen pops out.

## CHICAGO  2 — 3  NEW YORK

Top of the 6th. Mathewson's curve to Steinfeldt does not curve and Steinfeldt smacks it down the left-field line. The ball kicks along the contour of the wall past Spike Shannon. Browne in center picks it up and fires it in to Devlin as Steinfeldt cruises in with a stand-up triple.

Mathewson's next pitch is a fastball, sternum-high, that Frank Chance obliterates, the ball *buzzing* like a rocket-propelled beehive twenty feet above Blent's outstretched arm, splitting the outfielders and rolling into the expanse behind them. Steinfeldt scores. Browne tracks down the ball and fires it on a line to Blent, who wheels and zips it to Devlin at third. *"Safe!"*

## CHICAGO 3 — 3 NEW YORK

Gritting his teeth, Mathewson snaps his glove like a rat-trap onto the toss from Devlin. He inspects the ball, looking for lospidedness, a significant scuff mark, a frayed red stitch—something he can use to make the ball break hard.

Martin weighs pulling Mathewson. He glances at Wiltse, who raises an eyebrow, acknowledging the sticky situation.

Kling steps in. He, like his counterpart, the New York catcher, Bresnahan, is swift and athletic—unlike the more common thick-short-and-wide catchers. Mathewson throws a curve-ballish pitch—attempting to take advantage of a scuff mark, the scuff mark sloppily spinning at the ball's north pole, as the ball kicks in front of home plate, bouncing against Bresnahan's shin guards and scooting away. Chance starts in from third, Bresnahan pouncing on the ball, diving at the plate. Chance retreats.

Martin's nerve endings tingle, urging him to stand and rise from the bench to the mound and at least *talk* to Mathewson. But he knows that Mathewson, like all pitchers, will reply "fine," and "great," and "I'm good," and if Martin yanks Mathewson and it costs New York the game, his players will conclude that he was overmanaging, that maybe he *really is* as lame as Abernathy. On the bench, McGinnity asks, "Who needs a drink?" and everyone laughs. Even Donlin, in deep sulk, lets out a burp of a laugh. Martin's butt stays on the bench.

Mathewson's next pitch twirls perfectly, the scuff at the apex, dropping three feet and slicing the strike zone. The bench players clap along with the 10,434 paying fans.

Mathewson fires a fastball low and away that Kling takes for a ball: 2–1. Bresnahan calls for a fastball, away. It comes in over the fat part of the plate, and Kling swings hard *craaackkk!* the ball zipping over Velez's head—he barely hops—as it hits a foot inside the right-field line and clangs against the section of stands that juts out into fair territory. Kling hustles around second, chugs toward third, sliding in ahead of the throw.

## CHICAGO  4 — 3  NEW YORK

Martin glances down the bench at Donlin, who remains leaning back, arms crossed, expressionless. In the left-field stands, there is a small chorus of loud cheering accompanied by flying boater hats. *"Three Goddamned triples in a row!"* comments Hooks Wiltse.

Frank Schulte singles. Kling scores.

## CHICAGO  5 — 3  NEW YORK

Bottom of the 9th. Velez at third, Dahlen at first. Spike Shannon slices a lazy fly ball to right that settles in Schulte's glove to end the game, triggering a baleful chorus of booing. Turkey Mike Donlin struts toward the clubhouse. The knot of gamblers in left field hollers, hats spinning twenty feet into the air.

## CHICAGO  5 — 3  NEW YORK  FINAL

# 17

## Sure You Want This Job?

THE NEXT MORNING on the 8:05 train to Boston, Martin sits in the lounge, the day's newspapers on his lap, those newspapers' baseball writers' fleshy faces gazing down at him, flip pads out, pencils poised, their halitosis-afflicted questions imminent. F. C. Lane of *Baseball* asks, "Turkey Mike said he was feeling fine yesterday. Have a comment?"

"Not on that, thanks."

Some of the writers chuckle.

"Do you suspect Mike of consorting with gamblers?" Will Forrest of the *New York Times* asks.

"No. Why would I?"

All the writers laugh.

"Then why did you remove Mike in the third inning?"

"I wanted to get Spike Shannon some work."

"Spike went 0 for 4."

"Maybe he needs more work," Martin muses.

"Who is starting in left today?"

"Mike Donlin."

"You just said you wanted to get Spike Shannon more work."

"I did. He got it yesterday."

The writers laugh heartily, admiring Martin's skill at giving them useful quotes without stepping in the piles of runny manure that they plop in front of him with each question.

F. C. Lane asks, "Did it occur to you to ask yourself what McGraw would have done—whether McGraw would have relieved Donlin—in the same situation?"

Martin focuses for an extra-long moment on Lane's angular nose and the fringe of hair catching the sun through the window. Somehow Lane has guessed what Martin was thinking the moment before he went out to retrieve Turkey Mike. Martin answers, "What Mr. McGraw would have done—that's something we can never know."

| | NEW YORK GIANTS | | BOSTON BEANEATERS |
|---|---|---|---|
| CF | ROGER BRESNAHAN | SS | AL BRIDWELL |
| RF | GEORGE BROWNE | 1B | FRED TENNEY |
| 2B | JOHNNY BLENT | 3B | DAVE BRAIN |
| LF | MIKE DONLIN | CF | JOHNNY BATES |
| 3B | ART DEVLIN | LF | DEL HOWARD |
| SS | BILL DAHLEN | RF | COZY DOLAN |
| C | FRANK BOWERMAN | C | TOM NEEDHAM |
| 1B | ANDRÉ VELAY | 2B | ALLIE STROBEL |
| P | RED AMES | P | VIVE LINDAMAN |

Vive Lindaman is a twenty-nine-year-old rookie with a 2–7 record, 0–2 versus New York. He sets down New York 1-2-3 in the first inning. Boston chips Red Ames for runs in the first, third, and eighth, while New York scores single runs in the fifth and sixth.

## NEW YORK  2 — 3  BOSTON  FINAL

As he sits in the Copley Square Hotel bar drinking scotch with F. C. Lane and the writer from the *Brooklyn Eagle*, Martin is 2–2 as manager. New York is now fourteen games behind Chicago, who were rained out in St. Louis.

"That's baseball!" Lane states, "A yannigan pitcher—Vive Lindaman—out of nowhere, can have one great day." Martin's nodding head indicates agreement, while, inwardly Martin laments that he doesn't have hitting grids for the Beaneaters.

The next day is worse:

## NEW YORK  0 — 4  BOSTON  FINAL

Martin, Forrest, and F. C. Lane command the same corner of the bar, New York having been shut out by Irv Young, nicknamed Cy the Second, but of no relation to the great Cy Young by blood or talent. News of Chicago's win crashes like a tsunami through the barroom, meaning New York has fallen to fifteen games behind. For the first time as manager, whether in the twenty-first century or the twentieth, Martin drinks a fourth scotch in one sitting.

In his hotel room, Martin is blasted out of sleep by grinding fire alarm bells. He flicks on the light, reaches for his pocket watch: 3:45. He grabs his papers, his wallet. In the hallway, Mathewson and Wiltse are pounding on doors, yelling, "Fire! Get out!" From the row of Giants' rooms, only Blent emerges. Martin asks, "Where are the guys?" He receives blank stares and robotic shrugs—of course, the missing ballplayers are out in the night.

The clanging bells are unceasing as the hallways and stairwells fill with guests. Outside, hoses are hoisted up ladders eight, nine, ten stories, water pouring into a blaze that has punched a fist of fire in the face of the hotel. Four hundred guests, some wrapped in robes, watch the fire in the warm night.

Martin glances over at the pack of New York reporters, suitcases and cased typewriters at their feet, notebooks and pencils in hand, who nod in acknowledgment at Martin.

A hundred yards away a cluster of men in rumpled, torn suits, a multiarmed and multiheaded agglomeration holding fifths of booze and fat cigars, turns the corner. The flickering fire lights up the wet-eyed faces of the rest of the New York Giants, including Velez, who's holding something up to his eye. Dahlen's arm is wrapped in a tablecloth, dripping blood. Roger Bresnahan finishes swigging from a bottle of bourbon and asks, "What floor is on fire?" He is counting up, losing track, closing one eye and attempting the count again. Their rooms are on the sixth floor.

The drunken-pack logic enthusiastically responds to Donlin's declaration, "Gotta get my shirts!" And the pack rushes through the spectators, up to the blazing hotel, three bullet-helmeted policemen no match for the ballplayers. Martin rushes forward. Wiltse and Blent hang back, unwilling to confront wildly drunk teammates. Only Mathewson follows Martin.

The ballplayers rush through the deserted lobby, up the stairs, hopping over crisscrossing hoses leaking at their connections and soaking the carpets, smoke thickening at each higher story, surprised firemen screaming at them to get the hell out, the drunken ballplayers laughing and yanking on hoses. Donlin takes a roundhouse swing at a fireman, knocking him in the cheekbone, and the fireman drops. Donlin commands the brass nozzle and maniacally laughing, sprays the fireman, then sprays the fire, before he is tackled by a phalanx of firemen. It is a battle between firemen and ballplayers, an equal number of each. Soon the firemen retreat, some holding chins and mouths punched by Giants. Some Giants climb up to their rooms to retrieve possessions, while Donlin, McGinnity, and Red Ames man the hoses. Donlin pulls his Colt M1900 from his belt and shoots the ceiling while he sprays the fire. Four minutes later, the hotel is swarmed with police, who beat down the Giants and drag them out. Red Ames and Bowerman scurry away, but the Boston police manage to haul twelve New York Giants, corralling them, on foot, to the Beacon Hill precinct station. Lustily singing "Tessie," the Giants are herded into a holding cell. A shrunken, shrewish sergeant informs Martin that the ballplayers will likely be processed at municipal court at 9 a.m., while Mathewson signs autographs for twenty policemen.

Five and a half hours later, across from the courthouse at the Clink Restaurant, Martin, Mathewson, and Blent finish their fifteen-cent plates of eggs, sip their nickel coffee as they glance at the clock above the door, which reads 8:45. The phalanx of New York baseball writers, joined by Boston reporters, all keep one eye on Martin, who brings his cup over to their booths. In the irrational hope that the reporters have refrained from spreading the story of the ballplayers' off-field shenanigans, Martin asks, "The story already out?"

"It's a *crime* store-y," one of the Boston writers declares, "a police store-y more so than a baseball store-y."

Martin squints at the writer, whom he's never met. Martin's skin feels thick from lack of sleep and his lips are sticking together in a mixture of saliva, griddle grease, and coffee. F. C. Lane and A. B. Taylor, the latter of the *Newark Star*, chuckle, recognizing how far from the field of play this "store-y" resides. Again, the press is playing chess with Martin: If Martin blurts out, "no comment," some will interpret that he doesn't care that he has no control over his team.

Martin swallows his coffee. "The actions of many on the team are reprehensible"—he surveys the reporters, twenty of them crammed around him, scribbling—"and unprecedented."

F. C. Lane's diaphragm involuntarily contracts with laughter, expressing a jet of air from his mouth along with significant ounces of lukewarm coffee, spraying his colleagues. Martin's reply is both righteous and absurd. Because, certainly, there is nothing unprecedented about ballplayers drinking themselves deep into the realm of the idiotic.

Martin's morning is spent scurrying between the court and banks, phoning the office in New York. Brush, Sr.'s clipped words blast through the earpiece, as Martin arranges for the $2,400 bond money to be wired to the Chase National Bank on Cambridge Street. Martin retrieves the cash and walks it to the court clerk.

The day turns blazing, and all of the players show up on the field for noon hitting and fielding practice. Martin considers adding practice going first to third on a single, and first to home on a double, but, considering the heat, that would be vindictive. *They deserve it.* The players curse under their panting breath as they repeat the drill time and again.

As the team boards the 6:12 p.m. train to New York, the afternoon papers are gathered. The *Boston Herald*:

> It wasn't a pretty sight at the South End Grounds. The New York team, most of which had spent the better part of the night and early morning in jail on accusations that they interfered with public safety employees conducting their duty—the already-infamous obstruction of firefighters at the Copley Plaza Hotel —did not acquit themselves admirably on the ball field, though 'Iron Man' Joe Mc-Ginnity did

his part, holding the Bostons to
two runs and six hits. It would
seem that their nocturnal activ-
ities had a blurring effect on
their tracking of the ball.

|          | 1 | 2 | 3 | 4 | 5 | 6 | 7 | 8 | 9 | R | H | E |
|----------|---|---|---|---|---|---|---|---|---|---|---|---|
| New York | 0 | 0 | 0 | 0 | 0 | 0 | 0 | 0 | 0 | 0 | 5 | 3 |
| Boston   | 0 | 0 | 1 | 0 | 0 | 1 | 0 | 0 | X | 2 | 8 | 0 |

After the train disgorges the Giants at Pennsylvania
Station, Martin walks through the night to the Flatiron. While
sitting with a glass of scotch, studying Brush, Jr.'s new reports
on Chicago, Pittsburg, and Philadelphia, the latter of which
will be in town the next day, he loses himself in statistics on
Tinker, Evers, Chance, Steinfeldt, Honus Wagner, Fred Clarke,
Deacon Phillippe, and Philadelphia's Dooin and Doolan. The
updated standings:

|            | W L   | PCT  | GB    |
|------------|-------|------|-------|
| Chicago    | 39-20 | .661 | —     |
| Pittsburg  | 34-24 | .586 | 4½    |
| Phila.     | 36-29 | .554 | 6     |
| St.L.      | 28-32 | .467 | 11½   |
| Cincinnati | 28-34 | .452 | 12½   |
| Boston     | 23-34 | .404 | 20    |
| Brooklyn   | 20-33 | .377 | 21    |
| New York   | 20-34 | .370 | 21½   |

The clicking lock wakes Martin. He raises himself to vertical on the creaking office sofa as Brush, Sr. hobbles in. Martin
straightens his shirt. "Good morning, sir."

Brush, Sr. nearly topples from the surprise. Martin rushes
to steady him. "Off!" Senior barks.

"A lousy trip to Boston."

"What do you think the problem is?" Brush asks.

"Sir, first, I want to apologize for the conduct of the men at the fire—"

Brush holds up his withered hand. "No, sir. That is *your* purview: discipline. Mr. McGraw kept iron control."

"I prefer to treat the men as men."

"Again, sir, I say: It is up to you. But I have handed you a championship team." There is contempt, or disgust, in the words. Brush, Sr. aims his chin at the chalkboard standings.

Martin figures it is not a good time, with his record two wins and four losses, to ask for additional staff to cover more games. "Chief Velay is settling in nicely. Ten for twenty-four. .417 average."

A knock on the door. Brush's brow furrows. Martin opens it to reveal Harry Pulliam, president of the National League. Under Pulliam's right arm is a flat package the size of an unfolded newspaper. Pulliam comments, "Rough first week," winks at Martin, the wink accompanied, it seems to Martin, with a bit of glee. Pulliam tells Brush, Sr., "You're a creature of habit, John, and here you are, seven a.m.! Apologies for the early hour, gentlemen, but—" Turning to address only Brush, Pulliam says, "I can barely believe it." He holds out the flat package and lays it on Brush's massive desk.

"Should I go?" Martin asks Pulliam.

Pulliam shakes his head no. Brush opens the package, slides out a document that resembles a proclamation, roughly the size of the Declaration of Independence. Pulliam's large forehead glistens as he leans over, reading next to slender, sickly Brush, who asks, "Is it real?"

"Yes. Both league offices, and every team, is receiving one in the next day or two. All delivered by diplomatic courier. This will explode all over the newspapers." Brush motions Martin to the desk. The document reads:

*Dearest Gentlemen of the Major Leagues,*
*In honor of our Founding Fathers, who did so love, enjoy, invent, and play baseball, we, the New Glory Confederation of Baseball Clubs, find it our highest honor and privilege, to hereby challenge the winner of your World's Series of the year 1906, to a Solar Series—the best 4 of 7, or 5 of 9, to be decided—against the winner of the New Glory Confederacy of Baseball Clubs of 1906.*
*The prizes are as follows: the winning team's players shall be awarded a total of $300,000; the losing team's players, a total of $30,000; and the winning league $1,000,000.*

The document concludes with the multitude of names and titles of the officials of the New Glory and the New Glory Confederacy of Baseball Clubs. Martin deciphers the signatures of Robert E. Lee III and Henry Clay Johnstone.

Pulliam says, "Late last night, I spoke with President Hanna. He is hesitating to accept. Have an opinion?" he asks Brush.

"A million dollars for the league. Where's the harm in that?"

"The harm is sheer and utter humiliation—if we lose." To Martin, he asks, "Opinion?"

"Well, we're in last place. This is talking about the winner of the World Series. We haven't won anything. But"—Martin's mind flashes through the articles he's read about lynchings in New Glory, slavery, invasions of Caribbean islands and parts of South America—"that's a lot of money for the winners. I like that. My first question is: With so much at stake, who's going to umpire?"

"Good question," replies Pulliam.

"It would be nice to have four umpires—one at each base."

Pulliam, ever conscious of squeezing pennies, chuckles. "Overkill, don't you think?"

"Less room for deception," replies Martin.

Brush notes, "I read they have a stadium that seats fifty thousand people."

"That would be something to see!" says Pulliam.

Brush adds, "And the Cobb brothers."

"The Cobb *brothers?*" Martin's spine tightens. "You mean Ty Cobb?"

"That's one of them—Tyrus. The best one I've heard of is Augustus Cobb. And Josephus Cobb, the catcher, is said to be a marvel. Cæsar plays first base and is a monster, perhaps larger than your Chief Velay. Tyrus is the youngest brother, an up-and-comer."

"How many Cobbs are there?" Martin asks.

"Five?" Brush replies. "Six? They play every position except pitcher and there are stories that they've killed people—some on the field. I don't know if our boys will want to play against the Cobbs. They are said to be demons, something wrong with their brains." He asks Martin, "What is your opinion of how the players will react to the prospect of a Solar Series?"

"Three things motivate ballplayers," replies Martin, "And the first one is money."

Brush and Pulliam chuckle. Pulliam asks, "And the other two?"

"The second is winning. Ballplayers are competitive animals."

"And the third?

Conscious of his tenuous hold on his job, his 2–4 record, Martin states it as cleanly as possible: "Women."

*

At noon, Martin is hitting infield practice to Devlin, Dahlen, Blent, Velez, and George Browne, who can play any position. McGinnity is hitting fly balls to the outfielders. Martin considers his team, trying to figure out what, if anything, is wrong with them.

After two hundred grounders, Martin announces, "Enough!" He turns to the bench, trips on a divot, and falls to the scraggly field. He identifies the offending divot and is stomping it when Mathewson says, "Hi. I looked for you this morning—to give you a ride."

"Slept at the office." Martin's mind rushes back to the New Glory challenge and part of him wonders if he dreamt it.

"Would you like to come over tonight? Maybe we'll eat at home or get something in the neighborhood. And then I can beat you at checkers or chess."

Martin chuckles. "Wonderful. Yes. Thank you for the invitation."

Thirty seconds later, the writers have corralled Martin and are asking about the New Glory challenge. He discusses it, then asks if they know anything about baseball in New Glory, if any of them has been there. F. C. Lane's hand goes up.

Martin and Lane walk along the first-base line into the outfield, Martin kicking the occasional rock into foul territory. F. C. says, "It's a beautiful country. The natives are wonderful. The New Gloryers, not so much. You see Negroes in chains walking through the street led by white men. For a while, women of property were allowed to vote, but that's been taken away. Contraception is illegal. The prisons are full to bursting. There's public dueling—I saw a duel where one of the duelists was shot in the heart and died. But they love their baseball. They play beautifully. They have one pitcher, Walter Johnson, who is eighteen years old and might throw harder than anyone in the big leagues."

*"Walter Johnson!"*

"You've heard of him?"

Martin figures if it is *the* Walter Johnson, *the* Walter Johnson is/was one of the best, hardest-throwing pitchers in the history of baseball. But Walter Johnson was from Kansas. "How did Walter Johnson get to New Glory?"

"Probably born there." Lane continues, "And then, of course, there are the Cobbs. There's something wrong with them. A little slight, a hard slide into Hellcat Cobb at second base, a close call—anything is a pretext for a fistfight. And they're all ready at the drop of a hat. The country, though—they've taken over the Cayman Islands, Turks and Caicos, Anguilla, Dominica, Aruba, St. Lucia, Curaçao, part of Panama, mines and oil fields in Venezuela. It's all military, all the time. They seem to disdain, or distrust, peace. They conquer and enslave. But this series, this Solar Series—I guess they don't want to call it the Civil Series—" Lane smiles at his quip. "I suppose it's a way for them to try to soothe relations with the US. Or it's a way to gain equal footing—at least on the stage of baseball."

"Sounds like a very happy place."

"How much are they offering? No one at either league will say yet."

"Well, you didn't hear it from me. Three hundred thousand for the winning team, thirty thousand for the losing. A million for the winning league."

*"Three hundred thousand?* On a team of seventeen players, that's eighteen thousand each! That's more than Mathewson makes in a year!"

"Don't forget the manager." Martin winks. "But this team has a mountain to climb before we're in position to go to Cuba—I mean New Glory. This whole New Glory idea is a pleasant fantasy for the Giants. A dream."

"Whoa." Lane gazes up at the sky. "Look at that!"

The buzzing of an engine. A biplane cruises a hundred feet above the field, the pilot waving to the players below. Velez and Blent are standing in the outfield in their baggy, flannel uniforms and caps. Along with everyone else, they are gazing up at the yellow biplane.

| NEW YORK | | PHILADELPHIA | |
|---|---|---|---|
| CF | ROGER BRESNAHAN | CF | ROY THOMAS |
| RF | SPIKE SHANNON | 1B | KITTY BRANSFIELD |
| 2B | JOHNNY BLENT | LF | JERRY DONOVAN |
| 1B | ANDRÉ VELAY | 3B | ERNIE COURTNEY |
| LF | MIKE DONLIN | RF | JOHN TITUS |
| 3B | ART DEVLIN | SS | MICKEY DOOLIN |
| SS | BILL DAHLEN | 2B | KID GLEASON |
| C | FRANK BOWERMAN | C | RED DOOIN |
| P | C. MATHEWSON | P | TULLY SPARKS |

Martin sits at the end of the bench staring at the names on the Phillies lineup card. It's a bunch of no-names, except for Kid Gleason, who went on to become the manager of the 1919 White Sox—who intentionally lost the World Series for a gambler's bribe.

But the fact that this Philadelphia team is a bunch of fellows whose names didn't survive the test of time doesn't mean much; Martin's team was just swept by the equally-forgotten-by-posterity Boston Beaneaters. And the unsettling comparison is played out on the lumpy field:

|  | 1 | 2 | 3 | 4 | 5 | 6 | 7 | 8 | 9 | R | H | E |
|---|---|---|---|---|---|---|---|---|---|---|---|---|
| Phila. | 0 | 0 | 1 | 0 | 0 | 1 | 1 | 0 | 0 | 3 | 5 | 2 |
| New York | 0 | 0 | 0 | 1 | 0 | 0 | 0 | 0 | 1 | 2 | 5 | 1 |

That evening in the Mathewson/McGraw living room, Mathewson is contemplating a chessboard and a book of tactics, while Martin stares at the *New York Post* baseball page. Martin groans.

His eyes not diverting from a rook-king fork, Mathewson responds, "It will all turn around. We hit the ball right at 'em. Hooks pitched well."

"Losing is losing." Martin rises for the small table in the corner that serves as a bar. He pours a tall bourbon. He'd love a handful of ice for his drink—the Mathewsons' icebox is bereft.

Mathewson beats Martin in five games of checkers while they discuss New Glory and the Solar Series challenge. They dine on Mrs. Mathewson's pot roast—hard as a book cover on the outside, raw in the middle, juicy and aromatic in the in-between bands. After dinner, the men smoke cigars and play chess. Mathewson wins the first game in ten moves, the second game in seven. He plays the next without his queen and wins.

\*

Early the next morning, in a room on the tenth floor of the Hotel Seville on 29th and Madison Avenue, Velez is standing naked at the window and gazing at the rising sun. Nicole sleeps on her side. He glances over. *She's hot, man. And nice.* Niceness had never before entered into the equation. *And smart.* Got to get the trimmer out for certain patches of hair: a delicate discussion. He'd cut his hair any way she wanted. She's amazing, and he's ready again.

As he turns to the sun his smile evaporates with a mental image from right after yesterday's loss: Martin gritting his teeth as he trudged across the field to the clubhouse. Even the fans on the field, swirling around every ballplayer, balked when approaching Martin, sensing his surliness. To Velez, it was just one of those games where the team hit the ball hard, but the balls were caught—can't do anything about those. Another day, with the same sharply hit balls, they'd have piled up a dozen runs. Keep plugging along. Keep getting better. But sure, he doesn't want Martin to get canned.

*

That afternoon things suck further as balls clang off Giants' gloves, Velez is picked off first base, Chicago wins against St. Louis, and the Giants fall to eighteen games behind.

As Martin pulls on his street clothes in the clubhouse, the embarrassment has percolated to every pore of his body, and he considers not going down to the Flatiron. If this losing continues, he wonders how much longer Senior will stay with him. *Maybe the hitting grids, spray charts, and pitching charts don't work in 1906?*

Six glasses of scotch do not aid his sleep, as he feels the sword of Damocles hanging over him. The specter of selling shoes makes him groan, grunt, grit his teeth, and wince all through the night.

In the morning, the team coalesces at Pennsylvania Station for the ride to St. Louis. They'll play their way back through Chicago, Cincinnati, Pittsburg, and Philly. Two and a half weeks on the road. The ballplayers are cheerily greeted by porters and conductors.

"Mr. Donlin!" a tall, skinny porter in a white uniform gets Turkey Mike's attention, telling Mike, "I got the Cleer Beer! A new batch!"

"My old pal George!" Donlin exclaims.

After switching trains in Chicago, Martin is cozily asleep in a berth. Blent is a berth over, snoring faintly. Far away, a gun blasts. Martin and Blent do not stir.

Five cars ahead, in the dining car, Velez takes a shot of a drink the other players are calling Cleer Beer, but it is not clear, and it is not beer. It is a milky moonshine sold in half-pint bottles at forty cents apiece—three for a dollar—by the tall, skinny porter, who right now is screaming, *"No! No! No Mr. Dahlen! No!"* rushing at Bill Dahlen and Dahlen's smoking six-shooter, aimed at the roof, which a .38 caliber bullet has just punctured. Dahlen, whose fielding glove is on his other hand, snappily extends his glove arm and smashes the onrushing porter in the throat, crumpling him to the floor. The ballplayers laugh, tipple bottles of Cleer Beer, then drag the porter out of the way.

All other civilians have abandoned the dining car except for two fat insurance salesmen from Toledo imbibing Cleer Beer at the last table, enthusiastically smiling at the World's Champions. There's also a woman mid-car at a table with Bresnahan and Bowerman, the three of them before a small glass pitcher that is one-part Cleer Beer and one-part lemonade, while the woman squirmingly appreciates the two Giants catchers running their strong, smashed, and scraped fingers over her.

"That's first base!" Dahlen announces. He takes ten steps back, aims his gun at the roof, blasts a hole. "That's second base!"

"I can't see it!" Donlin complains.

Dahlen shoots three holes in a cluster in the roof. *"How's that?"*

"Better! Throw the ball!" Donlin wiggles the bat.

Eight feet away from Donlin, Velez, in his mind manning "third base," is wearing Bresnahan's padding and mask.

Wiltse rears and fires a fastball, a bit inside, Donlin pulling in his hands and turning, bat cracking ball into Velez's gut—somewhat protected by Bresnahan's padding. The ball bounces away as Donlin tears down the aisle. Velez grabs it and flings the ball halfway down the car to Wiltse under "second," who snags it and slaps the tag on the sliding Donlin.

*"Out!"* Ames shouts. The whole car erupts—save the porters and the woman being petted by the Giants' catchers.

Though tagged out, even Donlin is smiling, tickled at the game that he, with a bit of help from the others, has just invented.

*Bam!* The barrel of Ames' gun smolders. The window nearest is a shattered glass spiderweb centered by a hole the size of a grapefruit. *"One out!"* he announces.

"I'm hitting next!" Velez insists, shedding the mask and chest protector, as shots ring out.

Eight handguns obliterate windows and further puncture the roof.

*"Two outs!"*

*"Three outs!"*

*"Four outs!"*

*"Five outs!"*

Appearing in the window of the door to the dining car is the face of the train's conductor, whose expression of bugged eyes and screaming mouth was last triggered two months before as the train plowed into an Oldsmobile stalled on the tracks at a crossing outside of Jackson, Mississippi. *"Open up, Goddamn it!"* The conductor pounds on the door as porters frantically attempt to unstick the lock, which has been jammed shut by Bresnahan and Browne with the Cleer Beer porter's key. *"You're destroying Illinois Central property!"*

From the opposite side of the car, Martin pounds on the door. "Let me in!"

Mike Donlin puts his hand up to his ear as if he can't hear Martin, which convulses the drunk players in laughter. Velez's revelry vanishes as he spots the face of his manager, and for a moment Velez considers opening the door, then not wanting to piss off his teammates, Velez lays down, pretending to pass out.

An axe shatters glass. Ballplayers rush over Velez's outstretched legs, fleeing.

Martin pushes into the car. *"Stop!"* he screams at them. *"Stop! What the hell is wrong with you?"*

They flee like rats.

*

At 6:05 a.m., in a vestibule in the lobby of the Terminal Hotel, Bucky Martin holds a phone, breaking the news of the shot-up train to John T. Brush, Sr., who digests the information. "McGraw never had these problems. I expect you to gain control."

Martin replies, "That is my plan, Mr. Br—" before Brush hangs up.

Identical telegrams are sent, one to John T. Brush, Sr., the other to Bucky Martin.

```
BILL FOR DAMAGE TO TRAIN AND
EXTRA SECURITY FORCES SIX
THOUSAND, FIVE HUNDRED AND
FORTY DOLLARS AND EIGHTEEN
CENTS UNTIL REMITTANCE IN FULL
NEW YORK BALL CLUB "GIANTS"
AND ALL PERSONNEL BANNED
FROM ILLINOIS CENTRAL
```

# 18

## Sober and Clearheaded

SOBER AND CLEARHEADED, Martin, Blent, and Mathewson ride a taxi to Robison Field. Martin tells them, "I had to make a list of who I saw in that car, so I could telegram it to Brush. I got twelve names. It's about five hundred dollars each. Mr. Brush is giving them half pay until they make it up. Some of them might never make it up."

At the ballpark, St. Louis manager McCloskey approaches Martin. "Congratulations on the job. You owe me twenty-five dollars from when I sold Blent to New York. He didn't play three games for me, and our agreement was for fifty dollars for six games." McCloskey continues spouting his bizarre accounting as Martin's hungover players lug canvas bags of bats and balls toward the bench.

Martin finally cuts off McCloskey. "Where's the beef?" he says, hoping the non sequitur will sufficiently confuse McCloskey into leaving him alone.

"What the hell is that supposed to mean?"

"Where's the beef? You know—Where. Is. It?"

| | NEW YORK | | ST. LOUIS |
|---|---|---|---|
| CF | ROGER BRESNAHAN | RF | AL BURCH |
| RF | CY SEYMOUR | 2B | PUG BENNETT |
| 1B | ANDRÉ VELAY | LF | RED MURRAY |
| 2B | JOHNNY BLENT | CF | HOMER SMOOT |
| LF | MIKE DONLIN | 1B | JAKE BECKLEY |
| 3B | ART DEVLIN | 3B | HARRY ARNDT |
| SS | BILL DAHLEN | SS | GEORGE McBRIDE |
| C | FRANK BOWERMAN | C | MIKE GRADY |
| P | C. MATHEWSON | P | SLIM SALLEE |

Bottom of the 1st. Al Burch knocks an outshoot through the middle for a single.

As Mathewson winds up for the next pitch, in left field Turkey Mike twists away from the stands and vomits. Center fielder Bresnahan frantically waves his arms to get the field umpire's attention, yelling, *"Time! Time! Time!"*—too late—as Mathewson releases the ball and Burch takes off for second. Bowerman's throw to second sails over Dahlen, bounces in the outfield toward Bresnahan. Burch pops up and scoots to third. Blent takes the throw from Bresnahan, glares out at Donlin, who is wiping his mouth on the back of his wrist.

From the bench, Martin barks, *"What the hell was that?"*

Bennett singles. Burch scores.

## NEW YORK   0 — 1   ST. LOUIS

Murray bunts up the third-base line, Devlin charging, picking up the throw, too late to get Bennett at second or Murray crossing first. Bennett, rounding second, notices Dahlen wandering toward the outfield, and Devlin holding the ball while exchanging a word with Bowerman near home plate, leaving third base unattended. Bennett blasts for third, catching Mathewson, Dahlen, and Devlin flat-footed. Murray scoots in safely to second, laughing.

Martin yells, *"Wake the fuck up!"*

Mathewson strikes out Homer Smoot. Jake Beckley smacks a fly ball to deep left, all the Giants holding their breath as Donlin retreats on it, all the Giants wondering if Donlin is in any condition to catch the ball until it drops from the sky into his glove. He fires to shortstop Dahlen. Murray scores on the sacrifice fly.

## NEW YORK  0 — 2  ST. LOUIS

Harry Arndt pokes a fastball that Velez, with a leap, snares to end the inning.

Martin bellows, *"Everyone in here!"* He grabs Blent's elbow, keeping him from going to the plate to lead off. The motley crew of Giants hesitantly gathers. Martin takes a moment to look each of his players in the eye. "Right now is the time that most of you have to decide if you are ballplayers or drunks!"

Turkey Mike peeps, "How 'bout both?"

Half the team erupts in hungover chuckling.

Martin thunders, *"You can't be both!"* He spins to Donlin and screams, *"You want to go right now? I'll destroy you!"*

Velez, Blent, and Mathewson step between Martin and Donlin. They force Martin back. Neck veins bulging, eyes wild—reminding many of McGraw's expression the moment before he keeled over—Martin screams at Donlin, *"Answer me right the hell now!"*

Donlin's mouth opens. He glances at Devlin, Dahlen, Bresnahan, McGinnity—they're all waiting for him to do something, and he feels better since he threw up in the outfield. He rushes Martin, tackling him and driving him to the ground, the back of Martin's head whacking the dirt. Martin only knows two ways to fight—go for the eyes or punch the throat—and figuring that he doesn't want to blind Donlin, even though Donlin is on top of him, punching him, Martin rips at Donlin's throat, jamming his thumb into the Adam's apple, driving it back to his spine. Suddenly Donlin is rising off of Martin as if Martin's thumb has the strength of Superman's, but it is ballplayers all lifting handfuls of Donlin like he's a 180-pound sack of furious snakes. They drop Donlin on the ground and stand between him and Martin.

Mathewson screams at Donlin, *"Do not get up!"*

Martin rises. Bowerman gives him his cap. Martin's waving his hands bellowing, *"I'm fine! I'm fine! I'm fine!"* He looks for Blent, who's bent over Donlin. Martin pokes Blent in the ribs, *"Go hit!"*

Donlin shakes off help as he crabs his way to the end of the bench, surrounded by his friends. Taking a seat between Mathewson and Wiltse, Martin tells McGinnity, "Coach third." Martin rests his head back on the wall, crosses his legs. His head is ringing. Someone—Wiltse—is giving off an odor like rotten gouda cheese.

Rising, Martin gingerly jogs behind the St. Louis catcher, to McGinnity who's standing near third. "I'm gonna coach." As he turns to the field, a fan in the stands yells, *"Hey Buck! Nice fight! Did Donlin throw up on you, too?"* Martin gazes down at the sparse grass between his cleats. He has an urge to be alone, cordoned off from the drunken crap his team seems to revel in. He is trying to fend off feelings of hate for Donlin and any of the other guys. Hate will fester and bad decisions are made from hate. He exhales hard, then looks up at Blent in the batter's box, glances round at the half-full ballpark, recalling their few days in St. Louis as Blent resurrected his career.

At the end of the inning, New York having failed to score, Martin walks across the diamond. Turkey Mike is coming his way, grinning his stubby, tobacco-stained teeth. Mike extends his hand, and croaks, "Sorry."

Martin hesitates, then shakes the hand, looks up into the sun-creased face. "You okay?"

Donlin croaks, "Yeah." He attempts to clear his throat, whispers, "You got me good."

Top of the 3rd. Mathewson leads off with a single. Bresnahan, sweating alcohol, walks. Cy Seymour fouls out to first.

Mathewson leads off second, Bresnahan off first. One out.

Velez is batting third in the order, Blent batting behind, Martin hoping that opposing pitchers won't walk Velez so much.

Velez's stomach is sour from the Cleer Beer. "Damn," Velez mumbles, while the catcher, Grady, is prattling about a new brothel with Indian women and a woman *from* India. "You can find a squaw!"

Velez decides to wait for a fastball and if it's a curve to let it go, look for something on the outside corner and drive it over shortstop. He zeroes in on the spot where Sallee's left hand will release the ball and in his mind, tells Sallee, "You bastard."

Fastball *whoooooosh!* heading for the outside corner, Velez *craaaaack!* smacking it to left-center. Velez is slow out of the box, churning, arms pumping, as he sees the ball bouncing past the outfielders. He glances at first as he rounds it, hustling toward second as the strong throw zips in to shortstop, the second baseman yelling, *"Home! Home! Home!"* the shortstop wheeling and firing home as Bresnahan's slide jets up a cloud of dirt. *"Safe!"* Bill Klem bellows. Bresnahan pops to his feet, and to a beaming Mathewson, slaps a high five.

## NEW YORK  2 — 2  ST. LOUIS

Clusters of New York fans cheer.

Blent singles, moving Velez to third.

On the second pitch to Donlin—a sharp curve—Blent steals second. Donlin knocks a single to right. Velez and Blent score. They tack on another run.

Bottom of the 9th. Two outs. Mathewson pauses, his right hand and glove at his chest. He rocks back and fires a fastball over the outside corner that Beckley slaps toward third, Devlin charging, midstride flinging the ball to Velez, and the ball beats Beckley by a quarter-step.

## NEW YORK  5 — 2  ST. LOUIS   FINAL

The victory is sweetened when the team is greeted by the doormen at the Terminal Hotel with the news that both Chicago and Pittsburg lost.

Ten minutes after a bath, dressed and fresh, standing in the hallway, Martin addresses his gathered ballplayers (no one can find Cy Seymour). Martin scans the pack. Aside from Velez and Blent, the players' body language expresses varying degrees of apprehension, trust, hostility, insolence, and disdain.

"I am inviting all of you—each and every one—to dinner. I am paying." Bodies lose stiffness; face muscles soften. Martin tries not to single out Turkey Mike with his gaze, continuing, "Now listen. I like a drink almost as much as most of you." Some of the guys chuckle. "But at this dinner, there won't be any drinking." Shocked expressions indicate that digestion may well-nigh be impossible without alcoholic lubrication. "No booze. No wine. No beer. If some of you choose not to come along, that is your choice. After the dinner, though, we can order a round of drinks. Nice game today."

Most of the players have to modify evening plans, but all of them make their way to the two large tables in a corner of the Terminal Hotel main dining room. McGinnity examines the lime-painted wall, and holding his finger on an indentation, announces, "Right here! Last year Red's steak was so full of gristle that he got a hammer and a nail and pounded the fucking steak to the wall!" The Giants roar.

\*

At the expense of the St. Louis pitchers, the Giants carrousel around the bases over the next two days:

NEW YORK  7 — 2  ST. LOUIS  FINAL

NEW YORK  11 — 1  ST. LOUIS  FINAL

Meanwhile Chicago splits its last two with Boston, and Pittsburg loses two. The Giants are seventeen games behind Chicago.

Chomping steaks in the swaying dining car on the way to Chicago (Brush, Sr. having negotiated a settlement for damages with the Illinois Central), Martin dines with Blent and Velez. Sotto vocce, Martin says, "The 1978 Yankees were fourteen and a half games behind the Red Sox, and the Yankees won. I think that's the biggest deficit from July that a team has ever come back to win." He asks, "How're you guys adjusting?"

Velez stretches his arms; one hand assesses the other arm's triceps. "I'm weaker, man. I don't have anyone waking me up at six a.m. with a green smoothie and a perfect shot of espresso with a tiny sliver of lemon peel, then off we go work out."

Blent says, "Every time the train stops, I expect to see my wife and baby daughter waiting for me on the platform."

Martin tries to console with a crack. "It gets easier after three wives." He raises his fist, the knuckles a few shades of red and pink. "Just fighting for my job."

"I was impressed!" Blent laughs.

"I knew you had him," Velez comments. "He was sick and hungover. Probably saw six of you."

\*

John T. Brush, Jr. is waiting in the lobby bar of Chicago's Ambassador East Hotel when the team trundles in. Ten minutes later, in Martin's room, Junior and Martin pore over Junior's recent work, integrating significant numbers of at-bats for each of the Cubs' eight starting hitters.

Martin examines the nine-box grid of Joe Tinker's strike zone. It shows where, in the zone, or out of the zone, Tinker has made contact, and whether the result was an out or a hit. It notes whether the hit was a single, double, triple, or homer. The grid shows that Tinker gets a lot of hits with low-and-away pitches but has only gotten one hit with a pitch up-and-away. So he is potentially vulnerable to a high strike on the outside part of the plate.

"Fantastic work."

"Sometimes people ask what I'm doing. I tell them I am sketching the players. I have one ready." Junior pulls out a child-like scribbling of a batter hitting a ball. "That quiets them!"

While poring over the information, Martin says, "I am considering a lineup shift. Art Devlin's on-base percentage is .412. Bresnahan's is .355. I am batting Devlin leadoff. I like moving Blent, Velay and Donlin up one notch. Another at-bat per game can mean something."

Junior excuses himself due to a bit of intestinal distress, and soon there's a knock. It's thin, elegantly dressed Nikola Tesla.

As Tesla takes to the heavily indented, warmed chair Junior occupied, Martin phones the front desk to have a boy retrieve Blent and Velez, who soon arrive.

After trying to explain what went wrong at the Bellamy Theater, Tesla says, "I had a colleague in New Glory—a Swiss-German who has fallen in love with baseball. Ein-shtein. He goes to many games."

"*The* Einstein?" Martin asks. "*Albert* Einstein?"

"You've heard of him?"

"E equals MC squared."

"He was on a pair of shoes I had," says Velez.

Blent adds, "As were you, Mr. Tesla."

"You know of E equals MC squared? Is everyone so intelligent in the future?"

"As many idiots then as now," Velez replies. "More. You should see the destruction."

"We screwed the environment . . . " Blent shakes his head.

Tesla asks a long series of questions about twenty-first-century technology, transportation, communications, electronics, medical systems, societal structures. For the ballplayers it's a bit of talk therapy, to be revealing their past/future to a smart stranger.

Velez asks, "How you doing on getting us back?"

Tesla ignores the question for the moment. "Einstein and I were so very excited by his E equals MC squared discovery. We both grasped the implications immediately. We soon began searching for the heaviest elements in the world, wondering if it would be possible to observe a nuclear reaction, then wondering if we could control it. The uranium comes from Venezuela. The reactor design is mine. The bomb design is mine. But I've been cut off from Einstein. My most recent report from him is nearly three years old. Do you have nuclearized weapons in your century?"

"Thousands."

"How destructive are they?"

Martin tells him and Tesla scoffs, "Politicians! And Einstein despises New Glory as much as I, though I must say, they *do* support research and scientific construction. Mr. Ford is minister of science. Perhaps you're familiar with him?"

"Henry Ford? Yes."

"As long as we were building armaments—or if our research had even a tangential relation to armaments, the money came in. That society is all about armaments. Building and selling those armaments abroad. The amount of money they generate is staggering. A world awash in powerful armaments! *They* have no vision of the future. Everything is an all-consuming, angry present, or near-future dominated by accumulation and greed. Perhaps it is the definition of insanity."

Blent asks, "Where are all of your security guards?" to which Tesla chuckles, "Every so often I need a respite."

Velez asks again, *"Time travel?"*

"Actually, Mr. Velay, I am having difficulty with it. I do not see how it is possible," quickly adding, "though I do not dispute your claim to be from the future!"

Velez groans. "You came here to tell us you have no idea how time travel works?"

Tesla glances at the floor. "Since the, um, accident at the Bellamy Theater, my funding has been curtailed. Drastically. Fortunately, I have convinced Mr. Westinghouse that there is great potential in what you call 'the cell phone.' So with funding comes money that I can appropriate to experiments dedicated to time travel. This has not yet happened. But if you provide answers to my questions about cell phones, then I can provide more resources to time travel."

"I don't want to talk about cell phones!" Velez snarls. "I want to go back to my life!" He wonders about bringing Nicole with him to the twenty-first century. *Would she like it?*

Tesla says, "The situation is this: You were transported here. There must be a way to transport you back. Cell phones, gentlemen, please."

They teach Tesla about "on" buttons, satellites, speakers, earpieces, cell towers, nuclear power plants, uranium, tritium—Velez goes off about the lack of speedometers in 1906 cars.

Tesla is staring at Martin. "Sir, is that a normal growth? That bump?"

Martin's hand goes to his neck. Velez gently pulls Martin's hand down. There are lumps on the sides of Martin's neck as large as leeches. Blent is stunned.

"The cancer again?" Velez asks.

Martin waves a hand. "Let's not worry about it."

Blent asks Tesla, "Do you know a good oncologist?"

"If you will permit me to discreetly inquire with Mr. Westinghouse in this matter—the wealthy always know the best doctors."

\*

Arrangements are swiftly made and at 7 a.m.—July 4th—they meet Dr. Wessells, a vibrant, pasty man. He assures them of his discretion, though on the wall is a photo taken from the roof of the grandstand of a game in progress at the West Side Grounds, and another of him posing with Chicago's Frank Chance.

He pinches the enlarged nodes about as thick as a pinkie on each side of Martin's neck and ones a little smaller in his upper legs near his groin.

"What's your fee?" Martin asks.

"It's all taken care of."

"Mr. Westinghouse paying? I've never met him. It's really not right."

Velez bursts, "For God's sake, Buck, don't worry about the money!"

Doctor Wessells concludes, "I would like to look at a piece of one of these under a microscope."

Velez asks, "Cancer?"

Martin snaps, "Of course it's cancer!" And to the doctor, calmly, "Do you have treatments?"

"Once I have a look at the tumor under a slide, if it is cancer, I usually recommend a lumpectomy."

"What's that?" Velez asks.

"They cut the tumors off." Martin asks the doctor, "Do they grow back?"

The doctor scratches his ear, frowns. "Yes. But we have given the patients some more time." Reacting to the disappointment, he adds, "If you do nothing, you have, perhaps, two months before the enlarged nodes either cut off airflow or cut off blood flow causing a heart attack or stroke."

They wait for the doc to offer other options as he prods further.

Martin pushes the doc's hands away. "You have no medications?"

"For cancer?" The doctor chuckles.

"Is anyone working on medications?" Blent asks. "Working on treatment with certain kinds of poisons to poison the tumors?"

"Not that I know of."

Blent persists, "And is this the best research hospital in Chicago?"

"We consider it the best in the world."

In the taxi on the way to the ballpark, Velez and Blent can't convince Martin to commit to the lumpectomy or even to the biopsy.

"It's not going to tell us anything. I know what I've got. I've had it before. Let's play ball." From his portfolio he removes the grid for Chicago pitcher Ed Reulbach.

Blent asks, "Is there a cure in the twenty-first century?"

"When it came up before, I had one injection. Then pills. One pill a week. That did the trick—kept it away. I don't know if you call it a perfect cure, but it managed the cancer, sort of permanently. And there were some cures, but they were sort of drastic. Didn't think I needed it back then."

*

Sandwiched between marching bands, the Giants and Cubs amble onto the West Side Grounds in two sloppy parallel lines. Leading the parade is cheerful, drunk Mayor Eddie Dunne. The grandstand is decorated in red-white-and-blue bunting.

Mayor Dunne's July Fourth speech concludes, "We cannot in good conscience stand by while small sovereign nations of the Caribbean are overrun by naked New Glory aggression! Ladies and gentlemen, this war is not over until New Glory is completely and utterly defeated!" Most of the crowd roars in delight. Scattered pistols blast up into the sky. Blent glances down the line at Bucky Martin, who is toeing a clump of loose grass.

| | NEW YORK | | CHICAGO |
|---|---|---|---|
| 3B | ART DEVLIN | CF | JIMMY SLAGLE |
| 2B | JOHNNY BLENT | LF | JIMMY SHECKARD |
| 1B | ANDRÉ VELAY | RF | FRANK SCHULTE |
| LF | MIKE DONLIN | 1B | FRANK CHANCE |
| C | R. BRESNAHAN | 3B | HARRY STEINFELDT |
| SS | BILL DAHLEN | SS | JOE TINKER |

| RF | GEORGE BROWNE | 2B | JOHNNY EVERS |
|---|---|---|---|
| CF | SPIKE SHANNON | C | JOHNNY KLING |
| P | HOOKS WILTSE | P | ORVAL OVERALL |

In the first game of the double header, Cubs pitcher Orval Overall's curve is flatter than usual, and the Giants get to him for nine hits. None of the Giants outwardly complain to Martin about the reworked Giants lineup, as Wiltse keeps a clamp on Chicago.

## NEW YORK 4 — 1 CHICAGO FINAL GM1

In the second game Chicago bursts ahead to a 4–0 lead against McGinnity: a pair of runs in the first, one in the fourth, and one in the fifth. In the top of the 6th, Velez drives in Devlin with a single. Bresnahan knocks in two with a long double.

## NEW YORK 3 — 4 CHICAGO

Top of the 7th. After McGinnity and Devlin strike out, New York raps five line drives in a row, scoring four runs, Bresnahan knocking in two more.

## NEW YORK 7 — 4 CHICAGO

Bottom of the 9th. Steinfeldt, Chance, and Kling swat back-to-back-to-back singles, scoring Steinfeldt.

## NEW YORK 7 — 5 CHICAGO

Tinker walks, loading the bases. Evers works McGinnity to 3–2, fouls off two pitches. On a low-and-inside curve, Evers pops it sky-high between first and second. Blent settles under it as Evers screams, *"Motherfucker! Drop the ball!"* Blent catches it. Velez screams at Evers, *"Shut up, you jerkwad!"* Evers charges Velez, poking his pencil fingers into Velez's chest. Velez is a foot taller and a hundred pounds heavier, and he shoves Evers—a ball of wire. Evers ducks his head and plows into Velez's middle, rabbit-punching Velez's kidney as Giants and Cubs erupt from their benches. Evers keeps punching while Velez tries to rip off Evers' head as Chicago players and fans are swarming Velez and tearing at him.

Fans turn on New York players, punching them and getting punched in return. Devlin, Donlin, Bresnahan, Bowerman, George Browne, Cy Seymour chase down assailants and punch them to the ground. Bottles twirl through the air. Blood is running down the side of Blent's face near his eye, a bottle-wielding hooligan laughing and pointing. Heavy dishes brought from home become discuses, knives and forks bounce off players and fans, glass beer steins catapult.

Channeling McGraw assaulting that fan at the beginning of the season, Martin goes for the bottle-wielding fan, who screams as Martin's finger indents the assailant's left eyeball. Martin rips the bottle out of his hand, turns to Blent, who is up, holding his eye socket.

Chance is screaming, *"Stop! Stop Stop!"*

Chicago police club fans, and the field slowly drains of civilians.

Martin applies gauze and tape to Blent's cut above his eyebrow. "You want to come out?"

"No way in fucking Hell!"

As the most pugnacious and drunk Chicago fans continue screaming at the New York players, a dozen of them pounding on the wooden roof of the New York bench, McGinnity pitches a 2–0 curve to Frank Schulte who hits a medium-slow grounder right at Blent, who takes the easy out at first base, Frank Chance scoring.

## NEW YORK  7 — 6  CHICAGO

Kling at third, Tinker at second. Two outs.

Bench player Doc Gessler bats for Reulbach. Gessler chops the first pitch between Velez and Blent, Blent knocking it down, scrambling after it, tossing hard to McGinnity covering first, who snags it two steps ahead of Gessler. *Ouuuuuut!*

The Giants sprint toward the clubhouse as Chicago fans boil over onto the field, throwing bottles at the Giants, attempting punches, tearing at uniforms, grabbing at caps clutched in Giant hands.

## NEW YORK  7 — 6  CHICAGO  FINAL  GM2

Baseball writers revel in scribbling about subjects other than the movement of the stitched, horsehide-shod ball. The Chicago newspapers state that Chief Velay started the fight, while New York papers declare it was Evers.

The next day, under thunderous booing and shouting, a phalanx of policemen escort the Giants from the clubhouse to the bench, then disperse through the stands, keeping a lookout for disorder. As Velez approaches home plate, he is the focus of the afternoon's loudest booing. He tips his cap to the grandstand, to the outfield bleachers. Velez smiles at Kling and umpire O'Day. There's something relaxing about the booing, emanating, as it does, from the wooden grandstand and the ring of bleachers; it is not bouncing off concrete, steel, or plastic; there's no sound system blasting the most current pop song; right now—this—is a tidal wave of deep-throated humanity.

Four photographers squat twenty feet away in foul ground, pointing their boxy cameras at Velez. He holds his pose, "Got it, boys?" He smiles down at Blent at first who walked in front of him. He smiles at Martin, the third-base coach. Some of the booing turns to laughter as Cubs fans recognize and appreciate Velez's joyful insouciance.

Velez smacks a low-and-away slider to left. As he runs to first, he claps his hands, the Chicago fans screaming at him, and a bottle flies out from the stands, first-base coach Christy Mathewson ducking as the spinning clear bottle enters Mathewson's peripheral vision. Police flood the section of stands from which the bottle emerged.

The Giants lose this game, but win the finale.

*

The train ride to Pittsburg is happy, having taken three of four from Chicago. Velez and Blent share a dining car table with Mathewson and Turkey Mike, all having downed steaks, baked potatoes, and candied carrots. Patting his stomach, Velez asks, "What if you could take a little pill or injection, and it would make you stronger?"

Blent blinks, stunned that Velez is bringing up the subject of performance-enhancing drugs. Lord knows Velez doesn't need the drugs; he's hitting .410 / .517 / .599.

To Mathewson, Velez informs, "Your fastball would be a little bit faster." To Donlin, "You'd feel stronger batting. You'd sting more line drives. Your batting average would rise. Some of your singles would be doubles. Some of your doubles would be triples."

Mathewson responds, "That's why many guys chew. They think it gives them an edge. Of course, their body acclimates to it so they have to chew larger and larger portions."

Donlin nods, "Yup!" as he lights a cigar.

Velez persists, "But suppose there *was* a little pill, that you took once a week or so."

Blent adds, "But this pill and all those like it have been banned from baseball. They're called performance-enhancing drugs."

"They have them in California?" Donlin asks.

"No!" Blent assures them. "It's just something we talk about. Our imaginary world."

Donlin's eyes narrow.

Velez continues, "This pill can be the difference between being a career minor leaguer and being a major leaguer. It can be the difference between being an average major leaguer and being at the top. It can be the difference between being at the top and being one of the greatest players ever. On the other hand, you have to be a scientist to know what's going into those drugs and the negative effects on your body. Would you take it?"

"If it's against the rules, it's against the rules," says Mathewson. "My answer is no."

His crow's feet fanning as he grins, Donlin slowly emits a cumulus cloud of cigar smoke. "Intriguing."

Blent presses Donlin, "You'd take the pill?"

"Make me better? Give me that edge every day, that edge you lose when it's a hundred degrees and the sun is baking your head off and you're hungover; all you're thinking about is a cool shower but it's only the second inning? Yeah, I'll take that pill! Gladly! With joy!" He holds out his hand, faking an Italian accent, "Give-a me one!"

Velez chuckles at the insensitive raciscm. Matty's amused smile at Donlin's roguish personality oddly matches Donlin's smile.

*

Over the next seven games in Pittsburg and Cincinnati, the Giants win five and lose two. In the sole Pittsburg loss, a 9–2 blowout in which the speed of Mathewson's fastball diminished in the third, fourth, and fifth innings, for the players the highlight of the game was watching Martin stride out to the mound with a glove. All the infielders were laughing.

Martin threw curves and knuckleballs, occasional mid eighties fastballs, and one spitter which hit the dirt ten feet in front of Bresnahan. Enjoying working with Bresnahan, Martin's hips and arm aching, the Giants thoroughly amused, Martin let up only one run. In his one at-bat he sliced a low-and-away fastball down first that made Mathewson, the first-base coach, dance, and made the rest of the team bust a gut. But that's as close to a hit as Martin got, swinging over a curve for strike three.

The train screeches and lurches to a stop, shaking Martin awake in his seat. An unevenly-illuminated sign: Harrisburg. He flew in to Harrisburg once, a December a few years back, and spent a sleety, exhilarating day in wet sneakers touring the battlefield of Gettysburg, about 35 miles away. He wished he'd had more time. If he could get there now, perhaps it could give a clue about why General McClellan was there, answer why the South won the Battle of Gettysburg, and when this world's history diverged from his, Velez and Blent's. The train shudders forward with no answers.

In Philadelphia, Bowerman and Wiltse show up to the first game drunk; Martin fines each ten dollars. Bowerman threatens to fight Martin, but Bowerman is overwhelmed by all the Irish. McGinnity pitches a shutout. They sweep the three games from the Phillies.

That evening, train clacking, Martin stares out the window at the little brick houses of Trenton, then ponders the standings in his *Philadelphia Record*:

|          | W L   | PCT  | GB    |
|----------|-------|------|-------|
| Chicago  | 49-30 | .633 | —     |
| Pittsburg | 42-34 | .553 | 5½   |
| Philadelphia | 36-39 | .480 | 11 |
| New York | 35-39 | .473 | 11½  |
| Cincinnati | 38-43 | .469 | 12  |
| Brooklyn | 29-41 | .400 | 17½  |
| Boston   | 27-48 | .397 | 20    |
| St. Louis | 30-46 | .395 | 22½  |

In the pocket of his wool sports jacket, he removes the bill from the Terminal Hotel in St. Louis. On the back of the envelope, he scribbles:

$$1906 - 45 \over 1861$$

He is astonished. In this world, he was born the same year the Civil War started. Abraham Lincoln was president.

Christy Mathewson stops by and asks if he'd like to take over the McGraws' bedroom.

He ponders a moment. "What's the rent?"

One car back, Velez sits heavily in the seat next to Blent. Velez's eyes are red-rimmed from a night carousing with Turkey Mike and the Irish through the nether regions of Philadelphia. "Just told the guys about Buck's birthday."

Blent asks, "You think about your family, your girlfriends—you know, back in San Francisco?"

"Sure, man." Velez is ticked off by Blent's tone. "I think about them a lot, but the world is full of girls, and I'm having a good time learning about 1906 girls." His mind reels back to the previous night's foray with Donlin and Bresnahan to a pool hall and then to a place with a lot of girls on 18th Street. He likes the girls, but it's over with them. Building trust isn't a bad thing. Nicole trusts him. He misses her. He wants to buy her acting lessons with top-notch teachers, dancing lessons, pay to take her to every play she wants. "We gotta get you an actual woman, Blenty, old boy. One in each city. That's the way to enjoy life!"

Blent looks down at his scraped hands, notices the nail on his left thumb is split, thinks about Mrs. Mathewson.

Bresnahan announces, *"Here he comes!"*

The players' voices rise, *"Ohhhhhhhhhhhhhhhhhhhhhhhhh!"*

Martin enters the car. Bresnahan leads:

*"For he's a jolly good fellow—*
*For he's a jolly good fellow—*
*For he's a jolly good fellow—*
*That nobody can deny—"*

Turkey Mike Donlin adds, *"Not even Chicagoooooooooooo!"*

Everyone laughs. Blent and Velez rise, adding their off-key voices to the singing, all now segueing into the chorus of "In the Good Old Summer Time," the voices of their teammates very polished and pleasing, now harmonizing. Christy Mathewson, adding his voice, comes up behind Blent and Velez, and Mathewson's voice is sweet.

Martin stops halfway down the car, baffled, smiling: a birthday in a world into which he was not birthed. *As long as we keep winning, they'll keep singing.*

# 19

## The Cancer

BACK IN NEW YORK, Velez and Blent call on Mark Twain, updating him about Tesla and asking for the best doctor in New York for treating cancer. They tell him it's for a bartender at the Dublin House. Two mornings later, they're in the office of a pompous doctor who constantly strokes his "Ve Ri Tas" Harvard cuff links. His recommendation is the same as the Chicago doctor: lumpectomy.

Martin ponders his fate. "Okay."

Uptown, he moves his meager belongings across 85th Street, in with the Mathewsons, leaving more space for Blent and Velez.

Three mornings later, Martin is wheeled into the operating room. Ninety-three minutes hence, he's wheeled out. The Harvard-cuff link doctor tells Blent and Velez it was a success.

"What if the tumors come back?" Blent asks. "Can you do another lumpectomy?"

"There will be too much scar tissue. We've tried the second lumpectomy." His shoulder twitches. "The patients often bleed to death."

*

And so the summer goes. Martin steeps himself in batting averages, on-base percentages, slugging percentage, OPS, spray charts, and four-by-three batter grids. Many nights in the wee hours, a messenger stops by the Mathewson/Martin apartment and slips an envelope containing sheets of statistics in the mail slot. First thing in the morning, Martin opens the envelope, sips coffee and studies the updated stats. At 9:30 a.m., it's on to the ballpark, sometimes with Christy and his driver, Henry. Other times Martin takes the El, the train swaying as he gazes into the eye-level apartments along 9th Avenue, at people cooking, couples talking, couples arguing, babies crying. Sometimes the people in the apartments gaze back at him and wave hello. Then the train begins making its ninety-degree turn from 9th Avenue onto 110th Street; Martin can see no track and it's like gliding in air. One long block later, the train turns left onto 8th Avenue for the straight shot to the Polo Grounds, the Harlem River and the Bronx on the right, the natural escarpment of Coogan's Bluff looming on the left, like the Acropolis of Athens, lording over the open plain of the ball field.

Martin likes to be available in the clubhouse for his players, who shamble through the door in varying degrees of sobriety. He hits fielding practice, tosses batting practice.

Many evenings he dines early at the Ansonia Hotel, where reporters can get quotes from him regarding any late-afternoon baseball-world developments. Once or twice or three times a week he'll take a taxi down Broadway, through the excited crowds scurrying to theaters under the lights of Times Square, the traffic cop on a riser in the middle of the Square conducting a symphony of cars, trolleys, pedestrians, and horse-and-buggies. By 8:30, he and Junior are sitting in Senior's office with their charts, compiling stats as the clouds over Manhattan bloom in pink and purple.

Velez and Nicole spend evenings at the theater, out with Donlin and his fiancée, Mabel Hite. Velez, Nicole and Mabel are writing a murder-mystery play, the plot all Velez, remembered from an old *Murder by Dawn* episode. They plan to stage the play around Thanksgiving. Velez claims the role of the villain, because "the bad guys have all the fun."

\*

Observing Mrs. Mathewson clutching her Bible, descending her stoop one warm Sunday morning, brings Blent outside. She waves a gloved hand. "Mr. Blent, you are welcome to join!"

Henry steers the big car downtown. Mrs. Mathewson and Blent rush into the cathedral—"I want to show you something"—and up to the top. She pushes open the door to a room tucked in the roof, and there stands Theodore Roosevelt—the vice president of the United States—with two other older men.

One asks, "Who is he?"

"A ballplayer," Roosevelt replies. "A Giant."

Mrs. Mathewson turns to Blent, "Please wait in our pew. I'll join you shortly."

Blent slinks into the pew, and endures the service and an uninspired sermon—the church is only one-third full with high-crust New Yorkers away at Newport, Long Branch, the Adirondacks, Martha's Vineyard, and sprinkled along both sides of Long Island Sound.

Finally, Mrs. Mathewson joins Blent. He turns but does not see Roosevelt and the two other men. "What's going on?"

"Horse issues." She gazes down at the tops of the heads of the congregation.

"That's a load of malarkey."

"Mr. Roosevelt owns thirty horses."

"Who were the other guys?"

Her hand settles on Blent's thigh. She whispers, "You don't need to ask so many questions, do you? And please don't tell anyone about meeting Roosevelt. It's no one else's business. Follow me."

A parakeet-topped woman *shushes* them. Blent follows Mrs. Mathewson to the same room in which he met Roosevelt and the other men. She shuts the door. It's deadly silent except for the muffled intonations of Cardinal Donohue. She clicks the lock.

To Blent, it has been so very long. And maybe Velez is right—Darla's doing well with his life insurance; and she'd be able to find a man in about twenty seconds, even with a baby.

Mrs. Mathewson sits up on a table and pulls in Blent. Blent lets the enjoyable thing happen. He sets down his Bible.

*

The games go by quickly:

|  | Giants W-L | Cubs W-L | Pirates W-L |
|---|---|---|---|
| July | 23-7 | 18-8 | 13-19 |
| August | 24-5 | 23-15 | 18-21 |

The baseball stories of the summer are the Pirates' fade, the Cubs coming back to earth— somewhat—and Martin's 71–18 record. In the American League, the White Sox are scrapping with the Highlanders and the Philadelphia Athletics.

On September 1, the Giants are 6½ games behind the Cubs.

| | |
|---|---|
| Saturday, Sep 1 | 6½ |
| Sunday, Sep 2 | 6½ |
| Monday, Sep 3 | 6½ |
| Tuesday, Sep 4 | 5½ |
| Wednesday, Sep 5 | 5½ |
| Thursday, Sep 6 | 5 |
| Friday, Sep 7 | 5 |
| Saturday, Sep 8 | 5 |
| Sunday, Sep 9 | 4½ |
| Monday, Sep 10 | 4½ |
| Tuesday, Sep 11 | 3½ |
| Wednesday, Sep 12 | 2½ |
| Friday, Sep 14 | 3 |
| Saturday, Sep 15 | 3 |
| Sunday, Sep 16 | 2 |
| Monday, Sep 17 | 1 |
| Tuesday, Sep 18 | 2 |
| Wednesday, Sep 19 | 1 |
| Thursday, Sep 20 | Tied |
| Friday, Sep 21 | Tied |

On the misty morning of September 22, the Giants are riding the train through Connecticut, scheduled to play a trio of games against the Beaneaters, while the Cubs play three in Philadelphia. If the Giants and Cubs finish the season tied, a one-game playoff is tentatively scheduled at the Polo Grounds to see who will face the White Sox in the World's Series.

In the first two games in Boston, the Giants score first and never lose a lead. In the final game they are down 1–0 in the fourth, before they score eleven runs off Irv "Cy the Second" Young. Throughout the three days, every time a Chicago-Philadelphia update is related to the batboy, who sprints to the edge of the Giants dugout to announce the score in a high, piping voice, Chicago is always ahead of Philly. At game's end, Martin tips the Boston batboy seven dollars for the season.

An hour after departing Boston, Martin stands in the stinky lavatory—his only refuge of solitude on the train—and stares at his *Evening Standard*, folded into a small rectangle:

| Team | W L | PCT | GB |
|---------|--------|------|----|
| Chicago | 105-44 | .705 | — |
| New York | 105-44 | .705 | — |

It all comes down to this: The Giants and Cubs are converging at the Polo Grounds for a one-game playoff. *Will Brush fire me if we don't get to the World's Series? Or win the World's Series?*

\*

The next morning finds Martin sitting in his bedroom, studying the up-to-date Cubs and Giants statistics, compiled by Junior's at-times erratic, but reliably decipherable, hand onto crisp sheets of green ledger paper. Martin reaches over to his nightstand and lifts his pan of coffee, which is now lukewarm, and he renews his cup. He glances at his pocket watch—7:19. As he sips his coffee, he realizes that the stats have revealed all that they can reveal.

Screaming jars him, sending coffee down his chin.

*"I'm going to kill him!"* Mathewson's voice cracks on the word *"kill"* as he pounds his fists on Martin's door. *"Get out here! You know about it! You know about it! You know!"*

To the closed door, Martin asks, "What's wrong, Christy?" He cracks the door and is greeted by Mathewson's face twisted so violently the eyes point in distinctly different directions. Mathewson's hands reach up to wrap Martin's neck, choking Martin as Martin notices that Mathewson is wearing a Brownie camera on a strap. Martin croaks, "What—?"

*"That fucking yannigan across the street's been . . . !"* Mathewson squints, trying to conjure a word, a description that will lessen the humiliation, *"unfaithful with my wife!"*

He unclasps Martin's neck and Martin drops to his knees, gasping, feeling the indentations on his scarred neck where the lymph nodes were just removed.

Martin gasps, "What're you talking about?"

*"I'm not going to explain because you're all in on it!"* Mathewson rushes to his and Jane's bedroom. She slams the door shut. From behind the door, she weeps, "I'm sorry, Christy!"

*"'Sorry'?!"* Mathewson shouts. *"'Sorry'?!"* He kicks the door and it rattles violently, *"You bitch!"* He kicks the door, knocking a hinge off, and he stomps to the front hall closet, rips away umbrellas and her riding boots and rain slickers. He emerges with a chipped baseball bat.

Martin stands in the hallway in his underwear. "Christy! Calm down!"

*"I saw them screwing in the park! I saw it! In the Ramble! I took a photograph!"* He brandishes his Brownie camera. *"Fuck all you Californians! Blent! Blent! Blent!"*

"Blent? Are you sure?" Martin, stunned, myriad questions blossom in his mind, including, *Why take a photograph?* But Martin's main priority is to dissuade or restrain Mathewson from assaulting anyone, especially another Giant on the day of the one-game playoff against the Cubs. An equally important priority is to make sure that Mathewson, in his rage, doesn't hurt himself. "Why don't you put the bat down?"

Mathewson stares through Martin and shoots down the stoop, holding the bat, past Henry warily polishing the gleaming grille of his automobile, and across the street. He pounds the bat like an axe against the front door of 66 West 85th.

Her standard poodles barking crazily, Mrs. Critz leans out the second-floor window, blazing, *"What in God's name is going on?"* Mathewson derangedly looks up at her, and her tone changes, "Oh! Mr. Mathewson!"

"Will you open the door, please?"

His agitation making her hesitate, she asks, "Why?"

His scream echoes through the street, *"Open the fucking door!"*

From across the street Martin yells, *"Don't open the door!"*

Mrs. Critz looks at Martin, over at Henry who stands astonished next to the auto, and down at Mathewson. She suggests, "Perhaps you should go back home and settle down."

Recognizing that she is not going to help him, Mathewson resumes pounding the bat on the door. A cluster of children down the sidewalk playing jacks is stunned and horrified; a couple across the street scurry toward Columbus, giving wide berth to Martin in his undershorts. Mrs. Critz, halfway out the window, screams, *"Mr. Mathewson! Stop!"*

Mathewson's bat splinters against the front door, and he regards the broken bat as if he's never before seen a piece of wood. He ascends the red sandstone balustrade, and slashing with the broken bat like a sword—Mrs. Critz screaming—Martin yelling, "Stop, Christy!"—Mathewson shatters the window.

Velez and Blent stand in the living room staring at each other, dumbfounded, until deep and primal fear dawns on Blent as he realizes he is the object of Mathewson's rage. Echoing in the street is Mrs. Critz's voice, *"He's gone mad!"*

Mathewson crawls through the window frame and into the living room, broken glass on his shoulders and hair. He gestures the camera at Blent. *"I got you over in the Ramble! You filth!"*

It spills from Blent's mouth: "I love her!"

The full circles of Mathewson's crazy eyes widen. "She's married to *me!*"

Mathewson steps toward Blent, who's frozen. Behind Mathewson, Martin crawls through the window, slicing his forearm. Henry follows. Martin flings himself between Mathewson and Blent. But the combination of Mathewson's temporary insanity and his powerful right arm easily pushes Martin aside.

Mathewson cocks the bat, swings it at Blent, who ducks, but the bat nicks Blent's elbow.

Henry jumps at his boss, and Mathewson's bat *smacks* the back of Henry's head. Henry collapses to the carpet.

Blent grabs a sofa cushion as a shield.

Mathewson whacks bat into cushion, knocking Blent to the floor on top of Martin.

Martin yells up at Velez—who has refrained from getting between Mathewson and Blent—*"André! Help!"*

Mathewson's bat blasts into the sofa cushion protecting Blent.

Velez shouts, *"Guys! Stop! Guys! Guys! Guys! Stop!"*

Froth and snot dripping from his face, Mathewson screams at Velez, *"Shut up!"* as Mathewson pounds the bat into Blent, knocking the cushion away, ready to axe into Blent's face.

Velez yells, *"I fucked her too!"*

Mathewson blinks. His twisted stare turns on Velez.

From the floor, Blent screams up at Velez, *"You're a liar!"*

Velez rotates his hands out and shrugs, "Not lyin'."

Mathewson's bat remains raised, and he demands of Velez, *"What did you say?"*

"I made love to her. A bunch of times. Sorry, dude. You guys were on road trips. Won't happen again."

*"Bullshit!"* Blent shouts, scampering to his feet, shoving Velez backwards.

Mathewson screams at Blent, *"Shut up!"* and to Velez, *"That can't be true!"*

"Hey man," Velez presses a palm to his heart, "I like riding horses too." To Blent, "You ain't the first."

Mathewson, Velez, and Blent turn to Martin. Holding up his hands as if surrendering, he screeches, *"I never put a hand on her! Never even kissed her good night!"*

Henry is kneeling on the floor, touching a rising lump on the back of his head where Mathewson's bat cracked him. Mathewson demands, *"What's the truth, Henry?"*

Henry stares at Mathewson, at Blent, at Velez, at Martin, returning to Mathewson. Tears leak from his eyes. "I'm so sorry!" he sobs. "It will never happen again!"

Mathewson slams the bat into the coffee table, cup shards and bits of ashtray flying like shrapnel, part of the disintegrating bat demolishing the middle pane of the bay window. In the resulting second of silence, they all notice that a ham of a fist is pounding on the door.

Velez answers it, admitting a pink-faced policeman and Mrs. Critz. The officer is stunned at being face-to-face with the Giants: "Mr. Mathewson! Mr. Blent! Mr. Velay! Mr. Martin!"

Mathewson flings the bat handle, shattering the final pane in the bay window. A brisk September breeze blows in. Mathewson scoops up his camera, rushes past the policeman and Mrs. Critz, to whom he mumbles, "Sorry." He jumps down the stoop and jogs past the jacks players, past a rotund man walking a Chihuahua, who remarks, astonished, *"Christy!"* to Mathewson's receding back.

*

Two hours before game time, the Polo Grounds is packed to the brim. A passel of fans who have been denied entry form a crew that stomps and claws at a ground-level section of boards on the exterior face of the left-field bleachers, *craaaack!* The boards snap and they squeeze under like a line of rats.

Overlooking the left-field wall, a parked El train twelve cars long is jammed full of IRT employees, their families, and friends, all relishing an unobstructed, free-of-charge view of the field. A line of men sits on the train's roof. To the side of the stationary train, fans perch on the tracks.

Fans displace the seagulls and pigeons on top of the grandstand. Fans scale the vertical framing—beams no wider than a hand—above the right-field bleachers. Coogan's Bluff is thick with fans, like a company of soldiers massing on a ridge.

On Martin's advice, Blent is out of the clubhouse and on the field quickly, clearing psychic space for Christy Mathewson. Hauling a duffel bag of bats, Blent pushes through the spectators on the outfield grass and walks across the scrubby field, the crowd roaring, "Blent!" "Johnny Blent!" as if he's already hit a triple or made a great catch. He empties the bag in front of the dugout and picks out his three bats.

In the box next to the Giants bench, Brush Sr. is flanked by Junior and Mark Twain. A cloud of Twain's cigar smoke inadvertently drifts into Blent's face. "Apologies!" Twain exclaims. Blent smiles up at Twain, impossible to muster annoyance at him.

"How's Mr. Tesla?" Blent asks.

"Happy as a clam working for Westinghouse."

Ten minutes later, Mathewson is in the midst of his pregame warmups, pitching to Bresnahan along the first-base line. He notices Blent and Velay on the field, taking grounders hit by Wiltse. Mathewson tells Bresnahan, "One minute break." Bresnahan kneels in the dirt.

Mathewson strides at Blent, who backpedals. Mathewson blurts to Velez's back, "Chief!" indicating to a surprised Velez that he should come over too. Velez hesitates at the view of Mathewson closing, but joins them. Mathewson's eyes look crazy. Blent and Velez have never before noticed him unshaven for a ball game. He says, "If either of you ever say a word to my wife, or, God forbid, touch her, then I will kill you. Do you understand?"

Velez replies, "Yeah, man. Don't worry. Let's win this game."

Mathewson and Velez turn to Blent, who considers Mrs. Mathewson—her confidence, freedom, gorgeousness, sexiness, Southernness. If she screwed Velez, and Henry the driver, then how many other men have there been? Perhaps he was just another jaunt, another ride.

*"Answer the fucking question!"* Mathewson demands.

"Okay, Christy. I do understand."

"You said before that you love her. Is that really true?"

Blent's got a mess of emotions and concepts stirring—Jane Mathewson, Darla, present, past, future. "No. I don't love your wife . . . anymore. I'm sorry."

"I didn't ask if you were sorry!" Mathewson trudges away.

| | NEW YORK | | CHICAGO |
|---|---|---|---|
| 3B | ART DEVLIN | CF | JIMMY SLAGLE |
| 2B | JOHNNY BLENT | LF | JIMMY SHECKARD |
| 1B | ANDRÉ VELAY | RF | FRANK SCHULTE |
| LF | MIKE DONLIN | 1B | FRANK CHANCE |
| C | ROGER BRESNAHAN | 3B | HARRY STEINFELDT |
| SS | BILL DAHLEN | SS | JOE TINKER |
| CF | GEORGE BROWNE | 2B | JOHNNY EVERS |
| RF | SPIKE SHANNON | C | JOHNNY KLING |
| P | C. MATHEWSON | P | MORDECAI BROWN |

Mathewson sets down the first seven Chicago batters.

Top of the 3rd. Kling smacks a line drive that splits Browne and Spike Shannon and rolls into the thick arc of spectators sitting in the outfield, for a grounds-rule double.

Three Finger Brown slices a pitch that plunks beyond Blent's outstretched glove. Kling scoots around to home plate.

CHICAGO 1 — 0 NEW YORK

Bottom of the 3rd. Two out.

Blent knocks a curve past Brown's front ankle. He claps his hands as he takes his lead off first, eyes on Brown. The thought of Mrs. Mathewson, that he may never see her again, makes Blent step back to first as Brown fires a pitch to Velez. Coaching at first, Wiltse bellows, *"What the fuck, Johnny?"*

Velez takes a curve for a ball. Martin signals: optional steal. Blent leads, kicking at a pebble, and Brown fires over. Chance's glove comes down as the fingertips of Blent's right hand touch the canvas base a tenth of a second before Chance's glove touches his hand. *Safe!*

Blent dusts himself off. The volume of roaring and bellowing is louder than any he's heard in 1906. The coordination of feet stomping the slats of the left-field bleachers sounds like firecrackers, and those in the right-field bleachers and center-field bleachers admire the volume of sound so much that they start stomping, too.

Brown glances over at Blent. At the flinch of Brown's left foot rising from the mound, Blent takes off, legs churning. Kling catches, steps and throws, Three Finger Brown watching the ball zip past his face, high, the ball smacking Evers' glove seven feet off the ground and Blent slides in under. Ump Hank O'Day declares, "Safe!"

Two pitches later, Velez strokes a liner that bounces into the overflow crowd in left-center for a double. Blent scores. The Polo Grounds cheering reverberates off the rock escarpment of Coogan's Bluff, which, as Velez takes a quick glance above the rim of the ballpark, is thick with fans.

## CHICAGO 1 — 1 NEW YORK

Top of the 5th. Evers whacks a one-out double down the left-field line and cruises into second, smiling, serenaded by 360 degrees of booing.

Schulte cracks a liner, Blent diving to his left, snaring it, rolling and firing to second, Dahlen covering and Evers is out by a whisker. Double play. Evers screams at O'Day, *"You fucking blind bat!"* Evers' face is lobstering. *"I was safe!"*

Velez jogs toward Evers, who barks, *"What the fuck are you smiling at?"*

"Who's smiling now, Johnny?"

Evers rushes at Velez, but O'Day gets in front of Evers. Velez jogs away laughing, shoots Evers the finger, says, "I love it!"

Mathewson and Three Finger Brown pitch shutout ball through the sixth and the seventh.

Top of the 8th. Brown pulls a single over Dahlen; Mathewson reacts, *"Shit!"* Slagle bunts Brown to second.

Brown on second. One out.

As Mathewson walks Sheckard on five pitches, on the bench, Martin conducts an internal debate about removing Mathewson. The fire Mathewson ignited in himself has dwindled; his fastballs are down to the low eighties. Martin knows that, generally, a batter's love for low-eighties fastballs is greater than his love for sex.

Martin steps across the baseline, calls "Time!" and Mathewson has a look just marginally less menacing than the look he had a few hours ago when he was determined to kill Blent. Mathewson flips the ball in the air, the ball landing behind Martin. Then Martin attempts to slap Mathewson's butt and comes up with air as Mathewson trudges toward the bench, then veers toward the outfield and the clubhouse. Mathewson walks between Blent and Velez without looking at them.

The fans rise, roaring, and for those up on Coogan's Bluff, a boy in a tree is the first to see the white speck walking into the sunshine on the outfield grass, "There's Christy!"

On the field a dozen policemen flank Mathewson, cutting through the roaring outfield crowd. Mathewson does not raise his head to acknowledge anyone, spikes clomping up the clubhouse stairs.

McGinnity takes the mound. Martin tells him, "All right Joe, just do your stuff."

Martin replaces Bresnahan with Bowerman—the pitcher's spot is up second in the bottom of the inning—and Martin explains the substitutions to Rigler.

Three Finger Brown at second, Sheckard at first. One out. Score tied 1–1.

McGinnity's first pitch to Steinfeldt is a curve that starts outside and breaks over the plate. Then a fastball that Steinfeldt cracks into right. Brown scores, Sheckard to third. The Polo Grounds is silent except for scattered knots of cheering Chicago fans, who are immediately drowned out by screamed curses and threats. McGinnity angrily slaps the ball into his glove.

## CHICAGO  2 — 1  NEW YORK

Sheckard at third, Steinfeldt at first. One out.
The Giants play the infield in. Steinfeldt steals second.

Chance grounds to Velez, Sheckard breaking for home. Velez takes time to set his feet, fires a strike to Bowerman who, blocking the plate, presses his mitt into Sheckard's legs. *Out!*

McGinnity strikes out Kling to end the inning.

Bottom of the 9th. Evers smooths the ground. Over the first eight innings, Evers has picked out two dozen pebbles and tossed them into foul territory. It's Spike Shannon, not a strong hitter, now facing Three Finger Brown, but the Giants don't have any better bench options. On a 1–1 fastball, Shannon *knocks* a liner into right. The crowd screams hoarsely.

Shannon leads off first, no outs.

Martin considers waiting a pitch to see if Brown throws a ball to Bowerman, leading to a possible walk, but Brown has not walked anyone all day. Martin doesn't screw around and signals for a hit-and-run. Bowerman, a flabby face masking a keen intelligence, steps into the batter's box. A wicked curve ankle high, Bowerman slaps it slowly toward first. Chance rushes in, fields, and tags Bowerman, while Spike Shannon scoots over to second.

Shannon at second. One out.

On a 1–2 curve, Art Devlin strikes out. Two outs.

Blent twists his back foot in the batter's box. Evers is screaming something at him. Blent tells himself, *Just slow this game down. Just me and the ball. Hit the stupid ball. I wonder where Jane is.* He yells, "Time!" and steps out, reaching for his eyes, stalling. Rigler orders, *"Time!"*

Blent glances at the stands. Nicole and Twain are staring at him. Everyone is staring at him. He breathes in deeply, exhales hard, tests the pine tar on the bat, and now he's thinking of the World Series—the one in the twenty-first century—and of Darla. Pissed off at his wandering mind, he closes his eyes, lets the crowd noise in, finds his pinpoint of light at the end of the tunnel. He zeroes in on Three Finger Brown.

A 1-2 fastball, low and away, he whacks it over Evers' head. Shannon crosses third, then stumbles, limbs flailing. As Shannon falls in front of him, Martin can't believe this is happening. *"Back!"* Martin screams as do thousands of fans. Shannon scrambles up, Evers firing the ball to Steinfeldt, Shannon's toe catching the bag, *"Safe!"* Rigler calls it a third of the way up the line from home.

Shannon on third, Blent on first. Two outs. Velez is up. He's 2 for 3 on the day, batting .440 against Brown for the season, and Brown knows he has trouble with the Chief more often than is comfortable. After a quick discussion with Chance, Brown begins to intentionally walk Velez, who asks Kling, "Why you guys doing this to me?" Kling replies with a mixture of sarcasm and truth, "We're scared of you, Chief." As ball four is caught far wide of the plate, Velez turns to Rigler, "You believe this crap? Walking me to load the bases?"

Behind his mask, Rigler's forehead rises in acknowledgment.

Shannon on third, Blent on second, Velez on first. Two outs. Ninth inning.

The screaming is deafening, sore throats urging on the Giants. Behind the chicken wire, F. C. Lane gazes around at the densely packed multitude. Lane glimpses, out beyond center field, up in the line of men atop the Elevated tracks, a person dropping, disappearing behind the center-field bleachers. He asks his colleagues, "See that guy fall?" His question is met with an assemblage of blank stares.

It's Turkey Mike Donlin up at bat with the entire season on the line. A thought pops into Martin's mind: *It's been good, even if it ends here. I'll be okay. We'll be okay.* Martin says to Spike Shannon, leading off third, "Look alive for a wild pitch."

"From Brown?" Shannon replies, his back to Martin as Shannon takes his lead. "Never."

The count goes full. Brown winds up and sends a curve that dashes down at the strike zone. Donlin slices it foul.

Steinfeldt retrieves it, yellow and brown, and Martin jogs toward Rigler, complaining, "Get a new ball, Cy! Okay?" For once, Rigler complies with one of Martin's requests and tosses a fresh ball to Brown, who drops a bodacious gob of tobacco spit on it.

Donlin is a fine enough hitter to know to look for a fastball and fight off a curve. It's a fastball that zips in toward the inside edge of the plate, Donlin pulling in his hands and *whacking* the ball over Chance. Thirty-six thousand people hold their breath as Earth's gravity pulls the ball down, down, and the ball lands in right field a foot fair.

Sore vocal cords part, lungs blast out in exultant triumph as Shannon scores. Blent scores. The entire basin of Coogan's Hollow is reverberating, the sound spreading across the northern half of Manhattan, up to Washington Heights where the Highlanders' Hilltop Park stands empty, across the Harlem River, and to the Bronx. Everyone thinks it's over—nearly everyone.

## CHICAGO  2 — 3  NEW YORK

Chicago players are swinging elbows and fists at fans swarming the field. Giants players mob Turkey Mike.

Evers grabs O'Day's shoulders, screams, *"Second base! Velay didn't touch second!"*

O'Day is stunned at the implications of that statement—if the Cubs can find the ball and step on second base before Velay steps on it, then Velay is out, and as the third out, Spike Shannon's run doesn't count, and Blent's run doesn't count. *The Cubs would win the game and the pennant.*

Evers screams at Schulte and Slagle, *"Get the fucking ball!"*

Blent glimpses Evers, Schulte and Slagle slicing toward right field through the throng, and he figures they're getting past the mob to the clubhouse. Martin glances at Velez, who is surrounded by teammates in short right, Velez beatifically hopping in place, his head and chest towering above the crowd with each hop.

It is Martin who spots Evers in right field holding a ball aloft (having left a fan on the ground moaning and cowering). It is Martin who spots O'Day standing close to second looking out in the direction of Evers. And now Evers, Schulte, and Slagle are madly racing back toward the infield, toward second base.

Martin violently spins Bresnahan, who was coaching first. *"Did Velay touch second?"*

"Um . . . I don't know." Bresnahan's eyes widen in horror.

Bresnahan and Martin push through players and fans to grab Velez. Martin yells, *"Chief, touch second! Evers has the ball!"*

Wiltse, Devlin, Donlin, Dahlen, and Blent rush with Velez toward second base. But Evers is closer to it. Martin screams, *"Evers!"* Martin and Donlin and Blent veer off, knocking through fans. Donlin and Blent are momentarily stalled by a pack of soused Columbia fraternity brothers who attempt to bear-hug them and the brothers are the recipients of elbows and punches to the face, but Martin is ahead of them. Evers bowls over a passel of children at the edge of the infield dirt, Evers screaming at umpire Rigler, *"I got the ball!"* as Martin dives at Evers, grabbing his collar, pulling him down to the ground, punching his face—left, right, right, right—gouging his eye. Schulte rips at Martin, Evers reaching the ball past Martin to Slagle.

Martin screams, *"Stop Slagle!"*

Evers covers his injured eye as the one unassaulted stares up at Martin, accompanied by Evers screaming, *"You lose, fucker!"*

Martin thinks about losing this game this way, about accusations of inadequate managing, as a cheer goes up from the direction of second base. Martin scrambles upright, as does Evers, his two hands over the one burning eye.

Standing atop second base, Velez's arms are raised in triumph, while O'Day declares, *"Safe! Safe! Safe! Safe! Safe! Safe! Safe! Safe! Safe! Safe! Safe! Safe! Safe!"*

CHICAGO  2 — 3  NEW YORK  FINAL

\*

Martin accepts the offered ride in Mathewson's Cadillac, and even though a good hour has elapsed since the epic win, it takes an eternity for the car to crawl through the celebratory throng around the Polo Grounds and down 8th Avenue under the El. Behind them is Turkey Mike and Mabel, in his freshly purchased baby-blue Jackson. Mike's been smoking a fat cigar and beaming at the fans while squeezing the bladder of his window-mounted horn, chirping, "Hurry up, Matty-boy!"

Martin has been unnerved into speechlessness by the wild look that has somewhat faded, but still remains, in Mathewson's face, and he regrets accepting the ride. Mathewson suddenly blurts, "She was crying and clinging to me and swearing she wasn't going to do it again. She says she's not pleased by the whole thing"—Mathewson's "p" in "pleased" is accompanied by spittle—"I told her to go to Hell, but I don't know. I love her. I think. I don't know. What do you think?"

On the sidewalk, kids yell out, "Matty!" "Matty!" "Bucky!" "Bucky!" An adult shouts, "Great game, Christy!" Matty and Buck wave in acknowledgment.

"I am not the one to give advice on love," Martin replies. "I've been married three times, and three times a failure. I guess I'm married to baseball." Not wanting to pursue the subject further, Martin asks, "Wasn't that the craziest game ever?"

Mathewson closes his eyes and offers a small nod of agreement.

\*

On the overnight train to Chicago, the Giants savor the afterglow of having vanquished one's biggest enemy. After disentangling from well-wishers at the Ambassador East Hotel, the three twenty-first-century refugees take a taxi to the Chicago suburbs, to the Westinghouse office complex, and they are soon standing in Nikola Tesla's laboratory, irritated by the odors of burnt rubber and wire.

Tesla walks the ballplayers past monstrous metal machines, pointing out, "This is a turbine, this is a Tesla coil, this is a generator—"

"Whoa!" Velez stops next to a device dangling wires featuring a metal plate etched with "0," "10," "20," "30," "40," "50," and a red needle. "Speedometer?"

"What do you think of it so far?"

"Looks about right!"

"Brilliant suggestion, Mr. Velay! Many calibration tests ahead on the road itself!" Tesla gazes, a bit awkwardly, at Martin.

Martin pulls his collar and shows Tesla the scars from the removal of the tumors. Tesla leans in close and so does Blent. To Blent, alarmingly, the spots look a bit puffy, as if the cancer might be returning. The thought makes Blent feel faint.

Tesla flicks a switch on a machine about the size of a minivan and it hums to life. He steps past the ballplayers, to a matching machine about twenty feet away. He corrals them toward the second machine and sets them with their heads at the level of something that looks like a covered-up porthole. "Stay here." He retreats to the first machine. The second machine seems to be burning, as suddenly they hear through the porthole, "Am I coming through? Hello America. Hello future friends."

"We hear you!" replies Velez. "What is this?"

Through the mammoth speaker he tells them, the words crackling, "It is a cellular telephone!"

"This ain't no cell phone," Velez scoffs. "You're supposed to *walk around* with a cell phone."

"This demonstrates the *principle* of the cell phone."

"Principle shminciple!"

Blent leans into the machine's mouthpiece, which is as big as a wastebasket. "What about time travel?"

Tesla switches off the machines. He leads them to a wall of four blackboards crowded with indecipherable equations. "Tea or coffee, gentlemen? Because I would like you to tell me each detail of what happened when you went through time."

\*

In sports, as in war, as in the plenitude of competitive spheres of life, new enemies arise as surely as day follows the night. The Cubs' Frank Chance and Johnny "The Human Crab" Evers and Joe Tinker and Three Finger Brown and Ed Reulbach and Steinfeldt, Schulte and Slagle are exchanged for Ed Walsh and Doc White and Fielder Jones and Jiggs Donahue and the rest of the "No-Hit Wonder" Chicago White Sox, winners of the American League pennant.

During Game 1, top of the 4th inning, news explodes out of the telegraphers pit that $1,313,000 has just been transferred to a Swiss escrow account from New Glory: The Solar Series is set. It will be best of seven games; two games in Leeton, then one in Washington, one in Chicago, one in New York (if necessary), and two in Leeton (if necessary).

Hooks Wiltse lets up two runs in the fifth; Red Ames lets up two in the eighth; the Giants score five off Ed Walsh. Brush, Jr.'s pitching charts on Walsh help the Giants identify and lay off Walsh's best pitch—his spitter, and they smash his fastballs.

### GAME 1

|  | 1 | 2 | 3 | 4 | 5 | 6 | 7 | 8 | 9 | R | H | E |
|---|---|---|---|---|---|---|---|---|---|---|---|---|
| New York | 0 | 0 | 0 | 1 | 0 | 3 | 1 | 0 | 0 | 5 | 9 | 1 |
| Chicago | 0 | 0 | 0 | 0 | 2 | 0 | 0 | 2 | 0 | 4 | 8 | 0 |

Back at the hotel, Martin is offered congratulations and handed a stack of notes taken down by the telephone operator. There is an offer to endorse a shaving cream for a "sizeable sum," an offer for a free suit from a Chicago tailor, and the following:

*If you go to New Glory,
enquire Albert E.
—Tesla.*

In his room, as Martin changes into his best suit, he considers the absurdity of meeting Einstein, and the hope-against-hope that Einstein might have some insight into time travel. In the mirror, he checks the bumps on the side of his neck. Slow death.

Martin ties a new black necktie and, thankful that baseball is occupying his mind and not cancer, makes his way to Pulliam's suite. He joins Brush, Sr., Brush, Jr., Ban Johnson, F. C. Lane, and White Sox manager Fielder Jones. They plop into heavy chairs, sipping glasses of bourbon, scotch, and rye around a pair of low tables pushed together. They discuss the Solar Series. Pulliam and Ban Johnson have decided that ten or twelve of the best players in the Majors will be invited to join the World's Series winner to comprise the team representing the USA.

Names are tossed back and forth: Elmer Flick, a Cleveland outfielder, who hit .311; George Stone, the St. Louis out-fielder, who led the American League in hitting at .358 and stole thirty-five bases; Honus Wagner—"Of course," Fielder Jones says, seconded by Martin, "Yup"; Rube Waddell, the fireballing left-hander from the Philadelphia A's who is a dis-cipline problem—Ban Johnson warns, "I don't know if you gentlemen understand what corralling Rube Waddell means. He's driving Connie Mack to an early grave"; Napoleon Lajoie, the Cleveland second baseman-manager; Johnson notes, "Cy Young had another exceptional year"; Pulliam says, "Homer Smoot. And how about Red Dooin from Philadelphia?" They mention some of the Cubs; and Wee Willie Keeler, the dimin-utive, thirty-seven-year-old, tough-as-nails outfielder for the Highlanders, who hit .304, and stole twenty-three bases.

Junior opens a pack of cigarettes, pulls out one, lights it, pulls out the baseball card from the pack, glances at the stiff portrait of Honus Wagner against a mustard-yellow back-ground. Kids collect them. He rips and flicks the halves into the wastebasket. He brings out his pen and notebook to write down the names. Martin wants to ask about adding some of the great Black players, so he does it in this manner: "What do we know about the New Glory team?"

Johnson looks at Brush, Sr., who looks at Pulliam—who looks like a bank manager. He clears his throat, sniffs, wipes his nose. "The Cobb brothers. This new pitcher, Johnson. José Méndez, Martín Dihigo, both of whom are quite Black."

Fielder Jones and Ban Johnson stiffen. Jones says, "I'm not putting niggers in my lineup."

Martin remains silent. Brush, Sr. asks, "What about *playing* a team that has Negroes on it?"

"I don't like that either," replies Jones. "But if the money's right . . ." His face breaks into a wide, mirthful, tobacco-stained smile, which triggers laughter in the older men.

Martin, if he should beat Jones' White Sox and thereby helm the USA team, wants Philadelphia Negro League catcher Bruce Petway—just in case the Cobb brothers are as fast as they are rumored to be; he wants John Henry "Pop" Lloyd—nicknamed "The Black Honus Wagner"—who might be better than any white third baseman in 1906; and he wouldn't mind sitting on the bench next to Rube Foster, one of the best pitchers and baseball brains. Martin makes eye contact with Junior, who says, "Women are agitating for the vote and are likely to get it."

Senior barks, "What does that have to do with the subject at hand?"

"Rights are expanding. One day, Negroes will play in the Major Leagues."

"Not if I can help it," laughs Ban Johnson.

"Why not?" asks Junior.

"They'll take our jobs," replies Fielder Jones.

Junior replies, "You could expand the Major League rosters. No one would lose a job. Put a quota on it. One Negro the first year. Two the second. They're great players, some of them."

Johnson blusters, "We already have one idiot in our league—Rube Waddell—and I don't need them on each and every team."

Jones cracks, "Waddell *is* a white nigger, ain't he?" The others chuckle

"Well," Martin speaks up, "I wouldn't mind having a few of them on the bench against New Glory. I've studied some of the Negro players. They are fabulous weapons."

"Our players won't like it," Jones protests.

Brush, Sr. raises a bony finger. "What if the Negroes took a half, or a quarter share? Or even, we could pay them a flat salary. Three hundred and fifty dollars for a seven-game series? Simply add them as extra players."

Jones sniffs. "Nope."

\*

Junior's twenty-six games of Chicago White Sox scouting give the Giants an advantage in knowledge that dictates the course of hundreds of Martin's and his players' decisions.

### GAME 2

| | 1 | 2 | 3 | 4 | 5 | 6 | 7 | 8 | 9 | R | H | E |
|---|---|---|---|---|---|---|---|---|---|---|---|---|
| New York | 0 | 0 | 0 | 1 | 0 | 4 | 0 | 0 | 0 | 5 | 9 | 0 |
| Chicago | 0 | 0 | 1 | 0 | 0 | 0 | 0 | 0 | 0 | 1 | 4 | 2 |

McGinnity scatters four hits, lets up two runs. Donlin goes 2 for 5. Blent knocks a triple and a double. Velay is 3 for 5. Nick Altrock suffers the loss.

### GAME 3

| | 1 | 2 | 3 | 4 | 5 | 6 | 7 | 8 | 9 | R | H | E |
|---|---|---|---|---|---|---|---|---|---|---|---|---|
| Chicago | 0 | 0 | 0 | 0 | 0 | 1 | 1 | 0 | 0 | 2 | 6 | 4 |
| New York | 2 | 0 | 1 | 0 | 0 | 2 | 0 | 2 | x | 7 | 9 | 1 |

Each Giants batter gets at least one hit against Ed Walsh. Velez cracks two doubles. Mathewson baffles Chicago hitters. Chicago's fielding is sloppy.

## GAME 4

|          | 1 | 2 | 3 | 4 | 5 | 6 | 7 | 8 | 9 | R | H | E |
|----------|---|---|---|---|---|---|---|---|---|---|---|---|
| Chicago  | 0 | 0 | 0 | 0 | 0 | 0 | 0 | 0 | 1 | 1 | 5 | 1 |
| New York | 2 | 2 | 1 | 0 | 0 | 1 | 3 | 0 | x | 9 | 9 | 0 |

Hooks Wiltse shuts the door for seven innings. Ames pitches the eighth and ninth. The Giants destroy Nick Altrock. There is no joy in Chicago.

# 20

## The Cobbs

SUFFUSED IN A bright, invigorating October haze, a long row of men poses with their backs to the railing on the deck of the SS *Normandie*, the Manhattan skyline the backdrop, the steel skeleton of the in-construction Singer Building, at 612 feet, the tallest structure. A bevy of photographers barks:

*"Smile please!"*

*"Over here!"*

*"Again please!"*

*"This way, gentlemen!"*

The group is comprised of the entire roster of the World's Champion New York Giants; plus Honus Wagner of the Pittsburg Pirates; Homer Smoot of the Cardinals; large-bellied, weather-beaten Cy Young of the Boston Red Sox, and his teammate Jimmy Collins; Elmer Flick from Cleveland; George Stone of the St. Louis Browns; Ban Johnson, president of the American League; Harry Pulliam, president of the National; Wee Willie Keeler from the Highlanders; Ed Reulbach, Three Finger Brown, Johnny Kling, and Frank Chance from the

Cubs; and Vice President Theodore Roosevelt, whose calves ache as he has been standing on tiptoe while grinning for the photographers, nevertheless remaining diminutive between Chief Velay and Christy Mathewson.

As the photographers finish their work, Bucky Martin asks a cluster of players, "Anyone seen Waddell?"

Turkey Mike grins. "Last I saw him was about six hours ago being escorted out of the Landmark Tavern by three chippies."

Ballplayers babble quotes that are scribbled by reporters, while the photographers pack up. Soon all the press, excepting the ones who will continue on with the team, will descend to the tugboat awaiting to return them to shore.

Not in the photos and not quoted are Negro Leaguers Bruce Petway, Rube Foster, and John Henry "Pop" Lloyd. They are taking in the New York skyline one deck below. The plan is for the vice president to introduce them to the rest of the team at dinner, at sea. It was feared by Roosevelt, Martin, Ban Johnson and Pulliam that if the white players were told while the team was assembling in New York, a portion of them would go home.

Eddie Plank of the Athletics, who led the American League with a .760 winning percentage while compiling a 2.25 ERA and a 1.06 WHIP, cited his mother's acute encephalitis, refusing to leave her side rather than join the team. Addie Joss, the great Cleveland pitcher, who had an astounding year—.700 winning percentage, 1.72 ERA, .983 WHIP—agreed to join, but horribly drunk the night after watching Game 2 of the World's Series, broke his leg falling off a trolley. Jack Chesbro of the Highlanders refused to aid "The Enhanced Giants." Harry Steinfeldt, the Cubs' third baseman, was also asked to join, but in a night of drinking with Johnny Evers—who was not tendered an invitation—Evers twisted Steinfeldt into believing that helping Martin and the Giants' players win more fame and adulation was treasonous, and that Steinfeldt should instead join him boar hunting in Missouri. Cleveland player/manager Napoleon Lajoie telegrammed that he was ill with a stomach flu.

Out past Sandy Hook, Ban Johnson and Pulliam regard the clusters of players, the team they have assembled as Johnson successfully lights a cigar in the wind.

Pulliam notes, "No hide nor hair of Rube Waddell!"

"That is exactly why I am celebrating with this Cuban cigar!"

A dozen of the more fervent drunks form a pack and begin their exploration of the ship's seven bars, while other players smoke cigars on deck and reminisce about game situations and night-life situations, triggering convulsions of laughter.

Martin descends the staircase leading to the main dining room, very pleased to be at sea. There is a sharp tug on his elbow: Theodore Roosevelt. Behind the pince-nez, the pale-blue eyes bore into Martin, the gray-streaked brown mustache emphasizing the downturned line of the serious mouth. Roosevelt glances around to make sure that no one is overhearing. "When we arrive in New Glory, please keep your eyes open for anything unusual."

"Like what?"

"Technically we are still at war with them. England is sending over its latest ships." Roosevelt leans in, his nose two inches from Martin's chin. "And New Glory's modern inventions are bringing great wealth to their island. They outmaneuvered us in Venezuela, and are exporting quantities of steel and weapons. Their Mr. Ford's automobile is selling astounding numbers in Europe. They would love to sell to us, but we ban it. They are a growing monster." Roosevelt looks up and out, "We seem to be slowing."

On the top deck, Harry Pulliam observes, "That tugboat is trying to catch us."

Pulliam and Johnson gaze down, pondering the tugboat pulling alongside, and from its little cabin emerges a man who unsteadily tromps to the railing carrying a satchel and two bats; he tilts his head back; it is the slit-mouthed, wide-eyed, perplexed expression of Rube Waddell, locking eyes with the puffy oval face of Ban Johnson, the man who has had to deal with the most egregious of Waddell's antics these past years. *"Hey, Ban!"*

*"Waddell!"* Johnson raises a fist and yells with frustration.

On a roll of the tugboat, Waddell is nudged toward a gangway that swings out, where *Normandie* hands latch onto him. Waddell yells, *"Whoaaaaaaaa!"* as his fist slams against the ship, releasing his grip on his satchel and the bats, which drop into the ocean.

A score of ballplayers is craned over the railing, shouting, *"Ruuuuuuuuuuuuuuuuuube!"* and gut-bustingly laughing.

That night in the bar, Bruce Petway, Rube Foster, and John Henry "Pop" Lloyd mix with the rest of the team. Velez and Blent heartily shake their hands. Pop Lloyd and Rube Foster are as erect as royalty, and 5'6" Bruce Petway looks as tough as a duffel bag of bowling balls. Most of the other players welcome them. A group of grumbling drunk Irish at the far end of the bar doesn't make any effort. Velez and Blent bring Bruce Petway over to the table of Donlin, Dahlen, Devlin, Bresnahan, Johnny Kling and some American Leaguers. Wee Willie Keeler gets up to shake Petway's hand, and they all sit for a drink. Devlin reaches his hand across to Petway and says, "You threw me out in '02." He tells the others, "It was a game in March in DC."

Petway says, "I remember."

Bresnahan asks, "Who won?"

Petway smiles. The Irish laugh hard at Devlin's chagrined expression.

At the stop in Jacksonville, Florida, the last chance to quit the team, none of the whites disembark.

*

The contiguous marching bands, a thousand men in exact rows and squares, play a ragged "Star-Spangled Banner," followed by a precise, booming "Dixie."

The *Normandie* is docked. Vice President Roosevelt, Pulliam, and Ban Johnson are greeted by President Robert E. Lee III, Civil War generals, and other New Glory dignitaries, while the USA players stand off to the side cracking comments, marveling at the looming Victory Tower in the distance. At forty-nine stories, it is the tallest building in the world.

The huge crowd of white men in long beards, some white women, and clusters of Black men, push at ropes holding them back and point out, "Christy Mathewson!" "Honus Wagner!" "That's Three Finger Brown!" "Roger Bresnahan!" and every player is hailed by name except Bruce Petway, Pop Lloyd, and Rube Foster. After interminable speeches monumentally amplified by a contraption none of the USA delegation has ever seen (except Velez, Martin, and Blent), Roosevelt's voice screeches through the microphone, and ten thousand people cover their ears as a frantic technician in a white suit pulls it away from Roosevelt.

The Giants are led to a row of automobiles that look ridiculous to the 1906 Americans—the cars are half the size of Mathewson's Cadillac and Turkey Mike's Jackson. These automobiles are all the same black, dull.

Turkey Mike comments as he climbs in, "Looks like a roller skate."

"Hope it goes fast," says Velez, guiding Rube Waddell up into the car. Velez does not appreciate the constant goading of Rube Waddell by the other players, who like to get drunk with Rube and suggest that he do things such as chug a water glass full to the brim with whiskey, take a stroll *atop* all the tables in the bar, or climb the ship's smokestack and stick his head in so he can "resemble" the Negro players. Blent sits up front next to the driver. All the drivers wear gray army uniforms.

The cortege of fifty black Model 1s parades through the packed streets of Leeton, generating applause and booing. The citizens bloom out of open windows and balconies like over-grown Caucasian plants. Blent soaks in the tropical air and the soft Southern accents of the snippets of overheard conver-sations, the voices continually cascading little avalanches of memories of Alabama.

Donlin calls out, "Hey Chief!" Donlin is triumphantly dis-playing a fifth of white rum.

Velez calls back to Turkey Mike, a car behind, "How'd you get that?"

Donlin spreads his arms wide, "My reputation precedes me!" He tosses the bottle the twenty feet between cars, Velez snagging it with one hand. He pulls the cork and sips the fiery smooth rum. "Wow!" He winks down at Waddell and Blent. "You believe this place?"

"What part of it?" Blent replies. White fans boo them.

"We're in freaking Havana—or Leeton, or whatever the hell they call it—and it's 1906 and we're playing in something *bigger* than the World Series."

Blent takes a dip of Red Man and offers his pouch to Waddell. "I guess it's a beautiful thing—if we win."

*"Beat this team?"* Velez shoots a quizzical look at Blent. *"Honus Wagner, Christy Mathewson, Turkey Mike, Three Finger Brown? Us?* These bearded crackers? No way, man!"

Rube Waddell's spacey face contorts, guffawing, "No way, man!"

There's a large group of Black people—women, children, men—all barefoot, staring with no emotion at the players as they pass. Their Model 1 driver thrusts a finger in the air and proudly informs, "Our slaves!"

"What did they do?" Blent asks.

"Do? Nothing! They are an inferior race and happy we take care of them!"

Two cars behind, Bruce Petway stares in horror at the slaves, who return his stare.

"Baseball is too complicated for them." Blent and Velez's driver points to his skull. "They don't have the necessities."

Rube Foster yells at the slaves, *"Rise up! Rise up!"* The slaves break into laughter. Foster beams, turning to the passing white masses, *"Rise up! Rise up!"* The whites angrily *boo* Foster, who laughs in response.

The street opens onto a plaza that extends almost to the horizon. The cars stop in an arc about a hundred feet from a gargantuan stage backed by an equally gargantuan New Glory flag—the stars and bars—the size of half of a block of New York brownstones.

Blent asks Velez, over the cheering and booing, "What do you think about all this?"

"Wouldn't want to be a slave!"

New Glory dignitaries take the seats between the line of cars and the stage. Behind the cars are tens of thousands of people, the plaza about forty times the size of the Polo Grounds field. It is packed with New Gloryers—most in long beards; very few women. Amidst the white faces and Hispanic faces, there are islands of Black faces, who are not cheering. The heavy air is perfumed by the yellow and coral oleander trees bordering the plaza, the trees interspersed with dozens of bronze equestrian statues of Confederate generals on handsome horses.

Enduring another series of amplified speeches, the USA players slouch and bake in the penetrating tropical sun. Donlin's second bottle is tossed between cars. As Rube Waddell is sucking the longest drink, Velez gently scolds, "Rube, take it easy dude."

After the final New Glory speaker's word, "forever," dissipates through the plaza, President Lee III, erect of bearing, black beard, rainbow-colored hair, raises his right hand and brings it down, a signal for stagehands to pull cords that part the enormous stars-and-bars flag. A hanging platform the length of the stage is revealed, with nine nooses and nine hooded men bound hand and foot, each tended by a black-hooded executioner.

The crowd roars, whoops Rebel Yells, sings regimental songs. In the crowd behind Blent and Velez, a wrinkled white man in a gray uniform shouts, *"Killin' tiiiiiime!"*

Up on the platform, the line of hoods is removed on the convicted. All the USA delegation is shocked, except for Donlin who is sharing a laugh with Bresnahan, both incredibly drunk, the situation not having dawned on them.

The lines in his forehead deepen as Velez mutters, "Bastards."

Up on the platform, Vice President Roosevelt shrieks in the direction of President Lee III: *"What is the meaning of this?"* the shriek amplified across the plaza before the microphone is switched off. Roosevelt stomps toward Lee, who walks right past Roosevelt, Lee raising his arms and beaming out at the sea of New Gloryers. A wind gust blows Lee's black-dyed beard and lifts, in one woven nest partly anchored to his scalp, his rainbow-colored hair: stripes of red, yellow, blue, and purple.

The driver tells Blent, Velez, and Waddell, "That's his natural hair! It's so beautiful!"

The nine prisoners are gagged, as most of them grunt and squeal their innocence. Charges are read out—murder, theft, robbery, adultery, theft, adultery, murder, knowingly selling contaminated corn, murder.

"Gentlemen and gentleladies!" the amplified voice of the porcine mayor of Leeton echoes. "Let us please welcome the captain of our New Glory national team, Major Augustus Cobb!"

A roar from the 250,000-person throng greets the towering man in an army uniform, epaulettes glinting, as he mounts the hanging platform and waves to the crowd. The mayor continues, "May I please introduce Lieutenant Josephus Cobb! Lieutenant-Colonel Cæsar Cobb! Captain Tyrus Raymond Cobb! Sergeant Walter Johnson! Manager of our team, Colonel Dolf Luque!"

Eight ballplayers plus the manager fan out along the nine noosed men. There are nine trios: condemned man with a noose around his neck, ballplayer, hooded executioner who grips a lever that will open the trap door.

Vice President Roosevelt's face has transformed to the color of a sheet of paper. The rest of the USA delegation—even drunken Donlin and Bresnahan—are stunned. In the silence of 250,000 riveted, expectant faces, Rube Waddell bellows, *"I wanna get out of here!"*

A priest recites the Lord's Prayer, a cannon fires, and the nine executioners pull the nine levers and nine men drop through nine trap doors accompanied by a hurricane of cheering and Rebel Yells.

Nine ropes pull taut. Six of the men hang limply while three are frantically kicking, to much laughter from the crowd. The kicking spasmodically dissipates, and after a minute all has stopped. From the platform, New Glory dignitaries beam out at the crowd as the five Cobbs, Dolf Luque, young Walter Johnson, and the other New Gloryers wave. The USA ballplayers raise their middle fingers at the hanging platform.

\*

After the "welcome ceremony," the American visitors are toured through the Palace of Arts, the Museum of Science, and an elevator ride rising up the Victory Tower. Wee Willie Keeler, with rum breath, looks up at Martin. "Why do they have to kill people in front of us?"

"Trying to get in our heads." Martin says to the packed elevator, "Let's stay out of their war."

"You got that right," Velez agrees.

On the forty-ninth-story observation deck, all of Leeton and what New Gloryers have renamed the Gulf of Lee is spread before them. On the other side of the observation deck, rising over a carpet of palm trees at the horizon, is what appears to be a nuclear power generator's cooling tower. Martin exhales, "Oh my God."

Blent joins him. "See that?"

"Unmistakable. Old design. They've got the nuclear power plant. Do they have the weapons?" Blent glances at Velez, who's teaching Rube Waddell and Elmer Flick to high-five. "And what do they know about time travel?"

Martin smiles—a calm, faraway smile. "I'm resigned to staying here."

The nodes on his neck are now the width of a finger. Blent's thoroughly frustrated. "You've got to fight this, Buck."

Twenty minutes later, Turkey Mike leads the team into the players' gate at the Stadium of the Revolution. Through the under-the-stands clubhouse to the dugout, out into the sunlight, Donlin exclaims, "Holy mother of Christ!" as he gawks at the multiple tiers of stands that reach into the sky, four times as tall as any ballpark in the United States.

The players rush onto the field, where all are astonished, except Blent, Martin, and Velez: This stadium is roughly the same size as the original Yankee Stadium, the one built in 1923.

Wee Willie Keeler asks Roger Bresnahan, "Why don't *we* have ballparks like this?"

Velez and Blent bound to their territory on the right side of the infield, laughing in appreciation of the raked, pebble-free dirt. The dividing lines between dirt and grass are manicured.

Keeler, Donlin, Homer Smoot, George Stone, and Elmer Flick walk across an outfield that is bereft of swales, rocks, gopher and mole holes, divots, fists of crabgrass, or patches of dirt. Dahlen, Devlin, Honus Wagner, Pop Lloyd and Jimmy Collins are kneeling between second and third, rubbing their palms across the fine-grained dirt. Rube Waddell, wearing only his shirt, which fails to extend down to his penis, strides toward the pitcher's mound exclaiming, "My feetsies feel so good!"

Most of the players laugh at Waddell. In the twenty-first century, Martin figures, Waddell would be on medication, four hundred pounds, watching TV fourteen hours a day. Jimmy Collins admonishes, "Put your pants on, Rube!" Velez gently takes Waddell's shoulder and steers him toward the clubhouse.

The stadium reminds Martin of photos of Cleveland's Municipal Stadium—tall and vast. He announces, "Forty-five-minute workout right now!" The team whoops and jogs into the clubhouse to change into their new uniforms: white with USA stitched across the chest in dark blue.

Colonel Jackson is shocked. "It is not on the itinerary, Mr. Martin! I must forbid it!"

"We only have the one scheduled workout tomorrow morning. We need this." Martin finds the groundskeeper, who produces a tin bucket of baseballs and three bats.

Martin hits grounders and pop-ups to the infielders. Christy Mathewson and Cy Young crack fly balls to the outfielders. The New Glory baseball is a bit harder, flies a bit farther than the USA baseball—the players are relieved that they're acclimating to it now, rather than game day. Martin whacks a hundred pop-ups, so his 1906 infielders can get used to tracking a baseball as it drops along the backdrop of successive layers of seats and overhangs. The sound of bats rhythmically knocking baseballs echoes in the empty stadium.

They are ninety minutes late to the Palace Hotel, where their entrance into the ballroom is greeted by polite applause. At the sight of a small man at the side of the room—wimpy black mustache, tousled hair—Blent grabs Velez's sleeve. "Einstein!"

"The nerdy guy next to the fern? He looks like a teenager with a bad mustache."

Martin is stunned.

As calmly as possible, trying to avoid attracting any New Glory attention, the trio makes their way to Einstein, who is munching from a plate of canapés.

In an out-of-body experience, as if he were standing to the side watching himself, Martin quietly inquires, "Mr. Einstein?"

There is a jolt of acknowledgment.

"We are friends of Mr. Tesla."

In Swiss-German-accented English, Einstein asks, "You have seen Tesla?"

They quickly bring Einstein up to date. Martin says, "We are discussing time travel with him."

"Time travel! What does Tesla have to say about the subject?"

Velez states, "We're from the future, man. The twenty-first century."

Einstein recoils, drops the plate of food—caught by Blent at knee level—though the canapés crash onto Einstein's dusty shoes. "What is the proof?" Einstein asks.

Martin tells Einstein, "It's the thing we think about all the time. We're stuck here in 1906."

"We need to get back," Blent says.

Velez asks, "Do you have any way to help us?"

"Are you building a nuclear bomb?" Blent asks. "How far along are you?"

Einstein's mouth opens and he seems stunned by the questions.

"We saw the cooling tower," Blent explains.

"You know what it is?" Einstein asks.

Stern New Gloryers in dress uniforms and flowing beards are coming their way.

"They're always watching," Einstein tells the ballplayers. "Quickly, tell me one other thing about the future."

"You believe us!" Blent exclaims. Velez smiles with relief.

Martin: "Men and women walk on the Moon."

Velez: "The cars, man, just beautiful. A hundred and fifty miles per hour."

Blent: "We're polluting the hell out of our planet; some of the effects might be irreversible. Our galaxy is one of a billion galaxies."

Einstein smiles wanly, "A billion galaxies? How do you know this?" as his minders halt next to them, two chests of clattering medals. As tall and trim as Velez, one says, "Herr Einstein. We are finished."

Einstein says to the ballplayers, "You fellows won't beat us! I have placed money on our team! See you at the ballpark!" Einstein walks away, flanked by the minders.

In the gargantuan banquet hall, the two teams are arrayed on a dais as long as the span between third and first base, the USA team on the left wing, New Glory on the right, all dining on beefsteak, marlin, Cornish hen, suckling pig, and dishes of creamed corn and grits. As President Lee finishes a rambling story aided by florid hand gestures, about charging up a hill in Antigua with Lieutenants Josephus Cobb and Martín Dihigo, the one thousand diners spread out amidst eighty tables, and the voluminous wait and kitchen staff all rise and applaud, though most of the Negro kitchen workers don't seem too thrilled. Vice President Roosevelt leads polite applause from the USA side and it's then that Blent notices her.

In the second rank of tables, in a navy blue dress, wavy black hair unencumbered by a hat: Mrs. Mathewson, wearing a significant string of pearls, at a table of severe leonine men and fashionable white women. Looking straight up at Blent, she offers a slight nod and a raised eyebrow. He recoils, tipping backwards, chair crashing.

The players guffaw, assuming that teetotaling Blent's found an appealing island drink. He resets his chair. Seven seats down the line is Christy Mathewson, cutting into his steak. Blent elbows Bresnahan, asks for his pen and a slip of paper.

### Second table, Second row—Jane!

The note is passed to Matty, who unfolds it, looks up, spots Jane, and their eyes lock. She offers him the same expression she shined on Blent.

Then it's Roosevelt's turn to address the assemblage. His high-pitched "Good evening, assembled guests!" screeches through the amplification system. His ensuing lecture on economic and social freedom, democracy, letting Negroes vote and the prospect of women voting is heard at varying volumes depending on how far away from the microphone he ranges. Seventy-four minutes later, he's declaring, "Life is not a country club for white gentlemen!" when Rube Waddell emits a geyser of vomit across his plate, across the dais, dripping down the red-white-and-blue bunting facing the attendees. Rube's immediate neighbors back away as he is heaving afresh.

Martin's brow is moist as he shivers; Frank Chance burps and frowns at the odor erupting from within his body; Wee Willie Keeler raises a butt cheek and releases too-wet gas; Jimmy Collins groans and squints at Ed Reulbach, who says, *"I gotta go!"*

The assemblage dissolves. Blent jumps down from the dais, following Mathewson through the crowd. Mathewson grabs Jane's arm. *"What are you doing here?"*

"I'm here riding. It's very good."

*"Unhand her!"* It's a stern Southern voice having emanated from a man as tall as Mathewson, with ginger hair and beard, a young, reddish face.

*"You are referring to my wife!"* Mathewson protests, taking a quick, fierce glance at Blent.

Jane yanks her arm from Christy's grip, turns to Blent. "Hello, Johnny."

"Hi," he squeaks.

She explains, "There is marvelous horse country in New Glory."

Matty is perspiring. "Go home," he tells her, and turns away.

Half a dozen of the USA team is simultaneously being sick on the dais, and in that moment Mrs. Mathewson whispers to Blent, "The bar at the Estrella Club at midnight. It's *very* important."

She squeezes his hand for a moment and turns.

Blent is speechless. His stomach gurgles like an excited baby.

Up in the USA rooms, there is competition for the toilets, and when those are all claimed, the bathtubs serve the purpose. All the USA team is afflicted except Velez and Pop Lloyd, the only two who did not partake of the suckling pig. Near midnight, as the worst of the sickness seems to be passing, out on the lawn below their rooms, a hundred-piece marching band blasts "The South Is Marching On."

Some of the team wondered why their rooms were on the third floor of the ten-story hotel, and now they hear the reason. Martin peels back a curtain. As far as he can see, thousands of smiling New Gloryers are pointing up at him—his silhouette framed in the window—laughing at him and singing. They sit in trees, stand on benches, stand in Model 1s, and sit on horses.

Toward midnight, Blent wraps two pillowcases around his groin like a loincloth and stuffs himself into his pants. He stumbles out into Leeton. The air is moist, familiar, Southern.

It is a fifteen-minute walk to the Estrella Club, a cabaret in the middle of Leeton. Some version of a cancan is onstage with disembodied petticoats flying up into the rafters, delighting the audience. Blent's dizzy, sweaty.

At the bar he sips a glass of New Glory Cola, no ice—tasting a bit like Pepsi with extra sugar. Suddenly, there she is, at a crowded table, head tilted back, laughing at the cabaret, hair bunched up showing a lobe of ear, and the cool eyes. Surrounded by her well-dressed coterie, the same group in whose company she attended the banquet, she's made a costume change into a full-length blue dress with puffy sleeves, an open neck glittering with jewels.

Like an experienced hunting dog detecting an unmoving bird in a landscape, she picks out Blent. She excuses herself, rises, greets Blent with a gloved, extended arm.

*What a fool I was.* At the same time, he can't resist, eagerly touching her hand in greeting.

"I only have a second." She presses a tiny rolled-up notebook into his hand. "Give this to Roosevelt. Immediately."

Blent is stunned, understanding now. Jane Mathewson is a spy. Here is some intelligence to take to Roosevelt. He stuffs the notebook in his pocket.

"Meet my friends. Or else this will attract the wrong kind of attention, and *I* might end up with a noose around my neck."

She takes Blent to her table. "The second baseman for the USA, Johnny Blent! Johnny and I worshipped at the same church! He's a Southerner!"

Inquiries are made as to his provenance. He tells them about his wife at home. And this lie, or half lie, is making Darla more abstract.

Glasses are raised in Blent's direction. Gold watch chains glitter. The women are haughty and bejeweled, none as self-assured as Mrs. Mathewson. There's the red-bearded fellow next to her empty chair. A fat man across the table declares, "My plantation has a *fine* baseball team!"

The equally large woman next to him says, "You should see them run, run, run! Roger, here, is the manager." The fat man bows in Blent's direction.

Jane asks Blent, "Will you join us?" followed by invitations to have a drink.

There's something weirdly attractive for Blent—these elaborate manners and familiar accents—to be eagerly accepted by the Southern upper class. On the other hand, their slave society is repellent.

He tells them, "I have a friend who has cancer. It's advanced. I wonder if you or your friends know of any great cancer doctors. It's one of the photographers. He's going to die soon if we can't do anything."

Jane asks the table, "Who is the best doctor treating cancer in New Glory?"

The man to Mrs. Mathewson's left replies, "Anything serious, we sail for London, if possible! Or Canada!" He bows toward Blent. "We remain a poor country."

\*

Back at the hotel, all the doors to their rooms are open, the bathrooms overflowing with purging ballplayers. The native drumming and rumba bands cease. Three seconds later, a marching band strikes up "Dixie," and the thousands who remain outside sing full-throated. Rube Waddell lies on his back, hands on his stomach, moaning, a sound resembling that of a dying moose. In Martin's room, Blent discovers Wee Willie Keeler and Bill Dahlen on the bathroom floor.

There is an insistent knock on the doorframe. Theodore Roosevelt, wiping the underside of his mustache, seems wan. Blent fingers Mrs. Mathewson's hard, rolled-up notebook.

Roosevelt says, "Mr. Martin, this noise cannot be tolerated! They must cease and desist! There is a game to play later today!"

Martin gestures at the window. "Go ahead. Tell them."

"I already tried."

Wee Willie Keeler, in his Brooklyn accent asks, "Is dat what dey were laughing at a few minutes ago?"

Roosevelt *humphs*. His jaw unclenches. "I asked the French ambassador. We can shift everyone there. They don't have enough beds but at least there is a wall surrounding the grounds." Dahlen and Keeler weakly, slowly depart, Keeler mumbling, "Sarsaparilla," leaving Blent, Martin, and Roosevelt.

Martin asks Roosevelt, "Do you know who Albert Einstein is?"

"How do *you* know about Albert Einstein?"

"Have you ever heard of nuclear power, or nuclear weapons?"

Roosevelt is stunned. "Nuclear *weapons?*"

Martin and Blent share a glance. Martin asks Roosevelt, "Can you tend to our players? Get some hotel staff on our side? We need cool water and glasses in every room."

"Very good!" Roosevelt flashes vigor, sucks his lower lip. Blent follows him to the hallway. "I have something for you. In private."

In Roosevelt's suite, where the cacophonous music rattles the windows, Blent hands over the rolled notebook. "From Mrs. Mathewson."

"Are you in this?" Roosevelt sits at the desk and switches on an electric lamp, removes his pince-nez, examines the notebook. The writing is extremely small; to Blent it seems to be a form of code.

Roosevelt *humphs* again, then works his closed mouth as if sucking on a peculiar candy. He raises a finger. "You're not to mention this to *anyone*. And you didn't answer my question."

"I'm just a . . . friend of Mrs. Mathewson."

"That's all?"

"Yes. Is she a spy?"

"She's a patriot. She does remarkable work. Dangerous work."

"What does her husband have to do with it?"

"Mathewson?" Roosevelt snorts. "I hope that he's not aware. He has his own issues . . ."

Blent is shocked. "What kind of issues?"

Roosevelt touches his lower lip as he considers. "I will tell you this because, and only because, you put yourself in serious danger for your country." He strokes the little notebook. "Mathewson's issue is medical."

Blent's hands have explored Mathewson's spine and skull. Mathewson seems like the healthiest man in the western hemisphere. "Why can't you just spell it out? I'm discreet." And as Blent states this, the thing begins to make sense, and he guesses, "Something of a reproductive nature?"

"I'm not going to say anything about anyone's *manhood*. Do you have any children, Mr. Blent? By definition, reasonable people have reasons for their actions. I find Mrs. Mathewson a most reasonable person."

"She told you?"

Roosevelt raises an index finger, "No, sir. She did not divulge anything." He rises to the door. "Now let's find a jug of clean water and bread rolls for every one of our rooms!"

\*

Down in the enormous kitchen, they recruit Black staff, who are eager to help the team trying to vanquish their common enemy. Waiters bring pitchers of water and glasses up to the rooms.

Blent asks Roosevelt about an oncologist, and he replies with the name of the doctor they've already seen in New York, Dr. Harvard Cuff Links. "He's the best alive! Was a classmate of mine." It seems that no one in this world can help Bucky Martin.

As the first rays of sun strike the hotel, the last rumba drum stops, the last bugle ceases. The momentary silence is vanquished by the squawking of a parrot, followed, four seconds later, by the yelping of countless flocks of birds.

Most of the players stagger down to the dining room to ingest weak tea and toast. Martin's dry mouth is attempting to masticate a piece of a roll, when Roosevelt charges at him, sweeping his hand across the nearby table of half-keeled-over Frank Chance, bleary Roger Bresnahan, tea-sipping Wee Willie Keeler, and water-gulping Bruce Petway. Roosevelt shrieks, "These men are in no condition to play baseball!"

Keeler cringes and holds his ears.

"Well," replies Martin, toast in mouth refusing to decompose, in a tone quite demanding, "why don't you find out the condition of the other team?"

"The New Gloryers?" Roosevelt's pinched face nods once, and he rushes away, passing Christy Mathewson, looking pale.

Frank Chance slowly, sickly, tells Martin, "We've got a messed-up team."

"You think it was intentional?"

"To poison us with bad food and then blast that music all night?" Chance chuckles meekly. "Of course."

# 21

## Will Velez

AT 3:25 P.M. the line of Model 1s carrying the team of weakened, sleep-deprived players arrives at the ballpark. They are screamed at by red-faced fans leaning over the backs of the stadium concourses:

*"Down with the USA!"*

*"You're late, you pompous fools!"*

*"Yankees go home!"*

*"Gettysburg!"*

In his office in the visiting clubhouse, Martin sits with Chance, Mathewson, Ban Johnson, Pulliam, Brush Jr., and Theodore Roosevelt, grading the players by their health. This committee concocts a lineup of players graded C and above. Thus, they are left with Spike Shannon (.279 average) playing center field in place of Turkey Mike Donlin (.356), a weakened Blent (C+) at second, Velez in right, Chance at first, Christy Mathewson in left field and Ed Reulbach pitching. Roosevelt insists, "Mathewson is our best pitcher—at least for the first half of the game!"

Chance sneers at Roosevelt, "Do *you* want to play left field?"

Mathewson says, "Maybe one or two of our real outfielders will feel better as the game progresses."

"Maybe," says Martin, pondering putting himself in at short and Wagner in left.

"We can't do this," Roosevelt insists. "It's not sporting that the food poisoning affected us but did not affect the New Glory team one whit! We can postpone until tomorrow."

Frank Chance leans back, staring at the second-rate lineup. "I say we play this game and then when we get to Washington, we'll give them a taste of their own medicine."

The committee emerges into the locker room. Blent, Spike Shannon, Reulbach, and Velay are in uniform and appear ready to go. Waddell is on the floor, snoring. To Roosevelt, it looks like an army platoon after a losing battle. *"Come on now!"*

"No!" Martin snaps. "Quiet!" To the players, "Let Rube sleep. Anyone else too sick, stay here and rest. We're gonna delay some more and when you feel okay, come out to the dugout."

He turns to Pulliam, Johnson, Roosevelt and Junior, "Go to your seats."

Roosevelt dons his top hat, charges up the steps to the field, and is stopped cold by the sight of 62,000 screaming fanatics, arranged as if God has mixed humans with cake frosting, then spread the mixture thickly on the walls of a steep bowl. Roosevelt, along with Martin and the four umpires gathering at home plate, is the focus of the humanity spread on the walls of the bowl. "The Coliseum in Rome! Here I am! *Adsum!*"

At home plate, Martin shakes hands with Dolf Luque, the New Glory manager. Umpires Hank O'Day and Cy Rigler are two familiar faces, who do not look ill. Martin greets, "Didn't you fellows eat the pork last night?"

"Sure, we did," O'Day says. "I suppose you boys got a bad batch," adding sarcastically, "by mistake."

O'Day introduces Martin to the two long-bearded New Glory umps, Tiant, who is smoking a cigar as long as a baby's arm, and Jones, a little white guy who unsmilingly shakes Martin's hand. Martin tells the umps, "The most important people in this whole stadium are you four. This series is meaningless without fine umpiring."

"All under control," insists O'Day. Martin, just to add emphasis, again shakes each umpire's hand, and Luque's too. As Luque and the umps go over the rules of the grounds, Martin gazes around at the fans behind the dugouts, looking for Einstein, but doesn't spot him.

## SOLAR SERIES GAME 1

| UNITED STATES | | NEW GLORY | |
|---|---|---|---|
| 3B | ART DEVLIN | 2B | LUKE "HELLCAT" COBB |
| 2B | JOHNNY BLENT | 3B | AUGUSTUS COBB |
| RF | ANDRÉ VELAY | C | JOSEPHUS COBB |
| SS | HONUS WAGNER | SS | MARTÍN DIHIGO |
| C | JOHNNY KLING | 1B | CAESAR COBB |
| 1B | FRANK CHANCE | CF | BERNARDO BARO |
| CF | SPIKE SHANNON | RF | TYRUS COBB |
| LF | C. MATHEWSON | LF | SAM CRAWFORD |
| P | ED REULBACH | P | WALTER JOHNSON |

The afternoon sun is yellow-orange when the first pitch from Walter Johnson is thrown—a 100-mph fastball *whoosh* past Art Devlin. *Strike!* Devlin looks at the New Glory ump and the New Glory catcher, Josephus Cobb, the latter of whom chuckles at Devlin's stunned reaction to the fastest pitch Devlin has ever seen.

Walter Johnson, 6'2", his body not yet having filled out the frame of his fresh, young skeleton, face dotted with pimples, strikes out Devlin on three pitches. Devlin doesn't even attempt a swing. Blent strikes out on four pitches, swinging lamely late on the last. Velez fouls one straight back, indicating that his timing is good, and he manages to earn a ball before he swings over a super-bendy 92-mph curve for the third out.

Martin sits alone in the dugout. He calls to the batboy and, extending a ten-dollar New Glory bill, instructs, "Bring us fifty glasses of lemonade. And if you see a big cigar, get me one."

Blent takes the warmup throw from Kling, tosses to Devlin at third, who tosses to Reulbach. Blent looks across to Honus Wagner at shortstop, and asks, "What the heck are we gonna do?"

Wagner's almond eyes bore into Blent. "We're gonna play great. Don't be scared, Johnny Blent. If you get scared, you've lost already."

Blent is fully conscious that he's receiving a lecture from the greatest shortstop ever, and suddenly, like a shot of lightning into Blent's brain—and perhaps, it's the food poisoning—he realizes he doesn't believe in God at all. Doesn't *believe*. This is unlike his revelation about atheism in Pittsburg. This is spiritual. Life is just 62,000 fanatics, two teams on a field, umpires, one bat and one baseball. It's a feeling of profound solitude.

To the side of the New Glory dugout sits Jane Mathewson, unmistakable in a white dress and white hat with significant white plumage brushing the faces of those in the row behind her.

The first New Glory batter, Luke "Hellcat" Cobb, 5'8", thickly muscled and thin-waisted, crouches low. On a 2–1 Reulbach curve, Hellcat pops it up foul off third, Devlin ranging over, Wagner flying, and Devlin making the catch ten yards from the USA dugout.

"Way to go, Art! Way to go!" Martin's voice echoes in the empty dugout.

Augustus Cobb, the third baseman, slices a low-and-away fastball that curves through the air at Velez in right field. The ball smacks the heel of Velez's glove and drops to the ground. He throws in to Blent, and Augustus holds at first. *"Goddamn it!"* Velez admonishes himself.

The crowd in the right-field corner screams:

*"That is not the way a gentleman expresses himself!"*

*"Disgusting Yankee!"*

Augustus takes a massive lead, Reulbach spinning and firing to Chance: *"Safe!"* Reulbach tries the pickoff again to no avail. On the next pitch, Augustus takes off, flying across the hard-packed base path, Kling handling a fastball and firing to Wagner way too late.

Augustus on second. One out.

Josephus Cobb knocks a wicked-topspin-two-hopper to Blent, who fires to Chance at first as Augustus takes third. Two outs.

Bucky Martin is riveted by the sight of Martín Dihigo stepping to the plate, wiggling his bat. Many of the greatest baseball players look like they have emerged out of the clay of ball fields. They look like majestic trees. There's Honus Wagner. There's Mathewson in left field. There's Velez. Kling is good but not at this level. Mickey Mantle. Hank Aaron. Mike Trout. The Cobbs are phenoms and not yet categorizable, but just looking at Martín Dihigo—Bucky Martin has rarely seen a ballplayer with such presence. Bucky considers telling Kling to tell Reulbach to walk Dihigo, but Martin's never walked anyone just on the basis of looks. He doesn't have any charts on the New Glory players. Brush, Jr. is in the stands compiling them, but whether there will be enough at-bats to establish patterns before this is all over is debatable.

Dihigo works the count to 2–2. Reulbach twists the ball against a burr on his belt buckle. In his glove, his index finger traces the cut in the ball he's just sliced. He shakes off Kling so that Kling knows what's coming. It starts out looking like a hanging curve, then breaks four feet down. Dihigo whacks it—misses hitting it cleanly—popping it up high in the blue-yellow sky, high into shallow left. Wagner backpedals, then turns and sprints, looking up over his shoulder, screaming, *"Mine!"* the tone of voice fending off Mathewson. The ball drops over Wagner's shoulder into his glove. Three outs.

Top of the 2nd. Honus Wagner hops up and down, watching Walter Johnson fire a warmup fastball *whoosh, pop!* into Josephus Cobb's mitt. Wagner's hopping is priming the triggering mechanism connecting eyes, hands, arms, body, and bat.

The first pitch whooshes in, Wagner's bat whooshing louder. He cracks the ball and it gashes the air into right-center. Wagner runs like a bizarre crossbreed of rabbit and moose—fast, smooth, and monstrous—taking second base. He claps his hands. Walter Johnson looks blankly at Wagner as Johnson takes the toss from second baseman Hellcat Cobb, who reassures Johnson, "All right, kid. We got 'em!"

Kling strikes out; Frank Chance grounds to third; Spike Shannon strikes out on three pitches.

Bottom of the 2nd. Cæsar Cobb, a left-handed batter with a flowing red beard who is as large and broad-shouldered as Velez, wags his bat straight up. He bends to dig a Reulbach curve and smacks it on a line deep to right field, straight at Velez, the ball screaming through the air, Velez unsure for a couple moments about its trajectory as it flies at him. He takes three steps toward the line, sticks up his glove, and the ball smacks in, stinging. Trying not to shake his hand or wince, Velez tosses the ball in to Blent.

Bernardo Baro walks.

Ty Cobb stands in, the man many believe to be the greatest hitter in Major League history. He's slighter than his brothers, younger, his collar up, jittery: 80 percent intense and 20 percent crazy. He is clean-shaven, unlike older New Gloryers. Or perhaps Ty can't yet grow a beard.

"Hey!" Honus Wagner shouts at Blent, indicating that Blent will cover second in case Bernardo Baro tries to steal.

On a 1–1 curveball, Baro takes off like he's shot out of a cannon, sliding in almost a full second before Kling's throw arrives.

Ty Cobb pulls the next pitch toward the hole between first and second. Blent dives, knocks the ball down, grabs it with his bare hand, and fires to Chance: out by half a step. *"No!"* Ty Cobb protests to Rigler. Baro takes third. Remaining on his knees on the outfield grass, Blent watches Ty Cobb jog off. *I just threw out Ty Cobb.*

Baro on third. Two outs.

Bresnahan makes his way from the clubhouse to the dugout, and Martin asks, "Feel good enough to bat?" Bresnahan nods his head without taking his mouth from the glass of icy lemonade he's sucking down.

Sam Crawford battles Reulbach and works a twelve-pitch walk. Walter Johnson pops up the first pitch to Blent for the third out.

## USA  0 — 0  NEW GLORY

Top of the 3rd. Bresnahan bats for Mathewson and pops out to Augustus Cobb at third. Reulbach strikes out looking, shaking his head and mouthing, *Wow*, as he walks back to the bench. Art Devlin grounds to Martín Dihigo at short, Dihigo firing across the diamond to Cæsar Cobb.

Bottom of the 3rd. Hellcat Cobb doubles to right-center. Augustus Cobb smacks a screamer that sends Bresnahan back at full sprint, Bresnahan making an over-the-shoulder catch and firing to Wagner, who throws a 130-foot strike to Kling, keeping Hellcat from scoring from second on a sacrifice fly.

Hellcat Cobb on third. One out.

Josephus Cobb, the catcher, strikes out swinging. Two outs.

Martín Dihigo walks and easily steals second. Cæsar Cobb, the largest of the Cobbs, rips a Reulbach fastball into left, scoring Hellcat and Martín Dihigo.

USA   0 — 2   NEW GLORY

Cæsar Cobb steals second. Bernardo Baro walks. Two outs.

Ty Cobb rips a single into right, Velez charging and throwing in to second to keep Ty Cobb at first. Cæsar scores.

USA   0 — 3   NEW GLORY

Baro on third, Ty Cobb on first. Two outs.

Sam Crawford scorches a two hopper to Frank Chance at first. Chance knocks it down, corrals it, and steps on first base for the third out.

Top of the 4th. Blent flies out to center; Velez walks on five pitches; Honus Wagner bounces into a 4–6–3 double play.

In the box next to the dugout, Ban Johnson, Harry Pulliam and Theodore Roosevelt squirm. In the row behind them, Junior's chart of Walter Johnson's pitches is a rectangle heavily dotted on the lower borders and empty inside the box. Thirty-four pitches. Junior surmises that Walter Johnson has not made one mistake.

Bottom of the 4th. Hellcat Cobb singles and steals second. Augustus Cobb singles, scoring Hellcat.

USA   0 — 4   NEW GLORY

Bottom of the 5th. Martín Dihigo walks and steals second. Cæsar Cobb whacks a single to right, scoring Dihigo. Two more runs score, and the game is nearly out of hand.

## USA  0 — 7  NEW GLORY

Top of the 6th. To the outfield side of the dugout, Jimmy Collins and Rube Foster are tossing a ball. Martin watches them for a moment, then makes history, telling Collins, "You're going in to left," and to Foster, "Get ready to pitch."

Ban Johnson leans across Pulliam and Roosevelt and barks at Martin, "You can't do this!"

Martin calmly turns to Johnson. "It's my best option, Ban."

Moments after, Art Devlin strikes out for the second time of the day, and the New Gloryers jog toward their dugout. Rube Foster, a Negro, crosses the third-base line, headed for the pitching mound, the navy blue letters "USA" sewn onto the chest of his cream-colored uniform.

Top of the 9th. As Honus Wagner grounds to Cæsar Cobb, who steps on first to end the game, the 62,000 fans roar in deep satisfaction, the sun lighting the upper deck orange as the stadium lights buzz on. Pulliam, Ban Johnson, and Roosevelt gawk at the banks of bulbs illuminating the field.

\*

That evening, having moved to the French embassy, the glum team eats at a banquet table. The Irish and Rube Waddell eschew wine in favor of rum, which flows into them, lightening the mood. Martin wants to stand up and say, "We should not have played today. I thought it was important to play, but I was caught up in the fight of getting guys on the field. Looking back, feeling clear-headed, it was the wrong decision." But Martin remains silent.

He sleeps on a red velvet sofa in the attaché's suite, sleeps without stirring, and dreams that Bruce Petway's arm is a rifle and Hellcat Cobb is running toward second base and is shot dead, Hellcat's arm outstretched, three feet short of second base. Then Augustus Cobb tries to steal and is shot halfway to second. Then Cæsar, Josephus, then Ty. It's a line of five dead Cobbs, and one dead Martín Dihigo.

Bucky Martin rises in the big, dark room. Frank Chance snores in one of the beds, Velez in the other. The ceiling is so tall Martin can't see it in the shadows. He steps out onto the balcony. Palm trees rustle in the soft breeze. He's facing the first silver glow of predawn. His lips momentarily stick together before the word is whispered: "Petway."

"What did you say?" Blent's standing on the next balcony, after his second night of lousy sleep. He points beyond Martin. "Wow!"

A line of heads stick up above the French embassy's eight-foot brick wall. People wave at Martin and Blent. In silhouette, it's a line of men and women of African descent. They're standing on shoulders to glimpse the USA players. Many of them seem thrilled, waving their arms for the USA players to come down.

"This is a whole new fucking thing," Martin says.

"What do you mean?"

"Let's go meet some real fans."

Martin and Blent step out the front gate, not before a French sentry warns them, "Those *gens*—those people—are desperate! Careful!"

They are swiftly enveloped by the throng of hundreds. Almost all are barefoot, in patched clothes, skinny, some limping. A dozen of the men's necks are encased in iron collars, locks, and ringbolts. Preceding Blent and Martin have been Pop Lloyd, Rube Foster, and Bruce Petway, immaculate in their fine suits.

Foster says, "This isn't right, Mr. Martin."

"No it's not." Martin feels like he's at the epicenter of history: face-to-face with slaves. He adds, just to hear his voice, "For sure."

Blent's shaking every offered hand, returning pats on the shoulder, distributing his money even though no one's asking for it.

Martin tells the French sentry, "Go get the rest of the team, please." The sentry rolls his eyes.

And then Blent is struck by the sight of a tall man at the back of the group scratching the side of his scalp: the same wide forehead, head shape, little ears, and eyes as André Velez. The man is wearing one of the New Glory neck shackles. Blent approaches. "Are you a Velez?" he asks, and there's Mathewson and Wiltse emerging into the throng, behind them Frank Chance and André Velez.

"Yes," says the man, a shocking photocopy of André, except for darker skin and curlier hair.

Blent introduces himself. "What is your name?"

"They call me Will. Will Velez."

Martin steps forward and is astonished.

André Velez emerges through the arched gate, scanning the crowd, gaze latching onto Martin, then gobsmacked—the prominent cheekbones, the shape of his eyes, his ears, his nose, chin. It's like looking in a mirror, except that this man's skin is deep black. André Velez stands face-to-face with him.

Will Velez greets him, "You're a handsome fellow."

André Velez reaches up for Will Velez's iron collar, the redness where the collar rubs his neck. "Curaçao?"

"We were taken here six years ago, when New Glory invaded, took everything." A pause, then, "My children love baseball."

They touch each other's shoulders. "My name is André Velez. Velez, not Velay."

Will opens his big hand of oozing calluses and scrapes, holds it next to André's, to compare the matching open hands.

"Are you Bertrand's son or grandson?" Will Velez asks. "They left Curaçao fifty years ago."

"Bertrand Velez?" André Velez asks. He has never heard of Bertrand Velez. He considers how he can tell Will Velez that Will Velez might be his great-great-great-great-grandfather. He can't. "I'm distant. But obviously, not so distant."

Will introduces his five kids, his cousins, nieces and nephews, and André, disoriented by the thought, realizes that one of the boys is likely his great-great-great-grandfather. He asks Will, "You have a wife?"

"Working a plantation near Guantanamo. She was sold away three years ago."

"I'm so sorry, man."

André turns to Buck and Blent, whose astonished faces seem paler than usual. "We can't let these people go back to slavery." Andre's baseball-callused fingers brush the iron lock on Will's collar.

"Time," Will says. "Yes, it's time for us to get back. We are already late, and that will hurt." He raises his voice so all can hear, all the slaves and all the team that are out in the scrubby lot beyond the French embassy gates. "Go USA!"

"USA!" Blent shouts.

Some shout back, "USA!"

"USA!" Blent echoes.

"USA!" the crowd reverberates. "USA! USA! USA! USA! USA!"

Pop Lloyd tells Martin, "We're gonna walk back with these people. A lot are from Leeton, but some are from ten miles away."

Martin leans in to Lloyd, Petway and Rube Foster, brings them close. "I know you want to help, but listen. You're gonna play today." He points at Petway's breastbone: "You're my starting catcher. Get to the ballpark early so you can go over their lineup with Mathewson and me."

Nearby, André Velez is writing down as fast as he can the information Will is providing—the names of every family member, the location of the plantation, their home village in Curaçao. "I'm going too!"

Will tells his children, "Look, you have a new uncle!" Will Velez starts away with his kids. Velez takes a step after Will, then retreats. Tears form in the corners of Velez's eyes. There's a softness in his face.

"Stay with them," Martin says. He stuffs his wad of NG cash into Velez's hand. "Give it to them."

Blent asks, "Can I come with you?"

"Yeah, man. Of course."

Martin asks Rube Foster and Pop Lloyd, "Will you please make sure our guys get to the ballpark on time?"

Foster and Lloyd chuckle at the situation. "We'll take care of them," Pop Lloyd says.

*

Half an hour later, Martin soaks in the bathtub and asks Frank Chance, who's shaving in the mirror, about the idea of playing Petway.

"You're not really considering it, are you? Half the team will revolt."

"Ever seen Petway play? He squats closer to the batter than any catcher in the major leagues, and he's got a howitzer for an arm."

"What's a howitzer?"

Martin realizes that, probably, howitzers have not yet been invented. "A cannon."

\*

It's a dusty walk beyond the outer reaches of Leeton, the pack of a hundred slaves breaking off into clusters at roads and paths along the way, to return to their various plantations, not before Pop Lloyd, Rube Foster, Blent, and André Velez have employed Foster's and Lloyd's pens to sign every scrap of paper offered to them, scraps pulled out of ditches along the way, making sure to include the name of each person seeking an autograph.

Velez walks alongside Will Velez, dopplegangers asking questions of each other, André Velez trying to absorb every shred of information. Lacking a baseball, Blent lifts a small smooth stone and begins gently tossing it with the kids.

Two of Will Velez's boys, large kids about twelve and ten, remind André Velez of himself at those ages. He thinks of Nicole back in New York, and realizes it's quite insane not to miss the women from *his* time—Cookie, Arlene, or Gloria. He asks Will, "Have you tried to escape?"

"It's a big island. I could do it and hide. But if I escape they'll punish my family, just for revenge. They don't want to kill us, we're too valuable—labor."

"Would the person in charge of you let me—"

"The Missus."

"The Missus?"

"The Master passed away two years ago. His widow. She's harder than he ever was."

"Would she let me buy all of you?"

Will softly chuckles and glances at the horizon. Velez recognizes the expression; it's his. Blent recognizes it too. Will says, "That would give her no workforce. Slaves are expensive. It would rob her of her role of cruelty."

Will tells the Negro League players, "They can just seize Blacks on the road for doing nothing. I am warning you."

"We're Americans," says Rube Foster.

"They look at us as animals." Will steps across a ditch, followed in a line by his family and others from the plantation, up a berm and three steps along a path, down to the tobacco plants, each green leaf wider than a dinner platter, the plants spreading out in rows to the horizon.

Blent asks, "Does your Missus like baseball?"

Will laughs. "She likes money and buying things in Paris. If you want to help, you can help us pick starting tomorrow when the sky gets light."

"She goes to Paris every year for Christmas," says the oldest boy.

Rube Foster tells the ballplayers, "Time to get to the stadium."

"I want to meet the Missus," Velez insists. "What's her name?"

Will replies, "Mrs. Tramontine."

Blent tells Rube—the shining light of Rube Foster's round face—"This is incredibly important to him."

Rube asks, "So what is he, a Black man, or an Indian?"

Far away on the porch of the mansion stands a woman with hands on hips. "That's her." Will trods forward, head down, toward the house.

"Wait!" Velez implores.

The house is long, a new section going up, looking like a half-built chateau.

"You building it?" asks Pop Lloyd.

The twelve-year-old replies, "Pounding nails all day."

The ten-year-old holds up a bulbous pinkie, which has no final section. "Still hurts!"

They walk up along a garden bursting with flowers.

Will Velez tells the woman who "owns" him, "These are baseball players, ma'am."

Blent, André Velez, Rube Foster, and Pop Lloyd take in the sight of the woman on the front porch. "My niggers just love baseball. They're very good players, I'm told. I pay for them to go to games at the new stadium. Same architects as here."

The four ballplayers hide their disdain to varying degrees.

Pop Lloyd offers, "Very beautiful house. Very unusual."

"It's the style. Norman."

André Velez can barely control his rage. He wishes he had all his twenty-first-century money back and he'd buy her out, or at least buy all the slaves and take them to New York, or wherever they'd want to go. Maybe Curaçao, but that's a vassal slave state now. He asks her, "How much is it to buy a slave?"

She's a middle-aged woman with dyed red hair. She looks between André and Will. "Quite a resemblance!"

"My family's from Curaçao, originally," he tells her. "On my father's side."

Will tells the other slaves, "Get to work! Go on!" They turn away, some glancing up to gauge the prospective brutality of the day's sunshine, to the tobacco fields. Some climb ladders to start pounding on the house. The kids and some of the adults shake the hands of the ballplayers. André Velez tells them, "Wait!" He hurriedly unties his shoes and gives them to Will, who looks up at the Missus. She sneers and nods okay.

Velez gives Will his socks, gives his shirt to the twelve-year-old who's about six feet tall.

Blent kneels to untie his shoes, as do Lloyd and Rube Foster, along with expendable garments and bowler hats to protect from the sun a bit.

The Missus smiles at André Velez. "No one is for sale. Everything's working well here."

"What about for your whole spread? A million? Two million? Name a price."

From the porch, she looks down at him. "A million dollars? You're another unserious Negro. Or perhaps you can't count. In New Glory, it's rude to make such bald inquiries. We don't talk about money. One of my drivers will ride you back to Leeton. The ground must feel tender on your bare feet. You are not invited back here. Ever. Nothing is for sale except our very fine tobacco. *Adieu.*"

She turns inside, a screen door shutting.

"How about—" He starts up to the porch. Blent, Lloyd and Rube Foster halt him. He pleadingly looks at Blent, "Help me, man!"

Blent gazes around. The slaves have disappeared into the far fields. Way far away, he can see a patch of land with a very rough baseball diamond. A few fat white men stand to the side of the porch. Blent yells at the house, loud enough so she would, inside, possibly hear, *"Can we just take his family with us?"*

There is no reply. Just an indication from a driver to move to one of the plantation's pair of Model 1s.

Rube Foster says, "I don't even want to ride in her carriage."

"Let's walk back," agrees Pop Lloyd.

André Velez raises his middle finger at the house and at the two parked Model 1s. In walking out the same path they walked in, André cups his hands around his mouth and shouts, "Goodbye family! I will see you again! I promise!"

From a far field, bodies pop up, wave. From the face of the house they turn and shout, "André!" A boy crashes across rows of green tobacco—the twelve-year-old—running fast in his new shirt, already a sleeve has ripped. From the porch, one of the overseers shouts, "Stop! Nigger boy!"

He sprints and leaps up at André Velez, who catches him. André promises, "I'm not gonna forget you, okay? We'll get you out of here!"

Petway pats the boy's back. Pop Lloyd stuffs a twenty-dollar NG bill in his hand. Rube Foster comments, "What a *fucked-up* world."

*

That afternoon, the second game looming, Martin's mind disturbed with images of slaves, he sits in his clubhouse office, writing out his lineup. He's inserted Petway and crossed him out. He's inserted Pop Lloyd, who is an upgrade over the excellent Devlin, at third base. Now as he crosses out Lloyd, a little face with a wispy black mustache in the doorway, the unkempt hair squashed under a white NG baseball cap: Albert Einstein, brandishing a snow-white baseball and a pen. Martin yells to the clubhouse boy, "Bring Blent and Velay!"

"How did you get in here?" Martin asks.

"In New Glory you can bribe your way into almost any place. Mr. Martin, I didn't want to build a weapon to harness nuclear fission. The destructive capabilities are unimaginable."

"They're imaginable. We've seen it."

Einstein's face twists in horror.

The clubhouse boy tells Martin, "No Blent or Velay. No Rube Foster or Pop Lloyd or Petway."

"All right." Martin shuts the door.

Einstein continues, "I am attempting to take the project leaders down the wrong path. Without me, it might take them five years, ten years, or longer to build a bomb. I did not know this was truly possible, this bomb. *Mein in Got*, my life is torture."

It's then that Blent and Velez knock and enter, dusty and barefoot.

Einstein asks Martin, "Can you get me out? They kidnapped me from Bern. My wife—I miss her." They close the door.

"I know what you mean—missing your wife," Blent says.

Velez slumps in a chair, grabs a glass of water, drains it, tells Einstein, "Evil country." To Martin, "My relatives are slaves! Slaves! Who's the free-est man you know? Me! Right?"

"At what date did you arrive in our present?" Einstein asks.

"April 18th, this year," Blent replies.

Einstein touches fingers to nose. "Oh my God. Not again. We achieved a significant nuclear reaction that day—barely contained. The reaction does something strange, but I don't know how. It *might* be possible to move particles through time. It seems that we did that to you—seized you somehow—by accident. This is very strange."

A firm knocking on the door. The door opens and Einstein's two hirsute uniformed minders enter. One beard opens: "Herr Professor. We did not know you were such a fan of the USA team."

Einstein offers the ball and pen to Velez. "This is historic, no?" The ball and pen circulate to Blent and Martin before Einstein and his minders depart.

Velez crosses his big arms and rests his head back against the wall.

Blent says softly, "At least we know who's responsible for us being in 1906—Einstein."

"But he has no idea how it works. We have to get him and Tesla together."

Velez wipes his eyes. "How would you feel if your family were slaves?"

"Look, man," says Blent. "We ship out of here tonight. If you want to come back and see your family again, we've got to win at least two games out of the next four, so there *is* a Game 6 back at this stadium."

Velez sneers, "Now it's serious."

# 22

## My Head's in the Wrong Place

### SOLAR SERIES GAME 2

| UNITED STATES | | NEW GLORY | |
|---|---|---|---|
| 3B | ART DEVLIN | 2B | LUKE "HELLCAT" COBB |
| 2B | JOHNNY BLENT | 3B | AUGUSTUS COBB |
| 1B | ANDRÉ VELAY | C | JOSEPHUS COBB |
| SS | HONUS WAGNER | SS | MARTÍN DIHIGO |
| LF | MIKE DONLIN | 1B | CAESAR COBB |
| CF | GEORGE STONE | CF | BERNARDO BARO |
| RF | ELMER FLICK | RF | TYRUS COBB |
| C | BRUCE PETWAY | LF | SAM CRAWFORD |
| P | C. MATHEWSON | P | JOSÉ MÉNDEZ |

The entire USA team crowds the left-field foul line, twenty feet from José Méndez, who is firing warmup pitches. Méndez is a wiry 5'8", about twenty years old. He ignores the USA players and only throws fastballs. Martin sends three baseballs and a pen up the line of USA players for autographs.

Martin, Velez, and Blent step to the side.

"That is fucked up, what we saw today," Velez tells Martin.

Martin asks, "Do you think their owner will sell your relatives?"

"I asked. She says she won't sell. I've got to take them, somehow."

"Just play ball, man," Blent suggests. "We'll figure something out. As long as we get back here."

"Goddamn this world," says Velez as he autographs the baseballs and hands ball and pen to Martin.

Martin signs them and inscribes part of a panel on the last. "Stick close to me after the game. The three of us are gonna try to smuggle Einstein out of here."

After Méndez's warmups, Martin walks past the stands, spots Einstein six rows up. He hands out two souvenier balls to random fans, and tosses a ball to Einstein, who excitedly catches it.

Bottom of the 1st. One out. Blent glances over at Mathewson as he delivers a curve to Sam Crawford that breaks low for a ball, and Blent wonders what, exactly, Roosevelt was referring to in regard to Mathewson's manhood.

In the stands, Albert Einstein reaches into the pocket of his droopy canvas jacket and removes his autographed baseball. He reads the autographs of Hooks Wiltse, Cy Young, Christy Mathewson, Willie Keeler, Rube Foster, Bruce Petway, Honus Wagner, Johnny Blent, André Velay, Ed Reulbach, Frank Chance, and Buck Martin. Examining it closer, under Martin's signature, Martin has written:

*Palace Hotel —*
*90 mins after game.*

The USA strings together three hits in the fourth for a run. In the sixth, Martín Dihigo *whoosh crack!* crushes a fastball, the ball arcing high, higher against the blue sky. Donlin drifts back, back to the wall. The ball drops twelve rows up in the bleachers.

| Game 2 | 1 | 2 | 3 | 4 | 5 | 6 | 7 | 8 | 9 | R | H | E |
|---|---|---|---|---|---|---|---|---|---|---|---|---|
| USA | 0 | 0 | 0 | 1 | 0 | 0 | 0 | 0 | | 1 | 5 | 1 |
| New Glory | 0 | 0 | 0 | 0 | 0 | 1 | 0 | | | 1 | 6 | 0 |

Bottom of the 8th. Three Finger Brown takes over for Mathewson. Brown's uniform is already an agglomeration of gray sweat blobs as Ty Cobb strides to the plate to lead off.

Ty rips a first-pitch fastball into right for a single.

Crawford at bat. Ty takes a nine-foot lead at first.

Brown flicks a throw to Velez, Ty cramming his foot between Velez's feet. Safe.

Ty walks out to his previous lead and inches out beyond it. Brown throws over four more times, the New Glory crowd booing louder with each pickoff attempt.

The first pitch to Crawford is a fastball down the middle. Crawford swats it into left, Ty flying around second, sliding into third and popping up as Donlin fires the ball to Honus Wagner.

"Ladies and gentlemen," the electrically amplified PA voice grates on 59,000 ears, echoing, "hitting for José Méndez, Armando Marsans."

The New Glory crowd stands and applauds in appreciation of Méndez's excellent pitching performance: one run, five hits.

Armando Marsans is another baby-faced New Glory player, nineteen years old, a right-handed batter.

Martin turns to Rube Foster. "Warm up."

Foster and Kling jump up the dugout steps.

Three Finger Brown notes Foster warming up. Brown's body is suffering under the heat, still dulled from the food poisoning of a day and a half ago. But his mind is that of a warrior mid-battle.

1–0 to Marsans. Brown throws a curve that bounces on the edge of home plate and bounds toward the New Glory dugout, Petway breaking after it, Ty Cobb breaking for home, Three Finger Brown sprinting to cover the plate, the home-plate ump backing away to observe the expected play at the plate. But as Petway picks it up, the ball falls out of his hand, and Ty Cobb slides across the plate with the go-ahead run. Martin groans; everyone on the USA bench groans; Pulliam, Ban Johnson, and Roosevelt groan.

## USA  1 — 2  NEW GLORY

Top of the 9th. Walter Johnson looks fresh as he warms up. He strikes out Wagner, induces a weak Donlin grounder to second. As George Stone whiffs to end the game, the New Glory crowd roars, and the roaring soon subsides in favor of a chant, accompanied by index fingers and forearms repeatedly pointing at the USA team. "Los-ers! Los-ers! Los-ers! Los-ers! Los-ers! Los-ers! Los-ers! Los-ers! Los-ers!"

\*

It seems perverse to the USA delegation, but the last item on the New Glory itinerary is a bon voyage banquet at the Palace Hotel. The bar is filling up with dejected USA ballplayers. Martin sips a scotch on ice and puffs the richest cigar he's ever smoked. Reporters gravitate toward him as if he were Jupiter.

F. C. Lane asks, "Is the New Glory team the best you've ever seen?"

Martin's mind flicks through the greatest teams in baseball history. "New Glory is good. Obviously. But it's only two
games."

The reporter from the *Chicago Tribune* asks, "What can
you do differently?"

"Hit, run, catch, pitch."

Ed Dinkel of the *Pittsburg Courier* asks, "President Hanna
issued a statement that he was embarrassed by the performance
of the team. What do you say to that?"

Martin sips his scotch. "I was embarrassed by the outcome.
I was not embarrassed by the effort. Our boys play hard, with
honor and dedication and energy, and that's nothing to be
embarrassed about."

"Are you contradicting the president of the United States?"

Martin's eye turns reptilian. The reporter's self-satisfied
smile melts. "No."

\*

In the largest bar of the SS *Normandie*, the team has bifur-
cated: the drunks and the brooders. The drunks loudly command a corner. Meanwhile, Jimmy Collins, Frank Chance,
Christy Mathewson, Bill Dahlen, Cy Young, Hooks Wiltse,
Joe McGinnity, George Stone, Ed Reulbach, and Three Finger
Brown have pushed three tables together, like three humungous
lily pads. At a fourth table, not contiguous to the first three, sit
Bruce Petway, Rube Foster, and Pop Lloyd. Lloyd's suit is crisp,
his tie knotted perfectly, cuff links gleaming. McGinnity has
brought the Negroes beers because a waiter has let it be known
that the staff—all white—will not serve Negroes.

But Wee Willie Keeler has been left behind.

At the departing reception, Velez and Blent cornered Bill Dahlen, urgently explaining—without using Einstein's name—"the scientist" and the bomb, trying to convince Dahlen to switch places with the "scientist," so he could escape New Glory.

Dahlen replied, "Sorry. I got a wife and kids I need to get back to. I'm not gonna stay here. They'll hang me like those guys on that platform. The world's not gonna end with some crazy huge bomb. That's complete bullcrap." Dahlen wandered away to find a drink.

Then, recalling Keeler's rant about New Glory on the way over, Velez and Blent explained that they're giving Keeler an opportunity to "help destroy" New Glory.

Keeler replied, "Chief, Johnny, I'm all ears."

Exactly ninety minutes after the game ended, Einstein—tight-lipped, worried eyes—strolled into the bar, and Blent motioned for him to follow. In an empty dining room on the second floor, they introduced Einstein to Wee Willie Keeler, who said, "My price is a hundred bucks." That agreed, he departed.

Martin laid out the plan to Einstein. "You will dress as Willie Keeler. And you will come aboard our ship and depart with us. Keeler will stay here for an extra day, pretending to have missed the ship."

Einstein hesitated.

"What is it?" Martin asked.

"I must tell you. Until you arrived and told me your claims of time travel, I did not believe it. Because I have heard it before, with another baseball player."

*"Who?"* the three asked together.

"The shortstop. Martín Dihigo."

*"Dee-go?"* they said, astonished.

"I didn't believe such an outrageous claim. But now you three have made the same claim, independent of Dihigo, correct?"

"I've never said a word to Dihigo," Martin replied, stunned.

"Me neither," confirmed Blent.

"This disaster happened *twice*, to us and to Dihigo?" Velez whined.

"Unfortunately. And maybe more than twice—Dihigo claims it happened just to him twice. So three times in toto. You, Martín Dihigo once; then Martín Dihigo again. First he claims he went back to 1863, then to 1903. It seems that every time the nuclear reaction achieves a certain level, we are open to an accident of this type. Dihigo says he was taken out of March 27, 1933. Transported to 1863 in Virginia. And from 1863 to here, New Glory, in 1903."

"Wait a second." Martin raised his hands in double stop signs. "Dihigo in 1863 in Virginia? Did he fight at Gettysburg?"

"You and your Civil War hobby, man." Velez scoffed.

"But if Dihigo fought at Gettysburg, for the South, maybe that is the reason everything is out of kilter here."

"Dihigo changed the world's history?" Velez sarcastically asked.

"If a butterfly flapping can do it, so can Dihigo."

Velez and Blent shared a significant glance.

"To finish answering, Mr. Blent, it seems to have something to do with the quantity of power generated. But then, if this phenomenon explained it all, you, in your time, if there are hundreds of nuclear reactors in the world, you would be having this time travel problem on a consistent basis. But Dihigo is the only other person of whom I am aware to make this claim."

"So the nuclear power is not the only element," Blent asked. "Something else is going on."

"Nature doesn't reveal her secrets easily," noted Einstein.

"Should we try to grab some of your laboratory equipment for time travel?"

"Unfortunately, Mr. Blent, if I do not know how it functions, I don't know what I need—other than a nuclear reaction."

Keeler returned, inquiring, "What the hell're you guys talkin' 'bout?"

"Nothing," Blent replied, wiping a straight razor and dry shaving into Einstein's wispy mustache.

Martin slapped a wad of New Glory money into Keeler's palm, Keeler commenting, "Now I can really enjoy myself!"

Martin instructed Keeler, "Show up at the French embassy any time after noon tomorrow. We'll be back in the US. Just show up drunk."

"You don't have to worry 'bout dat!"

\*

Three hours after the switch, in their shared cabin, Albert Einstein lights a cigarette, and asks Wagner if he plays baseball in Boston.

Wagner requests, *"Stört es dich, nicht zu rauchen, Herr Einstein? Es ist unangenehm für mich."* ("Do you mind not smoking, Herr Einstein? It is unpleasant for me.")

Martin, Velez, and Blent join them in their cabin. Martin instructs Wagner, "Not a word about Mr. Einstein to anybody, okay? The vice president doesn't even know yet."

Wagner pantomimes buttoning his mouth, then pats his stomach. "I am starving. Herr Einstein, I will fill a plate for you and bring it back."

Albert Einstein bows to Wagner. As the door clicks shut, Einstein tells them, "Perhaps if I can reunite with Tesla, his mind will focus on time travel."

"The all-star scientists together again," Velez comments.

Blent asks, "What will it take to construct a nuclear reaction large enough to match what you have done before?"

"Enough fissile material. Uranium, preferably. A reactor."

"But there's only one reactor in the world, and that's in New Glory, right?" asks Velez.

"Yes," Einstein replies. "They are far ahead of anyone else."

"And we're sailing *away* from it," Velez says. "And we're losing 2–0. So we have to win at least two out of the next three games to get back to New Glory for Games 6 and 7." He grits his teeth, considering his enslaved relatives.

Blent reaches for Martin's collar. Martin flinches, then lets Blent reveal the angry-looking nodes. Blent asks Einstein, "What about this?"

Einstein reaches up to touch a bulging, reddish node. Einstein's mouth muckles. "What do the doctors say?"

\*

The moment that Martin's Solar Series consternations, combined with plans for getting Einstein to Tesla, all melt into a leaden sleep, an insistent knocking wakes him. He lets in Velez, reeking of rum and cigars.

Eyes red-rimmed and glassy in the light of the bedside lamp, Velez says, " . . . Being diverted to Jacksonville. Dock in an hour. One of the engines failed or something. Gonna kick us off in the morning. I thought you should know. How do we hide Einstein?"

"Please get Johnny."

At the door, Velez hesitates. "We should platoon. Send a left-handed-hitting lineup against Johnson and Méndez. They kill righties. Except Blent and Wagner." Velez exits.

Martin contemplates his best left-handed hitters: Elmer Flick, who mashed twenty-two triples, hit .311, and had a

.813 OPS for Cleveland; George Stone, who led the American League with a .358 average for the St. Louis Browns; and Pop Lloyd, and Donlin, and Velez. And Bruce Petway is a switch hitter, though not the greatest hitter; with Petway it's about the arm gunning out runners. Martin wonders how much booing will rain down from the Washington fans, or if they'll be violent, or even riot, at seeing a Black man behind the plate for the USA.

A few minutes later, Velez takes the chair, and Blent leans against the porthole.

"These seem to be our choices," Martin says. "We can either try to hide Einstein ourselves and get him to Telsa ourselves; or we hand Einstein over to Roosevelt and let Roosevelt deal with him. But Einstein needs to create a nuclear reaction to even have the *possibility* of getting us back, and the person who has the connections—either privately, or through the government—to help build a reactor is Roosevelt."

*"Roosevelt?"* Velez exclaims. *"That dickwad?"*

Blent explodes, "Do you know how many *years* it could take to build a device to control a nuclear reaction!" Blent motions at Buck but refrains from mentioning the lymph nodes.

Velez chimes, "You need a real doctor—a twenty-first-century doctor."

Shrugging his shoulders makes Martin wince. "Sore muscle."

Blent shouts, *"It's the cancer!"*

"Let's find out everything Dihigo knows," Martin underscores. At a gentle knock on the door, Velez lets in Einstein and Wagner.

Wagner tells Martin, "I am not leaving this man's side until he is safe!"

Einstein smiles. "Thank you, Honus. I am sure I am fine."

Martin tells Einstein, "We are going to introduce you to Vice President Roosevelt. He will know how best to protect you."

Blent explodes at Einstein, "You're responsible! You ripped us out of our lives! My wife! My baby I've never met! Figure it out!"

"Mr. Blent, as of right now I do not understand the phenomenon."

Velez rises to Einstein and softly punches the little man's shoulder. "You think when I go into the batter's box facing Walter Johnson that in my mind I'm thinking that I don't understand how he can throw so fast? No! I think, 'I can hit this motherfucka!' Every time I go to bat!"

Einstein smiles, eyes gleam. "I will keep that in the forefront of my mind."

\*

Twenty hours later, after stopping in Jacksonville to change ships, Roosevelt halts next to Martin on the deck of the SS *Thompson*. "Your man is safe. On land. He is now with our best agents from the Secret Service. Tesla and Einstein will meet tomorrow. I am being apprised."

"Very good. Can we get access to Einstein?"

"I hope to be able to arrange a meeting. During the time I had with him, he and I discussed nuclear power and a nuclear weapon. It is a thoroughly new age! Never be afraid of the future!"

A red razor nick on Roosevelt's neck vibrates as he hands Martin a sheet of paper. "I have Mr. Blent batting first!"—his proposed USA lineup.

# 23

## Nicole Knows

AT ANNAPOLIS, VELEZ rushes down the gangway and into the arms of Nicole, lifting and spinning her, both laughing. The New Glory ship is already there, having docked twelve hours earlier.

A few hours later in Washington, the parade down Pennsylvania Avenue draws a sparse crowd. The Cobbs and the other New Gloryers sit back in their horse-drawn carriages, unimpressed by the shabby town.

After sex, Nicole gazes out the window of the room at the Ambassador Hotel, looking out over Washington. From the bed, Velez assesses. She complains that she's thin, but he likes *thin*. Gloria was hot as heck, but hers was a workout hotness. Her body was *hard*. She was hard too.

"I met my relatives," he tells Nicole.

"Oh?"

"Slaves." She is stunned. He takes her hand and she nestles beside him. He recounts the visit in detail. He doesn't divulge that Will is his great-great-great-grandfather (give or take a great), because that would reveal the time travel part of his equation, and he's not ready to risk it. "I was told I had relatives in Curaçao. But they were captured and taken to New Glory and sold. Tobacco plantation. Some are in Guantanamo."

"Oh, André, I am so sorry." She goes to him. "I would love to meet your family one day."

His back against the headboard, Velez nods, looks at his right hand, the calluses, scrapes, a purple bump on his wrist where a batting-practice fastball pinged him. "I'd like to meet *your* family one day."

"Oh, I don't know. They don't like that I am an actress."

"Impossible!"

"I am the black ship!"

"'Sheep'?"

"Yes! My father's a lawyer and everything is very strict. They are not proud of me."

"I am proud. Tell me, which play, which role, do you want to do more than anything else?"

"Let me play Desdemona. But also, certainly, popular comedy. Gilbert and Sullivan. We could make our own Gilbert and Sullivan, but an American Gilbert and Sullivan."

"Yeah," Velez brightens. "Comedy. The world needs more comedy."

Velez holds her tight, moving one hand to her hip, the other to her shoulder, trying to hold the whole tenderly, solidly, reassuringly. He never did this with Cookie. Cookie was always attached to her phone.

\*

Amidst the odors of freshly cut grass and pine boards, which are the result of the massive array of bleachers that now enclose the outfield, the USA team assembles at League Park at nine the next morning. Rube Foster pitches batting practice, standing forty-five feet from home plate. Martin's idea is that Foster has a slinging, sidearm delivery that resembles Walter Johnson's, and positions Foster at forty-five feet because Foster's fastball is inferior to Johnson's. Foster pitches with a bitter expression, on the one hand feeling disrespect, on the other understanding Martin's strategy of the hitters practicing against fastballs fired from close range.

The batters choke farther up the bat, stand at the back of the batter's box, and shorten their backswing. By the last rounds of batting practice, most of the hitters, especially the lefties, are making solid contact. Lefties Elmer Flick, Donlin, Velez, and George Stone are hitting the ball sharply. Even Petway is confidently torquing his bowling-ball torso and lacing shots into right-center and down the line.

By game time, League Park is three-quarters full. The top half slice of the outfield bleachers is long rows of empty boards. The right-field bleachers are lined with soldiers and sailors in uniform, admitted for free. A quarter of Congress sits in the shaded grandstand. President Hanna is in the box next to the covered USA bench. Hanna has made sure that Roosevelt's box is on the opposite end of the bench.

The New Glory team takes the field to warm up, beards blowing in the breeze, garnering hearty booing. Dihigo and Bernardo Baro jog toward the center-field bleachers where a round, pink-faced man in the first row of bleachers screams, *"Get off the field, niggers!"*

Velez and Blent jog after Dihigo and Baro and catch up near the bleachers, 550 unmarked feet from home plate, 20 feet from the frothing-at-the-mouth, pink man screaming, *"Go back to New Glory!"*

*"Hola,"* says Velez.

Dihigo is almost as tall as Velez. Baro is a shrimp. Both have baggy eyes, the result of lack of sleep caused by an eight-hour concert of marching bands patriotically conducted through the night by John Philip Sousa.

Velez says to Dihigo, "Albert Einstein told us you're from the future."

Blent cringes, knowing it's reckless to mention Einstein after they facilitated his escape. And mentioning the future—it's also reckless.

Baro, who it seems, did not pay attention to what Velez has just said, comments, "Is this shitty field the best you've got?"

Dihigo tells Baro, "Go in. I'll be there in a minute."

Baro spits and jogs away.

Up in the bleachers, boys are screaming for autographs from Blent and "Chief." Velez and Blent stroll with Dihigo to the middle of the outfield.

"We are from the future too," Velez says. "And Bucky Martin. Our manager. The three of us. The twenty-first century." Martin, having sprinted across the field, joins them, huffing, eagerly staring at Dihigo.

Dihigo gazes into the faces, walking alongside for a few steps, his placid expression unchanging.

Blent and Velez recount how it happened. Dihigo offers: "With me, there was a voodoo doctor. He put me in a trance. I never woke up in my time—1933."

"A voodoo doctor?" Blent asks, "Did you tell Einstein that?"

"Yes. He didn't seem too interested. I went from 1933 to 1863 . . . northern Virginia."

"Gettysburg!" Martin exclaims. "That's when this whole world gets fucked up."

Blent spits tobacco juice, nods in agreement.

"The army on the way to Gettysburg swept me up. For the battle, I helped carrying soldiers to the medical tents. Got shot in my arm. The Union soldiers were coming at us. I picked up a pistol and shot it at them...I'm not happy about that. Two went down. We held the medical tents and the Unions retreated." He pulls up the sleeve on his left arm and shows them a bullet-sized scar over his triceps. "Ripped my arm. That was the third day. I got the bullet out, wrapped it up. I ran north and east, to Philadelphia. I was there eight months, working on the docks. Then I got sucked away to May 18, 1903, back in Cuba—what they now call New Glory, right where the voodoo doctor tranced me in 1933."

Martin interrupts, "But that moment, in July, at Gettysburg. That seems to be the moment that turned everything. What was the exact date and time you found yourself in northern Virginia, and exactly where?"

"June 28th, I think, around noon. I didn't have a watch. I was naked."

"We were too!" exclaims Velez.

"Naked next to a barn near Front Royal, Virginia. Bad place for a man with black skin. Rebels—Ewell's boys—put some clothes on me and stuck me with a mess unit. Then transferred to the hospital tent once the fighting broke out at Gettysburg. It definitely was not where I wanted to be."

"Was there an earthquake?" Blent asks. "In Philadelphia?"

"No." Dihigo gazes at the Capitol dome in the distance reflecting a spot of sun. "I found the voodoo doctor, but he was now a boy and did not remember me from the future. No one understood what I was talking about." Dihigo shrugs. "So here I am. I play ball. I miss many people in 1933. I don't miss 1863." He lifts his shot left arm. "But you know . . . I play ball. They treat me good."

"Did you have a wife and children in 1933?" asks Blent.

"No. Maybe that's what makes it easy for me. As long I have baseball. That's why 1863 was terrible. No pro ball. Einstein got me out of there."

"How did you meet Einstein?" Blent asks.

Dihigo shrugs. "I just had a feeling that he knew something. So I told him about going through time."

Velez asks, "Was there slavery in Cuba in 1933?"

"No slavery. It was *Cuba*. Very rough sometimes, but no slavery."

"My family are *slaves* in New Glory. Now! Today! They were taken from Curaçao."

"'Fuuuuuuck. Sorry, man. 'Life ain't fair.' I heard that a lot with the Confederates at Gettysburg, and on the docks in Philly."

"But was the world weird and different when you went from 1933 to 1863?" Blent asks. "This world, here, now. It's *different* than our history books from the twenty-first century. So moving between times *changes* the world."

"I don't know much history." Dihigo shrugs. "I just trust in God."

"You haven't lost faith?" Blent asks.

"Faith and baseball is all."

"But if we could go back and change the fact that New Glory invaded Cuba, then the slavery wouldn't have happened," says Velez.

Blent adds, "Also, if we can go forward—"

Dolf Luque, red-faced, is sprinting across the field. *"Dee-Go! Dee-Go!"*

"Anyone else you know of?" Blent asks, "Anyone else transported through time?"

"Never met anyone else. Just me, and you guys." Dihigo starts away.

"Hey!" Blent calls to him. Dihigo pauses. "Aren't you happy to know that we traveled through time too? That you're not alone? We're trying to figure out a way to get back! We've got scientists—great scientists—helping us. Come on, man, you should be thrilled!"

Dihigo shrugs. "Life is life. No one knows what will happen tomorrow!"

They watch him jog away.

Velez asks, "How could he not be excited-out-of-his-mind to find other time travelers?"

"I don't get him at all." A single chuckle of irony erupts from Martin. "Wow."

Blent pounds his glove. "I guess some people just roll with whatever shit the Universe dumps on them."

## SOLAR SERIES GAME 3

| NEW GLORY | | UNITED STATES | |
|---|---|---|---|
| 2B | LUKE "HELLCAT" COBB | 3B | POP LLOYD |
| 3B | AUGUSTUS COBB | 2B | JOHNNY BLENT |
| C | JOSEPHUS COBB | 1B | "CHIEF" VELAY |
| SS | MARTÍN DIHIGO | LF | ELMER FLICK |
| 1B | CAESAR COBB | CF | MIKE DONLIN |
| CF | BERNARDO BARO | RF | GEORGE STONE |
| RF | TYRUS COBB | SS | HONUS WAGNER |
| LF | SAM CRAWFORD | C | BRUCE PETWAY |
| P | WALTER JOHNSON | P | CHRISTY MATHEWSON |

As the announcer bellows the lineup through his megaphone and fans cross out pre-printed names on their scorecards and scribble in new ones, many in the crowd are already booing Petway and Pop Lloyd. When the USA takes the field, the fans amp up their booing as Petway squats behind the plate, and Pop Lloyd takes a warmup grounder at third base.

Someone deep in the crowd shouts, *This is not the real America!*"

On the bench, Devlin, Bresnahan, and Kling shift and shuffle their cleats, each feeling in his bones that he should be on the field. Bresnahan grits his teeth so hard—*crack!*—a speck of tooth comes out on his index finger.

Booing continues through Mathewson's warmups, through the first pitch, a foul straight back by Hellcat Cobb. The booing continues as Hellcat whacks a liner zipping twenty feet over Blent's outstretched glove into the gap between center and right, rolling, rolling, Hellcat racing around second, steaming into third with a triple.

Booing continues accompanied by shouts, *"It was the nigger catcher's fault calling for the wrong pitch!"* Someone in the third-base stands curses at Pop Lloyd, *"Screw you, nigger! Yeah, you heard me! You and your mother!"* Sporadic clusters of fans on the third-base side are standing and screaming at Lloyd, who ignores it. Various Congressmen cup their hands around their mouths and bellow, *"Niggerrrrrrrrrrrrrrrrrrrrrr!"*

Mathewson flips a pickoff to Lloyd, who applies the tag. *Safe!*

Mathewson kicks and fires a fastball. Augustus drag-bunts up the first-base line. Velez rushes in, and barehanded-sidearms the ball to Petway—far wide of the plate as Hellcat slides in. The crowd groans and jeers Petway.

### NEW GLORY  1 — 0  USA

The screaming and cursing at Petway and Lloyd increases, and more fans join in the abuse. Fans along the third-base line are yanking on the wall separating fans from field. Police rushing to the wall bash knuckles, and the wall stops moving.

Roosevelt scoots to President Hanna's box, inserting himself between Ban Johnson, Pulliam, Brush, Sr., and President Hanna. They quickly agree that in the interest of avoiding a riot, the Negroes must be removed, just as the third-base wall cracks and a section is pushed down. Police rush to the breach. The pulsing crowd behind it roars. A fan screams at Pop Lloyd, *"Gonna string you up!"*

Mathewson, so focused that he is oblivious to the crowd, looks in to Petway. Augustus takes a big lead off first. Pop Lloyd is staring in at the batter, ignoring the boiling crowd to his right. *"Tiiiiiiiiime!"* Honus Wagner raises his arms and turns to the New Glory second-base ump, who grants, *"Time!"* O'Day, behind the plate, bellows, *"Time!"*

Wagner slowly walks toward third base. Mathewson, his pitching rhythm interrupted, asks Wagner, "What are you doing?" Wagner ignores the question, stopping next to Pop Lloyd. Wagner reaches out his humungous hand. Lloyd, numb, looks at Wagner, who smiles, his eyes shining. Wagner says, "This is baseball, Pop!" Pop shakes Wagner's hand. Photographers scurry over and snap photos of Wagner with Pop Lloyd. Wagner puts his hand on Lloyd's shoulder and both stare into the third-base stands as bottles whirl toward them. A fan admonishes his seatmate, "Don't hit Honus!" Blent jogs across the diamond, glancing over his shoulder at Velez, who checks behind the first-base dugout that Nicole is okay. She offers a thumbs-up and a smile. He joins Blent and Wagner, and they pat Lloyd on the back, shake his hand.

Mathewson smilingly walks in to Petway, pats him on the shoulder. The outfielders jog in. Martin glances at his players on the bench as he heads out, followed by Frank Chance, Ed Reulbach, Three Finger Brown, Spike Shannon, Cy Young, the rest of the Giants, and the reserves. Jimmy Collins turns to Rube Waddell. "Come along Rube."

Waddell, oblivious, replies, "Why?"

Martin and the reserves crowd Petway, shaking his hand, laughing. Petway is smiling. The only ones left on the bench are Kling, Devlin and Rube Foster. Foster doesn't see the need to step onto the field and reignite racist fans. On the other hand, he realizes, *Hell, this is the moment of integration.* But there are two clusters of players—at third and behind the plate—and no one is anywhere near the first-base bench, so Foster would stand out rather than blend in, and he realizes that the moment has passed, and he will let Honus Wagner's great gesture live without further input.

The USA cracks Walter Johnson. Wagner launches a two-run homer. Petway nails Ty Cobb trying to steal—twice. Nails Augustus once. Blent goes 2 for 4. Velez knocks two doubles. Lloyd smacks two singles and a double. Mathewson pitches seven innings. McGinnity lets up a run in the eighth. Rube Waddell pitches the ninth, striking out Cæsar Cobb swinging to end the game. Waddell clenches his fist and screams up at the heavens.

| Game 3 | 1 | 2 | 3 | 4 | 5 | 6 | 7 | 8 | 9 | R | H | E |
|---|---|---|---|---|---|---|---|---|---|---|---|---|
| New Glory | 0 | 0 | 0 | 1 | 0 | 1 | 0 | 0 | 0 | 2 | 5 | 1 |
| USA | 0 | 2 | 3 | 0 | 0 | 1 | 1 | 0 | X | 7 | 6 | 0 |

### SERIES: NEW GLORY  2 — 1  USA

\*

Unlike Washingtonians, Chicagoans want to fête the teams. At the welcome banquet, icy platters of raw oysters are followed by quail, duck, boar, beefsteak, beef ribs, chocolate cake, raspberry sherbet, and quivering puddings the size of carriage wheels. On the dais, which is festooned with roses, carnations, and clumps of yellowing grass, Martin and Dolf Luque flank Chicago politicians and business leaders. The players are spared from sitting in a long row looking out at five hundred diners, instead seated at a series of round tables in the back of the room, drinking prodigiously, each team eyeing the other. At a table populated with Giants and Rube Waddell, Turkey Mike sneers, "Look at those long-bearded jerks."

Wiltse says, "Beards full of cat piss," as Waddell downs a water glass that was filled with scotch.

"Rube, slow down," Velez admonishes.

"I'm only pitching one inning a day! I can drink as much as I want!"

Dealing with a man beyond reason, Velez pats Rube's shoulder.

Ninety feet away, Ty Cobb has pulled a straight razor from his boot and is angling the blade so the chandelier light reflects into Bresnahan's eyes.

Bresnahan bolts up and shouts at Ty, "You ball of shit!"

Both teams scream imaginative curses at each other, rise and drift together. Martin jumps over the dais, Luque under it, both dashing to the back of the room. Bresnahan is red-faced, chest to chest with Josephus Cobb, whose beard is tickling Bresnahan. "Get that rat's nest out of my face!"

Josephus replies, "Sir, you insult me!"

Velez, Dihigo, and Blent coalesce at the edge of the crowd. Blent tells him, "We gotta talk to you more about Einstein." Dihigo says, "Now." They slip out a side door.

Bucky Martin and Dolf Luque shout at, push apart, scold their teams, as two gray hotel security guards shrink from four dozen athletes screaming at each other. Luque orders his team up to their rooms, on the fourteenth floor, all facing the court-yard, so New Glory cannot be disturbed by John Philip Sousa's bands, which line the hotel sidewalk, gulping coffee, ready to play all night.

Across the street in Lincoln Park, a wicked cold blasts Velez, Blent, and Dihigo. Blent goes over their extremely unusual common experience. "Yours was a cave, and ours was *sort of* a cave. We were in our manager's office. There was an earthquake and the ceiling came down on us." Velez asks Dihigo, "What did Einstein tell you?"

Dihigo shivers in the wind, and they follow him as he takes refuge on the lee side of a fat oak tree. Dihigo pipes up, his voice rather mellifluous, smooth, "Einstein doesn't know. He says maybe it's about moving one tiny particle at a time.

Something about the energy being too big to move a human body. Of course, though, we are here." Dihigo glances at the hotel. "I have to get back. They'll be looking for me. They can make me a slave on a plantation."

"Why put up with people following you? And *fucking* slavery?" Velez asks.

Dihigo's tone changes. "Maybe I'm just scared, man."

"How about getting slaves off the island? Do any ever escape?"

"It's hard, right? How you gonna get a boat?"

Blent implores, "Come along with us right now. Defect. We'll take care of you. If we can get to our century, the money is *huuuuge!* We got trainers and masseuses and cooks and houses!" Blent slaps Velez's shoulder, "This guy is mega-rich! Black guys play ball in the Major Leagues. We have Cubans, Dominicans, Japanese, Venezuelan guys, Curaçaoans, Mexicans, Koreans, Chinese, Australians. Everything! And if we can't get back, you could play for the New York Giants. Me and you, we'd be an unbelievable double-play combination."

"If you can't figure out time travel, then I'm stuck in this time, where your owners won't let me play in a whites-only league, right?" Dihigo asks. "How you gonna change *that*?"

"We're going to see Einstein tonight," says Blent. "Don't tell *anyone*. To meet with Einstein and another genius, Tesla, to discuss time travel. Come with us. Please."

"Can't do that. You're on your own. I have everything I need. Don't want to fuck it up." As he spits tobacco juice, a blast of icy air makes him shiver. "You don't freeze your balls off on the island."

"What's your chew?" Blent asks.

Dihigo slaps the pack into Blent's palm. "Dos Fuegos Maduro. The best. Here, a present."

"That's what we were smoking when we went through time!" Velez explodes.

Dihigo focuses on Velez. "I was chewing it. The same stuff. In 1933 and then again in 1863. Soldiers in Virginia had it."

"*That's what did it?*" Velez asks. "*The tobacco, plus the nuclear reaction?*"

A smile breaks across Dihigo's big face. "Could be. Yeah."

Blent examines the soft waxed paper pack with a print of a tobacco leaf.

Across the street, long beards flutter, a pair of New Glory officials possibly searching for Dihigo. "Enjoy. See you on the field." He jogs away.

\*

Midnight at Westinghouse Laboratories, they pass through multiple checkpoints consisting of mixtures of Pinkertons, Secret Service agents, and US soldiers. They are led past scores of glass globes housing filaments, past tables piled with nests of wires, to a corner of the large room where six blackboards crammed with white-chalked equations flank Nikola Tesla and Albert Einstein. Tesla brightens. "How can I ever repay you for bringing me my dear Einstein?"

Blent shows them the pack of Dos Fuegos Maduro. "You can get us back with this."

Tesla takes it and raises the pouch to his nose as Einstein's face broadens into a tittering laugh.

"You gentlemen were chewing the Maduro when transported!" says Einstein. "Like Martín Dihigo!"

"We weren't *chewing* it," Martin says. "We were smoking a chopped-up cigar. Bits of tobacco fell into my mouth."

"That's what fucking happened," confirms Velez.

"Then the earthquake hit," Blent adds.

Tesla presses the moist tobacco between his fingers, and to Einstein, says, "So there is some property—chemical property—combined with a nuclear reaction—amplified by their earthquake."

"That ripped us through time," Velez finishes the thought.

"Not a stable wormhole," says Blent.

The ballplayers share a look over all their fruitless San Francisco digging. The quintet discusses Dihigo going through time *twice*, and the fact that Dihigo doesn't seem to want to return to 1933.

Blent asks Einstein, "What happened the *second* time with Dihigo, when he went from 1863 to 1903?"

Einstein glances at Tesla. "That was one of our largest reactions ever, almost was out of control. It nearly melted down the core. It brought Dihigo to New Glory, 1903. Yes."

"Is there anyone else?" Martin asks. "Any other ballplayers get ripped through time. You've got four of us now."

"No, sir. No one has come forward. Since you claim that history is warped from your perspective, can you suspect any other people or baseball players, who do not belong in 1906?"

The twenty-first-century ballplayers glance at each other, shake their heads.

"And again," Einstein states, "we apologize for disrupting your lives so severely with our nuclear, and *tobacco*, accidents. But now that we have the tobacco. That's a barrier overcome."

Tesla squints at Martin's enlarged nodes. "Doctors helpful?"

The ballplayers' hopeful mood is blasted apart with the reality that if they can't get back to the twenty-first century, Bucky Martin is going to die from the growing nodes squeezing a vital vein, or suffocating him. Tesla palpates the nodes.

Einstein observes, "As if creatures have settled under your skin."

Tesla brightens, "But this!" He presses a button on a steamer trunk that's got wires poking out all over it, and the trunk begins to hum. He rushes across the lab to a matching trunk. The others hear him talking to himself. He scampers back. "Did you hear it!"

"Hear what?" Velez asks.

Tesla leans over the near trunk, clicking and unclicking buttons, checking wires. "They are the cell phones! A new edition!" *Pop!* A white light flashes out the side of the device, followed by a belch of smoke.

Blent erupts, *"Time travel! Not cell phones!"* He glances at Martin. *"We need twenty-first-century medicine!"*

Einstein tells them, "We will do everything in our power, gentlemen. But we are not creators of miracles."

Tesla sniffs, and says in German, "Albert, yes. Of course we are."

\*

Solar Series, Game 4.
West Side Grounds, Chicago.

The New York Times:

### U.S. VICTORS 9–2
### WEATHER, Brown BLAST New
### Glory

---

Series Knotted 2–2

---

### U.S.A. BATS SHINE

---

There were no tropical sun or balmy breezes gracing the West Side Grounds in Chicago today. Instead it was an end of October steel-gray sky, wind whipping in from Canada by way of Wisc-onsin, and a temperature of 43 degrees. No this is not the weather column, but the baseball column. All a way to let you know that the New Glory team found itself in unfamiliar conditions.

After the New Gloryers went down 1-2-3 to "Three Finger" Brown, who was cheered mightily by his home town fans, Jose Mendez, one of the pair of young New Glory phenom pitchers, escaped the first inning, the only chink being a Johnny Blent single, which was erased when Honus Wagner—batting an un-Wagner-ian .200 for the series entering the game—ended the inning by hitting into a double play.

Martin Dihigo whacked a double to lead off the second inning but the New Glory hitters' bats were as chilly as the day. In the bottom of the second, as he was warming up, the wind knocked the cap off young Mendez. Perhaps he should have followed the cap off the mound for good. For Donlin singled to lead a parade of U.S.A. hitters. George Stone struck a triple to left-center. Elmer Flick singled. The Negro catcher, Petway, doubled to right-center. Brown walked. The Negro third baseman, Lloyd, crushed a double down the line in right that Ty Cobb—the youngest of the Cobb brothers—bobbled into a double for Lloyd. Blent singled. "Chief" Velay place-hit a single to left. Honus Wagner blasted a double between Cobb and center fielder Baro. The U.S.A. tallied five runs in the second frame and did not look back.

Brown posted five goose eggs in a row on the scoreboard before allowing a run in the sixth and a run in the seventh. Chicago Cubs captain Frank Chance took the field for the eighth inning to thunderous applause from the fans who were stamping their feet and rubbing their hands in the gray, windy day. Another home-towner, Ed Reulbach, pitched the final frame for the U.S.A., garnering further applause. It is safe to say that Chicago baseball fans went home pleased, if not frostbitten.

|  | 1 | 2 | 3 | 4 | 5 | 6 | 7 | 8 | 9 | R | H | E |
|---|---|---|---|---|---|---|---|---|---|---|---|---|
| New Glory | 0 | 0 | 0 | 0 | 0 | 1 | 1 | 0 | 0 | 2 | 5 | 2 |
| USA | 0 | 5 | 1 | 1 | 2 | 0 | 0 | 0 | X | 9 | 20 | 1 |

## SERIES: NEW GLORY 2 – 2 USA

\*

Perhaps the happiest person on the train to New York is André Velez, who knows that even if they lose the next game, barring unforeseen events, the Solar Series will return to New Glory, and he will be able to again see his family. Maybe he can, at the least, arrange with the Missus to buy them in small groups, or one at a time. If he can't get them off the island, maybe he can set them up as free Blacks. Or even bring them to New York.

In a train car distantly redolent of vomit, Christy Mathewson sits across from André. "I heard that you met some relations in New Glory."

André Velez considers denying, lying—if he admits being a relative to slaves, then that'd make him Black, too. He settles on a distinct nod of his head.

Mathewson's lips pucker and he gazes out the window. He presses his big, white hand on the glass. "Mr. Velay, you're a one-man scandal."

"That may be," Velez replies. "Do you think they'll let me play with the Giants next year?"

"Not up to me. But you've certainly destroyed the notion that Negroes can't play at this level. I'd certainly want your bat in my lineup forever." Mathewson's right thumb runs across the tips of his pitching fingers, monitoring calluses and fingernail ends. "Ask some players to talk with me. We'll try to rally the team. If Bresnahan takes your side, he and I can go to Mr. Brush. The final judge is Pulliam, under the direction of all the owners. Perhaps getting Honus Wagner on your side wouldn't hurt."

The advice partly melts Velez's worries. He reaches across the aisle to shake Mathewson's hand, which is cold after being frosted on the window. "I'm sorry about everything, Christy."

Mathewson grunts, and returns his gaze to the Pennsylvania trees flashing by.

# 24

## Heroes

"MY BOYS ARE HOME!" Mrs. Critz commands the stoop, a cigarette between her fingers, poodles shaking against her legs. Velez and Blent are pulling their trunks from a horse-drawn carriage as Nicole steps down, beaming, having met the team at Pennsylvania Station. She folds her hands in a muff against the blustery day. Neighborhood kids round Columbus Avenue and zoom up to crowd the ballplayers and tote their luggage.

Velez lifts Mrs. Critz's hand and his lips peck her papery skin. "Feels like we've been away forever! May I introduce Miss LeVanche; Miss LeVanche, Mrs. Critz, the finest landlord in New York City!"

Blushing, Mrs. Critz replies, "Two games apiece! How's New Glory?"

The expanding pack of kids spots Mathewson's auto plonking down 85th Street. Halting, Mathewson's new chauffeur removes the luggage.

As Blent hauls his trunk up the red sandstone stoop, Mrs. Critz asks, "Would you have an extra ticket for me and a friend?"

"I'll see what I can do!" Blent thighs a poodle away.

Hesitating in the vestibule, Velez catches the eye of Mrs. Critz, as Nicole pretends not to notice. Mrs. Critz nods assent for Velez to show Nicole in.

At Delmonico's that night, the muckety-mucks of New York rub shoulders with the USA team, while New Glory has quarantined itself in the Knickerbocker Hotel. About half the USA team is absent, carousing familiar haunts rather than sitting through speechifying by greasy rich men. Petway, Lloyd, and Foster are dressed in spotless tuxedos, gleaming shoes, and are shunned by the majority of the crowd, though the more progressive dignitaries shake their hands and ask the questions they would ask of any fine ballplayer.

*

At dawn, there's a knocking, and Blent opens the door. It's Martin with the *New York Times* folded to an article:

## CHI GUN BATTLE

Three agents of the Secret Service were severely injured when they were involved in a gun battle following a traffic accident involving two automobiles at the intersection of West Ohio and North State streets. Witnesses describe one car ramming another, followed by a gunfire exchange in which multiple assailants emerged from their automobile and shot handguns into the auto containing the three agents of the government. The whereabouts of the assailants are unknown at this time.

A spokesman for the Treasury Department said that he is unsure whether the assailants were connected with New Glory, or with any other organization.

The New Glory ambassador, Henry Strickland III, issued a statement of denial which reads, "To insinuate responsibility for such a heinous act is merely one in an unending series of grave insults to the honor of New Glory."

The Treasury Department released the names of the injured agents. They are: Reinle, Davis, and McKenna.

*"Einstein and Tesla?"* asks Blent.

"I bet New Glory tried to get them back. Who knows if they succeeded?" Martin scans the living room, "Where's André?"

To Blent, this further cements the death sentence for Bucky Martin. The nodes might be bigger, or they only *seem* bigger because Blent's *freaked out* that they will *get* bigger. And Martin's breathing seems strained. "You can't die, Buck. Velez will be a mess."

Martin's lips press into a mocking half smile. He pats Blent's shoulder and his hand lingers a second longer than usual.

"Maybe Roosevelt can help find the scientists," says Blent. "Don't give up."

Blent watches Martin cross the street, looking both ways, climbing the stoop to his and Mathewson's apartment, as the El rumbles, a horse clip-clops at the head of a coal wagon, men shout as they greet each other walking toward the El and work.

The gravity of Martin's situation makes Blent feel like he's imploding.

Velez is striding up the block, the happiest smile Blent's ever seen on Velez's face. Velez bursts in. "There's a huge rally later today to promote the vote in November. You're going."

"What frickin' rally?"

"The Smash Segregation Rally."

Blent shows him the "Chi Gun Battle" article.

As Velez reads, his smile dissolves. "We're fucked."

\*

On the field before the game, Velez and Blent charge the box of seats containing Ban Johnson, Harry Pulliam, Brush Sr., and Roosevelt. Velez's eyes are afire. He grabs Roosevelt's overcoat and yanks him close, *"You're a moron!"*

Roosevelt's mouth shrivels. Secret Service agents chop at Velez's hands. Roosevelt's mouth opens: "Einstein was taken. Tesla escaped. He's safe. Seven agents died! Others are combing Chicago."

"*You* should be looking for Einstein!" Blent admonishes. "Get out of here! You lost him!"

Ban Johnson asks Pulliam, "Who's Einstein?"

"We are doing everything we can, sir!" Roosevelt tells Blent.

Velez spins away. "We are really stuck!"

Theodore Roosevelt calls after him. "In what way are you stuck, sir?"

Velez spits, *"Dickwad!"*

Bucky Martin walks in from the outfield along the first-base line, his hopes for returning to his twenty-first-century doctors all but extinguished.

The Polo Grounds fills, but there's no overflow arc of fans on the field. Looking up from behind second base, only a few fans are sprinkled atop Coogan's Bluff. A train parked beyond left field contains fans but is by no means packed. No one is sitting atop the train.

It's overcast and brisk, but not numbingly cold like Chicago. All of the New Gloryers are wearing their long sweaters with NG stitched over the heart. New Yorkers are screaming at them:

*"You killers!"*

*"You traitors!"*

*"You're gonna die!"*

*"You're gonna pay for Vicksburg!"*

## SOLAR SERIES GAME 5

| NEW GLORY | | UNITED STATES | |
|---|---|---|---|
| 2B | LUKE "HELLCAT" COBB | 3B | POP LLOYD |
| 3B | AUGUSTUS COBB | 2B | JOHNNY BLENT |
| C | JOSEPHUS COBB | 1B | ANDRÉ VELAY |
| SS | MARTÍN DIHIGO | LF | ELMER FLICK |
| 1B | CAESAR COBB | CF | MIKE DONLIN |
| CF | BERNARDO BARO | RF | GEORGE STONE |
| RF | TYRUS COBB | SS | HONUS WAGNER |
| LF | SAM CRAWFORD | C | BRUCE PETWAY |
| P | WALTER JOHNSON | P | CHRISTY MATHEWSON |

Except for one pitch in the fourth inning, Mathewson performs beautifully. That one pitch is a curveball that hangs sternum-high, spins without curving. Dihigo crushes it down the left-field line, the ball short-hopping the bleacher wall and kicking past Elmer Flick toward center field. Dihigo flies between second and third, Donlin's throw home sailing over Honus Wagner, bouncing next to the pitcher's mound as Dihigo slides across the plate for an inside-the-park home run.

The USA tries bunting on Johnson; they try screaming at him. They get some hits but can't string them together. He doesn't walk anybody. Not much success against his 100-mph fastball and his sharp, late-breaking curve.

| Game 5 | 1 | 2 | 3 | 4 | 5 | 6 | 7 | 8 | 9 | R | H | E |
|---|---|---|---|---|---|---|---|---|---|---|---|---|
| New Glory | 0 | 0 | 0 | 1 | 0 | 0 | 0 | 0 | 0 | 1 | 5 | 1 |
| USA | 0 | 0 | 0 | 0 | 0 | 0 | 0 | 0 | X | 0 | 6 | 0 |

## SERIES: NEW GLORY  3 – 2  USA

Blent watches Bucky drape a towel around his neck so no one will notice the bulging nodes while he changes into his suit, hanging a white silk scarf around his unbuttoned collar. *Where the fuck are Einstein and Tesla?*

\*

Velez pounds on the front door to Mark Twain's town house. Twain takes them inside, but Twain shakes his head no. He doesn't know. No. No Tesla. Nor Tesla's friend Albert Einstein.

Blent plops into a phone booth at the Ansonia Hotel. A series of connections are made to Tesla's laboratory. The phone there ringing forever, the operator finally hisses, "I do not believe anyone's present," as the line finally picks up.

"Hello." A scratchy male voice Blent's never heard.

"I'm a friend of Mr. Tesla. Has he been recovered?"

Three seconds, then, "Who are you?"

"Any word from him, or about him?"

"What's your name? Have *you* heard anything?"

"We are just friends. Thank you." Blent drops the earpiece into its cradle. The last thing he wants right now is to be in the midst of another huge crowd, but that's what he's promised Velez and Nicole, to go to the equality rally in Madison Square Park.

To Blent, it seems as if most of the Polo Grounds crowd has migrated downtown to 23rd Street, and many more people—particularly Black and Chinese—have tunneled in from around the city, all emerging into a chilly wind riffling the banners festooning Madison Square:

"Vote Equality For All!"

"No Banning!"

"EQUALITY!"

Velez is easy to find, towering over the crowd. Blent and Velez exchange glum experiences failing to find the scientists, while they pack in with Nicole, Mike Donlin, Mabel Hite, Rube Foster, Christy Mathewson, Pop Lloyd and Bruce Petway. Blent makes sure he's a few arm's lengths away from Mathewson. Buck has been left in his and Mathewson's apartment with a steak and a bottle.

Instead of trying to cheer up his manager, Blent's in a crowd of 100,000 people, spilling out onto all four sides of Madison Square Park, men sitting in trees like huge Christmas ornaments, all listening to a boring politician speechify from a platform. Blent takes a chaw of tobacco to quiet his rumbling stomach.

Gazing around, Blent notices that in a window of the Flatiron Building, stands the unmistakable slight silhouette of the owner of the Giants, John T. Brush, Sr., as a boisterous woman is firing up the crowd, *"This is incredibly wrong! Armed insurrection is the only way they will pay attention to us! Let's get them scared!"*

Velez shines a goofy look on Blent, mocking the speaker. The people around crack up at Velez. Mabel tries to keep a straight face but loses it in laughter as the speaker finishes.

Many near them recognize the ballplayers and Mabel, but Velez, the giant, is the most noticed. Velez says to some strangers, "We don't need to hurt anyone! Let's just show up, this whole crowd, and eat at these restaurants!" He holds up the list of the 206 restaurants on the boycott list.

Many laugh and applaud at his idea. This attracts, up on the platform, Nicole's gnomish, intense friend Tony, who points at Velez. *"You!"*

*"Me?"* Velez points a finger at his own chest.

*"Yes!"* Tony emphatically nods. "Come up here and address the crowd!"

Velez smilingly replies, "No way, man!"

Nicole encourages, "Go up there! You can do it!"

"Go ahead, André!" Mabel Hite seconds.

Those around them roar approval. Toasting with a glinting silver flask, Donlin yelps, "Speechify, Mister Velay! Here, this'll help!"

Through the megaphone, Tony announces, "The great Giant André Velay is here! Have you ever heard his voice? Would you like him to say something?" The crowd chants "Velay! Velay! Velay! Velay!" It echoes against the buildings on the four sides of Madison Square. Baseball fans cheer. Donlin and Rube Foster and Pop Lloyd are pushing Velez toward the platform.

Blent glances up at the Flatiron, the faraway triple speck of Brush, Sr., Pulliam, and Johnson, and he grabs Velez's coat, says in one ear, "Don't tell them you're Black! You could be banned from baseball!"

André turns to Nicole, who smiles up at him, a smile of love and admiration.

Rube Foster encourages, "Go ahead, man. Tear this segregation down!"

Velez and Nicole squeeze hands—a public kiss would be improper. He winks at Blent, at Foster, pats Mathewson's shoulder. The crowd makes a path for him and quiets.

To Foster, a Black man who's struggled to build a Negro league in the face of all this segregation, Blent says, "You're right. God help us all."

Eschewing the steps, Velez pulls himself up the side of the platform and vaults the railing. He's offered the megaphone and pushes it away. For a moment, he seems stunned to be gazing *down* at a sea of people; ballplayers are so used to looking *up* at a crowd. It's been such a long year. The crowd's cheering builds, reverberates. Velez raises his arms to try and bring down the level of noise.

From the base of the podium, the magnesium powder of photographers' cameras flashes at Velez. The crowd quiets. A female voice far in the back yells, *"I love you, André!"* which makes the crowd laugh and applaud. Velez laughs. His voice booms in reply, "I love you for all of the support you've given the Giants!" A huge roar, a roar of relief that he's changed the subject from violence. "I love you all for all the support of the USA team!" Another roar, though of shorter duration and volume. Velez's face is radiant.

Blent tells himself, *If I were up there giving a speech, I'd be shitting.*

"I have received my share of insults only because of the color of my skin, which people misinterpret all the time. It seems like it's a big deal in 1906!" Fear bolts through Blent that Velez is going to start telling a hundred thousand people about time travel. "First off, the vote next week. That's gonna pass!

It has to pass!" The crowd applauds politely, not raucously. "Most everybody in the world is *not* a racist. They're nice people. Only a small percentage have such small brains that they want to separate the world into groups based on the color of people's skin." The crowd quiets, listening. Up in the Flatiron, the three silhouettes merge. "With violence, with destruction of a person's property—say a restaurant—then that's gonna get a lot of the nice people against us." Now no one is talking or cheering. Pigeons, in the tops of trees, coo. "There's another way to change people's minds, and when the minds change the policies change, and when the policies change, the laws change. This is how we do it: we overwhelm them with friendliness, with love." Many in the crowd glance at their friends to assess whether this ballplayer is making any sense whatsoever. Velez raises his hands, and acknowledging the perplexed reactions, he smiles. "I'll tell you something. We were in New Glory. We got our asses kicked on the baseball field!" The crowd laughs. "But we saw *slavery*, man. Slavery." He looks down at Blent and Rube Foster, Pop Lloyd, and Bruce Petway.

Blent squeaks, "Oh shit."

Bruce Petway's smile beams.

"My real name's Velez, and I'm not an Indian Chief! Some of my relatives are slaves. Slaves!" The word echoes, fades.

Rube Foster raises his arms in a joyful expression none of the ballplayers have seen from him. Pop Lloyd high-fives Foster. Bruce Petway is crying. For her part, Nicole's expression of love hasn't changed, but now a myriad of worry is mixed in.

"We are all relatives! We are all related! That's what I can offer you as scientific fact from the future! Every fucking one of us is related to the other!"

Donlin yells, *"You tell 'em, Chief! I'm still calling you 'Chief'!"* A thousand baseball fans laugh at Turkey Mike.

Up in the face of the Flatiron, the silhouette of Brush, Sr. stands alone, unmoving.

Blent stares up at Velez. He wishes Martin were there, to witness this great moment in their insane journey.

"You all have been listening to speeches for a few hours. I bet you all are hungry!"

The crowd applauds and hoots. A man yells out, *"You're right!"*

"It's dinnertime!" Velez points straight at Blent. "My friend Johnny Blent, right over there, is gonna take a hundred of you to Carmelo's for dinner!"

The crowd roars. Blent is stunned. Nicole shrugs her shoulders at Blent, indicating that she had no idea Velez intended to enlist him. Not wanting to undermine Velez's effort, Blent slowly raises his arm and waves, and the crowd cheers him.

"The great Mike Donlin is going to take a bunch of you to Max's!"

The crowd cheers. Turkey Mike smilingly waves his flask.

"And I will lead a bunch of you to Süchow's! Let's fill the place up! Let's act nice. Let's *not* break anything!" Some in the audience chuckle, knowing that it was Velez who destroyed the windows at Süchow's. "Let's have some fun and some good food! I'm hungry! Who's hungry?! And I am paying for everyone's dinner!" The crowd cheers. "Our game today wasn't so great." A few scattered boos. "But when we played in Chicago a few days ago, I won a friendly wager!" Velez reaches into his jacket, removes a thick wad of money, and holds it like a trophy. Velez strains to raise his voice over the raucous cheers, "Let's be polite! Let's say 'thank you'! Let's use the correct fork and all that stuff! They know they're wrong! Let's make it easy for them to correct themselves. Let's make it easy for them to change! Come on! It's dinnertime! Remember: treat them with respect and love!"

As the crowd cheers, Velez starts down the platform steps where he is halted by a hundred hands extended to him. He shakes hands through the backslapping throng toward Blent and Turkey Mike. "Sorry to include you boys," he says as he peels off five hundred dollars for each. "I hope that's enough. Figured the New Gloryers couldn't handle the Chicago freeze. Gave away two-and-a-half runs! Got five to one!" He catches Nicole's concern, leans down to kiss her. His last words to Mike and Blent are, "Make sure there are Black people and Chinese at as many tables as possible. That will get the point across."

As Donlin asks, "What if we can't get in?" Blent realizes it's the first time he's seen Donlin scared, the most fearless, insouciant bastard in the world.

"Turkey Mike not getting in a place? Impossible!"

Blent grabs the arm of Rube Foster's suit, the triceps as hard as a hood of a car, pleading, "Help me, please."

"Sure, man," Rube Foster chuckles.

Soon Velez, Donlin, and Blent head in three directions, three huge portions of the crowd following each.

Blent fearfully asks Foster, "What am I going to say to the people blocking us at Carmelo's?"

"Be polite. Don't be a yannigan. Be cool!"

Foster and Blent lead a throng extending four blocks back down Broadway. Sprinting ahead, some reporters and excited boys are periodically grinning back at the oncoming crowd.

Down on Prince Street, the owner of Carmelo's and a passel of staff stand guard at the front door. Reporters and photographers and two dozen white men await. The owner is a wiry elderly man with a white goatee, thick white hair, a curving scar across his cheek.

Blent reaches out. The owner looks down at Blent's hand without moving, and says, "The reporters have informed me about what you intend to do. I didn't fight the Battle of Antietam to be forced to serve packs of monkeys in my establishment."

At a rhetorical loss, Blent turns to Rube Foster. Foster's hands are clasped behind his back. He glances at the owner, then, out the corner of his mouth, suggests to Blent, "Show him the money."

Blent pulls out the wad of fifty-dollar bills—ten of them. "People are people," Blent says, disappointed in his lame reply.

The owner's bare brow rises, revealing his droopy old eye, and he seems mildly impressed by the money but unconvinced by the argument. Meanwhile the crowd presses in behind Blent and Foster. Reporters' pencils are poised. Blent doesn't recognize any of them. They're not sports reporters.

Rube Foster tells the owner, "If you let us in today, we'll fill your tables every night for the rest of the year."

Glancing at his waiters and staff, the owner swivels back to Rube Foster. "How can you assure that?"

"We'll make a contract."

The owner rubs his thumb across his scar. "I *do* like contracts."

Foster encourages him, "Be a leader."

The owner sucks in a cheek. A cameraman's powder flashes. The owner mumbles to himself, then focusing on Blent and Foster in turn, "You two are responsible for any damages." He holds out his hand, and Blent gives him the money. Another camera flashes. The owner riffles the sides of the bills to count them, then asks Foster, "Like a brandy?"

"Certainly!"

"Come up to my office, and we'll write the contract."

Blent raises his arms with clenched fists. The crowd roars.

*

Velez ascends the Süchow's stoop, while Christy Mathewson and Nicole wait before a throng covering Broadway. The owner, Horst Schmidt, puts his hands up in Velez's chest. "You owe me for two front plate windows!"

"I do. Yes." Velez brushes off the man's hands. "We're coming in."

Motioning the crowd behind him up the stoop and into the restaurant, Velez announces, "Let's be polite! Let's be friendly!"

Horst Schmidt says, "This time you'll have to deal with the police!"

Once all the tables are packed, with no more chairs available, it's up to Christy Mathewson to stand atop the stoop and halt the flow of protesters. Inside, the waitstaff stands like stone, unsure whether or not to take anyone's order.

A police squad pushes up into the restaurant. They stand at the head of the main dining room. Everyone in the squad is white. The police captain approaches Velez, "The first baseman, right?"

"That's me."

"This is a whites-only restaurant."

"Captain, everyone's got a bit of mixed blood in them—somewhere in the past. Everyone."

"Not me," replies the captain. "Pure shanty Irish!"

"It's just skin, Captain. Were you ever banned from a place because you're Irish?"

The captain frowns, scratching the side of his fat neck.

"You hungry? Join us. The whole squad. On me!"

Horst Schmidt gasps, orders the captain, "No! Clear my restaurant!"

The police captain regards the restaurant packed with all sorts of white and Black people and some Chinese. They're all looking at him, about five hundred, the faces of New Yorkers, the kinds of faces he sees every day. The captain regards Horst Schmidt, who is fuming.

The captain turns to his squad of twenty, and his question, "Beer and sausage?" is met with twenty cheers. The police filter into the restaurant, taking seats here and there delightedly relinquished by protesters.

The legion of unmoving waiters stares at Horst Schmidt for instruction. He shuts his eyes and pinches his brow above his significant nose.

Velez softly encourages, "Come on, man. You can do this. And I'll pay for those windows."

Horst Schmidt's eyes flash open, and he screeches, *"Serve them!"*

Aside from some offended white diners, everyone in the restaurant, hundreds of protesters along with the policemen, cheer and roar, and unlike a ballpark open to the skies, the sound reverberates off the stained-glass ceiling. Word of victory is rushed outside and the cheers of the crowd on Broadway penetrate the dining room, which triggers more inside cheering.

Velez's smile is radiant. He offers his arm to Nicole. "Hungry?" Before they take three steps, a passel of joyous protesters shoves Velez toward the front door. Christy Mathewson, beaming, comes in, and the little group of protesters and Mathewson guide Velez toward the entrance to the restaurant. But Velez stops, shakes them off, tells them, "One minute!" He retreats into the restaurant and finds the stern-faced Mr. Schmidt, of whom Velez asks, "Ever have thousands of people cheering for you?"

*"Nein."*

"Come on."

Schmidt clenches his jaw, *humphs,* then accompanies Velez to the stoop where the crowd outside, all up and down Broadway, erupts in delight and triumph. Velez raises Schmidt's arm, and the crowd roars anew. Schmidt's stern face cracks into a big smile.

*

The celebrating of the triumph over the racist policies rolls throughout the city as restaurant after restaurant changes its policy. By morning, 186 of the 206 restaurants on the list have publicly agreed to serve anyone. Money has been pledged to cover the months of dinners that Rube Foster negotiated at Carmelo's, and the exploits of Donlin, Mathewson, Foster, Blent, and Velay fill columns on the front of the newspapers, and also the middle, where the failure of Game 5 of the Solar Series is recounted. Heroes on page one; losers on page seven.

At 10 a.m., the repaired SS *Normandie* sails without Cy Young, without Ed Reulbach, without Johnny Kling, each of whom complained about lack of playing time. Since prospects seemed tiny of reaping a share of victory loot, they decided against another voyage to New Glory. On deck, none of the thinned ranks of sports reporters are interviewing about baseball. They are fishing for tidbits about the protest. Rube Foster happily recounts the evening's events, and Blent corroborates. The USA team puts on brave faces, but no one is talking anymore about how they're going to spend $20,000 in winnings.

Velez smokes a cigar while watching the New York skyline shrink. He and Nicole were up all night celebrating with, it seems, the whole population of New York. After limited sleep, they stuffed themselves into Mathewson's grand automobile and rode down 9th Avenue. While being recognized along the way, they were cheered by not only baseball fans, but also a wider audience, people unconcerned with sports, who appreciated what they—most notably Velez—had done.

Mathewson declared, "I bet next week when there's a vote, all the racist laws are going to be wiped off the books! When we get back I plan to sit with Mr. Brush and Mr. Pulliam. Let them think about what's right and what's wrong. I'm ready to play with Blacks—as long as no one loses their jobs. We can expand the roster size."

At the dock Nicole buried her head in Velez's chest, her tears leaving blotches on his gray collar. He tried to soothe, "Just two more games. And then we'll have our own place and be rid of Johnny Blent's smelly feet!" He winked at Blent. She laughed, eyes wet, glancing at Blent. "I'm gonna get my family out of slavery. Somehow. Keep an eye out for a building for about fifty new family members."

She laughed. "André, you do not possess small dreams."

# 25

## Down So Long

VELEZ SMOKES DOWN his cigar and watches New York fade. Forty feet along the railing, Blent studies Velez, who somehow seems larger, as if another dimension has been added to his being.

Ninety feet away, Martin and Junior emerge on deck, in deep discussion.

Blent stops next to Velez. "He's gonna die."

Velez asks, "He tell you something?"

"He won't admit it. His body's fighting it. Making him tired. I can see it."

"You telling me he's on his way to dying?" They head inside to get a drink.

Down the railing, Junior asks Martin, "What about setting up a center-field system? I could hang my coat or a shirt over the outfield wall when it's a curveball."

Martin tries to clear his throat. It's hard to swallow. He says softly, "Stealing the catcher's signs?"

"Yes."

"Technically"—Martin's throat miraculously letting go its grip—"sign stealing when you include a spectator—it's cheating."

"Getting an edge. New Glory food-poisoned the whole team. That's an edge."

Martin concludes, "No. I don't want to do it."

\*

The next day at lunch, right fielder George Stone cradles his violin, skillfully playing a Schubert rondo. The ballplayers are transfixed.

There's a hard tugging on Martin's sleeve, and he is startled by Wee Willie Keeler's diminutiveness—exactly the same size as Martin's second wife. Keeler squints up, and with words tinged by his Brooklyn accent, Keeler says, "I got an idea about dat kid Johnson. I lean into a fastball. I get beaned. Pretend I'm dyin'. Put on a big ack. Make Johnson piss his pants. The trick is you gotta get me to our hotel—"

"The French embassy again."

"Okay. Don't let 'em take me to a hospital. 'Cause I'll be fakin'."

"Your plan is to get hit in the head by a 100-mph fastball?"

"I've done it before, Mr. Martin. In New York. In Baltimore. I know what I'm doin'. McGraw loved it in Baltimore. Especially against a very young and very good pitcher like Johnson. Johnson's not a killer like the rest of the New Gloryers. He's a good kid. We can use it against him."

Martin's never had a player offer to get hit in the head. And these guys *do not wear helmets!*

Keeler persists, "Look. I am here, right? I ain't jumped ship like Reulbach and Kling. I ain't played one inning. And I *want* twenty thousand dollars. This is a way to get it. It's gamesmanship. It's sport. It's not cheatin'. I know we can win."

"Are you ready to face Johnson if I put you in? Aside from getting hit in the head, what would you do?"

"Bunt down first. Steal second on a 2–0 or 2–1 count. Next at-bat knock an inside pitch over first. Chip at 'em. Hit 'em where they ain't."

That afternoon in his cabin, Martin is leaning against the porthole, while Roosevelt and Blent sit at the table, the trio discussing the oligarchic political structure of New Glory, when Martin collapses. Blent springs to him, rolls Martin on his back. Blent orders, *"Get the ship's doctor, and don't say it's for Buck!"* Roosevelt rushes out. Martin's turning purple.

Blent opens Martin's jaw, sticks an index finger far down his throat. It's all closed. Blent yanks his finger to one side, trying to let air pass through the trachea. Blent screams, "Breathe!" And Martin sucks in air.

Martin takes another breath, whispers, "I'm okay."

Roosevelt returns with the doctor, who asks a few questions and touches a node at the side of Martin's neck. There's not much to be said. Martin could asphyxiate at any time. In a loud whisper, Martin declares to Roosevelt, "If I die, Frank Chance is manager. Stay out of it."

\*

There are no banquets or tours. At the French embassy, Blent talks to an attaché who doubles as the embassy doctor. They discuss cancer. The attaché's knowledge of the disease is paltry. Blent asks, "What about New Glory? How is their medical research?"

The attaché chuckles. "They know nothing about medicine. About war machinery, yes."

The ballplayers are allowed off the premises—otherwise, being ballplayers, they would scale, tunnel under, or dynamite the walls. A knot of ballplayers including Blent and Velez heads to a swanky bar in Leeton. Blent watches Velez, Bresnahan and Donlin chat with the crowd that is forming around them. They're verbally bantering with the men, making pleasantries to the women while assaying them.

There's a poking in Blent's forearm: Mrs. Mathewson. Her skin sparkles, a wisp of black hair sways in the air currents blown by the ceiling fan. Without breaking her casual demeanor, she says, "Something is happening."

"What do you mean?"

She cups a hand around his ear—electrifying him— whispers, "They're trying to provoke an attack to justify invading Florida. The English will attack Miami and Jacksonville. New Glory will attack St. Petersburg and the West Coast. Tell Roosevelt. Now."

Blent pulls away. "Why? What's in Florida for them?"

"Nothing except glory. It makes no *strategic* sense, of course. They can't hold Florida. They will raid and terrorize. And one other thing."

"What?"

"They have Einstein. They brought him here."

*"Where is he?"*

"Likely in a black box site. Somehow they want to involve your team in a plot. I don't know any of the details."

"What are you saying?"

"I'm leaving. It might get very bloody, quickly."

"Don't you want to stay for the series?"

Her eyes narrow, reducing Blent to nothing. "You men and your games and your wars."

"Where will you go?"

"I have some offers. Tell Christy I'm sorry." She starts away.

Blent raises his voice to her back, *"I'm* supposed to tell him that?"

She's quickly swallowed by the crowd.

*I'm just a sucker.* On Blent's other side, a group of ballplayers is sipping fruity rum drinks that match the colors of the dresses of the ladies chatting with them.

Blent finds Roosevelt in his suite at the French embassy, at a desk, writing. The pruneish mouth, the drooping mustache, the pince-nez reflecting an electric lamp. Blent relays Mrs. Mathewson's information. "We've got to get Einstein back."

"We don't know where he is. And we can't very well ask for a scientist to be returned whom we abducted in the first instance."

Blent asks, "Why would New Glory attack Florida?"

Roosevelt's smile is wide. "Because they *can*, young man. That's the *raison d'être* of most armed conflict, whether it's with a bow and arrow, a club, or the most advanced munitions of this century! With the help of the British, they can take the coasts, and there's only one land border for them to defend. I've been wanting to build up the Navy, and well, no one listens to me! From any reasonable point of view, Florida is a vast swamp with few resources. But of course, we'll fight to the last man!" Roosevelt sniffs. It's his signal for Blent to depart.

\*

At 5 a.m., Velez is spotlessly dressed in a three-piece suit, holding a small wooden crate. Blent is bleary-eyed as a Model 1 drives them out to the open country.

"Don't you want to find *your* relatives?" Velez asks.

Blent chuckles. "I don't know, man. From what I heard, they were pretty hard-core Confederates. They were poor, but they probably owned some slaves. I don't think I could handle meeting them right now. I think I'm looking to find goodness in the world, you know? Not trying to explore every screwed-up piece of life. But this is important—what you're doing. Any way I can help . . . "

The plantation comes into view. Velez stands, scanning the fields. The Model 1 rumbles up the driveway. Emerging from the rows of tobacco plants, Velez's family appears, smiles beaming, eager, cheering, engulfing him. The tall ten-year-old tells him, "You're better than God!"

A white man brandishing a whip scoffs, "Back to work!" They do not move.

Velez and Blent are told to wait on the porch as a servant rushes in to inform the Missus.

A Black woman hands Blent a cup of coffee, asking if he takes milk, when the Missus emerges.

"You gentlemen did not call ahead."

Velez reintroduces himself and Blent, who thickens his Alabama accent, "Ma'am."

Blent earns an extra-long look. "We are in the middle of harvest, so everyone will have to get back to work. Today's especially important and this visit is, obviously, disruptive."

Velez asks, "Would you like me to say something to my family to get them back to work?"

"I have no need for your help. The best thing would be for you to depart immediately."

"May we go inside? I brought a gift for you."

She scans the crowd hanging just off her porch. "Mr. Velez, every second that you are here is a second wasted for my crop of Maduro. We take particular pride in it."

"Maduro?" Blent asks, turns to Velez. "That's the stuff that—"

Velez minutely nods. "Please, the gift."

Blent asks, "Any way you can let the people go to the game today?"

"During harvest?" she scoffs. "If you played after dark, well maybe, but no. I don't like them seeing you at all. You're wasting my daylight. Goodbye."

Velez steps closer. She must've been strikingly beautiful, but all her cruelty has brought out deep lines, especially around her downturned mouth. He says, "Just give me a price."

"My price is that next time you step foot on my plantation, my managers will have orders to shoot you. We have a pretty little graveyard. And you can be with your relations that way." She turns to Blent, "Do you wish to stay? I'd like to get to know where you're from, and why you're on the wrong team." She smiles at him, the lines in her face forced up.

"Practice, ma'am. Gotta get back." Quite freaked out, Blent sets down his saucer and cup.

Velez turns to his family, trying to let their faces and bodies burn into his brain. He rushes to Will and his boys, hugs them. "One day, I'll be back for you all. Don't give up faith in me. Please." They smile up at him. The twelve-year-old says, "Hit some homers."

"I'll try."

In the Model 1 returning to Leeton, Blent says, "I'm sorry, man." They watch the dusty scenery roll by. "What was in the crate for that fucking woman?"

"A French clock. Painted gold. Little cupids on it. Three hundred bucks. From Tiffany. Fuck. This all seems so stupid, this Solar Series. Baseball."

"Hey man, every person has their price. Good you left the clock. She'll let you back, maybe in the winter. Or you meet her in Paris and make the deal there. Suggest she buy a house in Paris. Get her drunk and buy her out."

"That wouldn't fix the whole situation. They won't let slaves leave New Glory. They're too valuable."

"You know what, you son of a bitch, I've got more confidence in you now than anyone I've ever met. I'll put money down that you'll figure out how to get them free."

\*

## SOLAR SERIES GAME 6

| | NEW GLORY | | UNITED STATES |
|---|---|---|---|
| 2B | LUKE "HELLCAT" COBB | RF | WILLIE KEELER |
| 3B | AUGUSTUS COBB | 3B | POP LLOYD |
| C | JOSEPHUS COBB | SS | HONUS WAGNER |
| SS | MARTÍN DIHIGO | 2B | JOHNNY BLENT |
| 1B | CAESAR COBB | 1B | ANDRÉ VELAY |
| CF | BERNARDO BARO | CF | GEORGE STONE |
| RF | TYRUS COBB | LF | MIKE DONLIN |
| LF | SAM CRAWFORD | C | BRUCE PETWAY |
| P | WALTER JOHNSON | P | CHRISTY MATHEWSON |

Top of the 1st. Wee Willie Keeler bunts the second pitch down the first-base line and the ball rolls foul. Keeler sets himself in the box, choking the bat two-fifths of the way up. Augustus at third and Cæsar at first creep in almost halfway to home. Johnson's next pitch sizzles and Keeler flicks his bat at it, popping it over Augustus, who, astonished, reverses himself, dives, and catches the ball two inches above the dirt. The crowd erupts in a volcano of vicious delight.

Pop Lloyd grounds out to Hellcat. Two outs.

Honus Wagner starts his swing early and cracks a double down the left-field line.

Blent works the count full. Walter Johnson sets, checks Wagner, who shouts, "Hey!" taking a step toward third. Johnson doesn't flinch and fires a fastball at the inside edge of the plate. Blent swings, jammed, and breaks his bat, hitting a soft one hopper to Dihigo, who fires a bullet over to Cæsar for the third out.

Bottom of the 1st. Hellcat strikes out. Augustus crushes a fastball into the right-field gap, Keeler tracking it down and slingshotting the ball to Honus Wagner, as Augustus charges into second base. *Safe!* New Gloryers are very surprised by the strong throw from the 5'4" Keeler.

Augustus on second. One out.

On a 1–1 pitch to Josephus, Augustus breaks for third. Petway nabs a fastball, and it's in his possession for less than a second before it zips to Pop Lloyd, who merely has to catch it and lower his glove to tag Augustus, who gratuitously spikes Lloyd's forearm. In reply, Lloyd smacks his glove across Augustus' face. Augustus scrambles to his feet, ready to fight, but third-base ump Rigler gets between them. Then, like a switch flicked off, Augustus frowns, turns away, patting dust out of his beard as he heads to the third-base dugout. Fans scream in delight at his ferocity.

On the next pitch Josephus pops out to Wagner for the third out.

Over the next few innings, the USA cracks isolated singles.

## USA   0 — 0   NEW GLORY

Top of the 6th. Mathewson leads off and smacks a clean single between Hellcat and Cæsar. Walter Johnson shakes his head as he takes the ball from Hellcat, who says, "You go get 'em big guy!"

Mathewson on first. No outs.

Keeler stands in, choking up, the corner infielders pinched in, the outfielders shallow. Keeler squints out at Johnson. Johnson glances over his shoulder at Mathewson. Johnson fires a fastball, Keeler slapping it above Cæsar, the ball dunking into right. Mathewson charges around second, Ty Cobb flying to the ball, firing it to third on one perfect hop, Augustus applying the tag to a sliding Mathewson. *Out!* Martin winces with the wrong decision to wave Mathewson on to third base, and the whole USA delegation winces with him. As Mathewson rises from the dirt, Martin apologizes, "I should've held you at second."

Pop Lloyd watches a pitch just off the plate in his estimation—called strike three. Two outs.

Wagner hits a flare foul that Augustus tracks down. Three outs.

Bottom of the 6th. Bernardo Baro works a walk.

Ty Cobb hits a grounder toward the hole. Pop Lloyd knocks it down, scrambling to his feet and firing across to nip Ty who, rather than stepping on the bag, crushes Velez's heel, spiking and twisting into it, Cobb tumbling across the bag and rolling up the line.

Velez, while crumbling to the ground, tosses the ball in Mathewson's direction to hold Baro at second. Velez roars at Ty Cobb, *"You asshole!"*

Ty Cobb can't get up, and neither can Velez.

Martin is quickly in O'Day's face. "You've got to kick that idiot out of the game!"

O'Day looks down at writhing Ty Cobb. "It doesn't look like he can play in any case."

*"Kick him out! Set a precedent!"*

*"Don't tell me how to do my job!"*

Blent and Mathewson push Martin away, Martin's neck veins and lymph nodes are deep red. He's wheezing. He says, "Get me a drink of water."

The fans are screaming at Velez as if he were the perpetrator, not the victim.

Blent glances up at the steep stadium of fans and wonders if they're all insane. Invade Florida? Why? Blent runs a glass of water to Martin, who takes a sip, clears his throat.

As McGinnity, Rube Waddell and Rube Foster raise Velez, who can't put any weight on his trashed, bloody left heel, a beet-red Roosevelt shouts at Martin, "That was a scoundrel's play! A scoundrel's!"

Martin gently clears his throat and replies, "Well said." Turning to the bench, "Mr. Chance, first base please."

In the dugout, Velez's ankle is a bloody mess as Foster and Wiltse remove the sock. The doctor from the French embassy leans down to the ankle.

Martin stops by. "How is it?"

Velez groans, "Not good, boss."

Baro at second. One out.

Sam Crawford at the plate. Crawford whacks a liner into left. Donlin dives, the ball short-hopping against his glove and bounding ten feet away, Baro racing around third, headed for home. Donlin retrieves the ball and tosses it in to Honus Wagner, holding Crawford at first. The crowd's delight is deafening.

## USA  0 — 1  NEW GLORY

Crawford takes his lead at first.

Walter Johnson sacrifice bunts up the first-base line, Chance grabbing it and tagging Johnson.

Crawford on second. Two outs.

Hellcat steps in. At 1–1, Mathewson throws a curve that hangs in the air and Hellcat *whacks* it *sizzling* over Mathewson's head for a single. Crawford races around third to score. Clusters of fans dance.

## USA  0 — 2 NEW GLORY

Hellcat on first. Two outs.

Augustus is up. Hellcat takes a huge lead. Mathewson fires to Frank Chance but Hellcat dives back safe. Petway calls for an inside fastball and the fastball zips inside, Petway catches and flicks the ball to first, where Chance catches and swipes the tag on Hellcat. *Out!* Three outs.

| Game 6 | 1 | 2 | 3 | 4 | 5 | 6 | 7 | 8 | 9 | R | H | E |
|---|---|---|---|---|---|---|---|---|---|---|---|---|
| USA | 0 | 0 | 0 | 0 | 0 | 0 | | | | 0 | 4 | 1 |
| New Glory | 0 | 0 | 0 | 0 | 0 | 2 | | | | 2 | 9 | 1 |

On the bench, Bresnahan screams, *"Kill those bastards!"* Goofy Waddell shouts, "Let's go, fellas!"

Keeler purposefully stops, hands on hips, directly in front of Martin. Keeler raises an eyebrow, silently asking Martin a question.

Martin exhales hard. "Okay."

Keeler's face lights up and he dashes into the clubhouse.

Top of the 7th. Matty strikes out. Keeler steps in. The first pitch is high and away. The second pitch is straight down the middle, and Keeler watches it: 1–1. The third pitch is inside, chest-high for Keeler, and from Martin's viewpoint as third-base coacher, Keeler ducks into it, *thump* on Keeler's head. The ball ricochets to the backstop as Keeler collapses. Both hands hold his head. The stadium is silent. Keeler's face is covered in blood. "Get a stretcher!" umpire Tiant bellows. Pop Lloyd takes Keeler's cap, and the doctor tends to Keeler. Roosevelt is in the huddle over Keeler, turning to Tiant, "You must eject Johnson! Our man here might die! Look at him!"

Keeler does not move. Martin wonders if Keeler's really okay, or if the ball got too much of his head and he's *not* okay.

At the side of the pitcher's mound, Walter Johnson stands stone-still, arms crossed, staring in at Keeler. The doctor wraps Keeler's head as blood streams down Keeler's face. Teammates shimmy Keeler onto a stretcher, carry Keeler through the dugout and into the clubhouse. Scattered fans applaud in a display of good sportsmanship.

Devlin jogs out to first base to pinch-run for Keeler, crossing Bresnahan in the first-base coacher's box, who is screaming at Walter Johnson, *"He's dying! You shit-for-brains! You murderer!"*

At third base, Martin remains mum. He wants to let Johnson think about the situation.

The first pitch to Pop Lloyd is way wide, Josephus diving to knock it down, holding Devlin at first. The next three pitches aren't close, and Lloyd walks.

Devlin on second, Lloyd at first. One out.

Wagner steps in, looks down the line at Martin, who touches elbow, chest, ear, tip of cap, chest, shoulder—a series of meaningless signs. Martin mumbles, "Get in there and hit!" There's a stab of pain in Martin's leg, and his vision pixelates. He tries to breathe deeply. If a foul ball is smacked his way, he can't see it. Two more breaths and most everything in his vision resolves.

The first pitch is in the dirt, Josephus smothering it. He calls time and jogs out to the mound to calm Johnson.

From the dugout, Dahlen shouts at Johnson, *"Keeler's going to the damned hospital! He might be dead! You fucking killer!"*

Johnson grooves a 3–0 fastball, but Wagner takes it for a strike. The next pitch is wide by a foot for ball four.

Devlin on third, Lloyd at second, Wagner at first. One out.

As Blent steps toward the plate, Dolf Luque strides out from the New Glory dugout. Head down, he's rubbing his nose. Josephus, Hellcat, Dihigo and Cæsar join Luque on the mound for his chat with Walter Johnson. In the USA dugout,

Velez hobbles from the clubhouse on crutches, his ankle cleaned, gauzed, and taped. Everyone on the bench comes up and pats his back or gives him a high five. George Stone comments, "Dirty mothers." Frank Chance informs Velez, "Bases packed, Chief. Your man is up."

Luque's attempt to soothe Johnson completed, Johnson is left alone on the mound. Blent coils like a wound-up spring. The first pitch is a fastball on the outside corner. Strike one. Blent whispers, "Come on, now." Removing a hand, Blent slaps the bat near the trademark, as if to wake it. He coils. Johnson, in full windup, slings a fastball outside for ball one.

"Murderer!" Bresnahan does not let up on Johnson, spittle running down the sides of Bresnahan's mouth. "Idiot diaper boy!"

Johnson winds and fires. Blent's uncoiling early, yanking the ball; there it goes down the leftf-ield line, hooking, hooking—four feet foul. Halfway to first, Blent yells, "Crap!"

Martin exhales, "Hell," because it's the type of result—a hard hit foul—that sends a jolt of fear through a pitcher, fear that can refocus an unnerved mind.

Blent reasons, *He threw a damned changeup. I've never seen a changeup from him before. No way I can gear up for the fastball* and *also be able to hit his changeup.* He rubs dirt on the bat handle, and decides he's guessing the next one is a fastball. *The kid wouldn't throw two changeups in a row, would he?*

Luque sees something different: a 2–0 lead, one out, bases loaded, and a pitcher grooving a pitch to get it over. Luque bolts out of the dugout, waves his hands to get ump Tiant's attention, walks to the mound, says, "Great game, Walter," and holds out his hand. Johnson relinquishes the ball and walks off to a sustained roar that serenades him until well after he disappears into the dugout.

All of the USA team are doubly astonished: to see Walter Johnson depart the mound, to see Martín Dihigo step to it from shortstop. He takes the baseball from Luque and starts firing warmups. Armando Marsans jogs out to short.

Blent stands with Frank Chance on deck, watching Dihigo fire a wicked curve, then a wicked fastball—though not as fast as Johnson's. An outshoot kicks the dirt behind home plate.

Blent glances into the dugout. Velez shakes his fist and bellows at him, "Go get 'em, dude!"

One ball, two strikes. Blent sets his back foot. Dihigo is almost as tall as Walter Johnson, but Dihigo throws straight overhand. Blent gears himself up. The pitch starts at his head and curves—inside at his belt as he jumps back: 2–2.

Now that he's been brushed back, he's looking for something outside. He calls, "Time!" Tiant confirms, "Time!" then to Blent, "What's a matter?"

Blent steps out of the batter's box and yells out to Dihigo, "You're a time traveler!"

Dihigo stares quizzically at Blent, as if he didn't hear or understand.

"Time traveler!" Blent repeats.

Dihigo hears it now. His eyes bug and jaw slackens. He shakes his head and smiles, then strides up the pitching mound.

Bucky Martin is frozen near third base, Blent's statement to Dihigo having smashed the two worlds together. Blent checks the dugout, where Velez is wincing from his throbbing heel, but nodding and giving a thumbs-up to Johnny Blent, despite the unknown risks of further entangling the butterfly effect, perhaps making it harder for them to ever get back. But now, with the series tilting away, Velez thrillingly agrees that it's a risk worth taking.

Josephus Cobb asks Blent, *"What the hell are you talking about?"*

In the dugout, the USA players confusedly ask each other what Blent and Dihigo's moment is all about. Dihigo stands to the side of the mount, licking his lips, shaking his head at Blent.

As Blent takes his stance, he's thoroughly relaxed and confident. Dihigo winds and fires a fastball, middle-in, and Blent unleashes, sending the sphere down the left-field line and fair by three feet. Devlin and Lloyd score, Wagner charging toward third, Sam Crawford picking up the ball just as Wagner's right foot pounds the corner of the third-base bag, Martin windmilling his arm, *"Go! Go! Go! Go! Go!"* coughing and chasing Wagner down the line, the throw pinging in to Augustus who wheels and fires right past Martin on a line to Josephus as Wagner's right foot spikes Josephus' shins out of the way and Wagner's left foot touches home plate.

*Safe!*

Spilling out from the bench, the USA players engulf Devlin, Lloyd, and Wagner. In the box next to the dugout, Johnson, Pulliam, and Roosevelt congratulate each other. In the center-field bleachers, Junior is muttering, *"Yes! Yes! Yes!"* On the bench, Velez is laughing. Blent's standing on second base. It's an amazingly powerful feeling to quiet tens of thousands of hostile fans.

## USA  3 — 2  NEW GLORY

Bottom of the 9th. Martin brings in Waddell. His warmups *pound* Petway's mitt, the sound like a heavyweight fighter punching a dangling training bag.

Augustus steps in. On a 1–1 fastball, Augustus lashes, the ball slicing foul into the stands down the right-field line.

Now Waddell rocks and fires, a curveball that surprises Augustus who tops it in front of the plate, Petway blasting out of his crouch. *"Mine! Mine! Mine!"* Petway sliding to the ball, his left cleat biting the grass, the momentum raising his body as he slings the ball to Chance. *Out!*

One out. Dihigo slaps a first-pitch curve up the middle, Wagner snagging it, spinning, firing to Chance who stretches out like a gymnast for the ball, Dihigo flying down past first, beating it out by a half step. *Safe!* The USA bench screams in protest, in frustration at Dihigo's speed.

Dihigo on first. One out.

Petway jogs to the mound. The infielders join. Petway tells Waddell, "When I make a fist, you throw to first."

Waddell pounds his glove. "Okay, Mike. We'll get a drink later, you wanna?"

Petway repeats, "When I make a fist, you throw to first, okay?"

Waddell's head pulsates, "Yes? To first. Sure."

Petway retreats to home, telling himself, *If Waddell's skin were Black, he'd be chained to a stone wall.*

Massive Cæsar Cobb steps in. He's hitting an even .300 in the series and does not have a hit off Waddell. On the day, he's 0 for 3 with a strikeout and two easy grounders to first. The first pitch is a curve that gets the plate for strike one.

Cæsar shouts, "No!" more at himself than the ump.

Petway puts down the fist. Waddell looks in and shakes his head. Petway rattles his fist. Waddell shakes his head again.

"Time!" Petway jumps out to Waddell, to remind him of the signal, Waddell replying, "Oh, okay, sorry Mike!"

Behind the plate, Petway puts down the fist. Waddell fires to Chance at first, and Dihigo slides in safe. Petway yells out, *"All right! That's the way!"* Petway calls for a fastball on the out-side edge and that's where the ball zips, Petway not having to move his mitt. Strike! Petway jumps out to Waddell. "Throw the next one high and away—a pitchout, so I can gun down this cracker."

Waddell looks in. Checks Dihigo. Waddell kicks, Dihigo taking off, Petway standing up, catching and firing toward second. Blent catches the ball and brings down his mitt. Dihigo's eyes go wide, and he frowns as Blent tags him.

Over the erupting USA bench, Bresnahan yells, *"Way to go Petway me boy! I deem you an honorary Irishman!"* Rube Foster belly-laughs at the crack. Two outs.

Cæsar hacks a curveball, sending it toward the hole between first and second. In pursuit, Chance puts on the brakes because he's doubtful that Waddell will remember to cover first. Blent dives for the ball, knocks it down, grabs it, fires to first, Chance covering it like a pitcher—catch and step on the base. *Out!* Game over.

The series is tied. There will be a Game 7.

# 26

## Three Neckties

THE MODEL 1s deposit the team, relaxed and celebrating, half of them already drunk, at the French embassy's wrought-iron gate. Awaiting them is a phalanx of New Glory soldiers in gray uniforms with flowing beards and fierce expressions. As Honus Wagner is about to walk through the gate, a baby-faced, wispy-bearded New Glory army captain steps in his way. In a serious, courteous manner, the young army captain states, "Mr. Wagner, if you would please stand to the side."

"Whatta ya want?" Wagner asks, as players flow past into the embassy grounds.

Stopping next to Wagner, Martin asks, "What's going on?"

The captain turns his determined expression on Martin, a dueling scar high on the right cheek. "Mr. Martin?"

"Yes?"

"Please stand aside with Mr. Wagner."

Martin asks Wagner, "Know what this is about?"

"No idea."

"Screw this." Martin takes Wagner's sleeve and pulls him toward the gate. The captain blocks them. Half a dozen soldiers fall in behind.

By now the rest of the team has become aware of the situation. Bresnahan, Donlin, Devlin, Mathewson, Blent, Velez, Frank Chance, Rube Foster, and Pop Lloyd push out from the embassy, their progress checked by New Glory soldiers who aim their rifles with fixed bayonets at the ballplayers. A soldier barks, "Back!"

Bresnahan retorts, *"No fucking way!"* and pushes between rifles, grabbing Martin's wrist, and Bresnahan pulls him toward the embassy. A rifle butt smashes Bresnahan's hand, another smashing him behind the ear, and Bresnahan goes down.

The players rip into the soldiers. Blent's twisting the shirt of one kid up around his neck as the kid's relentlessly whacking his rifle into Blent's right shoulder. The captain fires a pistol into the air. Pop Lloyd is smashed in the eye; Velez's gut is rifle-butted; a soldier bayonets Donlin's stomach, and he goes down, Rube Foster shouting, *"They stabbed Mike!"*

The French embassy guards are wide-eyed and stationary, Devlin yelling at them, *"Help!"* Seeing that the French are not inclined to move, Devlin screams at them, *"Nancy boys!"*

Theodore Roosevelt sprints out from the embassy, rushes into the melee, screaming at the New Glory army captain, at Wagner, at Martin. Donlin is on the ground holding his stomach with his white shirt stained in blood. Roosevelt orders the French, *"Get the embassy doctor!"* and the French are only too happy to purposefully retreat. Roosevelt pushes the sides apart.

Almost all of the players are inside the gate. They are checking wounds and eyeing the New Glory soldiers, who have surrounded Roosevelt, Martin, and Honus Wagner.

Roosevelt, red-faced and perspiring, rasps at the young captain, "What is your business here?"

"Are you Vice President Roosevelt?"

"Of course!"

"You and Mr. Martin and Mr. Wagner are under arrest."

Roosevelt screeches, *"You are about to cause an international incident! You are making a terrible mistake! Who is your commanding officer? This could be war!"*

He, Martin, and Honus Wagner are herded toward a pair of gray Model 1s.

From inside the gate Blent screams, *"You can't do this!"* but he is ignored. *"He's a sick man!"* Some of the players glance at Blent, wondering who is sick, but they don't ask Blent any questions.

Roosevelt, pausing on the running board of a Model 1, turns to the team, to Pulliam and Ban Johnson. *"We will be back by dinner! Set places for us!"*

Players cheer Roosevelt. The Model 1s speed away.

Blent attends to Donlin, peels back his bloody shirt, examines the puncture.

Donlin moans, "Nobody fights fair no more."

\*

Bucky Martin, Honus Wagner, and Roosevelt are driven to the edge of Leeton, through a dirt driveway lined by palm trees, to a low wood building. They're marched past flies loudly swarming a sweet-smelling mound of decaying pineapples. Inside the building, Roosevelt screams, *"I am the vice president of the United States! This is an outrage! Who is in charge?"*

They are led down a long corridor and into a windowless courtroom. There's a judge in a wig and black robe behind a bench. There is a jury made up of New Glory white men in white, blue, and gray uniforms, all with medals on their chests, epaulettes on their shoulders, flowing beards. There's a pack of New Glory reporters scribbling. Martin, Wagner, and

Roosevelt are led to a table where a short, nervous man with sparse hair looks up at them through a smudged monocle. "I am your defense attorney. The charges are serious."

Just then a door opens, the judge's gavel comes down, and in walks a group of six men. Among them is Einstein, his face bruised and bandaged, staring at the scratched wooden floor as he is shown to the witness box. Einstein sits.

A photographer's flash lamp ignites, sending up an eight-foot blast of flame, snapping a photo of Martin, Wagner, and Roosevelt. Momentarily blinded, Roosevelt shouts, "This is a monkey trial!"

In the French embassy, a series of telegrams are sent to Washington, DC, and Paris. The ambassador takes a telephone call from President Hanna. In less than an hour, the news of Martin, Wagner, and Roosevelt's arrest has traveled the globe.

At the French embassy, Blent's hunkered in a sofa with Frank Chance and Velez. Blent's worried that Martin will pass out, as he did on the ship, and die of lymph-node-enlarged strangulation, or a stroke. "Why would New Glory, at this moment, try to provoke the USA? What do they have to gain from it?"

Mathewson is towering over them, biting the edge of his thumbnail, his mind going through the calculations. "It's a thought-out move. They want something."

Velez adds, "Expand their empire beyond the Caribbean. Provoke us."

Blent looks over at Velez, because that's exactly what Jane Mathewson said.

"Why not keep going in South America?" Frank Chance asks. "The armies there are weak. Or Central America."

Velez winces as he tries to move his bandaged ankle. "Obviously they want the Old South. Past glory bullshit. Fucking slavery crap."

In the vast kitchen Blent finds a tub, negotiates a quantity of ice, brings it to Velez. The ankle is twice its normal size. Blent prods. "The Achilles isn't severed. Some of the ligaments are probably strained. I hope no bones are broken. Lacerations from Ty Cobb's cleat."

"Think I can play tomorrow?"

"You'll be lucky if you can walk to the bathroom."

Willie Keeler observes, comments to Blent, "If you played on the Highlanders, your new name would be 'Doc.'"

An army Model 1 halts outside the embassy, disgorging a white-uniformed, bemedaled, epauletted, gold-rope-aiguilletted general with a flowing white beard, a large sheet of paper rolled under his arm.

He is greeted in the dining hall by Ban Johnson, Pulliam and the French ambassador, the latter of whom, besides the irritation and incredible danger of this latest irrational outburst by New Glory, is exasperated to again be housing a passel of children's-game-playing American drunkards. But the French ambassador is gleeful and honored to greet General James Longstreet, New Glory hero of the Civil War.

Ballplayers shout at Longstreet, reporters bark questions. Longstreet smooths his beard with one white-gloved hand, then unfurls the twenty-by-thirty-inch sheet of paper, the officious blue seal at its bottom giving off the aroma of fresh wax.

Longstreet announces, "This is the verdict of our military tribunal, which cannot be appealed! Would you desire for me to read it aloud, or would you prefer to read it for yourselves? You will find the verdict rather sportsmanlike!"

"Enough with the flowery bullshit, asshole!" Bresnahan squawks.

"Gentlemen!" The French ambassador scolds, "Our visitor is one of the most esteemed citizens of New Glory!"

The general bows.

*"Go fuck each other!"* Bill Dahlen yells.

The general clears his throat and reads, "'Mr. Buck Martin, Mr. Honus Wagner, and Vice President Theodore Roosevelt are hereby convicted of espionage against the Republic of New Glory, and sentenced to hang. However—'"His words are swamped by shouting, cursing, and direct threats to Longstreet. Bresnahan shoves the general in his medals. From behind, Devlin punches Longstreet's shoulder in the decorative rope.

Longstreet turns to his attacker, his old, watery eye fierce. *"However!"*

Frank Chance yells, *"Let him finish!"*

Longstreet bellows, "'If the USA team should win Game 7, and thereby the Solar Series, by the good sporting graces of the Republic of New Glory, the sentences will be commuted and the accused set free.'"

\*

Sixteen hours later, at high noon, through the voice-amplified public-address system, the Southern-accented announcer elucidates, to a straining-to-hear crowd of 63,000; to the Cobbs, Dihigo, Baro, Sam Crawford, and Walter Johnson on the field; to the USA team in the dugout; to the center-field bleachers where Bucky Martin, Honus Wagner, and Vice President Roosevelt stand on a freshly constructed gallows, each with a noose around his neck: "If the United States of America team loses, Mr. Bucky Martin, Mr. Honus Wagner and Vice President Theodore Roosevelt will be hanged until dead by the three stars of the contest, voted on by the baseball writers of New Glory and USA!"

Tens of thousands of berserk Rebel yells and screams are let loose at a severity that none of the USA players has ever heard, a murderous/killing/bloodlust primal yell accompanied by individual shouts:

*"Die Yankees!"*

*"Go to Hell!"*

*"May the Lord* not *have mercy on your souls!"*

*"Hang them now!"*

On the USA bench, his stomach stitched and bandaged, and so sore he says it feels like an open wound, part of Turkey Mike Donlin's psyche appreciates the unadorned, twisted frenzy of the New Glory crowd. Looking up at Bresnahan, Donlin comments, "This is the most out-of-control thing I've ever seen!" Bresnahan spits a jet of tobacco juice. "Watch me get even."

Blent's standing next to Velez on the top step of the dugout. Velez is scrutinizing the far reaches of the stadium, in case the Missus changed her mind and let his family attend the game, and they somehow made their way in. He doesn't see them.

An hour earlier in the clubhouse, Frank Chance told Velez that, because of Velez's nonfunctioning ankle and heel, Velez would not play. Velez, painfully, got down on his knees, and pleaded, "That's my manager out there! I'm gonna play! If I hurt the team, then you can take me out!"

"You can barely stand up, André," Chance refused.

Now part of Blent is wondering, if Martin is hung, when he dies, will that make Blent and Velez disappear? Or will it sentence the two ballplayers to this stream of time until they die?

Blent glances at Mathewson, whose face is as white as a sheet of paper. This is a freaked-out expression neither Blent nor Velez has ever before witnessed in the months they've known Christy Mathewson.

Blent tells him, "Your wife says she still loves you. I saw her the other night."

"Why are you telling me this now?"

"Her exact words, 'Tell Christy I love him anyway.' She said she was leaving New Glory. She wouldn't say where she's going."

He looks down at Blent. "Whose side are you on?"

"I'm on your side, man. We gotta win this fucking game!" Blent gazes up at the war-whooping fans: in the third row, a man is screaming through his white beard, face full of pure anger and hate. A middle-aged woman in a frilly dress is pointing both arms at the hanging platform, her red face glistening and twisted. *"Die, Yankees! Die, Yankees! Die, Yankees!"*

At the French embassy last night, after General Longstreet departed, the team separated into factions—those wanting to take their vengeance out on the field, and those who did not want to continue. As news of the mobilization of the US Army and Navy filtered into the embassy, many of the team soon realized that if war commenced, it would be because they played Game 7 and lost it, or because they refused to play and therefore left the issue for the guns, bullets, bombs, bayonets, and the hangman.

The argument about whether or not to play boiled for three hours. And without Wagner, without Martin holding the team together—with Donlin gored, with Velez hobbled, with a bump on the back of Bresnahan's head the size of a golf ball from a New Glory rifle butt, with Devlin's eye turning black—there didn't seem to be a clear-cut, correct answer about whether or not to play.

At 11:30, a vote was cast by secret ballot, Ban Johnson and Pulliam insisting that they each have a vote. With twenty to seven in favor, Game 7 would be played. Johnson announced that, barring Martin's return, Frank Chance would manage. Right after the vote, Brush, Jr. waited for Chance to emerge from the bathroom, and Junior asked, "The gloves are off, right Mr. Chance?"

"Of course."

Junior explained his proposed signaling system. "I will sit in the first row in center field. I have a red shirt that I will hang over the wall if it's a curveball. If it's a fastball, I will remove the shirt."

At breakfast, while the players shouted to the waitstaff for more bacon, toast, and omelettes, while downing copious amounts of coffee, Frank Chance and Junior went around to each table, showed the silk shirt the color of blood to each cluster of players, and explained, "No shirt—fastball; red shirt on the wall—curveball." Junior stuffed the shirt in his bag with his binoculars, and rushed out to the ballpark, seven hours before game time, to secure a spot in the front row of the center-field bleachers.

Now here they are with US Navy warships massed on the horizon off Leeton, with the United States Senate debating a resolution to declare war, with José Méndez warming up on the mound, with Bernardo Baro and Ty Cobb playing catch in the outfield while stealing glances at Martin, Wagner in the middle, and Roosevelt, seated on a hanging platform built into the middle of the bleachers in right-center, with Frank Chance jogging back to the dugout from the outfield wall, having discussed the lineup with Martin, who, in a perversely lucid sense of fair play, is now being provided a microphone on a stand, which is connected by a wire snaking under the stands to a speaker in the USA dugout.

To one of the men setting up the microphone in front of Martin, a young man with a serious, jowly face, concentrating on adjusting the microphone stand, Martin asks, "How can you be party to all of this? This demented society?"

The jowly man responds without looking up, "Athens was founded on slavery. The light bulb makes the slave's life better too. Now, do not yell into the microphone and do not touch it with your mouth or you risk being electrocuted. Do you know what that is—electrocution?"

Martin speaks into the microphone, "Christy."

In the dugout, Martin's voice is metallic, emanating from the suitcase-sized speaker at the end of the bench. "Christy, we're going to save you for the second half of the game. We're going to start with Mordecai."

On the bleacher platform, Honus Wagner leans over to the microphone and says, "Go kick ass, gentlemen!"

The dugout cheers lustily, waving towels at Martin, Wagner, and Roosevelt, way out above right-center with nooses around their necks.

Martin coughs, feeling the compression on his windpipe, the noose pressing the swollen cancerous nodes. Wagner replies for Martin, into the mic, "We hear you loud and clear!"

Junior is seated in the front row of the bleachers, ten rows below the hanging platform, and Junior is trembling. He is fully aware that he should not make his sympathies known to those around him, but Junior refrains from saying anything, turns to the beautifully manicured field, and focuses his binoculars. He holds the red silk shirt on his lap. He has his sketchbook—the decoy—and by habit, his batters' and pitchers' charts, the compiling of which has been rendered irrelevant since this is the final game.

## SOLAR SERIES GAME 7

| NEW GLORY | | UNITED STATES | |
|---|---|---|---|
| 2B | LUKE "HELLCAT" COBB | CF | ROGER BRESNAHAN |
| 3B | AUGUSTUS COBB | 3B | ART DEVLIN |
| C | JOSEPHUS COBB | SS | POP LLOYD |
| SS | MARTÍN DIHIGO | 2B | JOHNNY BLENT |
| 1B | CAESAR COBB | 1B | FRANK CHANCE |
| CF | BERNARDO BARO | RF | GEORGE STONE |
| RF | TYRUS COBB | LF | ELMER FLICK |
| LF | SAM CRAWFORD | C | BRUCE PETWAY |
| P | JOSÉ MÉNDEZ | P | MORDECAI BROWN |

Top of the 1st. Bresnahan bunts up the first-base line, catcher Josephus pouncing on the ball, taking one step toward the pitcher's mound, and firing to Cæsar, half a step ahead of Bresnahan. Bresnahan veers into Cæsar, barreling him to the ground, landing on top, both hands pounding his face, pursuing as Cæsar rolls away. George Browne, coaching first, blasts into Hellcat to keep him off Bresnahan. O'Day, umpiring first, steps back, wary of Bresnahan's fury, and permitting him to vent his frustration in the wake of New Glory putting Martin, Wagner, and Roosevelt in nooses, plus Ty Cobb's spiking of Chief Velay.

The teams blast out of their dugouts, engaging in the area near Bresnahan and Cæsar, ripping into each other, punching and gouging. Scores of police and soldiers flood the field, pull the teams apart and form a thick cordon between USA and New Glory.

O'Day, figuring that he or Rigler must perform the act, and not one of the New Glory umps, catches Rigler's eye and Rigler nods assent. O'Day is sick to his stomach, on the verge of vomiting, because the action that he is about to take might tip the balance of the game and mean the death of three fine men and the reignition of the Civil War. O'Day raises his arm and ejects Bresnahan from the game.

Bresnahan screams incoherently at O'Day, spittle flying. Frank Chance bolts to O'Day. *"You can't do this! Those men might die because of you!"*

O'Day replies evenly, "I didn't attack the first baseman. Bresnahan did."

Cæsar's face is a bloody mess, and he is helped off the field. The Irish pull Bresnahan to the dugout.

On the hanging platform, Martin leans in to the microphone, "Calm down everybody! Let's not do anything else stupid!" To Martin, Bresnahan attacking Cæsar was moronic. Now the great leadoff hitter and center fielder is lost. Bresnahan is also the backup catcher, and now, with Kling having opted not to make the trip to New Glory, their only backup to Bruce Petway is Frank Bowerman. Martin clicks off the microphone. "What do you think, Honus?"

The overdeveloped nose, ears, mouth of Honus Wagner, the almond eyes, a noose scratching his neck, tightened to the top of his breastbone. "I'd love to be out there."

Beyond Wagner, Roosevelt blasts, "Bully! Bully! Honus! Bully!"

Regino García, a foot shorter and sixty pounds lighter than Cæsar, takes over first base, as every eyeball in the stadium watches Art Devlin settle into his batting stance. The first pitch is at Devlin's hip and makes him jump back. The stadium erupts in cheering.

Beyond pitcher José Méndez, Devlin does not spot a red shirt hanging on the center-field wall. Aside from the non-signal, Devlin already expects a fastball on the outside corner. It screams exactly toward there and Devlin swings hard, doesn't get the thickest part of his bat on it, hitting a high-arcing fly that plops into Ty Cobb's glove. Two outs.

Pop Lloyd lines out to Hellcat for the third out.

In the wake of Bresnahan's ejection, Martin clicks on the microphone and announces that Dahlen will go in at short-stop; Pop Lloyd will move to right field; George Stone will shift to center.

**George Stone CF**
**Elmer Flick LF**         **Pop Lloyd RF**
**Bill Dahlen SS**   **Johnny Blent 2B**
**Art Devlin 3B**         **Frank Chance 1B**
**Mordecai Brown P**
**Bruce Petway C**

Bottom of the 1st. Hellcat chops a curveball to third, Devlin backhanding and firing across the diamond to Chance. Hellcat refrains from barreling into Chance, peels off, head down, and jogs to the dugout. One out.

On the bench Velez bites his lip, extremely frustrated that he's not out there. From second base, Blent makes eye contact with Velez, flaps his glove. Velez salutes.

Augustus steps in. He's batting .343 for the series with six doubles. The second pitch from Three Finger Brown is a fastball that veers over the heart of home plate, Brown's eyes going wide at his mistake a split second before Augustus catapults into it, bat *cracking* ball, ball rocketing high in the baby-blue sky, Pop Lloyd racing back to the wall, looking up, and it's in the bleachers.

### USA 0 — 1 NEW GLORY

On the hanging platform, Honus Wagner deflates. Roosevelt blusters, "We'll get them!"

Near the front of the bleachers, a fan turns and makes eye contact with Roosevelt, the fan's smile humungous as he traces an index finger across his neck.

Three Finger Brown rubs up the new baseball, gazes out at the bleachers, at the three men on the platform. Petway slaps Brown's side. "Don't look at that! Look at me! It's just another ball game!"

Brown replies, "I like those guys out there. And Roosevelt said he'd get me and my wife a tour of the Goddamned fucking White House."

"Tell you what," Petway says, "I'll tag along with ya." Brown burps a chuckle. Petway continues, "You ready to get these motherfuckers?" Brown's square-headed expression of dead-eye seriousness restores.

Josephus fouls off six pitches before walking.

On the third pitch to Martín Dihigo, Josephus takes off, and Petway, like a giant eel, whips the ball: it arrives two feet to the right of second and two feet off the ground into Blent's awaiting glove: perfect. He applies the tag to Josephus' incoming cleat. Two outs.

Dihigo hits a long fly to center, George Stone camping under it, makes the catch. He turns and salutes Martin, Honus Wagner, and Roosevelt, and all three return the salute. Sixty-three thousand throats boo Stone's gesture.

Top of the 2nd. Digging in for his first pitch from Méndez, Blent witnesses Junior's red shirt appearing over the center-field wall: curveball. Blent adjusts his weight back. The pitch starts inside, and curves over the plate. Blent smacks it past Méndez's head, up the middle, Dihigo diving to his left, knocking the ball down, but it trickles away and Blent bursts across first. The USA bench erupts.

Frank Chance digs in. On a 1–1 count, Blent takes off, the ball fast and away, Chance flicking the bat at it, knocking it over first, and it drops foul by a foot.

1–2 to Chance. Méndez checks Blent, and Blent flinches, trying to get Méndez to balk. Méndez kicks and fires a fastball, Chance popping it up, shouting, *"Fuck!"* Dihigo and Augustus racing into foul ground, Dihigo shouting, *"Mine!"* and Dihigo catches it. One out.

George Stone strikes out. Elmer Flick walks, pushing Blent to second.

As the count to Petway goes to 2–1, Martin considers pinch-hitting for the next batter, Three Finger Brown, even though it's only the second inning; if Petway walks, the bases will be loaded, and they need runs. Replacing Brown on the mound isn't much of a concern with their stable of great pitchers. Brown will be pissed off as hell, but making the decision

430 feet from the dugout is somehow easier for Martin, even with a noose around his neck and increasingly weary from fighting an invasion of cancer. Petway works the walk.

Martin says into the microphone, "Jimmy Collins batting for Brown."

Honus Wagner nods, "Yes sir!"

Collins, the great Boston third baseman, takes his bat and twists his body, warming up. In the batter's box, he sets his back foot. Behind the center-field wall, Junior deciphers the catcher's signs, and the red shirt goes over the wall. A curveball comes in and Collins swings hard, popping it up, Regino García settling under it in foul ground. *Out.* The third out.

Wagner exhales, "Damn."

"It was a good decision despite the pop-up, Mr. Martin," Roosevelt comments. "We are stocked well with pitchers."

Martin, not seeing the need to contain himself, replies, "I don't need your approval or request it."

*"What?"* Roosevelt exclaims.

"It was under your supervision that this whole situation got so royally screwed up, and here we are with nooses around our necks! No more distractions from you, please! 'Nuff said!"

## USA  0 — 1  NEW GLORY

Bottom of the 2nd. Mathewson takes the mound. He is moving stiffly, tries to rotate his neck and winces. Blent steps forward. "You all right?"

He ignores Blent. García pops up. Baro strikes out. Ty Cobb pulls a two hopper, the ball bouncing off Chance's chest. He scoops it up and steps on the bag a stride ahead of Ty, who knocks Chance's shoulder as he passes, hopping on one foot, slowing, walking toward right. Chance shoots him the finger. Everyone on the bench is screaming at Ty. Three outs.

In the dugout, Mathewson grabs Blent's sleeve. "I'm all out of whack." They rush into the clubhouse where Matty lays on the training table. Blent traces the outline of his spine. Blent doesn't want to think about Mrs. Mathewson at this moment—he wants to score runs and keep the other team down—but he does think of her at St. Patrick's as he tells Christy, "Lie on your side." Blent's quick twist makes Mathewson's neck multiply crack; Matty's completely relieved.

Top of the 3rd. Even though Dahlen adjusts to the red shirt signal, he still swings over a Méndez curveball for strike three. Devlin hacks one up in the air to short left and to Hellcat. Pop Lloyd takes two strikes before the red shirt emerges. The next pitch curves over the plate and Lloyd whacks it *crack!* over Hellcat to right for a single.

Lloyd on first. Two outs.

Blent strides to the batter's box. Martin flicks on the microphone. "Play number two." It's a hit-and-run. On the next pitch Lloyd dashes for second. The pitch is high and in, and Blent pulls in his hands and cracks it over third. Lloyd rounds second, chugging for third. The left fielder, Sam Crawford, retrieves the ball near the line, Lloyd rounding third, blasting for home, Augustus taking the relay and firing toward Josephus, the ball bouncing, short-hopping Josephus' chest, and Josephus can't corral it as it bounces away. Lloyd slides in safe. Blent stands on second with a double, claps his hands, and extends thumbs-up toward Martin, Wagner, and Roosevelt.

## USA  1 — 1  NEW GLORY

Blent on second. Two outs.

The crowd screams encouragement at José Méndez.

After taking a wide ball for a 2–1 pitch, Chance sees the red shirt on the outfield wall. The curveball comes in, and he wallops it. The ball looks like it might make the left-field bleachers, but it short-hops the wall. Blent scores easily. Sam Crawford fields the ball quickly and fires in, Chance chugging for third, Dihigo taking the throw, slinging it to Augustus. Chance is out by fifteen feet. But the USA has seized the lead.

| Game 7 | 1 | 2 | 3 | 4 | 5 | 6 | 7 | 8 | 9 | R | H | E |
|---|---|---|---|---|---|---|---|---|---|---|---|---|
| USA | 0 | 0 | 2 | | | | | | | 2 | 4 | 0 |
| New Glory | 1 | 0 | | | | | | | | 1 | 3 | 1 |

Roosevelt and Wagner cheer. Roosevelt yells, *"That's the way!"* Martin saves his energy. New Gloryers jeer them.

Top of the 5th. Pop Lloyd whacks a red-shirt curveball for a single.

Blent pops up a fastball into short-left, Dihigo racing over and Blent thinks Dihigo's gonna catch it, the ball smacking the pinkie finger of Dihigo's outstretched glove and falling to the turf. Error.

Lloyd on second, Blent on first. No outs.

Chance steps in to loud booing. He takes three fastballs, 1–2. The red shirt appears on the wall. The curve comes in, and Chance crushes it. On the bench, to Velez, *It's gone.*

Sam Crawford and Bernardo Baro race back, back, Crawford reaching out, ball smacking glove, Crawford impacting wall. Crawford is unmoving for a moment, stunned, then crumbles to the ground. He removes the ball from his glove—he caught it—*Out!*—and meekly tosses to Baro. Lloyd has tagged up at second, rounds third, sprinting hard, eyes wide, arms pumping. Baro rifles the ball from deep center-left to Dihigo, who spins and fires home, Lloyd sliding in one second ahead of the throw. Blent was nearly at second when Crawford made the amazing catch, so Blent has retreated to first.

## USA  3 — 1  NEW GLORY

Teammates pour out of the dugout to greet Chance and Pop Lloyd, smiles of success and relief, but if Chance's whack made it over the wall they'd be hugely more comfortable. Crawford rises, checks the inventory of his moving parts, stays in the game.

George Stone lines a fastball over shortstop into left-center. Blent on second, Stone on first. One out.

Elmer Flick waits on a fastball and pulls it to right for a single. Blent zips around third and scores. The celebration is big.

Weightlessly trotting to the dugout, Blent beams out at the hanging platform, at Wagner, Roosevelt, Bucky Martin.

## USA  4 — 1  NEW GLORY

Walter Johnson rises from the dugout. Head down, carrying his glove and three baseballs in his left hand, he walks along the stands in a gathering wave of cheering that does not crest. As he takes the practice mound in foul ground, the stadium is roaring.

Josephus strolls to the mound, killing time for Johnson to get ready. As the umps converge on the pitcher's mound, Dolf Luque emerges from the dugout walking as if his shoes are three sizes too small, delaying so Johnson will have a few more warmups. Luque takes the ball from José Méndez, slaps Méndez's rear. "Good game!"

Out on the hanging platform, Roosevelt comments, "That's good—removing Méndez!"

"Be careful what you wish for," Martin retorts.

"We are in good shape. They're desperate."

"The game of baseball," explains Martin, "is like a speeding automobile with loose wheels driving down a steep rocky road."

Roosevelt considers. "It might come apart at any moment?"

Honus Wagner chuckles at Roosevelt's reaction, but his mirth is extinguished as the noose grates the back of his neck. Addressing the piggish face of the hangman, the plethora of glittering medals, he asks, "Would you please loosen this thing?" The hangman grunts, his rough hands tugging at the back of Wagner's neck, expanding the circumference of the noose.

The USA players pop from the bench and scream at Walter Johnson as he walks to the pitcher's mound.

First-base coach Bowerman yells, *"Keeler is in the hospital because of you! You murderer!"*

Stone on third, Flick on first. One out.

Frank Chance, coaching at third, meets Petway halfway to home, cups his hands around Petway's ear. "Don't swing. Wait for him to throw a strike." Petway nods.

He is short, squat, and swings a long, thin bat. He settles in from the left side. The first pitch from Johnson is low and away. Ball one. The next two pitches are outside, before a fastball shreds the air straight down the middle. 3–1.

Bowerman screams, *"You should be the one on the hanging platform! Wait till you're at bat! We're gonna put one in your ear and it's gonna come out the other!"*

Johnson checks the runners. He kicks and fires a fastball, inside edge, that Petway takes for strike two.

The corners of Bowerman's mouth froth, *"You shit-heel murderer!"*

The next pitch is straight down the middle, Petway swinging, popping it up to Dihigo. Petway's head bobs with each curse he spits out at himself as he jogs back to the bench.

Johnson throws four pitches to Mathewson, the last one a fastball that buzzes the inside edge of the plate for strike three. Inning over.

| Game 7 | 1 | 2 | 3 | 4 | 5 | 6 | 7 | 8 | 9 | R | H | E |
|---|---|---|---|---|---|---|---|---|---|---|---|---|
| USA | 0 | 0 | 2 | 0 | 2 | | | | | 4 | 7 | 0 |
| New Glory | 1 | 0 | 0 | 0 | | | | | | 1 | 4 | 1 |

Bottom of the 5th. Ty Cobb pushes a bunt up third. Devlin charges, reaches down his bare hand, the ball rolling off the top like a scoop of ice cream off a cone—plop onto the ground. Safe.

Crawford knocks a single up the middle. Ty rounds second, his eyes wide and insane, going to third, easily.

Petway calls time and trots to the mound. The infielders converge to decide what to do about Ty Cobb, at third, if Sam Crawford takes off from first. Petway suggests, "How about this: I throw to Johnny, who cuts it off and fires to third?"

Chance glances at the distinct, distant Martin, Roosevelt, and Wagner seated on wooden chairs on the hanging platform, nooses rising. "Good plan."

On the second pitch to Johnson, Sam Crawford takes off, Petway catching, firing toward second, but shading it toward Johnny Blent, who cuts in front of the bag, catching, firing to third, Devlin catching the ball to the outfield side of third, and turning to face Ty Cobb's spikes glinting like a dozen razor blades zooming at him; Devlin flinches, and Devlin's next thought is of Martin and Wagner on the hanging platform; he dives to the base, his glove coming down on Ty's foot, which is already in contact with the bag. Safe.

*"Fuck!"* Devlin admonishes himself. Ty Cobb grins.

Ty on third, Crawford on second. No outs.

Walter Johnson swings *crack!* turning around a fastball, sending it over second base. Stone, having positioned himself shallow, decides he doesn't have a chance if he dives at it, and so holds up and plays it on one hop. He zips it in to Dahlen. Ty Cobb has scored.

## USA  4 — 2  NEW GLORY

Crawford on third, Walter Johnson on first. No outs.

Hellcat swats a single over Devlin's head. Crawford scores. Walter Johnson stops at second.

## USA  4 — 3  NEW GLORY

Blent, noticing the pitches' reduced velocity, offers a significant glance to Frank Chance, who, silently agreeing with Blent's assessment, calls, "Time!" and steps toward the mound. The rest of the infielders and Petway converge. Maintaining the top of the mound, Mathewson stares over Chance's head and insists, "Let me pitch."

On the hanging platform Martin clicks on the microphone and says, "Keep Matty in!" Jimmy Collins runs the decision out to the pitching mound. The group on the mound glances out at Martin and Wagner. Then Frank Chance encourages Matty, "You're the man!"

Walter Johnson at second, Hellcat at first. No outs.

Augustus steps in, twirling his bat, cocky. Petway leans toward Augustus' knee, asking Mathewson for a pitch inside. The pitch veers away from Petway's mitt, over the plate and Augustus crushes it, sending it high and deep and far. Dahlen shrieks, "Noooooooooooooooooo!" as the ball disappears into the left-field bleachers, igniting the crowd into delirium.

Blent crumbles to a squat, staring at the ground. He can't glance toward the hanging platform.

From the bench, Velez screams out at Blent and the team, "Settle down!" but it can't be heard over the roaring crowd.

## USA  4 — 6  NEW GLORY

Behind third base, a man in a white suit scissors onto the field and dances a jig, eyes creased in mirth, igniting laughter all the way to the last row of the top deck. A sea of fans taunts Roosevelt, Wagner, and Martin, "Gonna die! Gonna die! Gonna die!" The chanting is picked up by 98 percent of the stadium. "Gonna die! Gonna die! Gonna die! Gonna die! Gonna die!"

Martin switches on the microphone, and states, "Foster. Rube Foster." Martin closes his eyes and slumps back. He turns to Wagner. "I left Christy in too long. Fuck."

Mathewson is waiting for Foster. Mathewson is white, hollow, his uniform soaked through. He tries to smile. "You get 'em, Rube."

Foster strikes out Josephus. He induces Dihigo to top a ball to Dahlen, who fires to first for the second out. Rube Foster tosses a changeup that has Regino García twisting and falling over for the final strike of the inning.

Sixth, Seventh, Eighth innings: Rube Foster and Walter Johnson each surrender one single and one walk, pasting the scoreboard with zeroes. Walter Johnson grounds out to end the eighth.

| Game 7 | 1 | 2 | 3 | 4 | 5 | 6 | 7 | 8 | 9 | R | H | E |
|---|---|---|---|---|---|---|---|---|---|---|---|---|
| USA | 0 | 0 | 2 | 0 | 2 | 0 | 0 | 0 | | 4 | 7 | 0 |
| New Glory | 1 | 0 | 0 | 0 | 5 | 0 | 0 | 0 | | 6 | 9 | 1 |

Top of the 9th. Roosevelt has withdrawn his attention from the game as he furiously scribbles, in a pocket-sized notebook, a goodbye letter to his wife. In the bleachers, fans are screaming at the American trio, blaming them for the Tallahassee Flotilla incident, cursing their children and grandchildren and great-grandchildren, spittle flying from thousands of faces.

As Walter Johnson takes the mound, the crowd roaring insanely, Martin turns to Roosevelt. "Are they *actually* going to hang us?"

Roosevelt sniffs. He wags his notepad. "I have written to each of my children and my wife. I have a second pencil, if you wish to write to someone." Roosevelt tears out three blank pages, extends them trembling in a sudden breeze to Martin along with a sharpened pencil.

Martin considers, realizes that there is no one special for him in 1906, other than Blent and André and the bonds he's forged with his players, and Junior, and his employer, John T. Brush. Martin replies, "I don't want to be distracted."

"Bully!" Roosevelt approves.

Frank Chance jogs to the base of the wall in right-center. He projects his voice up to Martin, but the voice is less assured than usual. "Petway's up. Then Rube Foster. On the bench we've got George Browne, Cy Seymour, Bowerman. Velay says he can bat. I don't think he can run; maybe limp. The little guy showed up. He's in the clubhouse." The "little guy" means Wee Willie Keeler.

Wagner roars at Chance, *"Get me off a here and into the game! Ask President Lee! He's a sporting man!"*

Chance replies, "I'll ask, Honus. Right now."

To Wagner, Martin says, "I'll send in the request," and to Chance, "What about Turkey Mike?"

"The stitches might come out. He's still bleeding."

Martin instructs: "Stone, Flick. Then Keeler for Petway, Velay—if he can swing the bat and hobble to first—for Rube Foster."

Frank Chance gazes intently, chin trembling, up at Martin, at Roosevelt, at Wagner.

*"Courage, Mr. Chance!"* Roosevelt bellows.

Frank Chance nods, and jogs away.

Martin switches on the microphone, and states, "I would like to speak with President Lee. This is urgent." Next to the New Glory dugout, in bemedaled uniforms, a pack of generals, President Lee, Vice President Johnson, and General Longstreet are given the message. Roaring spreads through the stadium as the generals and President Lee walk across the field, the president waving his cavalry hat up at the crowd, his rainbow-colored hair unmoving under layers of shellack. They stop below the hanging platform. Lee, with a Cheshire smile, projects his voice. "Mr. Martin! What is your request?"

Martin's voice is hoarse, his breathing constricted, "Let's have Mr. Wagner participate in this game. It's only fair. Why should we play with one less player? Let him determine his own fate, in part."

For a moment, Lee confers with his generals. He flourishes his hand and to Martin, says "We are nothing if not fair-minded," which draws Roosevelt's tear-blurred glare. "But I cannot undercut the authority of our courts. My hands are tied."

Martin sneers. Wagner growls, *"Bullshit!"* Roosevelt barks, *"You invite war, sir!"* to which President Lee offers, *"Adieu."* The crowd cheers him as he returns to his seat.

In the clubhouse, Keeler is putting on his uniform while Bresnahan sobs on a stool in the next locker, holding a fifth of white rum with only a few remaining ounces. "I shouldn't have started that fight! I can hit Johnson! I know it! Goddamn me!"

Nearby, Velez whacks a ball off a tee into a hanging blanket, and Rube Foster sets another ball on the tee. Velez does not look up, as he's feeling for his stroke, adjusting the pressure on his damaged back foot. Smelling Bresnahan's rum odor approaching, Velez barks, *"Get away!"* Velez orders the French doctor, *"More tape on the ankle!"*

Keeler swings his bat side to side, loosening his back. "We'll get 'em, Chief!"

Velez is so focused on the tape job he does not hear Keeler, who goes up the tunnel as a tidal wave of cheering blasts at him, as on the field George Stone is walking away from home plate, head down, carrying his bat, the ball going 'round the infield, Stone having struck out to start the ninth.

Next is Elmer Flick who has nine hits in the series and is batting .333. He's 5 for 13 against Johnson. The first pitch is on the outside corner. Strike. Johnson rocks and fires high and in. Ball.

Josephus yells out, "Come on now, big guy!" and to Flick, taunting, "You think you got a chance against him?"

Johnson fires a fastball on the inside edge that Flick decides is unhittable even though it's a strike. 1–2.

Flick inches back half a shoe length. He lets out his bat a corresponding amount, so he'll be able to cover a fastball on the outside corner. And it's a fastball on the outside corner that nightmarishly bursts over his flailing bat, the ball ticking off Josephus' mitt toward the stands, Flick taking off for first on the strikeout/passed ball, the USA dugout roaring, Flick racing with fear, first base four strides away, now two strides, the ball zipping *plop!* into Regino García's glove, Flick's foot stamping the base a moment after.

O'Day hesitates, knowing the USA will have only one out remaining, the lifeline. But O'Day does his duty. Out.

*"Gonna die! Gonna die! Gonna die! Gonna die! Gonna die! Gonna die! Gonna die! Gonna die! Gonna die!"* The stadium reverberates.

## USA 4 — 6 NEW GLORY

Wee Willie Keeler strides to the batter's box, hatless, a stained bandage on his head covering an insignificant mark made by yesterday's intentionally accepted beaning.

In the bleachers, the hangman asks Roosevelt, Martin and Wagner to stand. The chairs are removed, the nooses tightened. The hangman ties Martin's hands behind his back, and Martin mutters, "Holy mother of God." He gazes up at cloud islands in the blue sky.

Keeler grits his teeth. Off first base Bowerman screams at Walter Johnson, *"If you hit Keeler again you'll kill him!"*

Augustus jogs in to the mound from third, Josephus from behind home. Josephus pats Walter Johnson's side, says, "This little guy's faking. Ignore him. Pretend it's any player. Just strike out the dwarf. That's a lot of money we have coming to us." They gaze up into the stands behind the dugout where Mr. and Mrs. Cobb, the parents of the five Cobb brothers, expectantly look at them. Augustus asks, "You okay, Walter?"

"Yeah."

Augustus and Josephus retreat.

Johnson rocks, fires *shhhhhhhhhhhh!* straight down the middle. Strike! Keeler closes his eyes, pissed off that he didn't swing at it. But it's so damned fast.

Carrying his bat, Velez gingerly steps out to the on-deck spot. His left ankle is so numb it feels nonexistent, and it will barely support his swing. Velez takes a half swing. He decides to choke up four inches. He'd give all his money for Keeler to get on base so he can face Johnson.

Keeler coils. He wants something outside so he can pop it over third. But the ball zooms inside and Keeler jumps back. Strike! *"Nooooo!"* Keeler cries. *"Inside three inches!"* Chance runs toward the New Glory home-plate ump, Tiant, who turns on Chance, "One more step and you're out of the game!"

*"Ask for help!"* Chance screams, gesturing toward the men on the hanging platform. *"Three good men!"* With both hands, Chance wipes tears from his eyes.

Wee Willie Keeler exhales hard. He's mumbling to himself, bits of words, pieces, incoherent sounds. Johnson rocks and fires inside—the same spot as the lousy pitch that was just called a strike—and Keeler slashes it foul up the first-base line. Keeler bites his lip. Steps in. 0–2.

In the dugout, Blent can't even bear to turn his head to check the hanging platform.

Johnson rocks and fires *shhhhhwww* down the middle, Keeler whacking it over Johnson's head—his glove flashing up too late, the ball bouncing over second base into center field. The USA whoops and cheers and waves towels as Keeler flies past first.

Keeler on first. Two outs.

Velez takes small steps toward the batter's box, trying not to limp, but limping. A glance to right field: There's Ty Cobb. There's Martin up on the platform next to Wagner, both with ropes going down to their necks. Velez stares out at Johnson and hums, "I'm gonna destroy you, sucka." He takes a practice swing, humming, "Destroy you."

Johnson checks Keeler. Johnson rocks, Keeler running, Velez taking the pitch for a strike, Josephus catching and firing, the ball tailing high and wide on its way to second, Keeler sliding in safe.

The next pitch is, thankfully to Velez and the rest of the USA team, outside, because Velez didn't see it emerging from the background of Keeler's uniform.

Velez steps across the plate and motions to Frank Chance in the third-base coacher's box. "Tell Keeler I can't see the fucking ball! Get out of my line of sight!" Chance jogs out to Keeler and relays the message.

Velez resets, rocks his bat, stares out at Johnson, at the spot to the side of Johnson's shoulder where Velez expects the ball to emerge from Johnson's hand.

Johnson rocks, fires a fastball toward the outside corner. Velez lashes at it, fouling it off behind third. The sore left ankle isn't strong enough. It's making the body and bat too slow. He chokes up another half inch.

Keeler doesn't move. Sixty-three thousand are roaring, *"Gonna die! Gonna die! Gonna die!"* while the few Blacks in the upper reaches are standing and cheering for Velez. Martin, Roosevelt, and Wagner stare in. Wagner says, "I can't believe this shit!"

Wagner's face is contorted in fear; Roosevelt is trembling with rage.

Martin says, "Don't worry, Honus." Martin realizes it's an odd thing to say, perhaps his final utterance. But Martin is now ready. An odd sense of peace. After beating back the cancer once, and its recurrence now, after the absurd spitball of time travel, after finally winning the World Series with the New York Giants, after managing some of the best players ever, after helping Blent and Velez find success in 1906, he concludes it's enough for one lifetime. More than enough.

Johnson fires down the middle, up, Velez swinging, tipping it straight back. 1–2.

Blent's standing between Dahlen and Devlin and they're all holding their breath.

Johnson rocks, fires—the same pitch down the middle, up, Velez unleashing—the ball ticking off his bat—the chicken-wire screen reverberates. The crowd roars. Velez is pissed he missed that pitch, but oddly at this most pressurized moment, Velez's shoulders relax; Blent glances at the guys around him, but they don't seem to notice Velez's immense poise. Blent senses that it's all gonna be okay, that there's no way this kid, Johnson, is gonna get Velez. Somehow.

Velez sets his back foot without twisting it, rocks his bat, stares out. From center field, Junior sees two fingers go down; but since Keeler is on second, Junior isn't sure that Josephus and Johnson haven't changed their signs, so Junior keeps the shirt on his lap.

Johnson fires—it's a curve!—up in the zone—dropping from chest-high to belt-high, Velez turning, smashing, the ball rising, Velez starts out of the box, watching the ball curving toward the foul line, screaming, *"Stay fair! Stay fair!"* heard by most of the crowd in shocked silence, 63,000 pairs of eyes watching the five-and-a-quarter-inch diameter horsehide-covered ball rise high and far and begin to descend, Velez hopping toward first, flinging his hands and arms toward fair territory, *"Stay fair!"*

From the hanging platform Martin, Roosevelt and Wagner watch the ball drop into the stands, but cannot determine whether it's fair or foul. But Velez sees it, and Hank O'Day, the first base ump, emphatically motions both arms toward the field—*FAIR!*

*A HOME RUN!*

Devlin, Dahlen and Blent are hugging while they jump up and down and the USA players in the dugout erupt.

Velez limps past first, pumps his fist to the sky, pumps his fist to the hanging platform, jumps up with both arms extended facing the hanging platform, yelling out in triumph.

Right fielder Ty Cobb sprints in at O'Day, Ty screaming, "Foul ball!" All the Cobbs, Luque, Sam Crawford, Bernardo Baro coalesce into a mob around O'Day. Rigler and the two New Glory umps pull the players off. Fans in the right-field bleachers are gesturing that the ball was foul. But O'Day wiggles out from the mob, emphatically shaking his head no, his expression impassive, continually circling his forearm in a lasso motion: home run. The USA team celebrates Keeler at home plate. Velez limps past shortstop, slaps Frank Chance's hand as he rounds third. As he steps on home plate with his good foot, the team mobs Velez.

| Game 7 | 1 | 2 | 3 | 4 | 5 | 6 | 7 | 8 | 9 | R | H | E |
|---|---|---|---|---|---|---|---|---|---|---|---|---|
| USA | 0 | 0 | 2 | 0 | 2 | 0 | 0 | 0 | 2 | 6 | 8 | 1 |
| New Glory | 1 | 0 | 0 | 0 | 5 | 0 | 0 | 0 | | 6 | 9 | 1 |

The three nooses are loosened, three pairs of hands untied, three chairs returned to the hanging platform. Wagner and Roosevelt are trembling, Roosevelt mumbling, "Edith, Edith, Edith," wiping the back of his wrist into his eye. Martin, a kaleidoscope of emotions, crosses his arms and whispers, "Way to go, André."

Dahlen raps a single to right; Devlin bunts for a hit; Pop Lloyd walks.

Blent's up with the bases loaded and two outs. A single will most likely knock in two runs and put this game away. Blent glances out at the hanging platform, around at the box next to the NG dugout which has mostly emptied of generals and is devoid of rainbow-haired President Lee, at Christy Mathewson coaching at third, at Frank Chance on deck, at the 63,000 maniacs who are 99 percent silent on the verge of falling behind. On the mound, Dolf Luque is talking to Walter Johnson. Blent's trying to read their lips, but there's nothing discernible.

He closes his eyes and takes a deep breath. He hops a few times to get the blood flowing, his body primed for what he hopes will be the final, successful, at-bat of the year. With his bat he can save Buck's life, the lives of Honus Wagner and the vice president. Maybe a hit will forestall a war. The face of his brother returns, but unlike the other times, Mark's intense, stubbly face isn't distracting. It's there, occupying a portion of his mind, a figment. Johnny doesn't banish it.

He figures Johnson's nervous too, so Blent will let the first one go by. The crowd roars. Johnson rocks back and zips a fastball straight down the middle—hittable. Strike one. The crowd erupts.

Blent steps out of the box, reaches down for dirt, spits tobacco juice on his palms, re-grips the bat. He stares out at Johnson, Johnson, Johnson. Here comes the pitch, another fastball. Uncoiling, he slices it foul toward the dugout, watching it make a bending trajectory toward Frank Chance who is kneeling on deck, holding his bat, looking at a rag on the ground. Blent yells, *"Fr—!"* as the ball mashes into Frank Chance's skull just above the eye, sounding like a second foul ball. And Frank Chance goes down like he's shot.

The dugout empties to surround Chance. Blent walks over like he's in a nightmare. Blood soaks the grass. The French doctor pushes through. Towels are brought. Velez limps out from the dugout. Donlin gingerly steps up onto the field. Donlin notices Blent's freaked-out expression and jokes, "Don't worry, just a Cub!" Some of the guys chuckle.

Frank Chance moves, and eyes closed, says, "I heard that, Donlin!"

The guys help him sit up. One eye opens, the other covered in blood. Bone sticks through his brow. Blent kneels to him, "I'm so sorry, Frank. Shit. I'm—"

Chance asks, "The score still 6 to 6?"

"Yeah."

His one eye focuses on Blent. "Just get a fucking hit."

The team raises him. While the New Glory players watch Frank Chance, Blent studies Walter Johnson's blank, pimply, teenage face. It doesn't tell Blent anything.

No balls, two strikes. Two outs. Blent resets against Johnson. Beyond Johnson, the red shirt comes down over the center-field wall. The curve.

But it's a fastball that blows by Blent, as Blent tries to check his swing. Strike three. The crowd roars. It's hard for Blent to take a breath. He wants to whack the bat across his legs or his face. Failure.

Velez is limping onto the field, holding Blent's glove. A bandage is wrapped under Velez's cleat and around his ankle. Blent's shocked to see him taking the field. New Glory is going to think one and only one thing: bunt toward Velez. On the other hand, it's comforting to have Velez on the field. "How's your ankle?"

"Pretty bad. If I try to run, I think it'll give out."

"Why don't you play way in and I'll cover first behind you?"

"Yeah," he says. "That's about the only thing we can do. I'll force them to try to shoot it past me."

**George Stone CF**

**Elmer Flick LF**    **"Wee" Willie Keeler RF**

**Bill Dahlen SS**    **Johnny Blent 2B**

**Art Devlin 3B**    **André Velay 1B**

**Rube Waddell P**

**Frank Bowerman C**

The lives of Honus Wagner, Vice President Roosevelt, and Bucky Martin are in the hands of Rube Waddell, a man with an IQ of, perhaps, 85. As Waddell fires a warm-up *pop!* into Bowerman's mitt, writer Hugh Fullerton leans toward F. C. Lane. "This is the tensest I've ever been in my life. You have the current batting averages?" Lane hands over a sheet that is covered in division calculations, to come up with three-digit percentages, generating a list running down the side:

|  | New Glory |  | USA |
|---|---|---|---|
| .333 | Hellcat Cobb | .222 | Bill Dahlen |
| .277 | Augustus Cobb | .250 | Art Devlin |
| .377 | Josephus Cobb | .100 | Rube Waddell |
| .544 | Martín Dihigo | .476 | Johnny Blent |
| .188 | Regino Garcia | .188 | Frank Bowerman |

| .250 | Bernardo Baro | .333 | George Stone |
| .294 | Ty Cobb | .143 | Elmer Flick |
| .266 | Sam Crawford | 1.000 | Wee Willie Keeler |
| .200 | Walter Johnson | .444 | André Velay |

| Game 7 | 1 | 2 | 3 | 4 | 5 | 6 | 7 | 8 | 9 | R | H | E |
|---|---|---|---|---|---|---|---|---|---|---|---|---|
| USA | 0 | 0 | 2 | 0 | 2 | 0 | 0 | 0 | 2 | 6 | 9 | 1 |
| New Glory | 1 | 0 | 0 | 0 | 5 | 0 | 0 | 0 | · | 6 | 9 | 1 |

Bottom of the 9th. Waddell strikes out Martín Dihigo.

García bunts up the first-base line, Waddell almost colliding with Velez. Velez fields, spins, fires high and Blent's leaping, snaring the ball as García's little foot stomps the bag *before* Blent returns to earth.

Theodore Roosevelt exhales, "Oh no!"

On the bench, Petway says, "Frank's got to control Rube. Give him a sign to pitch over." Next to Petway, Mathewson asks, "Why don't you go out and tell him?"

Petway scratches his head as he flashes through the permutations: a Negro player usurping Martin's and Frank Chance's authority; the tag of "uppity"; hurting his opportunity of ever playing major league ball; helping the team and saving the lives of the men on the platform; the further breaking of the color barrier. Petway holds up his fist and replies to Mathewson, "Go out there. I give Waddell the fist to throw over."

Mathewson yanks Petway up from the bench and both jog to the mound, where Waddell greets Mathewson: "You already pitched today." The fist-pitchout sign agreed, they all return to their places.

García takes a nine-foot lead at first. Frank Bowerman, hand between his legs, makes a fist. Waddell fires over to first.

In the dugout, Petway comments, "Good!" and expectorates an arc of tobacco juice.

Mathewson nervously laughs.

Bernardo Baro flies to right, Keeler settling under the ball. Keeler seems conscious of Martin and the vice president and Honus Wagner at the gallows. Keeler's body is tense, as if he's telling himself, *Don't drop the ball, don't think about dropping the ball, DO NOT DROP THE FUCKING BALL!—smack* into his glove. Two outs.

Displaying a nervous smile, Ty Cobb affects a jaunty stride as he steps into the batter's box. He taps the outside edge of the plate and shines his grin on Waddell. The first pitch zips in, Ty turning, smacking the ball high and sharply down the line, García halfway to second, Keeler racing toward the line.

Keeler's only chance at keeping García from scoring the winning run is to not let the ball get past him. The crowd roars as the ball bounces four feet fair, Keeler diving headfirst, tip of glove snagging ball. He rolls once, pops to his feet, and fires toward Blent. Blent's next to the right-field line, one step in the outfield, Velez twenty feet behind him yelling *"Home! Home! Home!"* Blent spins and fires toward home, but the ball is veering slightly up the third-base line and Blent deflates and can't breathe at the sight of it bending away. He feels like all his skin is now contacting his bones, and he wants to cry: the ball is sailing above Bowerman's head as García barrels toward home—everything is over if this ball gets by Bowerman, Bowerman who is leaping as high as possible, shoulder rising to dislocation, ball smacking the top edge of his catcher's mitt and sticking. Arm and mitt wheel down like a breaking clock hand as García's body, arms and shoulders pass under Bowerman, and Blent's as sure that García is now scoring the winning run as he's sure his name is Johnny Blent, until Bowerman's wind-milling mitt brushes the back of García's head, knocking askew García's cap. *"Ooooooouuuuuuuut!"* bellows the home-plate ump, thrusting his fist high.

USA players burst from the dugout. Blent sprints in to hug Bowerman's sweaty neck. *"You saved my ass!"*

*"Your* ass?" Velez turns to the gallows.

Roosevelt exclaims at the sky, *"Thank God!"* Martin laughs. Junior cheers up at Martin.

Blent gathers Bowerman's mask and escorts him off the field. "I didn't know you could jump so high."

"Neither did I."

Top of the 10th. Bowerman strikes out; George Stone smacks a single up the middle; Elmer Flick walks; Willie Keeler pops up in foul ground to Regino García.

Stone on second, Flick on first. Two outs.

Velez limps up to bat. With his left foot, he smooths the dirt in the batter's box. Somehow he managed to crush a homer off Johnson in the ninth. Somehow he managed to move around almost adequately in the field. Now all he has to do is whack a single and make it to first to put the team ahead. But the question is, will Walter Johnson give Velez anything in the strike zone, or will Johnson pitch around Velez to load the bases, preferring to face Bill Dahlen? All of the USA wishes they could yank the noose off Honus Wagner and put him on deck, but they're stuck with Dahlen, who's a solid hitter, but no Wagner.

Velez looks out at Johnson and mumbles, "Kill you motherfucker." He's looking for a low-and-away fastball, and that's what's zipping in, off the plate. Velez flicks his bat, stroking the ball over Martín Dihigo's head, and the ball drops into left field.

The team screams like maniacs as George Stone races around third and is halfway to home as left fielder Sam Crawford comes up with the ball, and having no reasonable chance to get Stone at home, fires it to Augustus at third to keep Elmer Flick at second.

On the scoreboard, the USA's "6" slides out, replaced with a "7."

| Game 7 | 1 | 2 | 3 | 4 | 5 | 6 | 7 | 8 | 9 | 10 | R | H | E |
|---|---|---|---|---|---|---|---|---|---|---|---|---|---|
| USA | 0 | 0 | 2 | 0 | 2 | 0 | 0 | 0 | 2 | 1 | 7 | 12 | 1 |
| New Glory | 1 | 0 | 0 | 0 | 5 | 0 | 0 | 0 | 0 | | 6 | 9 | 1 |

The crowd moans and boos with all their remaining might.

Cy Seymour, who's coaching first, whacks Velez's back and the team's jumping up and down, shouting in exaltation, thanking God, high-fiving.

On the gallows, Roosevelt and Wagner are hugging, while Martin clicks on the microphone. "Seymour running for Velay."

A gigantic smile on his face, Velez limps to the dugout accompanied by foghorns of booing.

Dahlen strikes out.

Bottom of the 10th. Sam Crawford chops a roller between second and first. Cy Seymour fields it, springs back toward first, dives at the bag, slapping it with his glove before Crawford stomps down. One out. Walter Johnson taps a four hopper to Dahlen, who makes a perfect throw to Seymour for out number two. Hellcat smacks a liner to Blent's left that he leaps at, ball snagging in the little web between thumb and forefinger. Blent crashes to the ground. He turns his mitt to O'Day and displays the ball.

Hank O'Day's fist rises and he almost passes out with relief that Roosevelt, Martin, and Wagner are not going to be executed.

Game over. Series over.

Seymour and Dahlen jump on Blent, and soon the whole team is piling on. The crowd boos ferociously; some moan; some yell at the home-plate ump that they're gonna hang *him*.

The team swarms André Velay, and though he protests, they raise him to their shoulders. Blent gets in there, putting a hand on his lower back. With no place in particular to go, the swarm carries André toward first base.

"Let me down!" he laughs. "Give Bowerman a ride!"

Martin and Roosevelt and Wagner laugh in relief as their nooses are removed by the muttering-in-disappointment executioner.

The booing transforms into scattered frustrated wailing as the stadium of fanatics stares in silence at the celebrating USA team.

Sportswriters and telegraphers gape at the raucous USA players. Velay is set down. Bresnahan and Donlin yell up at the crowd, *"You're going to Hell!"* *"You slave-owning bastards!"* Junior and Wagner run across the outfield to join the party.

Roosevelt and Martin slowly walk in, Martin leaning on Roosevelt. Blent sprints out to them. The nodes on the sides of Martin's neck look angry, with red rope marks. "You all right?" Blent asks.

Martin's sore throat croaks, "Not dying today."

Blent sprints into the dugout and retrieves a bottle of water and then realizes he's forgotten drinking glasses. At the edge of the infield, Roosevelt and Martin take turns gulping from the bottle.

While the stadium drains of fans, Vice President Johnson offers the bulbous, shining silver Solar Series Cup to Bucky Martin, who accepts the trophy and refuses the outstretched hand, staring until Johnson's hand withdraws.

Martin transfers the forty-pound trophy to the cluster consisting of Pulliam, Ban Johnson and Roosevelt. Donlin snatches it, raises it above his head, and races it 'round the bases trailed by a ragged pack of celebrating teammates.

Twenty minutes later, the New Glory players, showered and in their military uniforms, stand in a line extending from their dugout. Many of the USA team is sitting on the grass, smoking cigars, passing bottles. But they rise to shake the offered hands of the New Glory team.

When Blent shakes Martín Dihigo's hand, he tells Blent, "You screwed me up yesterday—'time traveler.'" Velez joins. Blent steers them to a spot behind the pitcher's mound, and tells Dihigo, "We want to go to that cave, to see where you time-traveled, to try to figure it out."

Bucky Martin joins them. "Gettsyburg. Was history the same before Gettysburg? Or just the fact that you time-traveled in on June 28th change everything?" Bucky Martin can see that Martin Dihigo is perplexed and that these questions are, for now at least, unanswerable. "I wish I had been there, man. Gettysburg."

"No you don't. Slaughter like nothing you've ever seen. Bodies and piles of arms and legs." His mouth turns sour.

"Everything seems to get fucked up after that battle, that the South won in this world. And Vicksburg."

Christy Mathewson overhears and looks quizzically at the quartet before returning to downing a bottle with Bowerman, Dahlen and Rube Foster.

Honus Wagner approaches and pats Dihigo's back. "Why don't you come up to Pittsburg and join me on the team?"

Dihigo pinches the skin on his wrist, showing that it is, obviously, black. "That's the reason, Mr. Wagner."

"What if we let Negroes into the league? I can work on it. I have some influence." Borrowing a pen and scrap from a reporter, Honus Wagner writes his address for Martín Dihigo.

"Goodbye." Dihigo slowly strides away. Wagner joins a throng passing a bottle.

Velez asks Martin and Blent, "How do you think Dihigo'd do in our time?" as Rube Waddell, barefoot and giggling, sprints out of the dugout, holding four glass steins of beer in each hand. Art Devlin and Roger Bresnahan rip all eight beers from Waddell and douse him to hearty laughter from the players, from Ban Johnson, from Pulliam, from Junior, from Theodore Roosevelt, from Bucky Martin, and from eye-bandaged-and-beaming Frank Chance. Rube Waddell is giggling in his beer shower, bent backwards, as the beer soaks his uniform. In the center-field bleachers, seagulls are diving for scraps and the ropes from the three nooses are being pulled down.

Velez says, "Let's get the hell—"

# 27

## Gentlemen, Welcome

A DISTANT EXPLOSION induces the stadium's dwindling throng to scan the sky for fireworks, as Velez finishes his sentence "—out of here."

But there are no fireworks.

Fans on the upper concourse witness, on the horizon, continuous red-and-orange flashes at the waterfront near Leeton. The rumbling from the flashes ripples through the stadium. Rumors and panic cascade toward the field. In the upper deck, an ancient man, broomstick-skinny, leans over the railing and shouts to the emptying stadium, *"Git yer rifles, boys! They're attacking!"*

Martin rubs his neck where it was chafed. He's having difficulty swallowing. Blent hands him a bottle of water and tells him to take small sips to help open his throat. F. C. Lane returns from a discussion with NG reporters and informs, "They say that New Glory invaded Florida a few hours ago, claiming the US invaded Guantanamo at dawn, in the southwestern part of the island. Those are USA Naval guns we're hearing."

"Full-on war!" Ban Johnson exclaims.

Every player not yet too drunk to grasp what is going on gravitates to Bucky Martin. Many realize it wouldn't be too difficult to capture the entire USA delegation. Before Martin gets a word out, Roosevelt pipes, "Gentlemen! We must move en masse to a fortified position—inland! Then, when there is an opening, we connect with our invading forces on the coast!"

"How do you know we *have* invading forces?" Mathewson asks. "How do you know we are not just *bombing from offshore?*"

Roosevelt's eyes drift to Mathewson's groin, then back to his face. "I know these things."

A biplane buzzes above the lip of the stadium.

Pointing both fingers to the USA stitched across his uniform, George Stone tells Roosevelt, "We're completely defenseless!"

Roosevelt responds, "Change into civilian clothes and let us evacuate with purpose!"

The biplane circles low over the field, the pilot craning out, waving at the team. The pilot drops a package—a small parachute opens, supporting a box. Some of the players run after the chute and box. Bresnahan wraps both arms around the rapidly descending wooden box as it pounds his chest. The parachute is removed. Bresnahan cradles the box, which weighs about as much as a case of wine, and walks it to Roosevelt.

Wired to the top of the crate is a crowbar, which Dahlen grabs to jack open the box. He pulls out handfuls of straw and metal rods. Bresnahan rips the butcher paper off the package, revealing a device with looping wires, the size and weight of three bricks, wondering aloud, "What the fuck is this?"

Dahlen pulls an instruction sheet, confusedly hands it to Roosevelt, who remarks, "These pieces fit together!"

Velez starts to laugh, and most look at him like he's a madman. The entire USA delegation watches Velez screw the metal rods together, then screw the end into the device. He presses a button and a tiny white bulb illumes. Velez raises the device to his ear. "Hello. Can you hear me?"

*"Mister Velay?"* The hissing sound coming through crackles with the voice of Nikola Tesla.

"How'd you do this?" Velez asks into it.

"Happy to inform you later! The general here wants you to move toward the interior!"

The players are astonished at the talking box.

"It's a telephone," Blent tells them.

"Where are the wires?" Mathewson asks.

Roosevelt orders, "Give it here!"

Velez glances at Martin who nods his assent.

Roosevelt gets on the cell phone with Tesla and is instructed where to try and move the USA delegation. Roosevelt tells all, "We are to meet up with our invading forces at the French embassy!"

The pod of Americans is briskly led by Roosevelt away from the stadium. They walk parallel to the coast, through the massive plaza with its hundred-foot-long hanging platform. Most of the players did not change out of their metal cleats, which are scraping and clacking against the cobblestone street. All of them, not wanting to abandon the tools of their trade, are holding their gloves and bats.

Velez limps, one hand clutching a bat like a cane, the other entrusted with the cell phone, which is raised to his ear.

Rifle shots *pop, pop, pop* far and near, north and south, east and west.

Velez barks into the phone, "We need protection!" He listens for a reply and over the phone hears rifle shots overlapping like firecrackers. He bellows, *"Tesla!"*

Tesla shouts through the staticky phone, "We have problems!" *POW!* An explosion over the phone makes Velez jerk away.

Velez shouts into it, *"Tesla! Tesla! Tesla!"*

Velez stares at Martin and Blent. "I think I lost him." He holds the phone like it's a dead bird, then it squawks, "No you haven't, Mr. Velay! Tesla here!"

Martin and Blent chuckle.

As the team steps from the plaza onto a paved walkway lined with bronze statues, four boys are coming at them. Two carry rifles, another holds an open quart of clear liquor. One of them shouts, *"The baseball team!"*

The largest of them declares, "You cheated! We beat you fair and square!" He raises his rifle at the mass of players.

*"Put down your weapons!"* Roosevelt orders.

Much of the team crouches and covers their heads, while some charge the boys.

*"Go to Hell, Yankee!"* The boy blasts into the charging ballplayers. George Stone is shot in the stomach. The second armed boy shoots wildly, into the ground, and Bill Dahlen collapses, gripping his shin.

Rube Waddell tackles the biggest boy, and the others are smothered by USA ballplayers who smash bats into them, wresting away the rifles, bullets and four knives, then permitting the bloodied boys to skedaddle.

Honus Wagner and Rube Waddell wield the rifles. Bruce Petway asks, "Why does Waddell have a gun?"

"I've been a-huntin' plenty, Tommy!" replies Waddell, eyes wild, as he opens the bolt and inserts a bullet.

"Stay together, men!" Roosevelt commands. "Do not instigate a fight!" Roosevelt leads them to a square of crushed granite. Wagner points out a white stucco building. "That's where they put us on trial!"

A bit to the right of that building, in a gap between palm trees, the nuclear reactor cooling tower looms in the distance.

Roosevelt changes direction, leading the group north toward the Gulf. "A mile to the French embassy!" Above the trees ahead, smoke is rising from Leeton.

On the phone, Velez tells Tesla, "We're on a square. I can see the reactor in the distance!"

"Is there a fountain?"

Velez turns: A large fountain with marble water creatures. "Yes!"

"I see you!"

Velez spins. Behind him, across the square, Tesla wields the twin of Velez's phone. A heavy satchel is slung over his shoulder. He's wearing a lab coat, his chest full of medals, which as he awkwardly runs are clanging like sleigh bells.

"*Tesla!*" Velez yells, his voice echoing in feedback through the two approaching phones.

Tesla joins the ballplayers. "It works, doesn't it?" He pulls Velez, Blent, and Martin aside. "If you want to return—time travel—I believe I can tune it in. Now is the opportunity if we can take control of the reactor!"

George Browne informs a cluster of players, "That's the guy who burned down the Bellamy Theater!"

Velez, Martin and Blent are stunned at the statement as Tesla reaches into his satchel and removes a chunk of machined metal, pipes, and dials bolted onto it. "It's a regulator, designed to connect to the reactor—I hope."

Blent grips Tesla's arm. "*To the twenty-first century?*"

"Yes. I strongly believe so." Tesla shows a packet of Dos Fuegos Maduro chewing tobacco. "Einstein figured out how this particular tobacco most likely interacts with the nuclear reaction."

"If we go with you, are you sure you're not going to blast us to dust?" Velez asks.

Tesla stares up at Velez. "I cannot guarantee anything, Mr. Velay."

Rifle shots crackle from the direction of Leeton. Heavy guns rumble.

Blent weighs staying against going home to the future, being a star in 1906 against taking his chances as barely more than a replacement rookie in the twenty-first century. But he can improve, and perhaps through his season in 1906 he already has. And there's Darla and the baby waiting. And Buck, who is wheezing, hand to chest. If Blent can help get Bucky Martin back, that would be better than winning an MVP. Blent declares, "I'm ready."

Martin asks, "How long will it take to prepare the machine?"

"Perhaps one hour."

Martin doesn't want to abandon his ballplayers in the middle of a battle. Though this is not his century, it certainly *is* his team. He tells Velez and Blent, "You guys go. Help Tesla. I can't leave the team like this. It's the right thing for me to make sure they're okay. I'll try to make it to the reactor, but if I don't, go ahead. Go home, all right? Do it for me. Promise me that." To Blent, "You've got your wife and baby." To Velez, "You've got the Hall of Fame waiting. I believe it."

*"You can barely stand up!"* Blent blasts at Martin. *"This is our chance! Let's go! Come on!"*

Other players stare at them, confused, as Velez turns to Blent. "Buck is right."

Blent screams at Velez, *"We've got to go together!"*

Tesla interjects, "I might need an extra pair of hands."

Velez tells Blent, "I'll go with Tesla. You're the doctor. You go with Buck. Get the team safe, then get to the reactor."

"All right," Blent agrees.

Velez give him the cell phone and jokes, "Get to the reactor or I'll punch your lights out."

Rifle shots crackle to the west and to the east.

Roosevelt declares, "We can't wait!"

Martin tells him, "Mr. Velez is going with Tesla to disarm the nuclear reactor."

Roosevelt replies, "Bully!" and to Tesla, "Godspeed!" He smartly shakes Velez's hand. "Marvelous performance at the bat, sir!" He marches the pack northward, Martin wheezing next to Blent. They jog away and Blent turns back, watching tall, limping Velez, and little, intense Tesla, recede.

Roosevelt leads the USA delegation toward the French embassy, constant rifle fire like endless strings of firecrackers, and they walk into a cloud of bitter gunsmoke. Formed in two lines only sixty feet apart, NG and USA soldiers are shooting at each other.

The team pauses behind the NG line. Nearby, New Glory soldiers wheeling two cannons look at the USA ballplayers with curiosity and some recognition, but do not alter their course; they could easily turn those cannons at the team.

Roosevelt declares, *"We will attack from the rear!"*

Mike Donlin screams, *"We only have two rifles!"*

Roosevelt exclaims, *"Use your bats, boys! Your courage on the field was exemplary! Show your courage for your country!"* Roosevelt holds his pose, one arm raised like the Statue of Liberty.

A bullet whistles between Mike Donlin and Rube Foster; both heads turn to watch the bullet disappear; both heads turn and face each other in horror. A bullet crashes into the cell phone, and Blent jerks away. It shatters onto cobblestones in a loose confederation of wires, screws, and broken bulbs.

Martin shouts as loud as his throat will permit, *"We're going around!"* Martin starts away, the ballplayers cheering and running away from Roosevelt, who stamps his foot, *"Stop! I command you!"* Roosevelt stands alone.

Letting his ears guide him, Martin jogs away from the rifle fire. Baseball spikes scrape against the cobblestones, sounding like a workshop of stone chiselers. Then, about a third of a mile from the embassy, Martin stops. Ban Johnson looks like a sweaty melon about to burst. Fear is writ large on Johnson's face, and on Junior's and most of the ballplayers'. Martin tells the squad, *"Just a bit more!"* though he has no idea how far it will be.

New Glory soldiers are sprinting past them toward downtown, while other NG soldiers are scampering in the *opposite* direction, inland, bloody and frightened. A massive line of soldiers emerges silhouetted in the smoke, hundreds of soldiers blocking the way to the Gulf. Each is brandishing a bayonet-tipped rifle. Martin turns to face Donlin, Dahlen, Bresnahan, Bowerman, Wiltse, Mathewson, Frank Chance, Honus Wagner, Pop Lloyd, Petway, Blent, Rube Foster, and the rest. As they recognize what's happening, their bodies relax and Devlin and Donlin sprint past Martin toward the soldiers; soldiers are rushing toward them—USA soldiers! The soldiers roar, shouting:

*"You were aces!"*

*"Champions!"*

*"You showed 'em!"*

The USA soldiers are followed closely by hundreds of escaped slaves. Blent turns to Foster and Petway. "See the Velez family? I don't."

"No."

"No."

Pop Lloyd concurs, "No."

The USA soldiers pass along the information that, indeed, this is a full-blown USA invasion. NG has already invaded Florida. An officer takes Roosevelt aside.

Mike Donlin bellows, *"Three cheers for Bucky Martin!"*

With hundreds of USA soldiers and hundreds of escaping slaves adding their voices to the ballplayers, between the second and third "Hip hip hooray!" Blent removes his USA uniform top and hands it to a pimpled soldier, who's awed into speechlessness. Other players hand over uniforms to soldiers. Roosevelt interrupts and quietly tells Blent, "Einstein is safe. Shot in the melee. In poor shape. Being operated on presently I am told. But in our hands."

Meanwhile Martin approaches Junior. "Blent and I are going back to get Velez."

The players overhear and pack around Martin to tell him not to risk his life.

To Junior, Martin says, "If I don't make it back—don't worry about me. You're gonna own the Giants one day, all right? Keep those advantages to yourself."

"You're coming back with us on the boat, right?" Junior asks.

Reeking of rum, Donlin declares, "I'll go with you! I like a fight!" Bresnahan: "I'm coming with you!" Keeler: "I ain't leavin' ya!"

Martin tells them, "Stay here. Look out for each other. We'll be all right." Then, what he hopes against hope will be a lie, "We'll see you gentlemen later."

Mathewson offers his hand. "Thanks, Buck." The reaction strikes Blent as oddly tender, as if Mathewson does not expect to ever again see Martin.

Martin shakes Mathewson's hand. "You don't have to be the hero all the time, okay?"

Blent's double-play partner this past season, Bill Dahlen, is supported by Honus Wagner and Bruce Petway, keeping his weight off his shot leg. Blent takes a last look at Christy Mathewson, at Hooks Wiltse, at Pop Lloyd, at Turkey Mike Donlin who's tipping a soldier's silver flask up to the sky, at

Rube Waddell, at Keeler, at Frank Chance whose head and orbital bone is bandaged from Blent's foul ball, at Frank Bowerman and Roger Bresnahan, and Rube Foster and George Stone and Bruce Petway and Elmer Flick.

The ballplayers crowd Martin tighter. Martin addresses the cluster of Giants, "Gentlemen, go win another World's Series!" And Martin backs away, inland.

Blent shouts, "Goodbye fellas! Have fun spending all that money!" The team and many of the soldiers cheer. Martin and Blent run, Blent's cleats scraping the cobblestones as they head for the reactor.

*

Tesla and Velez make it the two miles out of Leeton, to a plaza in the shadow of the reactor's cooling tower, which looms above the palm trees. A New Glory squad, rifles shining in rows, marches toward them. Tesla jangles his dozen gold and silver ribboned chest medals. The captain salutes Tesla, bows and lets them pass.

Three seconds later Velez notes, "That was easy."

"Awards impress the servile."

After persistently knocking on the metal reactor door, Tesla is greeted as a returning hero by the half dozen technicians and scientists who have not fled. In German, Tesla asks for an assessment of the state of the reactor.

After twenty seconds of listening, he comments, "Not bad," then stares through a glass porthole in the lead walls that contain the nuclear reaction.

*"What does 'not bad' mean?"* Velez asks, following Tesla into a central control area that is cordoned off in a room of walls with large glass windows.

Tesla steps to a console, studies it, tweaks dials. "It means that this might just be possible."

As fellow scientists follow his every move, as rifle shots crackle outside, Tesla checks meters on the wall of the control room. He says something in German to the scientists, each of whom gasps. Unnerved, they quickly gather papers, slide rules, bits of unused equipment, paper files.

Tesla twiddles dials and checks his notes before the scientists say goodbye and depart. Velez and Tesla are now alone in the humming structure.

Velez looms above Tesla, who shoos him out of his light. Taking a step back on his barking ankle, Velez asks, "What did you tell them?"

"I told them that I'm going to melt down the reactor core, and they should go north and find the USA army for safety. I do not intend to cause a meltdown at all. I just do not want any other scientist observing this experiment in time travel." Tesla pulls the chunky metal regulator from his bag.

He attempts to yank a lug wrench on a nut on a pipe leading to the reactor. Velez elbows him out of the way, and with one yank, loosens the nut.

Stroking the regulator, Tesla says, "I hope to harmonize the nuclear reaction to the tobacco reaction, thereby finally controlling it. It is a very odd and delicate relationship. Einstein's were all accidents." They pull out the pipe, slide Tesla's regulator into place, and bolt it on.

A fist pounds on the outside door. Velez peeks through the little window in the door: Ty Cobb in his army uniform.

"Ty Cobb, that bastard!" Velez turns to Telsa. "With a squad of soldiers!"

Tesla dons the bemedaled lab coat and strides to the door, unbolts it.

*"What are you doing?"* Velez asks.

Tesla opens the door. Ty Cobb rushes up the steps, his face twisted with fury. He demands, "We need every able-bodied man at the fighting right now! That includes you!"

Tesla slowly explains, as if talking to a child, "We are doing important munitions work. We are arming a gigantic bomb that will kill thousands of Jankees. You are impeding our progress!"

At that moment, Martin and Blent make it to the edge of the plaza. The reactor looms. Armed New Gloryers are scurrying in every direction. "You all right?" Blent asks.

A hesitation. Martin croaks, "Something's definitely wrong."

Across the plaza, at the door to the reactor is a squad of New Glory soldiers and unmistakable, wiry, agitated Ty Cobb, jabbering at Tesla.

Martin and Blent sprint toward the reactor and Tesla, who, recognizing them, calls out, "Over here!" Tesla tells Cobb, "That man is bringing a vital ingredient for us!"

Cobb stiffens at the sight of Blent and Martin. He points at Martin. *"You!"* He stands in the doorway, blocking Blent and Martin.

Tesla insists to Cobb, "You are wasting time! Delay can cause an explosion!"

Shoving Martin and Blent in the chest, Ty Cobb orders his squad, "Arrest these men. Time for revenge!" Rifles aim at Martin and Blent.

Velez emerges from inside the reactor. "Let them go, Ty. You can take me if you want."

Cobb grins. "Good! Take them all!"

Three soldiers latch onto Velez, who shakes them off.

"Stop!" Tesla barks.

His back to the reactor, Blent glimpses—over the shoulders of the soldiers aiming rifles at him—two athletic men sprinting across the square at them, shoes *scrape, scrape, scraping.*

The soldiers turn to the approaching sound as Rube Foster roars, tackling four of them. Christy Mathewson snaps a rifle out of a soldier's hands.

The soldiers guarding Velez rush out the door, not before Velez tears at the head of one, who fires his rifle at the ceiling. Blent picks up Velez's bat and smashes it into one New Glory soldier then another, then another, chasing them from the reactor, the most primal hatred Blent has ever felt, so ashamed at this perverted version of his Southern society. He wonders if Mark would be proud of him.

Tesla screams at the New Gloryers, *"Idiots!"* as Velez, Mathewson, Foster, Blent, and Martin smash the soldiers, wrest away their rifles, and let them flee. Tesla shuts the fat metal door and cranks the two-inch steel bolts.

Velez, Martin, Tesla, Christy Mathewson, Rube Foster, and Blent are finally cut off from New Gloryers. Blent tells Tesla, "Einstein was rescued. He was shot. Being operated on." He tells Velez, "A lot of slaves are running to the US side. We didn't see your relatives."

"*Hundreds* of escaped slaves," Foster adds.

"None of my family?" Velez asks Foster.

"Looked at every face. Hopefully your folks heard about the invasion and are getting away," Foster says. "And another thing—"

"We're going with you," Mathewson interrupts. "To the future."

Velez, Martin, Blent are astonished. Blent feigns, "What do you mean?"

"We know all about what you're doing," Mathewson explains. "On the ship, Einstein talked in his sleep, about future men. In his sleep he mentioned Blent and Buck. Honus listened to it all, asked Einstein about the next day, and Einstein denied it. But then Wagner came to me."

"You really believe we're from the future?" Blent asks.

"Which we are," Martin croaks in a whisper, nodding his head. "We are. Just the three of us."

Mathewson's gaze settles on Blent. "I'm willing to find out."

"You're willing to give up everything?"

"For the future? Sure!"

"I just want to see a fair league," Rube Foster says, "where everyone is judged by their ability."

Martin whispers, "It's not easy adjusting to a new time. It was almost impossible coming to 1906."

"You really don't want to do this," Blent says. "Even if—*if*—Tesla is partly successful, we'll probably die in the process. A million things can go wrong."

Martin whispers, "I have to do this." He pulls away the neck of his shirt, revealing the puffy, red nodes. "This cancer will kill me if I don't get back."

Tesla stands at the control panel, tweaking dials. "We have plenty of Maduro. But the extra people make the calculations geometrically more complicated, lowering the odds for success."

A pounding on the door. From the other side of it, a demanding, muffled voice.

Peering out the little square window in the door, Rube Foster exclaims, "It's Ty! And his brothers are wheeling a cannon at us!"

"Morons!" Tesla blasts as he cranks dials.

The control room vibrates, hums louder. Tesla chalks a circle on the floor. "Sit on the line of the circle, everyone. Cross-legged. Knees almost touching, but not touching!"

Velez tells Mathewson and Foster, "You don't want to go to the twenty-first century."

"Pitchers don't hit in our time," Blent explains. "We've got something called the designated hitter—a guy sits on the bench when we're in the field and he hits for the pitcher."

"Where's the fun in that?" Mathewson asks.

"Exactly," says Blent. "Stay in your time."

Then Mathewson takes Blent by the arm, leading him away from the others. "In the future, can they fix—I don't know how to say this—people who—"

Sparing him the embarrassment, Blent tells him, "Our medicine is extremely advanced compared to now. They can fix a lot of things."

*"Blent!"* Velez and Rube Foster yell. *"Buck's out!"*

Blent finds Martin passed out on the concrete floor, Velez cradling his head. Mathewson and Foster look on, butts on the chalk circle.

Blent tilts Martin's head back, opens the jaw, sticks his hand in, prying for a passage for air. Martin's throat is tighter than it was when he went down on the ship. Now it's like jamming an adult hand in a kiddie baseball mitt.

Martin's turning purple. The control room vibrates harder. Blent pushes his hand in deeper.

Velez protests, *"You're hurting him!"*

Martin gasps. His eyes fling open.

"Sit him up! On the circle!" Tesla orders. He digs a teaspoon into the pouch and tilts a rounded spoon of the shredded tobacco onto the open palm of Blent, Velez, Martin, Foster, Mathewson, ending with his own palm. "Chew the tobacco! Swallow some of the juice!"

Martin is totally exhausted, barely masticating.

Velez leans close to Martin and Blent. "Goodbye, Buck. Goodbye, Johnny Blent." He gives Blent a hug.

Gently pushing Velez away, Blent asks, "What are you talking about!?"

Velez rises, smiling down at Blent and Martin. "I'm staying in 1906."

Martin gathers strength, croaking at Velez, "Come with us. I need you."

Velez smiles anew. "No, you don't. An MVP *doctor* is what you need, not a hitter."

Blent's speechless, gasping. "Are you crazy?"

"I'm gonna find my family and get them to New York. And I got a great woman waiting for me. I'm good."

"What about all the girls and cars in the twenty-first century?" Blent asks. *"The money?"*

Velez's smile doesn't fade.

Martin croaks, "Get a bunch of USA soldiers to help. Attack the plantation from *two sides*. Not one! Okay?"

"Good idea."

"Take over our place on 85th," Blent suggests.

"Sure. I got my play I'm working on with Turkey Mike and Nicole. And I want to see how that vote comes out in New York next week. No more banning people for the color of their skin!"

Blent argues, "But the league might ban you because you admitted you're Black. If you can't play, what will you do?"

"I'll figure something out. Right, Rube?"

Rube Foster replies, "It ain't easy. But you fight, man! Change it!"

"Thanks, Rube."

Blent's never seen a happier man than Velez.

Looking at Blent, Velez says, "Take care of my peeps, okay? It's gonna be a nightmare if they all think I'm dead. Check on my mom and my crazy sister."

Blent asks him, "Did you tell Nicole that you're not from 1906?"

He rubs his brow and smiles. "That's a hard discussion, man. I haven't told her, no. One day. She'll think I'm crazy. But maybe she'll believe me."

"Wow," is all the profundity that Blent articulates, staggered at Velez's decision.

Blent rises from the circle. "I'm proud of you, happy for you."

"Thanks, man. I'm proud of you too. You kicked ass in this league. You'll be great in the Majors. I got confidence in you. Keep that confidence."

Sitting back down on the chalk circle, Blent tells him, "If Mr. Tesla here fails, we'll all be stuck with you!"

Turning to Mathewson and Foster, Blent says, "This is your last chance. Go with André."

Mathewson tells Velez, "You can have my apartment!"

Velez chuckles, "How about your car?"

"Sell it. Sell everything. Give the money to people who need it. Have a nice funeral for me."

The chamber hums like helicopter blades. Martin reaches up for Velez, who kneels to Martin. Face-to-face, Martin asks, "You sure, André?"

"One hundred percent, two-time MVP sure."

"I won't be able to replace you."

Tesla screams, *"Take off your clothes!"* All except André Velez shed clothes, cleats, mitts, and toss them in a heap at Velez's feet. He kicks the clothes out of the control room. Tesla bolts the door behind him. Velez reaches down for a mitt—Blent's mitt—and his hands take comfort in the baseball mitt leather as he stares through the glass at the seated circle of ballplayers, and Tesla at the control board.

Tesla chews the Maduro as he tweaks dials and checks the glass gauges. "The reaction is increase—!" the word obliterates as the front door blasts, a cannonball skittering, glass and metal shards clattering against the window to the antechamber.

*"Troglodites!"* Tesla screams.

The Cobbs lead a band of soldiers through the smoke and debris.

Tesla checks the regulator, and noticing Martin about to spit, barks, *"Do not expectorate!"*

Ty Cobb pounds the butt of a rifle on the glassed-in control room, his face a gnarled ball of white hate. *"Get out of there!"*

Blent scans for Velez beyond the control room, doesn't see him.

Tesla ignores Cobb, checking the dials on the reactor panel and the regulator.

With the butt of his rifle, Cobb bashes the door to the control room. Pieces of glass rain down on the naked circle.

Tesla screams at Cobb, *"The radiation will kill you!"* To the naked ballplayers, Tesla shouts, *"Do not move!"*

Cobb reaches through the shattered glass for the inside door handle.

The reactor roars, the ceiling vibrates. Pieces of concrete ceiling are falling.

Ty Cobb laughs as he raises his rifle, aims at Tesla, calms his laughing, and fires. Tesla falls away from the control board, falls to his side and drops onto Blent and Martin, Tesla's shoulder bleeding. The floor is undulating. Blood floods onto Blent's hands. Christy Mathewson shouts, *"I'm staying!"* and explodes up from the circle, as the others shout, *"No!" "Get back!"* and he knocks past Cobb, and out of the control room.

*"Are the calculations screwed up?"* Blent asks Tesla.

Tesla jumps up, tweaks knobs, rejoins the circle, which has shrunken with Matheweson's departure.

Blent screams, *"Stop it, Ty!"* as Cobb reloads, and the others notice Velez creeping up behind Ty.

Ty Cobb raises his rifle, sighting, relishing his choice of ballplayers to kill, and aims at Martin.

Velez smashes his baseball bat into Ty Cobb's head. Cobb drops the rifle and staggers forward toward Blent, Cobb's eyes going in different directions, his hands reaching out as he lurches, falling into the circle, blood streaking the side of his face.

The noise drops to a low hum. Cobb is not moving, knocked out, a piece of scalp flapped forward, exposing his bloody cranium.

Rube Foster is whimpering.

Blent's strangling Tesla's shoulder, attempting to slow the outflowing blood.

Martin is gagging as if he hasn't had a full breath in a long time.

Blent orders Martin, *"Lay back!"* and Blent sticks his free hand down Martin's throat. Blent looks around for clothes to wrap Tesla's arm above the bullet hole, but the clothes are outside.

Ty Cobb lies motionless in the middle of the circle; he's in his army uniform and Blent's considering using Cobb's shirt as a tourniquet for Tesla's wound. Blent's right hand is trying to stanch Tesla's bleeding while Blent's left hand is far down Martin's throat, trying to keep Martin breathing. *"Frickin' disaster!"* Blent screams as the humming ceases.

They're shocked by the silence.

"What happened?" asks Rube Foster.

Tesla seems faint. He groans from the bullet in his shoulder. "What happened is . . . failure."

"We need a doctor!" Blent shouts. "Two doctors! Martin's dying and Tesla's losing blood!"

Ty Cobb moans. His hands cover the pain on the side of his head.

"Where are the rest of the Cobbs?" Foster asks.

"They got the hell out," Blent says. "They'll be back. Then we're really screwed."

Foster rises, nods at supine Ty Cobb. "Maybe we can use him as a hostage, to negotiate us out of here." Foster assesses the half-dying crew on the floor of the reactor control room, and the lack of gunfire outside. "I'll look." He heads away.

*"Get Velez!"* Blent yells after him. "We need help!" Blent continues choking Tesla's wound with one hand, the other feeling the air from Martin's wheezing lungs move past his fingers.

Rube Foster is shocked to see the front door intact, unblasted, the paint and hinges perfectly fine. He shoulders the door, which rustily creaks open, emitting stark sunshine.

As Blent's explaining to Tesla where to squeeze the bullet hole in his shoulder, Foster's deep voice reverberates. *"Holy Christ! What is that?"*

Blent helps Tesla and Martin up. They leave Ty Cobb moaning on the floor. Tesla, Blent, and Martin walk out onto a fresh sidewalk and a dried-out lawn which none of them remembers.

"What were you doing in there?" a woman in a lab coat warily confronts the naked men. She's about Blent's age, tall, athletic.

The air is exceedingly dry. The palm trees are gone. The crushed granite square in front of the reactor has been replaced by a ribbon of black pavement and a vista of yellow hills studded with wind turbines, the blades of which are turning.

"We need doctors," Blent tells her. *"What year is it?"*

Glancing at Tesla's bleeding shoulder, at Martin's weak state, she digs in her red handbag, and without looking up, asks, "You're the Giants, right?"

Martin and Blent gape in astonishment. Blent says, "I think we did it, Buck."

"How'd you wind up here?" she asks. "Part of the stadium collapsed."

"Ma'am, where are we?" Blent asks.

"Livermore. Don't you guys know? You're exactly forty-five and a third miles from the stadium. I'm a big fan. You're Johnny Blent." She talks into her watch, "Nine-one-one."

Tesla, Martin, Rube Foster and Blent gawk at each other, and a split second later Ty Cobb bursts out of the doorway, holding his bleeding head, screaming, *"You fucking Yankees! You're gonna—"* Eyes crazy, listening, he says, "The fighting's stopped!" Unlike the naked men, Ty Cobb has been transferred to the future in his gray army uniform. *"Where're my brothers?"*

Taking a glance at the other ballplayers, as if they would take this opportunity to capture him, he sprints away, then, at the sight of cars and huge trucks zipping on the highway, and the scores of enormous white wind turbines poking up from the hills, Ty Cobb stops cold.

Blent chuckles at Ty's predicament.

Bucky Martin pulls Blent's hand from his face. Martin tests one breath. He reaches for Rube Foster's hand and shakes it, then shakes Tesla's hand. In a whisper he says, "Gentlemen, welcome to the twenty-first century."

*

Nikola Tesla shares a room with Bucky Martin in the crowded Livermore, California, hospital. Tesla's shoulder is bandaged, having had bullet fragments removed and a mesh tube inserted to repair his punctured brachial artery. As the anesthesia fog has thinned, Tesla's been contemplating the medical apparatuses, particularly the digital display of his vital signs.

Bucky Martin is propped up in bed, watching the TV. It's three days after the magnitude 9.2 earthquake that jolted the Bay Area and sent Blent, Martin, and Velez through time. The news is telling Martin that estimates range from 700 to 1,500 people dead, 5,000 structures destroyed, and three trillion dollars in damage. The ballpark is half tumbled down. There's no mention of any condo towers tumbling down, so perhaps Martin's condo is okay. A section of bridge near Oakland dropped into the Bay.

A tube going down Martin's throat ensures that oxygen is getting to his lungs, and modern medications have already reduced the pressure on his throat, his inhalations and exhalations slightly constricted but in no way blocked. His neck nodes have shrunken, and their aching has dissipated. On the hospital tray there's a fresh orange-yellow bottle with his name on the label, containing 180 pills of a type that has proven effective for his cancer: it's an amazingly reassuring sight. *Man, it's good to be back. But am I ready to be* THAT GUY, *answering two hundred questions a day from the analytics department and the front office, taking calls from annoyed player's agents, answering another hundred questions from reporters, tending the social media garden of garbage? I won't be able to rant and scream at umpires anymore, won't be sitting on the bench just me and a handful of reserve players. Outside of the condo—if it's still there—I'll have to be in check all the time.*

He pulls himself up and swings his legs over the side, feet-in-socks touching the linoleum floor. He pulls the tube from his throat, takes a relaxed breath. Pulls out his intravenous line, wraps his arm.

"What is the mechanism for this display of lights?" Tesla asks. "They're so precise!"

"You'll have to find a smarter person than I am to answer that." Martin takes a slow, deep breath. "Mr. Tesla, how did you move us—not only to our time, but from New Glory, to here—only forty miles from where we disappeared? And you moved Ty Cobb while he's still wearing his *uniform.*"

Tesla offers a smile so pure it reminds Martin of the smile of a ballplayer circling the bases after a walk-off home run—a smile of absolute triumph: "I am Nikola Tesla!"

Outside, Johnny Blent's standing in the shade of the hospital, signing autographs for a pack of fans and reading the news on a borrowed phone. He's wearing rubber sandals, baggy Nike sweatpants, and a UC Santa Cruz Banana Slugs sweatshirt. He's got an urge to join rescue workers digging through the rubble for survivors. He's got experience.

Rube Foster and Ty Cobb observe Blent and these people—Cobb's head stitched and wrapped in a white bandage. Foster has donned shiny black track pants, hiking shoes, and a T-shirt for Garcia's restaurant, Albuquerque, New Mexico. Ty Cobb's still wearing his blood-and-dirt-streaked New Glory army uniform.

When they arrived at the emergency room with the ambulance sheets wrapped around them, the coalescing knot of fans recognizing Johnny Blent and Martin, snapping their pictures, eagerly dug through their cars for clothes for Blent and Martin. Blent asked for clothes for his two friends. Ty Cobb refused to touch the clothes.

Now Rube Foster and Cobb are staring goggle-eyed at the parking lot full of shiny automobiles, up in the sky at airplane contrails, and at the lumpy fans getting autographs from Johnny Blent. Ty Cobb, trying to make sense of this dream or nightmare, asks Rube Foster, "What kind of baseball do you think they play?"

Foster replies, "They promised me that it's the kind where Black men can play on any team."

*"What the hell are you talking about?"* Cobb scoffs.

Trying to avoid the fans' attention to this matter, Blent softly asks Cobb, "Were you chewing Dos Fuegos Maduro?"

"Only the best!" Cobb pats his stomach. "When I got bashed on the head, I swallowed my chaw. Listen, it's not fair. I don't want to be here. I don't want to deal with a new set of pitchers, a new league. Fuck this, all right? Get me home."

Blent stares into the weird mixture of intensity, confusion, brilliance, and fear registered on Ty Cobb's face. "Decent players in our league make millions of dollars a year."

Ty Cobb's mien changes. "How much does the *best* player make?"

Martin emerges into fresh sunlight wearing blue jeans and a Garth Brooks T-shirt.

Blent admonishes, *"What are you doing?"*

Martin rattles the plastic bottle of pills. "This takes care of it. The rest is just overkill."

Fans surround Martin and scraps of paper and pens and baseballs appear. They snap photos.

Ty Cobb elbows fans aside and begs Martin, "I'm a good guy, Mr. Martin. I really am. I can get along with people. I can. I don't like it here."

Martin places a hand on Cobb's wrist. "Try to relax, Ty. If you behave well, we'll take care of you. Take off the bloody uniform. Blend in."

"How's Tesla?" Blent asks.

"Shoulder's taken care of. Asking questions I can't answer." Martin adds, "Thanks for saving my life, kid."

"I didn't do anything."

"You did everything."

"Well . . ." Blent tries to deflect the thanks.

While a fan hands Martin a Sharpie pen and an orange-and-black Giants cap to sign, another fan offers a phone.

"Thanks." He takes it and gazes at the reflective screen. Fans keep snapping photos. Martin knows he should try, immediately, to contact the Giants and let them know that he and Blent are okay. *I'm not ready yet.* He returns the phone to its owner. "I'm good. Thanks so much. Got any clothes for a friend of mine inside? He lost everything."

Martin gathers a bundle of clothes for Tesla and returns to the hospital, waving to shout-outs and stopping for a selfie.

Blent googles "Rube Foster" and reads it aloud to Foster and Cobb: "'Andrew 'Rube' Foster was a pioneer baseball player, manager, and team owner. He was instrumental in creating the first commercially viable Negro league. His teams won the league title in 1902, 1904, 1905, and 1906. On November 2, 1906, a train he was riding in derailed near Allentown, Pennsylvania, killing six passengers, including Foster.'"

Foster's stunned. Blent is stunned. Ty Cobb asks, "That little *thing* told you that?"

"Watch this!" Blent asks the phone, "Ty Cobb, bio. Baseball player." The computerized voice, in an Australian accent, declares: "In his first full season with Detroit in 1906—"

Cobb and Foster are startled, frightened, Foster exclaims, *"Who's talking?"*

"—Ty Cobb led the American League in hitting, batting .326. He knocked in one hundred and five runs, and stole thirty-four bases—"

Cobb nods, "Not bad."

"—On the morning of November 3, 1906, he was found dead on the floor of his room at the Terminal Hotel in St. Louis, the victim of poisoning."

Cobb smacks a fist into his palm, *"I know who it was! That bitch!"*

Foster and Blent share a glance regarding being stuck with Ty Cobb.

Blent tells them, "It's technology. You'll get used to it." He pokes in the number for Darla, explaining, "Now I'm calling my wife!"

It answers: "Cherokee Lawn Service!"

Blent hangs up. Examines the number. Tries again. "Cherokee Lawn Service!" And again. "Chero—"

He tries Darla's mother. He's amazed he remembers the number. It rings.

Ty Cobb and Rube Foster stare at Blent holding to his ear the odd contraption that everyone in this world carries with them.

Foster asks, "You all right, Ty?"

"The fans look fat," Cobb replies. "Their clothes look like sacks. They look like prisoners, or slaves. But in worse condition than prisoners or slaves."

"Maybe it's because we're outside the hospital."

On the phone, Darla's mom answers.

*"Hey! This is Johnny! I can't find Darla! Know where she is? How is the baby? Healthy? How's Darla?"*

"Which Johnny?" she asks.

"Johnny Blent. Your son-in-law."

"I know who you are. You're that cocky baseball player who grew up with Darla."

"I'm also married to Darla!"

"Are you drunk or on drugs right now?"

"No ma'am. I was caught in the earthquake out here in San Francisco. Where's Darla?"

"I'm sure Darla and Dave remember you. But it's been six, seven years since high school. You want them to call you? Want me to give them a message?"

"We were having a baby. Who's Dave?"

"They met at work. Stop saying you're having a baby with Darla. That's outrageous talk!"

Blent pauses. "You're saying I'm not married to her?"

"You are definitely not."

"Really? Does she have kids?"

"A boy and a girl and another on the way. She works at Fine Trail Capital in Jackson. Head of human resources."

"Okay, ma'am. Please have her call me. I beg you. I'm sorry."

"Get some help, son. You sound very odd. Maybe call *your* kin." She clicks off.

He feels like the earth has fallen away. He glances up at Foster and Cobb who seem extremely concerned. He calls his parents. His mother picks up and the instant she hears his voice she sobs.

"I'm fine!" he tries to soothe her.

"Where you been the past three days?"

"Have you heard from Darla?"

"Darla? My hairdresser? Which Darl—"

*"Darla my wife!"* he screams. *"Darla! Darla! Darla!"*

"Your *wife*? Thank you, Jesus! Oh Lord! *He's married!"*

His stepdad chimes in, "Who's the girl?! You're gonna have a good Christian ceremony down here, right? None of that San Francisco stuff!"

*"You've met Darla a million times!"*

His stepfather asks, "Did you call Charlene?"

*"What the hell are you talking about?"*

Tossing his thumb in the direction of the phone, Ty Cobb comments to Rube Foster, "These things seem to cause significant irritation."

Foster asks, "Do they force everyone to carry one on their person?"

"What kind of society is this?" Cobb asks.

The driver of a silver Porsche eagerly, frantically waves at Blent. The car rolls to a stop along the red-painted "no parking" curb, and out bounds a young, muscled man, obviously an athlete in the eyes of Foster and Cobb and Blent. His smile breaks a trim beard. Big biceps and triceps bulge the sleeves of his golf shirt.

*"Johnny!"* He bear-hugs Blent.

Blent doesn't hug in return. He does not know this guy.

"You're are all over the news! 'Giants Manager and Player Found!' How's my dad? He doesn't look too good in the photos. He okay?" The man brightens at Ty Cobb. "JoJo! What are you doing here? I thought you live in Dallas? Were you at the stadium too?"

Cobb is thunderstruck. "My name's not JoJo."

The man points at Rube. "Dude! I got you good in spring training, right? Big dinger! You're good, you'll be up soon! You hangin' with JoJo?"

"Who do you think I am?" Foster asks.

Blent realizes that this is Bucky Martin, Jr., his eyes clear as glass, and he seems to be friends, and maybe teammates, with Blent.

"You came up for a few games in September," Bucky Martin, Jr. replies to Foster. "You all right, John?" he asks Blent.

"My wife—I don't know—my wife. My wife."

Junior laughs. "You've got more girls than anyone! You don't have a wife, at least one I know about."

"Did I ever mention Darla?"

Junior shakes his head. "No Darla."

Blent quickly, quietly leans in to Cobb and Foster. "He's Martin's son. Wait here for Buck to come out of the hospital. I gotta be alone for a minute. It seems that my wife isn't married to me and everything is all fucked up again."

"I'm sorry," says Rube Foster. Ty Cobb frowns and shrugs his shoulders.

Blent bolts across the parking lot, crosses the street to an embankment leading down to a scrubby Little League field. In the outfield, a little kid making a strong throw, and his mom, are playing catch.

Up at the ER exit, Bucky Martin slowly accompanies Tesla, whose arm is in a sling, Velcroed over a tie-dyed T-shirt featuring Jerry Garcia's head.

Junior sprints up the driveway and hugs Bucky Martin, Sr., who beams, *"Damn! Look at you!"*

"Good to see you too, Dad!"

Senior's eyes leak tears. "This is something special. You look fantastic."

"Everyone's so happy that you're all right. Especially the team."

Senior is thunderstruck. He glances at Tesla, then back to Junior. "Did everyone get out okay?"

"Luckily. Barely. All of us. But about three hun—" The last words are obliterated by a helicopter hovering, then tilting away. Tesla ecstatically follows it.

Down by the Little League field, Blent sits on a paint-chipped board in the bleachers, crying. He looks around, expecting to see Velez; but there's no Velez. His mind latches onto Mrs. Mathewson. Darla. There's a wrenching in his gut worse than anything. He *feels* different; he doesn't want to *feel different*. He craves a tall drink with Turkey Mike and Roger Bresnahan and Bill Dahlen and Velez.

Martin steps down the embankment. Blent's back is to him, alone on the small set of bleachers.

"Hey," Buck says, "I'm so sorry, Johnny. Rube told me about Darla. Can it be a mistake?"

"Her mom says she married some asshole named Dave. They have three kids. She knows who I am. We went to high school together, but we never dated. My folks don't know her.

And there was the girl, you know? There's no baby." Blent sobs. "I met your son. I think he plays with us. I'm glad for you. Seems like a good guy."

"*You're* a good guy. Think about how many games you've played in the last year, between minors and majors and postseason and World Series. Two World Series in one year! And that crazy, fucking Solar Series."

Blent bites the edge of his thumbnail. "I don't care at all."

"The Giants finished in fourth place this year! Losing record! How do you like that? You're a starter, man."

"What about Scuttario?"

"Not on our roster."

"Holy shit. What did I hit this year?"

"Don't know. I should've checked. I asked Buck, Jr.—we were in the clubhouse after working on drills. After the season. I guess you live in San Francisco, or near San Francisco full-time now. Can you believe my son is on the Giants—with us—with you! A guy named Cornell is our first baseman. Never heard of him! My son's the backup infielder."

Blent snorts with the new reality that he'll have to fend off Bucky Martin's son for his job next season.

"Johnny Blent!" a voice squeaks.

Striding down the embankment is a soldier in camouflage, helmet and thick wraparound sunglasses partly blocking the soldier's wide, young face. The beaming soldier removes the helmet, shakes out shoulder-length hair. She rushes up and hugs Blent hard.

"I was helping with training at Fort Irwin and they deployed us up here to help with recovery. When the news flashed, my CO gave me a green light to take the bird and see my big brother. They found you!"

Blent stares at her, dumbfounded.

Bucky Martin offers his hand. The army sergeant shakes it. "Charlene Blent. Great to meet you. You two must've had quite an adventure to wind up here."

"Nice to meet you," replies Martin, confused as heck—Blent never mentioned a sister. A *brother* in the Marines, the hero, yes.

"What about Darla?" Blent asks.

"When you gonna settle down, Johnny?" Charlene Blent laughs. "You call mom?"

"And Mark? Memories of Mark?"

"Who's Mark? You two Giants need a ride? I can set you down right next to the stadium—what's left of it."

Martin tells her, "There are five or six of us."

"I can accommodate." She charges up the embankment in her jumpsuit.

Blent turns to Martin. "I don't have a sister."

"I know."

They watch her climb the embankment. Martin says, "Well, you've got a sister now. And she's thrilled to see you."

"My memories of Mark have not changed. I feel different. You?"

"Like a different person? Not really. I'll let you know if I notice something. We gotta compare notes all the time."

"That means you won't cut me next spring training?"

Martin chuckles. "*That's* what you're worried about?"

"It's high up the list."

A shiny black Ford truck halts next to the field. Rube Foster and Ty Cobb have difficulty with the door handles, are helped, and then step out. The driver emerges with her husband. Two little kids scramble out the back hatch.

Buck, Jr.'s Porsche halts behind the truck, with Tesla in the passenger seat excitedly asking Junior questions about the dashboard displays.

Martin says to Blent, "We've got three guys we have to take care of. They can stay at my apartment, I guess, if it's still standing. We gotta get our stories straight. Let's figure out something before we step off the helicopter." Martin checks his pockets. "I need a phone."

Rube Foster, Ty Cobb, Tesla in his sling, Buck, Jr., and the family of four step down the embankment to the field. They're holding baseball mitts.

Foster notifies Blent and Martin, "There are some people here excited to see you!"

There's a tall woman and a man and the two kids. The man seems a bit awestruck to be in the presence of Manager Bucky Martin and the Giants.

The woman stops just a few feet from Blent. "My name is Veronica Velez Wilson. My great-great-great-grandmother was Nicole Velez. My great-great-great-grandfather was André Velez."

Blent closes his eyes. It's hard for him to believe what he's hearing.

"I think we're missing a 'great' in there," the husband adds.

Blent opens his eyes. The woman *does* remind him of André—dark, large eyes. She has Nicole's broad forehead and the fine, dark hair is reminiscent of Nicole's.

She continues, "It was sort of a legend in our family: after an earthquake takes down the stadium, find the second baseman for the San Francisco Giants."

"That's me," Blent tells them, with a glance at Buck, Sr., who nods yes.

She hands Blent a mitt—his 1906 glove, now faded, flattened, cracked through in two fingers—the mitt he bought with Velez and Martin in St. Louis and used for the entire season. Out of habit he slips his hand into it, feeling the century-old leather. He pounds his right fist into the pocket.

He tells Velez's great-great-great-granddaughter, her husband and kids, "Thank you so much! This is awesome!"

She adds, "Open it."

Blent opens the glove. Along the pinkie finger, there's some writing.

Bucky Martin, Sr. asks, "What does it say?"

Blent steps close to Martin and reads the faded ink aloud:

*To Johnny Blent.*
*Game 6. World Series.*
*I should've let you make that catch.*
*—André*

ENDS

# ACKNOWLEDGMENTS

## THANKS TO:

—Jackson Haring for a discussion about life as manager of the rock band Camper Van Beethoven, and his comment about old-time ballplayers: "A lot of them were probably packing heat."

—Leila Samrad and Van Nightengale for MVP copyediting.

—Joe Paulino for conspiring on a fun publication game plan gone awry.

—Writers & buddies Richard Polsky and Matt Geyer.

—Café DiVino and Sartaj Restaurant for sustenance and understanding.

—Neighbors Lila and Jenny LeCoq, Joe Burns, and Ricky, Robert, and Liz Gallardo for being fabulous.

—Devin Crowley, Kirk Davis, M. George Stevenson, and Lia Miller for getting me through the '90s.

—The inventors of the Strat-O-Matic baseball game. Playing games with Strat cards and dice sparked some of the game description in this novel.

—The wonderful librarians at the Baseball Hall of Fame; baseball-reference.com for letting anyone dig into their statistics gold mine.

—Charles Mandel and the Helmar Baseball Art Card Company, for great friendship, and art.

—My folks; and Ellen Hermanos, Hall of Fame sister.

—Leslie Daniels for asking, "Do you have a baseball novel in you?"

—Lamar Herrin for showing me a path from playing baseball to writing novels; it only took me thirty-five years to follow.

—The Inkshares team: Adam Gomolin, Barnaby Conrad, Avalon Radys, Kevin Summers, and Dan Crissman.

—To everyone who laid down their hard-earned dollars to participate in this crowdfunding endeavor. I hope that you found it worthy.

—And to Karin and Ansel, who rode the losses and wins of *Going, Going, Gone!* with me over many years. Without them, this book would not exist.

A note on the characters: The novel is a mixture of completely fictional characters and those from history, and more specifically, baseball history. All of the 1906 players described actually took the field around that time, except the fictitious brothers of Ty Cobb. And if anyone is passing through West Long Branch, New Jersey, "Turkey Mike" Donlin is buried in an elegant cemetery there. He deserves a visit. Leave an old baseball or a splash of bourbon.

I had a heck of a lot of fun researching baseball in 1906, studying the old ballparks. I especially fell in love with the Polo

Grounds. An escarpment above the site still stands and will outlive us all: Coogan's Bluff. From up there you can look out at the plain where the ballpark stood. Eighth Avenue is across the plain, and that's where the Elevated train stopped to let off fans and players.

The Mathewsons. The only intentionally distorted historical character in this novel is Jane Mathewson. By all accounts, Christy and Jane Mathewson were a loving couple. Jane stood by him during his stellar pitching career, when he exhibited legendary acts of sportsmanship. As many baseball fans know, Christy served in World War I, where, during a training exercise, he was a victim of a chemical gas accident. The gassing made him susceptible to tuberculosis, and after a lot of suffering, he passed away in 1925 at age forty-five. Heartfelt apologies to anyone offended: descendants of the Mathewsons, historians, and the spirit of Jane Mathewson. As to Christy Mathewson's unhinged outburst in this story—well, during a fight on the field one day in 1911, it is documented that he slugged a teenage lemonade vendor.

Twenty-first Century biographers have questioned the veracity of their Twentieth-century predecessors' depiction of Ty Cobb as a seething racist. Seething, perhaps, but racist perhaps not. History, after all, is changeable. In either case, we now have Ty Cobb in the Twenty-first Century, so we'll see what happens next.

Finally, it should be underscored that the implication regarding the structural integrity of San Francisco's beautiful baseball stadium is fictitious. The ballpark was engineered with the seismic history of San Francisco fully in mind. I'm so thoroughly confident in its stability that, when the big one hits, I hope I'm there with you. Hopefully, we won't be chewing tobacco.

# GRAND PATRONS

Adam Klausner, Ithaca Royal Palmists, P
Adam Klein, Halifax Oyster Shuckers, CF
Adam Tattlebaum, Dalton Tigers, 2B
Alistair Goldfisher, Brooklyn Trolley Dodgers, RF
Ansel Hermanos, S.F. Bay Breakers, CF
Anthony Piana, Corte Madera Maderas, CF
Arthur Orduna, New York Lookouts, P
Alex Shulzycki, Geneva Pondulets, RP
Ariana Cuervo, DaVino Espresso, CF
Babette Cohen, New York Diamonds, SS
Barnaby Conrad, Washington Absinthe Sippers, P/2B
Benjamin Knapp, Phoenix Fanboaters, SS
Bennett Johnston, Mill Valley Millers, RP
Bill Forrest, Albuquerque Isotopes, CF
Bradford Peck, New York Rangers, Forward
Brian E. Walder, Ithaca Royal Palmists, 2B
Brian Stadtmiller, Dog Patch Reclaimers, GM
John and Mimi Burnham, Nantucket Reds, Ownership Group
Christine Fuetsch, San Rafael Hairclippers, P
Carla Pollard, Sausalito Salts, Uniform Designer
Carol Fink, Napa Survivors, P
Charlie Crawford, Toll Builders, SS
Charles Denby, MHS Fog Chasers, Coach
Charles Garner, New York Limo Hailers, CF
Charles Gaspari, Florida Beach Combers, CF
Charles S. Mandel, House of David, Signage Architect/P
Chloe & Spencer Braunstein, Weston Yankees, P
Chris Ryan, B & H Filmmakers, CF
Van Nightingale, O.C. Proofreaders, 1B
David Blinken, Rutherford Casters, Secretary of Fish
Dave Geisler, Wisconsin Stockpickers, 3B
Devin Crowley, Roswell Filmmakers, Captain/OF
Dick Knowse, USA Baseball, LF
Dan Fost, Mill Valley Millers, Hitting Coach
Darell Krasnoff, Bohemian Mountain Dads, Cornerback
Doug Simon, N.Y. Frisbee Flingers, 3B
Douglas Zang, Albuquerque Isotopes, Third Base
Duncan Plexico, Dalton Tigers, Right Field/P
Edward M. Burns, San Francisco Seals, SS
Eivor Taylor, Sausalito Sense Diviners, P
Elizabeth Burns, San Francisco Seals, 3B

Elizabeth Cuervo, DiVino Espressos, P
Elizabeth Krasnoff, Team Navy, GM
Elizabeth Lawrence, Santa Fe Tortillas, CF
Ellen Hermanos, Wellesley Wonders, C
Erik Taylor, Sonoma Stompers, RF
Gabby Chan, Sausalito Salty Dogs, 3B
Gail Stark, S.F. Property Flippers, 2B
Gerry Larson, Ecuador Sierra, Wrangler/CF
Geoff Potter, New York Giants, P
Grace Cricket, Eau Claire Hank Aarons, Manager
Helen Y. Fung, Sausalito Architects, SS
Jackson Haring, Palm Springs Geysers, Music Booker/P
Jacob Knapp, Phoenix Microscopes, Half Back
Jacquie Lopez-Wyman, Mill Valley Millers, Futurist
James A. Caldwell, San Francisco Seals, Housing & Finance
James Redford, Dalton Tigers, P
Jared Polsky, Larkspur Lookouts, SS
Jarom Fawson, Mill Valley Millers, Entertainment Director/OF
Jason Abrams, Trader Vic's Scorpions, CF
Jennifer Crawford, Philadelphia A's, P
Jennifer Fragetti, New York Metropolitans, 1B
Jim O'Neil, San Francisco Giants, P
Joan Metsch, Green River Polar Bears, P
Joanna Prasinos, New York Stockflippers, Owner
Joe Burns, Sausalito Oyster Shuckers, Bass
Joe Paulino, Sausalito Voiceovers, P
John Cecchi, Sausalito Salts, 3B
John Scott, Helmar Hellians, P
John M. Bader, Puerto Rico Windersurfers, P
Jonathan Rutchik, Mt. Tam Timbers, Dr./P
Jonathan Weintraub, Trader Vic's Scorpions, P
Joseph V. Paulino, Sausalito Voices, 2B
Jeff R. Vervlied, Team USA, 2B
Julie Ovadia, NYC Tech Crunchers, CF
Julie Sessions, Albuquerque Isotopes, P
Karen C. Hubble, San Francisco Seals, Analyst/P
Karin Taylor, Sausalito Salts, MVP/Pitcher
Katie Zang, Albuquerque Isotopes, RF
Kendal Taylor, New York Giants, P
Kenneth Palmer, Houston Gyros, P
Kerry Barlas, Mill Valley Millers, SS
Kirk Davis, Arizona U.F.O.s, P
Kris Gaspari, Florida Beachcombers, P
Laura Metsch, Brattleboro Bombers, SS
Leila Samrad, Sausalito Sartajians, 1B
Leo Valiquette, Inkshares Inkstains, P

Leon Silverman, Sausalito Mets, SS
Louis Farese, Team USA, C
Louise Iyengar, New York Yankees, Webmaster
Melissa Jo Potter, Boston Braves, C
M. George Stevenson, New York Tunnels, Replay Review Coordinator
Mark Humphries, San Francisco Rookie Collectors, P
Michael Knapp, Green River Lake Diggers, Third Base
Mike Hart, Atlanta Slicers, 1B
Mike Hood, S.F. Realtors, CF
Mike Testa, Team Free Solo, Safety Advisor
Miles Rubin, New York Yankees, Drums
Nikki Johnson, Belvedere Bridge Viewers, RF
Pamela Bingham, New York Giants, Artistic Consultant
Patrice Cromwell, Baltimore Squash Conquerors, Center Field
Patrick Taylor, Sr., Sausalito Brain Mixologists, Captain
Patrick Taylor, Jr., Wisconsin Fate Deciders, P
Paul Levitan, Philly Specialists, C
Paul Winston, New York Cosmos, Goalie
Peter Gelfman, The Stan Keys, Center Field
Philip Taylor, Team USA, Poet
Regan Ural, Tam Junction Linchpins, SS
Richard Polsky, Warhol Authenticators, P
Dr. Robert Gelfand, New York Cartoonists, CF
Robert Hermanos, New York Giants, Ownership Group
Robert Michener, Jr., San Rafael Pacifics, Dir. Of Souveniers
Robert Taylor, Organic Farm Director
Ronald Grelsamer, New York Kneecappers, P
Sara B. Khan, San Francisco Tycoons, Real Estate Liason
Scott Jampool, S.F. Bay School Breakers, P
Scott Knapp, Ithaca Royal Palmists, SS
Scott Wilder, Google Algorithms, C
Stefan Smith, Team USA, Play-by-Play Announcer
Stefano Scali, Sausalito Floating Homers, C
Stefani Adler, Baltimore Friends, LF
Stephanie Morris, San Anselmo Hikers, SS
Steven J. Rubenstein, Team USA, C
Susan Hermanos, New York Yankees, Commentator
Tammy Wexler, L.A. Dealmakers, SS
Ted Hallman, Albany Dustjackets, SS
Thomas Skunda, Sausalito Salty Dogs, 3B
Tim Ural, Sr., Bohemian Mountain Dads, 2B
Tracy E. Dutton, Walden Pond Plungers, LF
Veronica Perez, Mill Valley Flag Football, RB
Victoria Huerta-Miller, Mill Valley Millers, Attitude Coach
Yovani Castillo, Sausalito Salty Dogs, Chef

# INKSHARES

INKSHARES is a reader-driven publisher and producer based in Oakland, California. Our books are selected not by a group of editors, but by readers worldwide.

While we've published books by established writers like *Big Fish* author Daniel Wallace and *Star Wars: Rogue One* scribe Gary Whitta, our aim remains surfacing and developing the new author voices of tomorrow.

Previously unknown Inkshares authors have received starred reviews, and been featured in the *New York Times*. Their books are on the front tables of Barnes & Noble, and hundreds of independents nationwide. Many have been licensed by publishers in other major markets. They are also being adapted by Oscar-winning screenwriters at the biggest studios and networks.

Interested in making your own story a reality? Visit Inkshares.com to start your own project or find other great books.